He came to the door the washing in the scullery and Margaret was lying on her couch in front of the fire. I went in and said, 'There's someone to see you, Margaret.'

She thought it was the vicar or kind Mrs Lansdowne from the shop or Mary Test, an old friend of Mother's, but when Nat's large frame filled the doorway she cried out, shrieked almost, and her face flamed up. She threw off the blanket, but before she could stagger to her feet Nat was across the floor and on his knees by her side with his arms around her, burying his head in her wild curls.

I was shocked to the core by what I had done, thinking it would be kind words, a stilted meeting of decorum and neighbourliness. Heavens, what did I know about this sort of passion?

SMALL GAINS

K M Peyton

Definitions

SMALL GAINS
A RED FOX BOOK 0 09 944387 2

First published in Great Britain by David Fickling Books
a division of Random House Children's Books

David Fickling Books edition published 2003
Red Fox Definitions edition published 2004

1 3 5 7 9 10 8 6 4 2

Copyright © K M Peyton, 2003

The right of K M Peyton to be identified as the author of this work has
been asserted in accordance with the Copyright, Designs and Patents Act
1988.

Papers used by Random House Children's Books are natural, recyclable
products made from wood grown in sustainable forests. The manufactur-
ing processes conform to the environmental regulations of the country of
origin.

Red Fox Books are published by Random House Children's Books,
61–63 Uxbridge Road, London W5 5SA,
a division of The Random House Group Ltd,
in Australia by Random House Australia (Pty) Ltd,
20 Alfred Street, Milsons Point, Sydney, NSW 2061, Australia,
in New Zealand by Random House New Zealand Ltd,
18 Poland Road, Glenfield, Auckland 10, New Zealand,
and in South Africa by Random House (Pty) Ltd,
Endulini, 5A Jubilee Road, Parktown 2193, South Africa

THE RANDOM HOUSE GROUP Limited Reg. No. 954009
www.kidsatrandomhouse.co.uk

A CIP catalogue record for this book is available from the British Library.

Printed and bound in Great Britain by Cox and Wyman Ltd,
Reading, Berkshire

To David and Annie

1

I was riding Tilly home from the village on a fine October day, my favourite time of year, and I was thinking good thoughts, not gloomy ones for a change. (We have a lot to be gloomy about in my family.) I had been talking to Nicholas, the vicar's son, who, in spite of being consumptive, always made me laugh, and Tilly had been admired by some strangers outside the Queen's Head.

'Is that the famous Garland's Tilly?' they had asked curiously, getting down from their cart behind steaming, over-driven horses.

'Yes.' I made her stand out to be admired, laughing to myself as I saw them trying to find something complimentary to say about her, and failing. She was a terrible ratbag to look at.

'Well, she's won me some money in her time.' The older man gave her neck a grateful slap and I caught the rein sharply to stop Tilly biting him. 'It's time you had her out again, and I can win some more.'

'She's too old now,' I said.

7

'They get better with age, these Norfolk trotters,' the other man said.

Not like you, I thought, and rode on.

Our farm was half a mile out of the village. The fields on either side were alive with birds in the stubble, gleaning, their voices shrilling in the clear autumn air. The ruby-chestnut breasts of the cock pheasants were like jewels in the sun as they strutted down the hedgerow, but the little pipits and dunnocks and sparrows were almost invisible, peasants to the kings. The hedges were shedding ditchfuls of golden leaves and starting to liven their branches with berries. I loved the changing of the seasons, save for the portents they brought with them – work, work, work. Winter was cruel for labourers working out in all weathers in a land where the wind came from the North Sea and Siberia beyond (so they said, I had no geography). But now was lovely, and I sniffed it in, the lovely distant smell of woodsmoke and the air cool and clear. The sky was cloudless from horizon to horizon, of a blue so pale it was hardly a colour, with an errant moon fading away over the windmill sails.

But coming towards me – my heart sank abruptly – was Nat Grover on his new horse, Crocus. From a distance I could see the horse was lame but it was typical of Nat Grover to take no notice. He was going to pass me by with an arrogant nod but I could not help myself pulling up and saying, 'Your horse is lame, sir.'

I could see by his look he thought I was completely out of place – I was only eleven after all – but he must have been aware of the damage he was doing. He wasn't stupid. And Crocus was truly beautiful, one of the best I had ever set eyes on. My eyes were all over him.

He noticed, grinned, and slipped down. 'Take him home for me, if it concerns you so. I'll walk.'

He went to toss me the reins, but I declined angrily. 'Take him home yourself!'

He was so used to giving orders and being obeyed that I could see my refusal surprised him. He looked at me sharply. I knew my sister Margaret was sweet on Nat and at that moment I could see why, for he was undeniably as handsome as his horse. His arrogance gave him stature, somehow. He was tall anyway, but at eighteen still slender and lithe in his smart black cut-away coat and tight breeches, his cravat wound high and fashionably under the commanding chin. His hair was black and curling and his eyes very dark. They called him the gypsy Grover – all the others were fair. What a waste that he was so horrible.

He wasn't sure what to do after my rebuff, and I was half regretting my refusal for I would have liked to study his new horse more closely. But I wouldn't kow-tow to a Grover. Luckily there were some labourers working on the road, filling in potholes a little farther down, and one of them was old Sim, who knew all there was to know about horses.

'Ask Sim. He'll see what's wrong and take him home for you.'

So Nat bawled for Sim and Sim came up slowly to take orders.

'Miss Clara here tells me my horse must go home.'

He spoke with heavy sarcasm, and threw the reins at Sim. 'Take him.'

With which he walked off.

'What a bastard,' said Sim.

We laughed. Sim was in his seventies, down on his luck if it had come to road-mending. His last employer, a country vicar, had died in a hunting accident and Sim was out of work.

Nat walked off, and Sim and I went on together. The horse he led was a chestnut trotter, as handsome as Tilly was ugly.

Sim said, 'They say he gave three hundred guineas for this one. A fortune! Only a three-year-old, but Mister Nat can't wait to match him, they say. He'll probably be challenging old Tilly here as soon as he's got him fit enough.'

'Ugh! I hate Nat. I couldn't bear for him to beat us.'

It was the custom in our county to match trotting horses one against the other, over twenty miles or more. The best horses were really valuable and Tilly was one of the best. But, alas, now she was in her late twenties.

Coming down the road, approaching the two properties which stood opposite each other – the Grovers' to the left, ours to the right – it was easy to see which was the rich property, which the poor. The contrast was painful. The Grovers' large newly-renovated house lay at the top of a freshly-gravelled drive lined with young lime trees and a neatly trimmed yew hedge. The farm buildings were laid out to one side of the house in neat yards, the roofs all sound, with the hayricks beyond them in soldierly lines, perfectly thatched.

As for ours, a potholed right-of-way meandered off the road towards a distant wood, Gridswood, which belonged to the squire for his shooting. Our farm was halfway down on the right of the track, a tangle of ancient, leaking barns, cowsheds and stables. Our row of ricks was only roughly thatched and one or two were leaning slightly, giving a slightly drunken appearance. Our gates sagged too, and our hedges had holes filled in with the odd bedstead or broken plough. The house fronted the track, the back giving on to the yards, and although it was pretty enough with its pinkish old bricks and thick thatch, it was less than a quarter the size of the Grovers'. We had barely a hundred acres, and of that the water meadows between our place and the wood belonged to the squire.

I rode slowly up the drive, wondering if Margaret had bestirred herself to do some baking. I was hungry, not an unusual circumstance since Mother had died. Just to think of Mother's baking, and the pans of cream set out in the dairy, the cheeses waiting to go to market, the ham hanging on hooks in the kitchen . . . all memories now. No wonder the family had fallen so glum since her death, and our father aged far beyond his forty years. She had been so strong in their partnership, even when she was ill. I could still remember the strength of her will, the courage, the *life*, even when it was almost extinct. And her awesomeness in death when she had lain in her coffin on the big polished table in the parlour looking so incredibly young and beautiful – a sight I could never get out of my head although it had happened three years ago now. She had been beautiful in the usual consumptive way – the disease for some reason conferred a fine-bloomed complexion with high colour in the cheeks and lips. With her mass of blonde hair, she had made what the villagers called with awe 'a lovely corpse'. They had trailed in, all of them, young and old, to pay tribute and have a good look.

Margaret had inherited Mother's beauty, but I had missed out. As well as the cloud of golden curling hair, Margaret is tall and lissom with long legs and a tiny waist, but I, her sister, am stocky and square. My hair is brown and fuzzy, my eyes grey, my mouth determined, my jaw likewise. I frown a lot, I am very strong. Am I jealous? I try not to think about it.

For I could not be jealous of Margaret, who as well as inheriting Mother's beauty had inherited her disease as well, and was not likely to be with us for long.

No wonder I was an earnest, old child, who everyone said should have been a boy, and who worked as hard as a man with the horses. I knew what they said about me. I even rode astride when I was around the fields, in my breeches, although I used Mother's side-saddle and riding apron to go out on the road. Smart Nat had seen me at my best, such as it was.

I put Tilly away in the stable and gave her a feed and went indoors. The smell of bread baking met me at the door and my heart lifted – so much so that I pandered to Margaret and said, 'I met Nat on the road.'

She was putting out plates and cold meat and dripping and onions for the men coming in shortly, and looked up sharply.

'Did he – was he—?'

'Coming this way? No. He is horrible, Margaret. You can't possibly like him.'

'He's so handsome,' she said dreamily. And smiled.

I thought there was probably more going on than I had noticed. I had seen Nat riding past at times, through the water meadows and into Gridswood. Perhaps he had been eyeing the water meadows for his father. There were rumours that his father Eb had approached the squire to buy them. But maybe that wasn't his reason.

I put a loaf of the new bread on the table. The table was covered in candle grease and hadn't been scrubbed for days. I didn't say anything, but thought I kept my stables in a better state than Margaret kept the kitchen. The range was unpolished and even the fire only smouldered, when for Mother it had danced and sparkled on gleaming pans and shining glassware. The copper pans were now tarnished, the glasses dull, all the pretty cushions and rugs faded and torn and dirty. I tried to clean up sometimes, but my job was in the stables and with seven carthorses besides Tilly, it was heavy work. I had to do the washing too, because Margaret was too weak to wring out wet sheets and carry them out to the line.

Ellen, our younger sister, was only nine and kept

herself out of the way at school. She was wild and out of hand but there was no one to teach her better. None of the rest of us, Margaret and Jack and myself, had been to school because Mother had taught us, and taught us better than old Crackpot, the village schoolmaster. Cheaper too, for it cost twopence a week each to go to school. Most of the villagers couldn't afford it, and sent their children to slave on Grover's farm to earn sixpence instead. We were an ignorant lot, all in all, but we could read and write and knew about the French Revolution and our fat King George.

I put out the ale and glasses. Father came in at twelve, crosspatch as usual.

'What's this talk about Eb Grover wanting to buy our water meadows?' he growled at me. 'You hear anything about it down in the village?'

'Not today. I've heard it said though.' I nearly said, Ask Margaret, but bit my tongue back in time.

'So where does this gossip come from? There must be some truth in it.'

'Jack will know,' I said.

Jack came in five minutes later with Martin, his friend. They had both been clearing a ditch where an old elm had fallen across it, and were covered in wood chips and lichen. Mother would have made them wash in the scullery but her nice habits had been forgotten. The fresh bread and dripping and jug of ale were too much for them. They fell on it like wolves and I got up to fetch a second loaf. Margaret moaned to see it go so fast.

14

Father asked Jack.

'It's alehouse talk, Father. But probably true. Those water meadows, if they're drained, would be useful to the Grovers.'

'Aye, to us too!'

But we couldn't afford to drain them. We rented them quite cheaply from the squire and would be in trouble without them, our own land being so small.

'The squire wouldn't sell to the Grovers,' my father said.

I saw Jack and Martin exchange glances. Martin was Jack's friend, our friend, from childhood, as good as family. They got about, Jack and Martin, and knew everything.

'No. Probably not,' Jack said affably. It was cruel to encourage even more doubts in our father, Sam, who, with age, bereavement and rheumatism, was beginning to wonder where life was leading him.

Jack dropped the subject with a laugh. 'Alehouse talk is all about a match between Tilly and that new horse of the Grovers.'

At this, Father perked up. 'Aye. Nat Grover challenged me, thinks that new colt of his can beat Tilly over twenty miles. And the little beast hardly three years old!'

'Yeah, twenty-five years younger than Tilly!'

'It'll go out like a light after ten miles.'

I butted in. 'The Grover horse is lame.' I told them (proudly) how I had challenged Nat.

Jack laughed. 'Good for you! Picked up a flint probably. Yeah, Nat told me he wanted a match.

Saturday week he said, but I said Tilly was past it.'

'Rubbish,' Father said shortly. 'She'll go.'

'Tilly'll drop dead at the post, Father, the way you treat her! You're going to kill the goose that lays the golden eggs.'

'She's not past it! Two hundred pounds at stake. We need it.'

It was true that our Norfolk trotting horses improved with age, and matches were often wagered between horses in their twenties. But Father had wagered Tilly too often and now she looked like a scarecrow. People scoffed when we pulled her out, the ones that didn't know. But later when after twenty miles she came home flying, ears pricked, eyes blazing, their laughter turned to amazement. They lost their money. We made ours.

'It was Nat as made the challenge, not me,' Father said.

'Yeah, well, he's no more sense that you have. Ruin both of 'em, ours too old and Nat's too young and the ground coming either frost-hard or deep mud the next few months.'

Jack could talk like that to our father, but we both knew he would have to do what Father said. Jack rode Tilly in her matches since Father had got so rheumaticky, and if Father said go, Jack went. Jack was fifteen, a dear boy with a heart of gold. He loved the horses too, but had far more sense than Father, who gambled on them and lost nearly as much as he made. Between them, they were saving for a new horse to take over from old Tilly. There was a pot of money under the kitchen floor. Our poor farm was well named Small Gains. While Small Gains fell apart, the pot was filling. Slowly.

'Win a match against Nat Grover and with a good bet we'll make enough to go to the horse fair and bid with the big boys,' Father promised.

Jack looked at me and winked. It should have made him despair, Father's crackpot optimism, but it just made Jack laugh.

'Aye, Father, we'll give it a go then. But when it comes to the match I'll not thrash her, she can choose her own pace.'

'She knows how to judge a race better'n you'll ever learn,' Father growled.

You could crack him one sometimes, for being so daft. But I suppose he had ridden Tilly for over twenty years and knew her better than he had ever understood his son. The passion of his life was matches between trotting horses. They talked about it for hours in the alehouses, how Old Shales trotted twenty miles in the hour carrying seventeen stone, how Fireaway could trot two miles in five minutes, how Paulson put his farm mare to a blood stallion descended from Flying Childers and got a horse that could trot fifteen miles in fifty minutes carrying twenty stone . . . the stories got taller and taller.

But Tilly in her prime had trotted a hundred miles in twelve hours, that was the truth. It was unlikely that we would ever find another so good with the money we had in the pot. That was my opinion, but of course I kept it to myself. We lived on dreams in

17

our family, for there was not much else going for us.

I was the one who looked after Tilly. When I fed her that night, remembering the lovely Crocus, I moaned, 'Oh, Tilly, if only you were ten years younger!'

She tried to bite me, but I knew her old tricks and clapped my hand over her nostrils. 'You old toe rag!'

It was too much, I suppose, to expect a horse like Tilly to be as loveable as she was brilliant. But I would have loved a horse of my own, a horse to me like Tilly had been to Father, that you had had all its life and *knew*. I knew Tilly well enough, but I had never known her, as Father had, when she had been digging deep into all the courage she possessed, fighting, winning. Or not winning, and being angry together with Father, two cross-grained souls at one. Their lives were entwined.

'That's why he should look after you now, now you're getting past it,' I murmured as I tipped her bucket of oats into the manger. How she ate! But to look at her you'd think we starved her. She twitched a long rabbity ear back at me. She suffered me because I looked after her, only savage when food was in the offing.

'You're too old to beat Nat's horse. Fancy, three hundred guineas!'

Tilly had been bought in exchange for a cow and five pounds. But she could trot faster than a Newmarket horse could gallop. None of the spectators in her matches could keep her in sight, even rich farmers on their hunters.

'Father should have another try at getting you in

foal,' I told her. 'A nice retirement, with a baby to look after, that's what you want.'

But Father rarely did the wise thing. Tilly had never bred a foal, although she had been put to a stallion a few times.

But I couldn't waste time with Tilly. Her stall was clean, there was hay in her rack and her scarecrow frame was wrapped in a rug of potato sacks and the remains of an eiderdown. In the next stall was Ben, our favourite carthorse, a great slow Suffolk, as kind as he was stupid. Father had collected him after a pulling match when he had been left for dead after hauling an oak tree out of a quarry. Father had no truck with these cruel matches but, such was his gambling nature, he could not resist enquiring as to the winners and betting. Going along for a drink and the chat when the match was over, he had returned afterwards to the scene of the competition and sat for a while on his own, caressing the dead horse's ears. He then realized they were warm. He stroked and talked to the horse well into the night, and at last the horse recovered and stood up. Having been stripped of its harness, it followed Father meekly home, led by a piece of string. Dear Ben – he had been with us ever since, earning his keep a thousand times over.

I went out. The sun was low over the Grover fields, its sinking rays catching Gridswood so that it glowed crimson against the slate-grey sky. How lovely was the landscape if it could be left to its own devices! Our workload was prodigious to keep it in the manner Father decreed, decent and productive. Our hedges were neat, our ditches ran, our muck was tidily stacked. But we had little time to admire it. We did most of the work ourselves.

Across the way, the Grovers employed a gang from around the neighbourhood, mostly children, who came every day all the year round and worked from light till dark in the winter, and ten hours in the summer. They were poor little things, some as young as six and seven, and some of them had to walk miles to get to the Grovers' before they started and miles back at night. Their 'ganger', who organized their employment, was Martin's father, old Ramsey. I knew quite a few of them, the ones from our own village, Gridstone. In winter the poor workers were still out in the fields, and ate their bait at lunch time under a hedge, even in the rain and snow. The Grovers never invited them into a barn, said they'd eat slower and waste time. They were right, naturally. The Grovers were always right.

I was glad I wasn't a Grover, in spite of their riches. Nat's father Eb beat his workers with a horsewhip if they played him up (and was said to beat his wife and children too if gossip was to be believed), and even if they did have a horse like Crocus they hadn't won a match yet.

We had won lots and were likely to win another. In spite of what Jack said, I knew Tilly wasn't past it yet.

2

Nat crashed into the kitchen, shouted to the boy for his boots to be pulled off and flung off his heavy caped riding coat. He was starving! In the kitchen, a large joint of mutton was just being taken out of the oven. Roast vegetables steamed in their bowls. The maids scurried about, taking plates to the sink and draining cabbage and sprouts.

'They didn't wait for you, sir. The soup and fish have already been served,' the cook said.

'Ah well, I'll make up on the meat!'

He was in a good mood, Crocus so full of going and the match coming up to look forward to. All the neighbourhood would be out to put their money on. That scarecrow Tilly! Yet her reputation was enormous. If only Crocus would learn not to break . . . Tilly never broke, ever. If the horse broke trot, the rider had to circle, wasting valuable time and getting out of rhythm. Crocus was the most promising horse they had ever had, and they had had plenty.

He went through the kitchen and out across the hall to the dining room. This was the new part of the house, the front, only lately completed by Mr Nash. It wasn't nearly as cosy as the old Tudor hall which he had knocked down, too airy and precious for Nat's liking, with its pale plaster twirls and the nimby-pimby marble mantelpiece instead of the great old brick arch of the original fireplace. You couldn't walk through this sort of place in your outside boots like you could the old hall, and stand with your backside warming before the great logs that the old fire used to burn. His mother loved it and wanted to give parties like the squire, but they weren't in with those sort of people, not yet.

Their friends still preferred the old study that Mr Nash hadn't touched, where the dogs lay on the chairs. Their friends weren't in the squire's league: they were brute farmers like themselves, made good on Norfolk corn and cattle and turnips all selling at high prices during the war. Times were harder now. All the more reason to grab what you could, like the squire's water meadows. The squire, for all his smart friends, wasn't as rich as they were. He was said to be cutting down on staff. At Grover's, they could still use all the workers the ganger could supply, even the six-year-old children. People in the village didn't like this, but the six-year-olds still came, pulled out in the dawn light by a desperate mother to make a few pence a day. What else was there for a child to do but mewl about at home, after all? The Grovers were proud to supply so much employment for their neighbourhood. They were proud of all they had achieved, and expected everyone to respect their strength.

Nat crashed into the dining room and got soundly scolded for being late. His mother, always trying hard to make her uncouth family behave more in keeping with their improving circumstances, said, 'It's not as if we're still in the kitchen, coming and going with the men. Dinner is served at seven, here in the dining room, and you've got to learn to be punctual. It's not asking much. And why do you have to ride in the dark?'

'I want to practise him on the road and I don't want anyone to see how good he is.'

'Anyone would think this is Newmarket, not back of beyond.'

His mother looked peevish, as usual. Her husband and relations called her Maggie, and the common diminutive annoyed her. She was always trying to make them change it to Meg. The whole name, Margaret, was obviously beyond them, yet it was not beyond the poor people across the road whose eldest daughter was never known by anything else but her full name. In her family, Nathaniel was Nat, her husband Ebenezer was Eb; her eldest daughter Elizabeth was Lizzie and poor absent Philip had usually been known as Pip.

Pip had run away from home when he was fifteen after a beating from his father, and had never been heard of since. Someone in the village had a son in the navy who said there was a high-ranking commander called Philip Grover, but whether that was their Pip – how to find out? She had no idea. The squire had been in the navy as a young man but she hadn't the presumption to ask his advice, in spite of the fact that he was a friendly and unpompous man who did not stand much on ceremony. He did not like her husband – along with just about everyone in the neighbourhood – and this inhibited her. No one liked her husband, herself included. But as a poor dairy-maid with a large purple birthmark on her face, she had been glad to accept the lifeline of his marriage offer, being already pregnant with Philip. At least she had never been hungry again or had to work in the fields for her living.

'And how did he go?' Grover asked Nat. 'No problems, I hope.'

'No, sir. No problems. He's a real winner.'

'Should be, what he cost.'

Meanness was Eb Grover's most striking character-istic. He spent to enlarge his holdings, to impress, to invest in assets, but not to be kind or charitable. His lack of success considering the money invested in his horses riled him. Expensive horses were supposed to win. The thought of that scarecrow Tilly owned by the paupers across the road beating Crocus on Saturday was insupportable. Yet still the old ones in the village were putting their money on Tilly.

'That mare can't possibly beat him,' Nat said. 'They were ploughing with her yesterday, and this morning Jack was carting straw with her.'

'That's the reason she's so fit, you fool. A twenty-mile spin on the road is nothing to her after the work she's used to.'

'I'm not having Crocus pull a plough,' Nat growled.

24

'Aye, well, you make sure you beat her. The whole neighbourhood will be out to watch.'

Nat was scared of his father, as they all were. He could use a leather belt with precision and was not above slapping the females of the family. He was forty-five, lean and strong, clever, ruthless and ambitious. If he bought the water meadows, which he intended to do, he was thinking about how he could acquire the farm that lay between them and his own place. Those paupers only hung on there by a thread – and by matching the mare Tilly. He wanted to bring them down.

Out in the stable yard, old Sim put Crocus away. Since bringing the horse home a few days ago – at young Clara's instigation – he had got himself employed in the Grover stables. Old Ebenezer had met him in the drive, enquired as to what he was doing with his best horse, and gave him a job on the spot. The pay was hardly above that of stone-bashing, but beggars couldn't be choosers. Old Sim loved to be with the horses. Old Eb knew of Sim's expertise and the man's age was no barrier to a man of Eb's ruthlessness. He employed six-year-olds. Seventy-five-year-olds were the same to his way of thinking. If they worked, he paid them. If they showed weakness, he threw them out. It came hard to Sim to jump to attention when being shouted at by those he considered his inferiors, but the job was worth it. The young boy Peter who worked with him was a good lad and strong, and glad to help.

Sim tied Crocus up in his stall and unsaddled him.

Crocus was a chestnut, fifteen hands high, a true-bred Norfolk trotter by Burgess's Fireaway. He was built short and strong with hard, clean legs, a wide chest and a fine proud neck. Perhaps a dash of Newmarket blood had decided the shape of his beautiful head and the fire in his eye, the slash of the white blaze and the curl of the nostril, but the whole was pure Norfolk trotter.

'There, my young Crocus, my beauty. It's an honour to do you, my lovely boy.' It was Sim's habit to talk continually in his soft voice to a horse while he groomed him. Peter thought he was a nutcase.

'Which will win on Saturday, d'you reckon?' he asked, anxious to place a bet. He could make something if he was lucky. Everyone at Grover's was betting on the master's horse, of course, but in the village the old boys still fancied Tilly.

'Aye, it's very even,' said Sim. 'I'm afraid our young Grover will be hard on this one – he's no sense – and young Jack will be easy on Tilly because she deserves it, and that might decide it.'

'The riders?'

'Aye, the riders. We're all at the mercy of the riders, Peter, horses and servants alike. That's the rub.'

Definitely a nutcase, thought young Peter.

3

I was fearful about this match. Usually I wasn't
bothered. After all, she didn't always win and if she
didn't this time . . . well, her time was nearly up and
one couldn't expect miracles. But we were used to
Tilly's great days: the excitement, the crowds, the
enthusiasts who rode miles to witness the race and got
happy and drunk, the villagers who made on the
betting. It made a wonderful, rare day out, full of
excitement and fun. The only other entertainment
like it was the harvest supper.

But this time, matching our neighbour, was
different. We usually matched farmers whose interests
and friendships were the same as our own. It was
always friendly, informed. But this time we were aware
that there was an added dimension: the bad blood
between us. All the villagers were on our side, the
Grovers being universally detested. But for the sake of
common sense, the chance to make money, quite a
few were betting on Crocus. I wasn't surprised. I
thought Crocus was the best horse I had ever seen.
I would have given my soul to own Crocus.

'Not like you, you old scumbag, Tilly. He's a real gentleman horse, so handsome, so smart, so well-mannered.'

I was grooming her with all my strength, determined that she would look as well-cared for as her rival. But her colour was roan, pale now with age, and never a colour to shine like a bay or chestnut. She was a gaunt thing, well made but not handsome with her sour eye and Roman nose, her manky tail and bare hip bones. But if you knew horses, you could tell she was a good one: deep, deep through the heart and well sprung in the ribs that housed a gallant engine. No, there weren't many like Tilly. If only she could have her clock turned back ten years, or twenty!

Tilly stood four-square with her ears back. She knew a match was imminent. I knew she knew, I knew the way her brain worked. Thank God, so did Jack. Poor girls didn't ride, more the pity; only sideways on, to market on an old jade, although rich girls like lovely Charlotte the squire's daughter went hunting and rode thoroughbreds. Oh, lucky Charlotte! I loved to ride Tilly. I loved the feel of her, to see her great shoulders moving beneath the slidy silk of her fine coat. Her stride was enormous, flung out from those shoulders. If I had to ride far, I still rode astride and pulled an old hat down over my hair and people thought I was a boy. You couldn't imagine Margaret passing for a boy, not in a hundred years!

'I'll make up her feed,' said Jack, coming to see what sort of a job I was doing. I could tell he was nervous this time, not liking this confrontation.

'Everyone will want the Grovers beat,' I said. 'Even those, in their hearts, whose money will be on Crocus.'

'I'm not fearful for want of support. Just fearful for Tilly. The road's had ice in it for a week – I'd rather deep mud than that jarring.'

'Her legs are like iron, you know that. She's never been lame in her life.' I wanted to cheer Jack up, although I agreed with his doubts.

'If we win, that'll make up the kitty for a new one, at least – although the odds are against getting anything as good.'

Oh Crocus! I thought. Three hundred pounds! We could have a new house for three hundred pounds.

I didn't say anything; just, 'Put an apple or two in the oats, she'll like that.'

Saturday was bright and cold, good weather for an outing. And they came, all those people, from miles around. The big village green was packed with horses and carts, smart turnouts with grooms alongside donkey carts, and a crowd of lads and farmers mounted to run along with the match as best they could.

The match was five miles out and back, and then again. It was a perfectly straight road leading to the turnpike which went to London, but few of us had been that far. There were plenty of stewards along the way to see fair play, and a crowd, no doubt, at the turnpike to see them round the old oak tree that did for a post. The finish was outside our local alehouse, the Queen's Head, which stood on the left side of the road opposite the green. Houses straggled round it but most of the village was at the other side, along with the mill that ground our corn – a windmill, not a water mill, although there was one of those farther on, where the road crossed the river. The green was triangular, going to a point away from the road, and at the point were the gates of the squire's place, Friars Hall, with the park beyond and the drive up to the big house. On the far side of the gates at the top of the green was our church, St Mary's, with the rectory beside it hidden away in a tangle of trees, where the rooks squawked all day long. All around were the usual decrepit cottages with their pigsties and vegetable plots, and the rough ground where the villagers pegged out their cows or their donkeys. Thank God, we were better off than them, lords by comparison.

The road that ran through our village was fairly busy, and a great load on the parish to keep it in repair, as it was used by long-distance traffic and smart coaches. Hence the children's job of stone-picking all the hours God sent, to add to the piles the road menders were always requiring. (Three pailfuls before school was normal, taken off the arable land before the corn got too high.) But the passing trade was good for the village and especially the Queen's Head. It wasn't a posting inn, but the stable yard was well used and the landlord kept several liveries for hire. (He wanted Tilly when we retired her, but no way was she going there, or anywhere else come to that.)

And for the match, the squire himself came down

from the hall on foot with a party of friends, and the vicar (who loved a bet) came out from his study with his consumptive son Nicholas smothered in scarves, and the Grovers came in their carriage – what swank! – too proud to walk half a mile! What were they coming to? we all asked. That was Maggie, of course; the old man would have walked. We all saw Maggie bob to the squire and turn red, and the squire doffed his hat and said 'Good morning' but made no move to introduce her to his friends, who were obviously gentry. But not above taking brandy in the Queen's Head along with the throng. Grover rarely went in the Queen's Head; only when he took visitors. Martin was in there, helping out. I wanted to be with him when the match started. He was my friend and would keep me calm. Martin did all sorts of jobs round the village, a lot on our farm. Although his father was the ganger, he refused to work for him at Grover's.

I went up with Margaret and Ellen, having got Tilly ready for Jack. Jack was dressing up for the occasion in his best breeches, a white stock and a gorgeous bright red waistcoat under his smart dark jacket. His topper was slightly ancient but his boots were new and shone as well as the saddle that I had polished. With his bright face and blonde hair he looked lovely. He *was* lovely. No one had a better brother than me.

Of course Margaret didn't want to stay by me. Dolled up in her green velvet with the cold brightening her already bright cheeks, her mass of blonde curls scarcely hidden by a silk shawl, she knew perfectly well that all the men were eyeing her. She was like an actress on the stage. I wished I could love Margaret, but I couldn't. Nor could Jack or Ellen. But because she is the image of our dead mother, poor old Father doted on her. To him she could do no wrong, although it was perfectly clear that she was lazy and selfish.

She went off with her admirers and Jack came down the road on Tilly and gave me her to hold while he went into the tavern to report to the starter. Everyone crowded round and I shouted at them as Tilly lashed out behind in her usual prima donna way. But most of them knew her well and laughed and stayed clear.

'She's in the right mood,' they said, knowingly.

Yes, I knew she was.

Nat Grover rode down and jumped off beside me. I thought he was going to give me Crocus to hold too, but old Sim came out of the crush and took the reins. Nat grinned at me. He too looked the part, only his gear was shining new and he was three years older than Jack, a man really, with his smart black sideburns and shaved cheeks.

'How's the old mare?' he asked.

'She's in good heart,' I said.

'She'll need to be.' But he smiled. He wasn't so bad really, and certainly was attractive. Even I could see what Margaret saw when he came down our track on the chestnut colt. But he had a notorious temper and was unsparing on the people who worked for him, taking his cue from his father. I could see that he, like Jack, was nervous. There was a lot at stake: pride for him and the money for us.

Sim kept Crocus well clear of Tilly, although Crocus stood amongst all the excitement like a lamb, kind and well mannered. The horsemen all stood round admiringly. Even so, most of them had bet on Tilly. I had no money to bet.

Then Jack and Nat came out and mounted, and the crowd fell back. I stood close, checking the girths and the stirrup leathers. Jack was silent now, concentrating. Tilly started going up on her hind legs as she usually did at the start, but I held on to her and led her to the tavern signpost on the green that marked the start. The stewards held back the big crowd of riders that was collecting to follow – most of them would quickly be left behind, although some Newmarket horses generally kept up for the first few miles.

'Ready, boys? Off you go then.'

The starter dropped his handkerchief, I let go and Tilly went off with a plunge, immediately into the trot that she could keep up for ever. Crocus, slightly bewildered by what was happening, did not find his stride until Nat had given him a clout with his whip – typical, I thought – and Tilly was already well ahead. That was experience. But youth was on Crocus's side, I knew. I felt a pang for poor old Tilly, who would now always have a younger horse to beat.

We all stood back as the great crowd of followers jostled past – farmers, boys, young toffs, some of the squire's guests, doctors, blacksmiths, millers – everyone who could lay hands on a horse for the day, even a few children on donkeys and ponies. The iron shoes struck sparks from the flinty road, several people fell in the ditch, a cart was upset . . . it was always the same with such a crowd and plenty of ale drunk already. After the cavalry had passed, all the men barged into the inn and the women wandered off up the green to gossip and watch their children play. I stood in the road and watched the departing army, feeling sick with worry. I longed for it to be over – it would only take a little over the hour.

The old vicar came up with poor Nicholas and enquired kindly after our family. 'I hope the mare wins for you.'

I always felt embarrassed with the vicar, for since Mother died our father had refused to go to church, and none of us went either, only Margaret sometimes so that she could dress up and be seen. But the vicar's wife had died too, and Nicholas was fast going the same way, yet the vicar still believed. I remember Nicholas as a young boy hunting on a fierce little pony: he had been a great rider and a wild boy before falling through the ice while skating four years ago and catching pneumonia. From that illness he had never properly recovered and now, at fourteen, was a pale shadow of his former self, only able to walk slowly a short distance. But he was always cheerful, still care-less and jokey. I really liked him. He had thick blonde hair that always needed cutting and very blue eyes. I took butter and eggs up to the rectory quite often and I used to go in and he always came to talk. He led a very boring life now, not able to go out, and was always pleased to have a visitor.

'Pa wouldn't get the trap out. I wanted to follow a bit,' he said to me. 'He said it's too dangerous.' Nicholas shrugged dismissively. 'I used to like following.'

'I would if I had a horse,' I said.

'You can go up the church tower at the end if you like,' he said.

'Yes, thank you. I will.' You could see well from there about two miles down the road; people went up there by invitation only, otherwise the mob would jam it. 'Father asked Sir and his party, no one else. They won't mind you.'

Nicholas always called the squire Sir. He was Sir Alderbrook Bart, correctly, more often known as His Nibs around the village or, properly, Sir James. He made whacking bets on horses, mostly at Newmarket where he had a few in training. People quite liked him, he didn't throw his weight about and was much better to work for than Eb Grover. Mind you, he didn't mix much with the village usually, only when it was a sporting event, like now.

Martin came and found me. We always waited by the post for the first rounding. I told him I had been invited up the church tower. 'I'll ask if you can come too.'

I did and the vicar, looking worried, said, 'Yes, my dear, but no one else. Because I promised Sir James, you understand.'

'No, only Martin.'

When it came to the important things in life, like now, it was always Martin I relied on. Martin and Jack. Together they were invincible, so strong, so funny;

they always found a way round trouble, always bobbed up from disaster. Martin helped us a lot, and worked in the Queen's Head livery yard and in the bar. His family lived on the verge of real poverty, for there were eight living children out of thirteen born. Martin was the oldest. He was at our place a lot, for peace and quiet, he said.

He knew how I was feeling. It was how he was feeling too. My father was drinking with the farmers naturally, the day promising triumph or disaster, both equally hard to stay sober about. We hung around by the post along with most of the crowd, trying to picture how it was going out there, watching the time on the church clock. People were now betting on the first horse to come into sight this time round. Crocus was clear favourite for this. Everyone knew how Tilly picked up her power later on, grinding down the opposition.

They were right too. Crocus came back with Tilly out of sight until he had already rounded. Nat was sitting up there, red in the face, spurring away, and Crocus was still going great guns, but there was an expression of disquiet about his beautiful head, his eyes rimmed white. He wasn't enjoying it. But when Tilly came – oh, she was enjoying it, you could tell! Even though her ragged ears were flat back on her head there was that blaze in her eye that everyone knew, and the swagger of her great stride, still steady, saving herself, made everyone put up a cheer. She was a real sight, making every real horseman feel weepy, for they didn't come often like Tilly. She was as great in her trade as some of those horses that won the Derby or the great matches at Newmarket.

Jack was grinning. He never wore spurs and only used his whip on bystanders taking a liberty. He shouted to me, 'Don't worry, we'll catch him easily!' Tilly went round the post without any guiding from Jack and was back up the road with her great backside working away, her mothy tail floating wide and sparks flying from her iron feet.

I saw old Sim shake his head and say to young Peter, 'He's got our horse unsettled. It's no way to ride a youngster, frightening him.'

'But he's winning!' shouted Peter.

Sim shook his head again. 'He won't win.'

Martin almost knocked me over with a bear-hug and I felt my confidence flood back. All the Tilly backers were shouting and a fist fight had broken out down the street. Margaret was talking to one of the squire's party, a very handsome young man. Trust her! There was nothing coy about Margaret. But the squire himself, His Nibs, was already strolling up the green with his friends accompanied by the vicar. Martin and I fell in behind and Nicholas joined us. His cheeks were flushed and his blue eyes as bright as Tilly's.

'She's a wonder! Nat will never beat her.'

Well, we all thought that.

We made our way towards the tower steps, keeping several steps behind the smart party. Nicholas of course had to stay at the bottom. He sat himself on the church wall and huddled into his scarves. Martin went on, but I stayed with Nicholas for a bit as it was a rare occasion to talk to everyone. There was a boy about the same age as Nicholas on a white mare, who I didn't know. He looked like Nicholas would if he were still fit, sitting so easily on the mare.

'Who's that?' I asked.

'Prosper Mayes.'

'Mayes?'

That was a big farmer the other side of the turnpike, some twenty miles away. Mayes had no less than seven sons working for him and his farm was even bigger than Grovers'. The Mayes were very rich and, unlike the Grovers, were liked. Prosper Mayes was very handsome, with longish curling brown hair, curling lips and an aristocratic nose.

'You should marry him, Clara. Later on, of course. He's lovely and rich and likes horses. That mare is an Arab, strange, eh?' We weren't into Arabs in our part of the world, although rich people were importing them all the time.

'He wouldn't want to marry me, I don't think,' I said.

'Why not? You're coming on nicely. I'd marry you, but what good would that be?' Nicholas, unlike Margaret, had no illusions about his brief future.

'I thought you wanted to marry Miss Charlotte?'

'Well, yes. She's my number one, but she's got to marry some lordship or other, hasn't she? Go to balls and things and be shown off like a pedigree cow. You know what they're like.'

I laughed. I did like Nicholas.

The sun was shining but it was very sharp, and a

cold wind was rising. It was certainly cold on the church tower. But the view was stupendous. We could see our farm, Small Gains, some half a mile away down the road, with the wide curve of the river Grid encircling our lower fields as it made its way behind the village to the water mill on the far side. The willows and alders that lined the river were red-twigged in the sun and our woods gold and brown in the last of their leaf. How pretty it looked! If Tilly won her two hundred and Father came up on his bets, we would go home laughing today! What a bonus that would be! I was shivering with excitement, not cold. From our viewpoint you could see the road as it went out of the village; then it was lost behind a rise in the ground. It was all Grover's land on the left opposite ours, right to where it came up against the ancient wall that surrounded Friar's Hall. Inside the wall was all parkland with very ancient trees and deer and cattle, and the old house at the top with woods behind it.

Sir James nodded kindly to me and said, 'Your horse looks the likely winner, I think. That young chestnut hasn't the experience.'

'I hope so, sir.'

He was a nice old buffer. He had commanded a ship under Nelson and lost an arm at the battle of Aboukir Bay, blown off by a cannon-ball, which was bad luck as he loved to shoot pheasant. He still did, but not very well any more. He had a ship's telescope, which he was balancing on the church battlements. He let me have a go and I had a better look at Prosper. Yes, he was certainly very desirable, but how was I likely to get in with a rich farming family like that? It didn't happen. I would marry Martin when I was fifteen. Before, or shortly after, I became pregnant. That's what we all did if we could, to be safe and decent.

It was nice looking down on the green all crowded with people, and we could see more people on horseback coming into the village from the other way, just to see the finish. We could no longer see the church clock as it was underneath us, but everyone knew almost to the minute what time the horses would hove in sight again, and you could tell by everyone crowding towards the post that they were due.

Of course we saw them first.

'Tilly!' we all screamed, even Sir James.

I felt all my insides swell up and nearly burst with pride at seeing the tiny speck of her, unmistakable, pounding round the long curve. Now her trot was into top gear and she came along in front of a great crowd of followers all on *galloping* thoroughbreds, half-dead, yet I knew there was no speck of sweat on Tilly.

'She's a marvel,' murmured Sir James.

Martin's red face was like a beacon, his ginger hair clashing gloriously. His smile stretched from ear to ear.

'Good old Jack. His arse'll be sore for a fortnight.'

Yes, I knew that. Moans and groans.

A great cheer went up from the green as they first sighted her. Of Crocus we could see no sign. Strange how it never occurred to us that it wasn't in the bag, that the post was still a quarter of a mile off. Still no sign of Crocus.

So, what happened?

It was hard to make out from where we were, but afterwards Jack said it was a drain that gave way under the road. In mid stride Tilly suddenly pitched forward and fell on her knees. Such was the rate she was going at that she turned a complete somersault. Jack went flying. I screamed. But Tilly, quick as a flash, was on her feet again and at that my heart blossomed with relief. It was everything, whatever happened, that she was not killed. But Jack, instead of leaping back on, lay in a rolling heap. Like a real pro he had kept hold of the reins, but I thought I could hear his scream from the church tower. Something awful was wrong. And then the spectators and crowds engulfed him and we couldn't see what was happening. But round the bend came Crocus, pounding away, and drawing fast towards the stricken rivals.

Well, they got Jack back on. How they did it I have no idea, because he was screaming with pain. But they didn't care, those gamblers whose money was on. They held him on and clapped Tilly across the buttocks, but Tilly's heart was now with Jack. She was going to look after Jack. Besides which, Sir James with his telescope said her knees were broken and pouring blood.

I was weeping buckets.

I saw Crocus come up and could almost feel Nat's amazement and elation at the sight before him. Poor old Tilly was sort of crow-hopping along, knowing just like a human that the post was nearly there and she really ought to win, but so anxious for Jack and for her own knees. She saw Crocus go past and snapped out at him, and then she stopped because she knew it was all over, and Jack was allowed to slide out of the saddle.

Crocus, poor darling, came gasping to the post and was received in dead silence. Not a wave nor a cheer, even from the people who had backed him. It was just too awful, the match in ruins. Nat pulled up but even he could see it was a hollow victory that he had won. I almost felt sorry for him – it was so embarrassing, the feeling against him. Sim came forward and took Crocus, and patted his neck and gave him something out of his pocket, but poor Crocus was too done in to take it, and stood head down, flanks heaving. Tilly never finished like that. Young Peter loosened his girth, which Nat never bothered to attend to.

On the top of the tower we all stood stunned, as one, me and the squire. He put his one arm round my shoulders and said, 'I'm so sorry, my dear. What deuced bad luck! She didn't deserve that.'

I saw the vicar's distress and supposed he saw it as God's will. No wonder my father had given up going to church! Jesus did not love us, no way. We stumbled down the stairs. There were tears on Martin's cheeks.

'Whatever happened?' Nicholas asked. 'I couldn't see a thing.'

Leaving the others to explain, Martin and I ran down the green. You could feel the anger and discontent like a wave engulfing us, such a crowd milling round and the stewards trying to clear the road. Fights and arguments, riders pushing through from every-where. I hated them all suddenly. I wanted Tilly. I shoved my way through furiously.

She stood by the post, very subdued, Jack still holding on to her, crying. He was white as a sheet, holding his shoulder.

'Clara!' he gasped. 'Oh Clara!'

'It wasn't your fault!' I put my arms round him, he was so distressed. I took Tilly's rein and hugged Jack.

'What have you done?'

'Oh, it hurts so! My arm, my shoulder, I don't know what. Look after Tilly.'

He was almost fainting, but luckily Dr Roberts, the local quack, arrived on the scene and took over.

'Carry him into the inn,' he ordered, and the crowd began to disperse, arguing and cursing.

I bent over Tilly to look at her knees. They were bleeding, but the wounds did not seem too deep. The sooner I got her home to bathe them the better. Martin had gone in with Jack, and as I led Tilly away I found I was accompanied by old Sim and Crocus. Crocus had got his wind back but looked half the horse from an hour ago, tucked up and distressed. His head was tossing up and down, up and down. Tilly walked dispiritedly, more fed up than tired.

'That was a bad business,' said Sim. 'She was the winner all over.'

'As long as she's all right,' I said.

'Aye, well, this poor boy will get a panning from the master. He's no patience, Mister Nat. He doesn't understand, you can't hurry a young horse. It does them no good to get a hiding before they're ready.'

'Sell him to us if Nat wants to be rid of him!'

'Oh, he won't get rid of him. He's not that much of a fool.'

We walked along, not saying much. I liked old Sim. I took Tilly into the yard and unsaddled her, rubbed her down and put her tattered rug over her back and led her down the track to where it crossed the river. There was a gravel sort of ford where it was shallow enough to pass, and I led her there and into water deep enough to cover her knees. The ice-clear river washed away the blood and dirt. She knew the sense of it and stood calmly, reaching out to munch the passing weeds. Of course although I tried to stay on the ford she pulled me in and I was up to my knees in the icy water. What I did for that horse! Devotion knows no bounds. I tried to pull up my skirt but it was hopeless keeping dry. Well, it had to be done.

After the excitement and clamour up on the green, it was lonely and silent down by the river. I had time to stand and reflect on the day's disaster: Jack's injury which would keep him out of work for weeks by the look of it; Father's despair; Tilly's knees ... even Margaret's growing desire for Nat Grover ... all bad news on a day that had promised such joy.

I was worried by the effect it would have on Father. He got depressed very easily these days. He seemed to have lost heart and strength since our mother's death, growing old before his time. He suffered from quite bad rheumatism and was often in pain which made him bad-tempered. It wasn't all sweetness and light at home any more. Ellen went away down the village with her friends and said she couldn't wait to get a job in service, it was too miserable at home. I didn't really blame her. She was high-spirited like Jack, not patient like me, and had no interest in the horses or the farm. If it wasn't for Tilly and the hope of getting another like her, I might have felt the same. But now the prospect of buying a new horse had faded. So much for our hopes.

The sun slanted across the golden stubble where the gleaners had still left seeds for the pheasants to pick up. We daren't take a pheasant, even off our own land; they were all Sir James's. But they were lovely to watch, their amazing colours gleaming in the sunshine. I was often heartened just by looking at our fields and the woods. I couldn't stomach the thought of going away, like Margaret and Ellen with their hankerings. 'This old place,' they muttered. 'The sooner we get out of here the better.' But not me. The harvest had been good at least and the horkey afterwards on the village green had been great. That was when Nat had first approached Margaret. I had sat with Nicholas and that was the first time he had said, 'If I was to get married, Clara, I would marry you.' And we both laughed then, because we both knew he would be dead before he was old enough to marry. But he was no farmer. I wanted to marry a farmer who would come to Small Gains and make it pay. Could Prosper possibly be as nice as he looked?

And standing there with Tilly, warming my hands under her rug, I thought that worse things could happen than happened today. She wasn't hurt badly, she was still a winner, we owned our farm. How many could say that? It had been in Father's family for four generations, when our great-great-grandfather had got rich on cloth. He was the Eb Grover of his day, ruthless and talented far beyond his descendants. True, Small Gains had shrunk and become a lot poorer since his day, but it was still ours.

I walked slowly home and dried Tilly's legs. Her knees were no longer bleeding but I wrapped cloths round them to stop the straw sticking when she lay down. I fed her and left her to rest. I went in and took off my boots and skirt and stockings and stood steaming in front of the range. Unlike Margaret, I only had two skirts, both cut down from Mother's. And only one pair of boots, which I could see I would have to wear wet when I went out again. I stuffed them with straw and stood them in the hearth. Then I boiled the kettle and made myself some tea, and waited for the others to come home.

4

Martin brought Jack home later, both riding on a horse from the livery yard which Martin would return when he went. Jack was now fairly cheerful as his injury was not a fracture but a dislocation of the shoulder, which Dr Roberts had mended. It was all bound up and still very painful, but not as bad as a fracture.

'He just pulled it back,' said Martin gleefully. 'A great big yank and Jack didn't half holler – you should have heard him! Then he looked really surprised to find he was cured.'

'And he didn't charge anything, the old sawbones,' Jack said.

That was rare for Dr Roberts, who only let the really poor off. He was on the surface a miserable old sod, but, deep down, was sometimes known to act kindly.

'That's because he'd bet on Crocus,' Martin said. 'He was really pleased old Tilly turned somersault.'

I had put some onions and mutton in a pot because I knew Margaret wouldn't be back in a hurry and I ladled them out the broth and cut bread. My skirt steamed over the fire. I told them Tilly was all right.

'Even if we didn't win, I still reckon we should go to that sale next week at Diss. We might have enough money for a yearling,' I said.

'We want another horse, trotter or not,' Jack said. 'It's daft to have to ride two on Tilly now you and I go to market with Father.'

We had six other carthorses besides Ben – Matchem and Duke (who was a mare!), Boney and Blücher, Blossom and Ted – but you'd be all day if you rode them anywhere. I agreed with Jack. He was right. I noticed how he was taking decisions over from Father these days.

'We'll use the money,' Jack said. 'Getting a winner is a freak, anyway. Look what they paid for Crocus, and he didn't really win, did he?'

'He will, I reckon,' said Martin.

I reckoned too.

'Tilly's still good for a few more wins yet,' Jack said.

It was good, the three of us together, and no one else. Rare. I loved being with just them and I never was, save out in the fields sometimes, working. I liked being alone too, but there was no privacy in our house: I had to share a bedroom with Margaret, Ellen had a tiny room and Father and Jack shared the other. Father's depression, Margaret's airs and graces, Ellen's rebellious tantrums ... without them it was lovely. I fetched some home brew out of the scullery and we sat round the range, drinking and eating apples. Jack was white and in pain, I could see, but he liked it too. He sat staring into the fire opposite

Martin, in Father's chair. They were both fifteen, he and Martin, and strong and ardent, but life did not offer much in the way of fulfilment. I thought of Nat Grover, with all that his money could buy and his great inheritance and all the pretty girls after him . . . and then I thought of Nicholas . . . what was there to say? Martin fetched some more apples.

'Both our fathers'll come home legless tonight,' he remarked.

Yes, we knew that. We would heave Father up to bed and he wouldn't wake up till lunch time. He was like that these days.

Jack needed to go to bed so I put a hot stone in for him and we saw him up the stairs. The doctor had sent a dose of laudanum to see him through the night so we gave him that and I promised I'd try not to let Father disturb him. With luck he'd be too drunk to get up the stairs.

Martin and I sat on for a bit.

I said to him, 'You ought to get a horse job.'

'Pigs might fly.'

'Sim got one. That was a miracle.'

'Yes, it was. Grover doesn't pay him what he's worth though. He knows Sim'll never get another job. He pays him a pittance.'

'I hate Grover!' I shouted out.

Margaret chose that moment to appear in the doorway, and heard me.

'Tut tut, you're jealous,' she said.

I felt like strangling her, standing there looking like a holy angel with her bright cheeks and blown bright hair and the light of love in her eyes. She was alight with life, our doomed Margaret, and I could not bear the thought of hating her when she had nothing to look forward to. Unlike poor Nicholas she was quite heedless of her future apart from the next day or the day after that. And quite obviously the next day and the day after that was filled now with the image of our vanquisher, Nat Grover.

'Pa Grover we were talking about,' I said sulkily. 'And Jack was really the winner today, you know that.'

'Yes, even Nat said so. He was over the moon at his luck.'

And, remembering his fine figure and laughing face, how could I blame Margaret for going with him?

'How is Jack?' she asked.

And I didn't hate her any more, but fetched her a drink and told her Jack was in bed. Martin stood up and said he'd be getting along. He was always uneasy with Margaret. He was probably not immune to her charms, being a strong lusty lad, although I knew he didn't like her. He liked me but I had no charms. At eleven I wasn't much of a child, not like Ellen. I understood all these things. It was the animal background, I suppose.

So Martin left and then I sat over the fire with Margaret and she told me she loved Nat Grover and he loved her, and whatever were they going to do about it?

'Nothing,' I said.

She groaned. 'His parents will never have me! They scarcely pass the time of day. That Maggie Grover –

she stares at me like I'm dirt, yet we all know she was only a dairymaid, and an ugly one at that. The old man – well, the way he looks at me – it's like he would have me for himself if he had half a chance! And of course Nat can't marry if they don't say so, for he's nothing of his own. That Maggie will never allow it, I know she won't. She wants Miss Charlotte for him, at least, if not some title out of Norfolk.'

Then, after a pause, she said, 'The old man says Nat can't marry a sick maid like me. That's what he called me!'

'Why, has Nat asked him?' I was startled to hear things had gone this far.

'Nat said that, so I suppose so.'

Or was Nat just saying it, I wondered, to string Margaret along? She wasn't a good marriage save for her beauty; even he with his ambition must see that. The Grovers wanted to marry more land, there was no doubt about it. That's what the big farmers always did. Love rarely came into it. Charlotte would bring a few acres, and our water meadows, for nothing.

'He's too young to think of marriage, surely,' I said.

'Well, I'm not,' Margaret said tartly. 'I'd give anything to get out of here!'

She spoke with such a sudden burst of passion that I realized, yes, she knew time was short, she wanted some comfort and she wanted it soon. She burst into tears and for once I loved her dearly. I reached out and took her hand and said, 'Don't cry, Margaret. He loves you, that's the main thing. Things work out.'

'Oh Clara, I do love him so!' she wept. 'What shall I do?'

'He'll come and see you, you won't lose him. Don't cry!'

'It will never happen! I want a nice place, Clara – I want – oh – I want—!' Coughing choked her. She could not cope with this sort of emotion. Her crying became hysterical; the colour was hot on her cheeks and the dreaded fever that we all knew so well started to shake her.

I put my arms round her and tried to soothe her but she shook me off and howled.

'It's all right for you! You're ugly but you're strong! He'd never call you a sick maid!'

Well, I know she was hysterical, but I never forgot those words she came out with. Plain, perhaps, but *ugly*? It was like being hit with a stone. Like Maggie Grover? It implied sourness as well as bad looks. Yes, like Maggie Grover. Like Tilly! Because I never *felt* ugly, that was the truth. All the same, I'd rather be ugly than consumptive.

I calmed her down with one of her drinks and pulled her chair up to the fire to stop her shivering and told her Nat would be true to her, of course he would, she was so lovely, and even if they never married she would have him for ages . . . she would get tired of him before he did of her. Now she could not stop coughing – oh, that dreadful cough, which brought up specks of blood on the white boiled rag I gave her. Just like Mother's. No wonder poor Father got drunk, to think of going through all that again with Margaret and being helpless to stop it.

'You should have come home earlier, out of the cold,' I said.

'And miss all the fun, like I always do?'

'Well, it wasn't much fun for the rest of us,' I said a trifle shortly.

After she had gone to bed I sat there thinking, yes, I am just like Tilly, sour and ugly at eleven years old. I cried a bit, because of poor Tilly and Jack. And then I thought, if I had a heart like Tilly, I would get by.

5

I was going to market with Father with the pot of money, to buy a new horse. We only had Tilly to ride the twenty miles there and it was too far for her to carry Jack as well as Father, so I was going. I rode behind and Tilly scarcely knew I was there. Her knees had healed very well.

Jack was furious not to be going and gave me all sorts of instructions about what not to let Father do and what sort of a horse not to buy. But he knew we both knew what we were about. Jack and I realized now that Father was failing to see how much we had depended on Tilly to make us money. The money we lost when she turned her somersault was sorely missed.

So we set off, Father and I, me sitting behind on a cushion that I tied to the saddle – sideways of course, as I was wearing what were laughably known as my best clothes. Market day in town was an occasion, after all. I was the lucky one. Margaret and Jack were furious not to go. It was just before Christmas, a festive time, but Margaret was too ill for the journey and

Jack could not be spared. We did desperately need another horse, even if it never won a race. We had had an old cob, but he took the colic in the spring and we couldn't save him.

So we set off, muffled up to the nines, as it was bitterly cold. The road was hard with frost which was marginally preferable to deep mud, although dangerous. But Tilly was catlike on her feet and we trusted her. We fell in with other farmers all going the same way, and Father chatted, and then let Tilly hurry on as she loved to do, until we met the next group. Tilly was so well known: it was nice sitting up there and being recognized and admired. I had turned her out the best I could, but when Nat sailed past on Crocus with his father on another horse even more handsome, I felt a pang of jealous rage. If only Tilly had her life ahead of her instead of behind!

They were a motley lot, these travellers, mostly farmers and their wives. The wives rode behind, like me, or walked. Lots of people walked. But about halfway on our journey we came up with a couple on a fine big trotting mare which had an unweaned foal running behind it. This wasn't uncommon in the summer: mares often went to work with their foals. We supposed they were going to sell it.

But the farmer laughed and said, 'No, he's only out for the ride. The mare'd not go without him. He'll be coming back with us tonight.'

The foal was in his winter coat, thick and black. He could not be considered pretty, but he had a grand stride on him. I couldn't help noticing. And there was something about him: a boldness, a great interest in the goings-on around him. He was all over the place, not tired at all, although the farmer came from beyond our farm, nearly out to the turnpike. Of course he knew Tilly and we had to explain how she fell in the drain. While Father chatted I watched the foal. And I fell in love with him.

Funny, this thing about horses. You can see the most beautiful in the world and you admire but remain unmoved. I admired Tilly but did not truly care for her as Father did. I do not think Nat cared for Crocus save as a money-spinner, but Crocus was my unattainable dream. I saw hundreds of horses all the time but I did not covet them in this special way. But this foal, he was different. He had rather a big head, with short alert ears and big inquisitive eyes, a nice face in short. There was a white star but no other white. He also had an enlarged hock, but it made no difference to his action.

I asked the farmer and he said carelessly, 'He got kicked, by a cow.'

'What is his sire?'

At this the farmer looked rather shame-faced and said, 'Truth to tell, I've no idea. I graze the mare on the common at times, and some randy nag must've been running loose or got out from somewhere – she just dropped this foal out of the blue – we didn't even know she was expecting it. She made no show, save just a week before, and I thought it was a false do, you know. She'd never bred before. Well, right put out we were, for she works hard on the farm, all day and every day.'

'Poor girl, she only got a day or two off,' laughed the farmer's wife.

As the wife weighed as much as a heifer behind the saddle, and the farmer too was as good as two or three bushels of corn, I saw that the mare was as tough as they came, trotting steadily with that burden after fifteen or so miles.

I said to Father when we parted, 'You ought to make an offer for that foal.'

But he said, 'I don't want one as'll do nothing but eat for three years.'

'They're cheaper like that. We've got the food.'

'I want one now. I'll be dead three years from now.'

With this happy thought to sustain me, I watched the foal behind me as Tilly forged ahead. He came with us for a bit, for fun, and his stride matched Tilly's for fifty yards. I could see those baby shoulders moving like our mare's, the forelegs covering a great pace and the hind legs coming past longer, the sign of a good horse. I just hoped no one else noticed. I thought, Wait till I talk to Jack. We're going to get that foal. I rode on in a dream, thinking up names for it. For once I felt happy and excited, going to the market, all the bustle and people and fun. Everyone loved it: it was the only time they met up and gossiped and ate in a roaring inn and maybe made some money.

Well, the sale ring was offering trotting horses by famous Norfolk trotting sires, or out of mares by the famous Fireaway, Pretender, Hue and Cry,

Bellfounder (if you could believe them), and one or two of them were marked to fetch big prices. All the best horses would be offered in March at Downham Market when all the European and American dealers came over to buy, and these were, I suppose, second best, but the sort the likes of us might be able to afford. We left Tilly with a man Father knew on the edge of town and went on with the throng, first to the White Hart, of course, for a brandy to warm us – mine was mostly hot water – and to find out what was being offered. What a babble! I slipped out and went looking on my own, but my head was full of 'my' foal. Horses were everywhere tied to posts and doorknobs, and I wandered up the street looking. The 'cream' for sale were in the back yard of the inn but I knew that any of them Father deemed worth bidding for would go for more than we had. Father had an eye for a horse; he wouldn't make do with second best, not after Tilly. Farmers were complaining bitterly about hard times now that the big prices they got during the war were a thing of the past, but when it came to finding a price for a good horse, most of them could do it. When it came to paying their labourers – that was a different thing altogether. The big farmers were ruthless exploiters of the hapless workers. The Grovers were not alone.

Fortunately, although I didn't find the foal I saw the farmer who owned her and his wife buying at a harness shop and I went up to the woman and asked her where she lived. She recognized me and told me the name of their farm and I asked her if they were going to sell the foal later.

'Oh, I don't know about that. He's a strong beast and might be useful to us in time.' Then she added, 'He's not an easy one though. He'll lead us a dance, I dare say.' She laughed. 'Your father fancy him then?'

'Oh no. He wouldn't buy a foal,' I said.

I daren't say I fancied him. Children didn't buy horses. I just said, 'I like him. He's sweet.' The sort of thing a child ought to say. He was anything but sweet.

At least I had her address. I had no plan and no money, but I really wanted that colt.

The upshot of our day out was that yes, we bought a horse, and it was cheap, but it wasn't the horse Father wanted. That was a dark brown ten-year-old by Jary's Bellfounder, a sire since exported to America. It was the best horse at the fair and went way beyond our pot of gold, although Father stayed in the bidding long after it was wise. With his last bid the pot would have been completely bare, leaving nothing for the second riding horse we desperately wanted. I stood shivering by his side, praying for him to stop throwing our dearly-earned money away on a *ten-year-old* which had proved nothing. Father said it would go if it was matched, which it hadn't been so far, but I saw nothing of the steel about it that a match-winner needed. It had mean eyes. Couldn't Father see? Sometimes I thought his brain was getting fuddled with the drink. He was getting old, fortyish, I suppose, at that time. Certainly by the end of the sale he had had a skinful and when the Bellfounder horse went for two hundred and eighty guineas he swore and said to me, 'Get a horse for Jack, but nothing over thirty pounds.' And made off back to the White Hart to drown his sorrows.

I stared at him in disbelief. The sale was nearly over, a few sad old nags left, and everyone was leaving after the excitement of the Bellfounder horse. Father departed and I was left with his stupid instructions, the first few flakes of Christmas snow drifting over my hair. There was only rubbish left.

I examined them hastily. I didn't want an old one, nor one not strong enough to pull a plough beside Ben, like Tilly did. That left about three, and the only one of these that shaped up – without any glaring flaws of conformation – was a sad and very·thin brown gelding. I tried to see him well-fed and well-groomed, but it was very difficult. He looked congenitally a loser, somehow, as if he never expected anything of life but the worst. This rather warmed me to him, although I knew sentiment was fatal. We couldn't afford sentiment. I gave him a caress and he lifted his head and looked kindly at me. His eyes were right.

I bid and got him for fifteen pounds. The auctioneer knew who I was and took my father's name and told me to fetch the money before someone stole it off him. As it was sewn into his trousers I didn't think this would happen, only that it would take me a time to unpick it. I was more worried about whether our poor horse would make the journey home.

Father was not pleased when he saw it. He wasn't pleased about anything at all, save that he grudgingly acceded that the horse I had bought was worth the money – if it lived.

'It's not that bad! Only starved,' I said.

We stayed to eat, although I would rather have set off for home. But it was fun in the inn and Father cheered up when the food was inside him, and took no more drink, thank God. He bargained for a length of pretty cloth as a present for Margaret and even bought me a little piece for a blouse, not nearly as nice as Margaret's, but no matter. It put him in a good mood again. The hot sweat of the bawling farmers, the pipe smoke and cooking smells were better than the cold outside, but I couldn't help thinking of that poor horse waiting in the snow. As were lots of others, no doubt, but at least Tilly was in a stable on the edge of town. When we went out it was only the lot number that told us which horse was ours, for it was pitch dark, and we had to ask a groom with a lantern to help us find it.

We collected Tilly and got on her, with me holding the lead-rope of the other horse, and of course Tilly set off for home at her best trot, and the other horse couldn't keep up and I had the lead rope pulled out of my hand. What a journey! It was hopeless trying to slow Tilly down and after about halfway when I was exhausted with being pulled in two by the lead rope, I got down off Tilly and said I would walk the rest. Father grumbled but was quite pleased really, with the prospect of a fast ride home on his dearest possession. As for me, I thought it was wiser to walk with our new horse than ride him, in case he had tricks I didn't know about. It was not the time to find you'd bought a bolter or a bucker. So I plodded on, pulling my cloak hood well over, leading the horse. He was willing enough at this pace and had no thoughts about jibbing or wanting to go back the way he'd come, so we got on fast enough. It was dark and snowing softly but the road was good and quite a few people passed with cheery good nights. Only the Grovers, father and son, rode past too close and too fast and made my horse shy away in fright. Typical, I thought. Not a word to their neighbour. They hadn't bought another horse though, I noticed.

I decided to call our new horse Hopeful – maybe he was. As I walked I thought up names for *my* horse, the dark foal from Cribb's Farm. I determined that night to have him. His raking trot was engraved on my mind – I only hoped that no one else had noticed it. With luck he did not show it off too often, only a few strides at a time between gambols and bucks. I would tell Jack my secret. I know he would be on my side. He might not be too enamoured of poor old Hopeful, but he might have been landed with worse.

I had about ten miles to walk and it was late when I got home. Father had thrown feed at Tilly and rugged her up but not cleaned her. It was too late for that now. Everyone was in bed and asleep. I went in to fetch a lantern. There wasn't a stall for Hopeful and I had to leave him tied in the cartshed for the time being. But I gave him a deep bed and water and a small feed of oats besides a load of good hay. He couldn't believe his luck at the oats and wolfed them down greedily. I brushed all the snow off him. The shed had its back to the wind and made a good shelter, so he was happy enough, and I went in to bed. Margaret as usual was sweating like a pig with her illness so I snuggled up to her and was warm in no time.

6

She came marching up the drive as bold as brass. In the frosty morning her colour sparkled: red shawl thrown over the golden curls; bright pink cheeks; radiant blue eyes and her best green velvet – not man enough to keep out the cold but just the colour to set off the pink and the gold. Margaret did not need furs when her love for Nat kept her fever burning.

Sim was full of admiration for her daring, his old heart not impervious to the girl's beauty.

'Nat said he would meet me here at eleven,' she called out to him. 'Am I early?'

'No, miss, but he had to go in with his father's visitor. If he knows you're waiting, no doubt he'll be out in a trice.'

'I don't want to see Eb! Nat told me he'd be closeted with the Enclosure man all morning and he wouldn't see us. He doesn't approve of me – you can guess?' She laughed.

'He don't approve of much, miss, that's for sure.'

How could anyone not approve of Margaret? She was the spit of her mother, but without her mother's steel. She was thistledown, blown before the wind of delight. Strange how that family had thrown up such different siblings: heedless, lovely Margaret; strong, brave Jack; the stern child Clara and wild little Ellen – not one of them dull or unworthy like so many of the village puddings.

'I reckon you're better company for Mister Nat than the Enclosure man, miss, don't fret. He told me to get Sunbeam ready for you, so he's expecting you.'

'He said we would ride out together. Oh, it's ages since I rode out!'

'Go steady then. Don't set yourself a-coughing.'

But she only laughed. 'I suppose Eb is conniving to get the common land for himself? They say he gives the Enclosure men backhanders. My father wouldn't do that.'

The village of Gridstone had so far escaped 'enclosure' – dread word to the villagers who used common land for grazing their odd cows and pigs. Now the government was fencing it off and turning it over to good farmers to make it more productive. The villagers were paid off with lump sums which pleased them for a year or two. They sold their animals and enjoyed spending the money without a thought for the future.

Money in the hand, Sim thought . . . that's all they thought of, to scamper off to town and buy new waistcoats. Then a year or two later, they realized they had lost a lifetime of cow-fodder, not to mention their firewood and kindling from the now-ploughed woodland. There had been far more common land when Sim was a boy. Grover had already taken twenty acres on the far side of the squire's place.

'He's very successful, old Grover,' Margaret said, half enviously.

'Aye, he's that,' Sim said shortly. Better not to add how he got his success – through ruthlessness, crookery and greed. And Margaret had no part in Eb's plans – of that Sim was sure. Nat would be forced to marry to add to the family's wealth, or land. Nat probably knew it, and would drop Margaret as soon as his father came down on him, or when he tired of her, whichever was first. Margaret had no future at all.

Had Nat remembered his careless promise? Sim wondered. But, thank the Lord, he came swaggering out and shouted for Crocus to be got ready, and Sunbeam, one of the quiet hacks, with a side-saddle. Peter came running. They brought the horses out and Sim took Sunbeam to the mounting block and helped Margaret on. She had ridden well as a youngster, like all the Garland children. But it was a long time now since she had been on a horse, not since their old cob had died. She never rode Tilly, who was a hard puller.

Well, he thought, they made a handsome couple! Nat, laughing, his dark eyes alight, his expensive clothes, his gorgeous horse, and Margaret radiant, the bright curls falling out over the red shawl . . . he had to smile, although he knew it was all wrong. In reality, it was a selfish brute idling his time with an unsuitable girl below his standing. Children! It happened all the time. Even he could remember his first love, at fifteen, and how you thought no one had ever known love like you suddenly knew it. But when you eventually married, it was long after those early fires had died down and you married for stability, or convenience, or because the girl was pregnant. Lucky the man who married the love of his life! Old Garland had, of course, and where did that get him? At less than fifty, a broken man. And when Margaret went – it did not do to dwell on what would happen to him.

And when they came back, after an hour, they gave Sunbeam back to him and Nat took Margaret on Crocus, in front of the saddle, to take her home. His arms were round her and his cheek lay against her hair. Crocus walked away kindly, perhaps aware of his precious burden.

Sim did not know whether to cry or laugh or swear, to think what lay ahead of them.

7

I couldn't believe my eyes when I saw Crocus coming up the track with Margaret riding in front of Nat on the saddle. And you could tell what they were up to, laughing and canoodling, all alight in the bright morning. If it had been anyone but Nat, it would have lifted my heart to see Margaret so happy. But as it was the sight came like a clap of doom. Nat Grover, of all people!

She slipped off clear of the house and came walking home, while Nat set off back. She came carelessly into the kitchen, where I was setting out bread and cold meat for the men's midday meal. I looked at her and hadn't the heart to say what was in my mind. I had never seen her look so happy.

She saw my face and said, 'What have you got against Nat Grover? He's really kind and funny. I love him!'

I said reluctantly, 'He's a Grover. You know how they are. Father says—'

'Oh, Father! He's jealous because he's not got on like Eb Grover.'

Maybe she was right. I didn't want to argue. I really

did want her to be happy and she was happy now. It was lovely to see her all smiles, instead of how she usually was, grumpy and sour.

'He's very handsome,' I agreed.

'We saw you, we saw you!' Jack and Martin came crashing in from work, two great gales of wind, more like six boys than two.

'Kissing Nat Grover!' Jack whistled.

'Up there on his best horse – heavens alive! I hope his old father don't see you!'

'It seems like the whole family's been spying!' Margaret said, but she wasn't upset, more proud. 'He said he'd take me into town, to see a play.'

We were all staggered at this. This was life beyond our expectations.

'To see a play!' Jack couldn't believe it. But he was impressed. 'He's that serious? Does his mother know?'

'His mother doesn't have to know! He won't tell her! She can think what she likes!'

I wondered, what about our father? But didn't say anything. Like Jack, I was terribly impressed.

'When you're mistress of Grover's you can give us all jobs,' Jack said.

'Give me Crocus,' I said.

'Nat won't be master. There's his older brother Philip,' Margaret said.

The eldest son got everything. It always seemed to be terribly unfair, these rules of property.

'Oh, he's probably killed by now. They've never heard word from him,' Jack said. 'Not that I've heard tell anyway.'

'Nat says he's got command of his own ship. He never writes, but old Grover found out from the Admiralty.'

'And he's still alive?'

'Nat says he sailed to St Helena with Napoleon. Not on the ship Boney was on, but with an accompanying ship.'

We were all terribly impressed. Philip Grover and Boney himself! Had he met him? Seen him, at least? What fame!

'I can't see him wanting to be a farmer, even if he does come home,' Jack said.

'No, that's what Nat says. He'll never come home. Nat will have the farm.'

We all looked at Margaret, wondering if she was seeing herself as the mistress of Grover's.

Jack said, 'If you've got Nat's ear, find out what the Commissioner was cooking up with the old man this morning. Grover's snatching some more land, I bet.'

'The common up by Cribb's,' Margaret said. 'The edge of the common joins the Grovers' farthest turnip field, and they reckon they can get a share of it and add it to the turnips.'

The government was very pro-turnip, we all knew. If you grew turnips – a fairly new idea – you did not have to kill your cattle in the autumn for want of food during the winter, and that meant you could actually improve your beasts year by year by clever breeding. Sheep too. The only thing was the Grovers didn't have any cattle. Their land, like that of all the rich farmers, was purely arable. Their turnips were a ploy to extend on to the common land.

'Maybe if he gets Cribbs he'll give up wanting us,' Jack said. Jack was terrified that Father would give in one day and sell our farm to the Grovers, and he would have no living to look forward to. Jack loved the farm passionately, whereas Father didn't care any more. With the money he could live comfortably for ever, but even that wouldn't make him happy. When he came in the atmosphere changed as it always did. It was difficult to laugh and joke with him around, although he didn't lose his temper with us. He was just sad, that's all. He was a quiet, good man whose life had fallen apart with the loss of our mother. Our mother had been the sharp one, the boss really. When she was alive we had had a herd of dairy cows and she had run a thriving dairy with the help of two girls, sending milk and butter and cheese off for sale. But now the dairy stood silent, save when we brought in the milk from our remaining two cows, Lucy and Lizzie, and I made butter. I couldn't be bothered with making cheese – I was the horse-keeper, after all – Father didn't employ another, and that took most of my time. The work horses had to be turned out nice every day. It was a horse-keeper's pride to see a good shine on their coats, their legs brushed clean and their harness gleaming. What was cheese to a sight like that?

Our father was tall and attractive looking with his steady air and melancholy blue eyes. Several women in the village had made advances since the death of our mother, some who would have made good dairymaids

71

– and wives as well – but he never took any notice. We could have done with one, Jack and me. Margaret, of course, would have made the woman's life a misery. And in Father's eyes, Margaret could do no wrong. He would always side with Margaret. But going with Nat Grover? If – or when – he found out about that, he might come out of his dream. The whole village probably knew by now and certainly would when Martin went home.

'Where's Ellen?' I asked.

'She's gone to school,' Father said. 'I sent her. She needs a bit of discipline. She's running too wild.'

'There's a new teacher,' Martin said. 'She's smart. All the kids are terrified of her.'

'That's what I heard,' Father said, and actually smiled.

The old teacher, dear Mr Potts, or Mr Crackpot as he was known, had finally retired. He had never noticed who played truant or who didn't.

'She's from Norwich, hard as nails,' said Martin. 'But she's only young,' he added. He grinned at me. 'You could start going.'

'Go yourself! I'm too old!'

I reckoned I knew all I needed to. I could read and write and add up, and I knew some geography from the war, and history too, if Napoleon counted. And I knew about how farming worked, and had worked in the past. And I knew about horses. Oh yes, I knew about horses.

Talk of Cribb's reminded me – as if I needed it! – of my foal. If the farmer there lost his grazing to the

Commissioner, he might well want to be selling his foal and even his mare too. But I knew I'd have a job talking Father into it. Now we had Hopeful there was no urgency. He had turned out all right, as I knew he would, and after two months of good feed and lots of grooming he was a credit to the farm. Jack rode him a lot and liked him. He would also pair in harness with one of the big horses if necessary and pull the gig and the carrying cart into the village.

'Yes, she's an eye for a horse, that littl'un,' they said, the fairest compliment I was ever likely to get.

The only hope I had of buying the foal was with a gold brooch I had from my mother. It was in a little box in my clothes drawer, and I was pretty sure everyone had forgotten about it. It did seem rather a dreadful thing to do, but I think my shrewd mother would have approved. If it hadn't been for that, I would probably have abandoned my dream by now. When I talked to Jack about it, he scoffed, of course, but then wisely said, 'February's a good time to buy.'

Which was true, as most of the animals were starving by February and a lot killed off. If I was actually to buy the foal and bring it home – well, whatever Father said or however angry he might be, the deed would be done, with no going back. I could not stop thinking about it.

Ellen came home and we questioned her eagerly about the new schoolmistress. A new person in our small village was bound to make an excitement. We didn't have much to talk about ordinarily.

Ellen tossed her head (she had curls too, but brown

ones) and said crossly, 'She's awful! Like a weasel. She fixes her eye on you till you get all hot and wriggly. You daren't move.'

'Cor, not like with old Crackpot,' said Jack.

'What's her name?'

'Miss Frobisher. She's old. Thirty-something, they say.'

'What's she look like?'

'Very straight, starchy, cross.'

'She sounds just right for you,' said Jack.

I saw her soon after and she wasn't as bad as Ellen made out, not when she smiled. She was in the shop, buying ribbon. She had very white skin and curly hair pulled back and wore very dark plain clothes. She was the sort of person you would look at twice. Her first name was Ann, I found out. I, unlike Ellen, liked the look of her. But I wasn't going to school. I was too busy.

One morning, I took Hopeful, or Hoppy as he had become, and went out when Father was at the miller's. It was a bright day with the birds singing fit to bust in the hedgerows, thinking spring had arrived, and the larks shrilling overhead. The birds always made me feel happy, even with everything that hung over us. I was riding on my (Mother's) side-saddle in my best (Mother's) riding skirt, which was miles too big but looked all right when I was on. Hoppy was pleased not to be carting and went gaily. Once on the road I put him into his trot. He was nothing like Tilly but good enough, and very smooth and willing. More comfortable than Tilly, dare I say it, who always wanted to get there in half the time. He was the same size as Tilly, just under fifteen hands, but lighter in build. His dark bay coat came up beautifully under my hard grooming and shone now with health.

'Lucky old Hoppy, that I saw you!' I told him, remembering how sad he had looked standing in the snow.

He was a nice character too, unlike Tilly. He twitched an ear back at my nonsense, then forward again as the mailcoach came into sight. I pulled into the side to make way – it ran you down if you didn't, it gave way to nothing – and the coachman gave me a nod. The horses on this coach – always on time, almost to the minute – were good ones, four matching chestnuts, and I loved to see them. They did twelve miles between posthouses, and our village was about halfway on their stint. Martin wanted to be a coach-driver but didn't have much hope. How could he learn, without the opportunity? It was a job that passed down in families, like most jobs did. That's why he worked in the inn stables most of the time, trying to pick up tips or a chance. He certainly could change a pair of post horses quicker than anyone I knew, but the mail didn't change horses in Gridstone, barely stopping to exchange bags and parcels, or a passenger, before setting off again at a canter.

Being a coach-driver was a great job on a fine morning like this, but in the winter in the dark when the snow was coming down and the road full of potholes it wasn't very funny. And then there were robbers to contend with, and London at the other end with all its terrible traffic. We thought Martin was a bit cracked wanting it. But it was a highly regarded job, not surprisingly, with its exacting standards – a letter posted in Norwich in the morning would be in London the same day without fail (if stuck in deep snow or if the coach got damaged in a pothole, the guard would get off and ride one of the horses on its way with the post) – and Martin could have done with a bit of glory. He was more ambitious than Jack, who only wanted the farm. Father called him a firecracker, but perhaps that was because of his ginger hair. 'He'll make trouble one day, that lad,' Father would say. But Martin was kind and honest as the day was long. I loved Martin.

Our road wasn't very busy, just the odd farmer's gig or heavy cart, and a tramp walking. There were people working in the fields, hoeing, or digging out root crops, laying the new hedges and clearing ditches, the never-ending jobs. Bonfires smoked here and there, their blue smoke lifting the lovely scent into the thin winter air. I kept clutching at the hard little box with the gold brooch in it in my top pocket, terrified of losing it. I was so excited, hardly believing my mission could be successful.

When I got to Cribb's, I was too nervous at first to approach the house. I pulled up on Hoppy and sat there, looking. It lay near the road on the side of a small hamlet, a poor collection of buildings but carefully mended, a tidy place. It adjoined the common, and some cows were pegged out there, but no horses.

I got off Hoppy and led him up the track to the house. It suddenly seemed terribly cheeky, to try and buy a horse that wasn't for sale with a gold brooch. Of course I had no idea how much the brooch was worth. For all I knew it was worth far more than the foal.

I knocked at the door.

The farmer's wife came. She didn't recognize me.

I said, 'My father owns the trotting mare, Tilly.'

'Oh yes, you're from Small Gains then.'

'Yes. I want to talk to you.'

I could see then that a girl of eleven couldn't really buy a horse on her own, and be taken seriously. I could see the look of amusement in the woman's face at my self-importance. But she wasn't unpleasant, just a trifle impatient. Her hands were floury and I guessed she was making bread. A nice smell was floating out of the door, making me feel hungry all of a sudden.

'I want to buy your foal from you, in exchange for this brooch.'

I snatched the box out of my pocket and opened it. The brooch was certainly very pretty, a scarf pin in the shape of a butterfly, with tiny blue stones for eyes. I knew my mother had got it from an old aunt. It wasn't anything my father had given her and was of no sentimental value.

The woman didn't know what to say, not surprisingly. But the brooch took her eye. I could see she liked it.

She said, 'Tie your horse to that nail a minute, and come inside.'

I did what she said, and entered a kitchen not unlike our own, where bread was cooking in the oven and pies were being made. It was like ours when Mother was alive. Margaret wasn't keen on baking. For a moment it made me feel quite weepy, seeing everything set out on the kitchen table in this homely way.

I handed the woman the brooch and she looked at it closely, smiling.

'Why, it's beautiful!'

I saw at once that she thought it was worth more than the foal, and my heart lifted a little. 'Have you still got the foal?'

'Why, yes, and a right load of trouble he is. I'd rather the brooch than that animal any day.'

That was plain enough!

'Why's he trouble?'

'Oh, he wants his own way all the time. You can't do anything with him. I say cut him, but my husband won't get round to it.'

Cut him! It wasn't in my plans to buy a gelding. My plan was to have a great trotter and make a fortune in travelling it as a stallion. The best trotters were taken round the countryside in the spring with a stallion man, to serve the farmers' mares. A good horse could make a lot of money. I wanted to breed great trotters. I didn't just want a pet. Of course I completely disregarded what this woman was telling me about the character of my darling foal.

'I wouldn't want to buy a gelding,' I said.

She looked at me in a funny way. 'You're a rum'un,' she said. 'Does your father know what you're up to?'

78

I blushed fiercely and did not reply.

'Your brooch, is it?'

'Yes, my mother left it me! It's mine. My father doesn't want it.'

'Does he want a troublesome horse, your father?'

'It will be mine! I am the horse-keeper at home. I do all the horses, even Tilly. It won't be anything to do with my father.'

'It's a man's horse, this one.'

Well, I'd heard say that I was as good as a man when it came to horses. I should have been a boy, they all said. She wasn't going to put me off that way.

'If you sell it me, my father will accept it.' I knew this was true, even if we had an almighty row first.

'Well, I must say, I'd fair like a bit of jewellery. What a treat! We'll have to see what my husband says. After all, a bit of gold is always money in your pocket, like. Sit yourself down and have a bite to eat. He'll be in shortly.'

She buttered me a flat scone which I ate gladly. So far so good. My heart was thumping with excitement. What was I getting into? It didn't sound like plain sailing, but I had nothing to lose. I didn't want the old brooch anyway. And if this colt was so naughty, a bit of ploughing alongside Duke would tame him. Horses worked hard on our farm. And a good horse usually had plenty of spirit.

She was a nice old girl and gave me a second scone, and then her husband came in.

'This is the little girl from Small Gains,' the woman said. 'She's got a proposition for you.' She explained the deal and showed her husband the brooch. He examined it in his great calloused hand where it looked very strange, so pretty and out of place.

'Her father know about this?' he growled.

I suppose I had been a bit optimistic, thinking I was going to hand over the brooch and ride away with my foal, no questions asked. The main thing was that the farmer agreed to the deal, as long as he first 'saw someone' about the brooch.

'If he says it's real gold, you can have the foal.'

'Of course it's real gold! You can see the mark.'

He turned it over.

'Oh go on, George, it's a lovely piece. And the colt – you say it yourself – nothing but trouble, and starving like the rest of them. It's three months before the grass starts growing. If you decide to sell him, then he'll be nought but skin and bone. Let the child take him away.'

'It'll take more than a child to take him away if he doesn't want to go!'

'I'll come back with my brother. Or three of us. We'll manage.'

'Well, if he goes, I don't want him back. If your father complains, too bad.'

He had given way. He couldn't help but see the brooch was genuine. He said he'd take me out to see the colt and I might change my mind. He laughed.

So now I was frightened, as well as excited. What had I done? It was what I wanted but all the same I couldn't help feeling scared. I was really out on a limb, no going back. Whatever would Jack say, let alone Father?

I went out behind the farmer, past dear Hoppy – well, I had got *that* deal right – and into the stable beyond. Two carthorses which had been working were tied up eating their bait, and the mare was in the next stall. The far stall was boarded across and when our footsteps approached, loud kicks made them shudder.

I don't know what I had expected. I should have thought ahead a bit more. After all, it was the end of the winter and most of the animals on poor farms were starving. My colt had obviously been shut in his stall for weeks, and fed what could be spared for an animal that wasn't working. The others looked well enough but my poor boy was just skin and bone under a thick filthy coat. He looked terrible. I was so taken aback I couldn't think of anything to say. He didn't look worth tuppence, let alone a fine piece of gold.

He turned round – he was loose in the stall – and poked his head over the boards. Then I saw what I remembered, that characterful bony face with the large mettlesome eyes – that had not changed. Nor, if he had the opportunity, would he have lost the raking stride that had so impressed me. I told myself this, firmly. For, in truth, he was the worst scarecrow I had ever seen. Even worse than poor Hoppy.

But then, Hoppy had turned out all right. The art was to see what was underneath the ragged coat and dirt, and I told myself that I had an instinct for this. I had to believe in it, believe in myself. But whatever would Father and Jack say? They would think me ripe for the lunatic asylum. My courage faltered.

The farmer's wife laughed. 'He's not as pretty as your little brooch, you're thinking.'

How right she was! I wanted to die for being so stupid.

But then I shut my eyes and thought back to the day I first saw this animal. It was so branded on my memory, it was no illusion . . . those thrusting shoulders and the way the forelegs had flung out, toes pointed, the action floating . . . I hadn't imagined it.

I must have the courage of my convictions.

'He looks very poor,' I stammered.

'Well, it's take him as he is, no part exchange,' said the farmer. 'It's you as wanted him, not like I advertised him for sale, after all.'

'No. I understand.' I took a deep breath. 'Yes,' I said.

And as I said it a great shudder of pure delight went through me. I couldn't be mistaken! I *knew* I was right. I just had to hold out against the scorn and ridicule I would be held in, a small price to pay. A vision of the lovely Crocus floated before me and died. I would show them!

'Good girl,' said the farmer. He put out his hand and I shook it. 'You can take him when you like. He's very wild, I warn you.'

'I'll come back with help, with my brother,' I said.

'If he won't go I can bring the mare part of the way, perhaps.'

The deed was done. I was trembling all over,

whether with fear or excitement I could not say. I stared at my colt and he stared back with his great bright eyes. It was hard to see what colour he was under the dirt.

'Is he a bay?'

'Yes, very dark.'

Not another grey or roan like Tilly, thank goodness! How I loved to put the shine on a good dark horse!

We went out and the farmer bunked me back on to Hoppy.

'If you was my daughter, I'd be a worried man,' he said, and laughed.

8

Everything I most feared happened, of course.

Father beat me. Jack and Martin nearly died laughing. The colt wouldn't leave the farm and it took the three of us five hours to beat and cajole him home, riding Hoppy and Tilly between us. Father wouldn't give him shelter and made me turn him out in the water meadows with the two cows for company.

Well, that made them stare.

He hadn't been out for months, not since he was on the mare. He stood inside the gate with his big bony nose up high, sniffing the sharp air, then he let out some huge bucks and set off at flat gallop down towards the river. As he went he threw more great bucks out behind and clods of mud flew from his hooves. And then he wheeled round and came back towards us at that enormous trot. If it had looked good when he was a foal, it looked fantastic now. He tucked in his nose and flung out his legs as if he would beat the earth into submission. His back legs came up high with a great action and powered him along so that he came back faster than he had galloped away –

one of the best and truest Norfolk trotters you could ever wish to see.

Both Jack and Martin were awed.

'That's what I saw when he was a foal!' I crowed.

Perhaps that was the only day he had ever been loose and free before today. He had never given the farmer a chance to see what he could do, pegged out on the common and shut in that stall. Those great water meadows were a paradise to him, giving him the freedom of what must have seemed the whole world to him. His hideous shaggy coat steamed in the spring air. Fortunately, it had turned mild and he would come to no harm.

Jack said, 'Father should have seen that!'

'Tell him,' I said, remembering the beating. 'You tell him.'

Martin said, 'You don't want the Grovers to see him go. Don't say anything to Margaret, or they'll know.'

'Too late,' said Jack. Margaret told Nat everything, we knew. On the other hand, we learned from her quite a lot about the Grovers. To our amazement, Father hadn't stopped her going with Nat Grover. Maybe he remembered his early days tumbling round the fields when he was a lad, because he said to Jack, 'The lass needs her happiness. I'll not deny her.'

I don't think our mother would have allowed it.

'There can't be any future in it, not with a Grover,' Jack said.

And Father said, 'Margaret's got no future.'

Whatever the ways of it, it was a pleasure for us all to have Margaret all smiles as she was now. Nat took her to the play, driving in his smart curricle, and she snuggled up to him under the big leather apron, and she couldn't stop telling us all about the magic of it. I just wished she'd stay at home and bake bread and pies like the farmer's wife at Cribb's. Our comfort was scratchy, to say the least, and I worked as hard as the men keeping the horses and the cows, milking and making butter and running all the chores. We needed a good housekeeper but Father never got round to finding one. I think he was frightened a housekeeper would want to marry him. He was what counted as an eligible bachelor in our village.

'My mother would come like a shot,' Martin said.

'Yes, that's what he's frightened of,' Jack replied.

Martin's mother was a terrible shrew. The whole family was feckless and skint and lived hand to mouth. This was probably why Martin spent more time at our house than at his own.

Martin was full of admiration for my cleverness in acquiring the foal. 'You could have him trotting timed distances at three and make a mint out of stallion fees.'

A good horse could trot sixteen miles in one hour, a hundred miles in twelve. Or two miles in five minutes. We knew all the figures. You had proper stewards to time them and word quickly got round about the good ones.

Jack said, 'You've got to break him in first.'

He had a good point. Certainly, the horse wasn't easy. I spent as much time with him as I could, just talking to him and handling him all over, lifting up his feet and suchlike, teaching him to tie up. That wasn't easy.

He broke several ropes and took half a fence away with him before we got him to settle. The boys helped me quite a lot. We turned Tilly out with him in the spring and the mare's company quietened him considerably, although she was always ready to kick out at him if he came too near. I prayed her iron feet wouldn't harm him. It was a risk I had to take. Father wasn't going to give him the prime treatment of a field to himself. Father listened to our eulogies about the colt and I think he came to know that there was something good in the offing, but he didn't say much as usual, only, 'He'll be a good one if he comes half as fast as Tilly.'

Tilly went out in the afternoon when her work was over, along with the big horses. They lived out at night in the summer. It meant the great chore of mucking out was finished, which the men did for their own horses but I did for Tilly and Hoppy. Instead there was the chore of going to fetch them in in the morning at four o'clock, which I did alone. Grooming them was much harder, as they had usually rolled in the mud. No farmer worth his salt sent a dirty horse to work, even if it was where no one would see it. The big farms like Grover's even braided their horses up with coloured ribbons in their manes and tails just to work. It was the horse-keeper's pride to see them so pretty. How I wished I could do the same! Even old Duke would look a treat. I only did them if we took them to a fair or somewhere and Jack helped me, grumbling all the while. I kept the ribbons in a box by the feed. It was quite an art to get it right. Tilly didn't get this treatment, of course, only the big horses were decorated.

But when the spring came it was lovely to see the horses all out on the new grass with their winter coats moulting away to show their fine summer colours. And my colt, when he was revealed at last – his coat was bay, hard and dark, almost black, with a lighter brown round the muzzle. When I groomed him it came up like a polished oak desk. He was unrecognizable from the colt I had brought home from Cribb's.

I spent a lot of time thinking up a name for him and eventually he was called Garland's Black Rattler. Most good horses had the owner's name in front. And the expression 'a rattling good horse' was common for a trotter, so Black Rattler he was, Rattler for every day. It suited him – as Jack said, 'He fair rattles around.'

With the arrival of spring, we were so busy I didn't have a lot of time to spend on him, not as I would have wished. Father hired some of Martin's rackety brothers to help out, so much hoeing to be done. He insisted on doing all the sowing himself, save for some Jack was allowed, to learn the skill.

As Margaret was out cavorting with Nat a lot of the time, I got lumbered with most of the cooking. When Ellen went off to school I really envied her her quiet life, and sometimes wondered if it was too late for me to enrol after all. Ellen was keen to go since she had got used to Miss Frobisher, quite a change. This was good as she had less time to get into trouble, and she took her work quite seriously. She was starting to know more than I knew about outside things, about how Napoleon had risen to power and where the battles had taken place, and how William the Conqueror was really a Viking, not a Frenchman, and things like that. I think Father thought it was a waste of time in some ways, except that it was making her kinder and more of a lady. 'Her mother would have been pleased,' he said. All rich farmers' wives and daughters were ladies these days, it seemed.

Margaret was becoming a lady through her friendship with Nat. He bought her pretty things and a good woollen cloak for driving out. She was coughing more and getting thinner by the day and, with her love, more and more beautiful. It was well known that consumptives with their transparent skin and high colour could be very attractive, and Margaret was certainly proving the adage. Everyone was remarking on it. They shook their heads, or course. I guessed that Eb and Maggie Grover were not preventing the liaison, knowing that time would sort things out. Nat was not for marrying, it was obvious, although Margaret longed for him to propose.

She talked to me about it in bed at night when I was trying to get some sleep. She couldn't sleep, and if she did she often woke pouring with sweat. I was forever washing out sheets and hanging them out, nearly every day. I just swilled them under the pump in the yard, not worth lighting the boiler for. I worked so hard that I was half-asleep while she talked. It was all about how marvellous Nat was, and what they would do when they married.

'He's going to take me to Europe. To Paris and Rome and Florence! Just imagine, Clara, how wonderful it will be!'

It was the fashion for rich young men to do their so-called Grand Tours of Europe before they came home to get on with making more money. Maybe Nat would go, but with Margaret . . . ? Why was he so cruel as to lead her on? She would never stand such a journey. Yet she believed it. She fantasized, lying in bed, about the house he would build her, the children she would have. I couldn't credit the stories, the power of her imagination. Surely he had never sketched out this future? She was making it all up.

'I've such a pain in my side,' she would say.

I would get out of bed and give her a few drops of laudanum in a spoonful of sugar. It comforted her.

One night she started coughing and couldn't stop. I sat her up and held her shoulders. Then all of a sudden there was a great shoot of blood all over the sheets. It was a bright night of full moon, and I didn't need a candle to see what a haemorrhage it was.

I leaped out of bed and fetched a bowl. I held it to her mouth while the blood poured out and talked to her all the while. 'It's all right, Margaret, it's all right. I'm looking after you.'

'Don't tell Father,' she gasped.

'No. No one will know.' I knew what to do, after all. I had seen it all before with my mother.

When it was over I fetched a clean sheet and a clean nightdress and changed her. She was now icy-cold and very weak. I propped her up on pillows and covered her with all the blankets and fetched her hot water to drink. The tears ran silently out of the corners of her eyes and she made no more talk about her marriage and her children. She just cried without a sound. I sat cuddling her until she fell into a sleep of exhaustion.

I went downstairs with the bloody washing. I knew I wouldn't sleep any more so I put on my coat and boots and took it down to the ford. I weighed it down with stones and the linen streamed out in the current, the blood flowing out. I would leave it there till morning. I stood watching it, smelling the clear, icy water, watching the moonlight flooding our fields in the utter silence of the night. Nothing stirred, not an owl or a fox or even a mouse. I loved it then, our land, our farm and everything it meant. It would stay and be here for ever, when Margaret was gone, and Father and Jack and myself. It mattered far more than anything else I could think of, Grand Tours and all. Margaret was staving off her future with all her stories, deluding herself and knowing that she was deluding herself. She knew all right. But when she was gone, my dearest love would still endure, and always would. It was the only comfort I could take, the night was so sad. I needed my comfort.

So I walked back up the track to the dark house. In the curve of the river the horses were grazing, all in a bunch except Tilly, proud independent Tilly. Over the river the great black mass of Gridswood divided us from the squire's acres. If Grover bought the squire's water meadows, we would be pincered by Grover land. It did not bear thinking about. I could not bear it. There was a gang of strong Grovers: the parents, Nat, the absent Philip, a younger son and two daughters, all wanting lots of money for life and pleasures. Money from the land.

Margaret was in bed for a week or two after that and took a while to recover her strength. Nat enquired after her from me. I think he was frightened of asking Father or Jack. He really did seem to care. After all, Margaret had never been short of suitors.

I said, 'I think if you paid her a visit it would do her a lot of good.'

'Your father wouldn't allow it.' It was half a question, which I answered.

'He needn't know. Come round the back woods when he's working in the front. He doesn't come in till twelve for his dinner.' I just wanted to see Margaret smile again.

He visited her and Margaret flamed back into spirits. It was wonderful to see. He came to the door the next day, when I was washing in the scullery and Margaret was lying on her couch in front of the fire. I went in and said, 'There's someone to see you, Margaret.'

She thought it was the vicar or kind Mrs Lansdowne from the shop or Mary Test, an old friend of Mother's, but when Nat's large frame filled the doorway she cried out, shrieked almost, and her face flamed up. She threw off the blanket, but before she could stagger to her feet Nat was across the floor and on his knees by her side with his arms round her, burying his head in her wild curls.

I was shocked to the core by what I had done, thinking it would be kind words, a stilted meeting of decorum and neighbourliness. Heavens, what did I know about this sort of passion? I never read any books or saw any sign of it where I lived, only the rough puppy play of the boys on the green. (Or did my baby memories stir and resurrect visions of my parents once? I think they did, as I gaped.) Nat was covering Margaret's face with kisses. I turned and fled.

Crocus was tied outside the door for the whole world to see. I took him into the nearest barn to hide him, and stood with my arms round his neck, my face buried in his sweet-smelling mane. Oh, horses! I knew where I was with horses! I cried for Margaret and her terrible future. Perhaps forbidden love was the sweetest kind. I didn't know anything, save that Margaret got better from that day and all the sparkle came back into her. If my father knew, he said nothing. He had never been known to deny Margaret anything, so why deny her now her greatest desire?

And when she was up and about again, there was no longer the need for Nat to visit, for she went gaily down the drive to meet him where he waited for her on the road in his beautiful curricle with a pair of grey horses. There was no secret then and the whole village saw them drive past. It gave them something to gossip about. And how they gossiped! Why didn't Father stop it? That's what everyone said. But if they saw Margaret as we did, and her happiness, and how she was without it, how could they say that? What did she have? Nothing at all, save this love. Jack was furious and hated it and said dreadful things to her, but she took no notice.

Of course the gadding about did her no good, and although she was so happy she was also getting thinner and her breathing was getting worse. Some days she had to stay in bed and then Nat stayed away. What with nursing her and doing the cooking and washing and cleaning, I hardly had any time for the horses. With harvest coming up and all the extra men there would be to feed, I didn't think I would be able to cope and I said so to Father.

Jack took him up on it. 'It's not fair on her, she's only a little kid. You must get a woman to cook and clean, Father. Margaret's no good any more.'

An agonized look came over his face. 'Who will come?'

'Any village woman'll come,' Jack said. 'It's a good job. A decent cook, for a start.'

I took that as an insult and hit him and we had a fight. I bit him and he held me by the wrists so that I danced and kicked in front of him. We often fought, Jack and me.

Ellen was laughing. She said, 'Miss Frobisher'll know someone.'

Miss Frobisher knew everything. We heard this a lot.

'Tell her then,' Jack said. 'Tell her to find someone, because Father never will. Tell Miss Frobisher to find someone.'

To my consternation the next day, when Ellen came home from school, she brought Miss Frobisher with her. I was in the hearth with my bottom in the air scrubbing off some spilt soup, and Margaret was sitting on her couch sewing some fancy blouse with

94

beads. The table was in a mess and there was a pile of washing off the line filling the best armchair.

I got up in a great flurry. But Miss Frobisher was smiling, not a bit stuck up, and spoke in a friendly way.

'Ellen's been telling me you need some help,' she said. 'It would be a pity if she had to give up school, for she's a clever girl.'

I might have been too! I thought.

'I think Father would like it, yes,' I said. 'A good cook,' I added for Jack's sake. 'There's the harvest coming up and all the men to feed.'

Mother used to make beer and we hadn't made beer since she died. All farms made their own, and most houses too, but Margaret had never learned. It was hard to remember how it was when our mother was alive, with all the jams and chutneys she made and the butter and cheese from the dairy.

I bundled up the washing off the chair and bid Miss Frobisher sit down.

'I just came to see what the situation is, as I'm sure I can find you a suitable person. Quite a few of the mothers at school would like a position, I know. They ask me.'

Miss Frobisher was the sort of person people would ask, I could see. Although she had only been in the village a short time, she had made herself very respected. I could see that she was a cut far above the usual village schoolmarm, a warm and intelligent woman. I had no feeling that she had come prying, although I could see by her quick sideways glances that she was taking in Margaret's state. No doubt she had heard all the gossip surrounding her.

Ellen said, straight out, 'An old, ugly one is what we want. Father's frightened of getting someone who will want to marry him.'

'Ellen!' I shrieked.

Then we all laughed, Miss Frobisher too.

'Perhaps I can find a well-married one,' she said. 'Elderly perhaps. If that is what your father wants. I would have to ask him before I make a move.'

'He won't be in until dark,' I said.

But, unexpectedly, just as Miss Frobisher was leaving, Father came into the kitchen. He had cut his hand quite badly and wanted it bound up so that he could carry on working. He looked put out at seeing the visitor, although he recognized her. She was very tactful.

'I think you should run it under the pump to clean it,' she said, seeing his hand. No doubt she was well versed in tying up cut knees and elbows. She went out into the yard with him and I watched them standing there together, talking, while Father held his hand under the water. I saw him laugh, a rare occasion. It was wonderful to see him laugh. Oh, Miss Frobisher, I thought, you are good for him! He looked so young then, and I saw him – yes, as a good catch, with his hat doffed and his blonde hair showing pale against the weatherbeaten skin, his eyes very blue. Everyone in our family was like that, except brown me, a throwback to a gypsy or something. How unfair life was! Not only was I the drudge, I wasn't even pretty with it.

But the upshot of it was that we got ourselves a housekeeper and I wasn't a drudge any longer. I wasn't any prettier either, but that didn't matter. The woman that Miss Frobisher sent was sixty years old and happily married to one of Grover's regular workers. She was a principled sort of woman, not given to gossip, quite severe in a way, but nice with it. She let Margaret alone, not fussing her or giving advice, but she saw that she ate well and she made her special milky possets and tempting things, I noticed. I never had, I didn't know how. Yes, she was a good cook and we all loved her for it. She was not intrusive, not taking over which we had feared, but was quiet and hard-working and altogether a perfect choice. Her name was Mrs Ponder.

Ellen of course took all the credit. 'I knew Miss Frobisher would find the right person.'

We all agreed Miss Frobisher was brilliant. I couldn't get out of my head the little scene in the yard, Miss Frobisher with my father, making him laugh. And then a really terrible thought followed it: if only it was all over with Margaret we could forget, get on with our lives and start to laugh again. What a wicked thought! I was shaken by it. Worse than that, in my heart I knew it was true. We were all harrowed by Margaret's ordeal. The strange thing was, when I went to see Nicholas up at the vicarage – which I usually did when I was in the village to shop – I never got that feeling with him, although he was in exactly the same state. Unlike Margaret, he was so calm and philosophical. If he had the same resentment and despair for the future – and how could he not? – he didn't show it. He spent most of his time studying (what for, after all?) and trying to play the violin, and reading books Charlotte the squire's daughter brought him. He was always pleased to see me, always with something funny to tell me. Every time, I wished I could stay longer.

Having Mrs Ponder was a huge relief for me, like a ton weight off my back. Back to the horses and turning them out as they should be turned out – I was so happy, the summer arrived, the crops all coming through and my lovely Rattler growing more handsome by the day. Margaret said Nat had noticed him and was asking where he had come from. How much did we give for him? How was he bred? Margaret said she didn't know, which was true. She never cared for the horses.

Now I had the time, I handled Rattler as much as I could, to make him obedient. He was very opinionated, not easy at all, and I was at a disadvantage being rather small. I couldn't handle him by strength, only by guile and kindness, which of course was by far the best way if one had the patience. I had the patience. He became very kind towards me, which he wasn't towards others. Jack and Martin called him bad names and said he was worse than Tilly, and that he should be cut.

'Don't be stupid!' I shouted. 'How will he make us money if we cut him? He's going to be the most wanted stallion in East Anglia – you wait! I didn't get him just to be a farm horse.'

Father agreed with me. He was coming to be interested in Rattler and praised me for my good eye. He advised me on feeding, and got me some special cake that he said was good for bones.

'He's worth it. He's going to be a good one, you can see. You're a bright girl, Clara, seeing that stride when he was a littl'un. We'll have to keep a look out for a little jockey for him, if he's good enough for matches.'

Young horses were ridden in matches or in timed demonstrations by lightweights, often children. You didn't put a heavy farmer on a young horse if you had any sense. Later on when their bones were fully mature, they did matches with heavy weights. Martin said his nephew Billy (one of dozens) was tiny and could stick on any horse.

'He's a natural. We'll train him up.'

I knew Billy. He was an imp of six who already worked in the Grovers' gang. His mother was a harridan who had four older children in the gang and worked in it herself. On these wages they just about got by. Her husband had died in an accident soon after Billy was born. Martin brought him in one day to introduce him to Rattler.

'Would you like to ride this horse?'

Martin lifted him up so that his face was on a level with Rattler's surprised eye. Billy stroked Rattler's nose, unafraid.

'Yes.'

They called Billy Boney, not after Napoleon, but because he was such a skinny little thing. When we lifted him on to Rattler's back, the colt hardly felt him.

It was good for Rattler to feel a rider, even such a shrimp, and to get used to a hand on the reins. We wouldn't break the horse in properly until next year, but if Billy was going to ride him, the sooner they got used to each other the better. Billy needed no encouragement. He was born a horseman, you could see; he was a natural. He had no fear. We just led the horse round the yard and Billy sat there grinning. He had a grin like an apple slice. For all his skinny frame he was as hard and strong as Rattler himself. The hard work on Grover's land either killed or cured the weak, and Billy was a survivor. He had a shock of dark blonde hair and endearing sticky-out ears and, in spite of the brutality of his upbringing, there was a natural gentleness in him. Martin, not endeared to his many relations, adored Billy.

'He'll go far, that one,' he used to say.

On Rattler, I hoped.

9

Harvest was always the high spot of the year.

Poor Margaret didn't see much of Nat for he was officiating over the fields across the road. Their harvest spread for miles, and Nat rode round on Crocus carrying a horsewhip to show his authority, shouting at the little children. Women worked a ten-hour day, and many of them had their babies in cots in the hedgerows, but only dared feed them when no one was looking. Mostly they were the wives of men who worked for Grover full time. They would have preferred to come to us, but were too frightened to, in case it meant their husbands were laid off. How Grover was hated! He had no feelings for the less fortunate. One longed to pay him back for his inhu-manity, but there was no way.

Margaret said our father was too soft and that was why he wasn't a Grover. She kept saying, 'Nat says . . .' this and that, but I wouldn't listen to her.

'Tell Jack,' I said. 'Tell Jack how it's done.'

Jack worked far harder than Nat Grover on his horse. Nat didn't harden his hands with field work, while Jack and Martin scythed their two acres of wheat in each ten-hour day with the grown men, and afterwards helped with the pitching, the hardest job of all, tossing the sheaves up on to the top of the waggon. Jack and Martin seemed to thrive on hard work. They loved the harvest, with its larking around with the girls at bait time and lying out for half an hour at four o'clock with a jug of beer in the hot sun when we brought it out to them. Their hair was thick-furred with dust and their faces burned brown. They were always laughing. In the evening they would strip off under the pump in the yard and even then they had the energy to horseplay around. Even I could see that harvest – for all it was such hard work – was a better time than the eternal spring hoeing in the rain or beet lifting in the February winds. It was the high spot, the gathering in, the reward for the months of hard labour. And this year it was good, and even Father smiled. Little Billy helped me with the horses, leading them in and out and filling nosebags. He loved them as much as I did. I was always terrified he would get under one of the great iron-shod hooves, but he was wise to the dangers, and quick as a little monkey.

Rattler of course was too young to work and grew fat in the field. Tilly worked but I made sure she never had to overstrain herself. In the autumn we hoped we would find her another match – someone with a young horse who hoped to topple her, as one day no doubt she would have to give way to a better. She looked good now, almost fat, not the scarecrow she would revert to when the summer grass faded.

Margaret helped Mrs Ponder a little and sometimes came out to the fields, but the dust got her coughing, and most of the time she just sat about. It was clear that she was fading. I made her a seat out of some logs and cushions under the apple tree across the track and she sat there sometimes, looking down the drive to see if Nat was riding down the road.

'He'll be back,' I said. 'You can't expect him now, not with his father telling him what to do. Wait till the supper – he'll be out then.'

It was the custom to have a big turn-out on the village green when all the harvest was in. Everyone came, even if they had had a supper at home for their own workers, and generally there were dancers and a band and a bit of a fair. I always looked forward to it. The bigwigs came – the squire, and the distant eccentric lordship from the far side of the village who was rarely to be seen out of his greenhouses. He collected rare plants in forays to Turkey and the Himalayas and was said to be very fair. To have a job in the house or gardens at Oakhall was the best the village could offer. There were six gardeners and six in the house and any vacancy that came was always over-subscribed. Not like when the Grovers advertised, nor even the squire whose wife was said to be a tough taskmaster. His lordship had a young son, Edmund, whom all the girls dreamed of marrying. He was very handsome and very sweet, a botanist like his father, not into bloodsports at all, although he rode a very decent horse. He was a great admirer of Tilly and I knew him a bit through that, because he used to talk to me about her. What a pity, I used to think, that we had the bad luck to adjoin the Grovers, when our fields might have run up to Oakhall and they would have been our neighbours! If Edmund had been Margaret's admirer instead of Nat . . .

But I think it was Nat's arrogance and power that attracted Margaret, the attributes that made me hate him.

We had our own harvest supper and Mrs Ponder excelled herself in the cooking of ham and sirloin and plum puddings, all served out in the orchard on a long table made of two old doors. Margaret and I covered it with a white sheet and put out jars of wild flowers that Ellen brought in from the riverside. Jack was in charge of the beer cask. We all wore our best clothes, such as we had. Margaret shortened one of mother's cotton dresses for me and took it in down sides, and I felt quite grand, all pink and white with a white silk shawl round my shoulders. Martin said I looked like a rose: he went quite red; I think he had had too much beer. I laughed. Later in the evening, when he had had even more beer, he asked me to marry him. I laughed so much the tears ran down my cheeks. Then even he saw it was funny and laughed too, but he gave me a sort of kiss.

'I don't mind waiting a bit,' he said.

It was quite nice in a way, as the day was Margaret's: I could well have been jealous. She looked so radiant and beautiful, sitting at the head of the table where our mother should have sat. The men couldn't keep their eyes off her. Yet she had done none of the work, save arrange the flowers. She wore a dress of turquoise silk (made from the length our father had bought her the day we bid for Hoppy) and the soft sky colour set off her wonderful pink cheeks and golden hair, and she knew she was beautiful and she was laughing and being her very nicest, so that our father opposite her at the far end of the table was laughing too, so proud and happy . . . why couldn't it always be like this? I wondered. It was wonderful to see Father laughing. He had had a good harvest, of course, and his immediate worries for the coming year were over, but it was Margaret who brought the sparkle to his eyes. I could never have had that effect on him, however hard I might try. He valued me for my way with the horses, but he didn't love me as he loved Margaret. So when Martin gave me that silly kiss, it was a sort of comfort and I was glad of it.

Anyway, I wouldn't have changed places.

Nat was not invited, of course, for the Grovers had their own harvest supper. Even old Grover was forced to supply the best, and from hearsay it was a great evening, with so much beer drunk that they all forgot their grouses and indulged themselves so hugely at his expense that most of them never got home that night but lay comatose in the ditch all the way from Grover's gates to the village green. The only time he gave anything away, they all said. It hurt him so much he only stayed for one course, and was gone by the time the singing and dancing started.

We had singing too, and some bounding about (one could scarcely call it dancing) to the wheezy strains of

Martin's uncle's fiddle. Ellen was a great dancer and whirled about with Jack and little Billy and Martin's siblings until she could whirl no more. Martin couldn't dance of course and sang instead. He had quite a nice voice and knew all the words – through spending so much time in the yard of the Queen's Head, no doubt.

I stayed up helping Mrs Ponder clear away and it was dark by the time I went up to bed. I looked out of the window and saw the white-sheeted table below in the orchard, the wild flowers wilting, their pollen spilt amongst the beer and gravy stains and a white owl sitting in the apple tree above. What a happy day, and so rare, the excess of food and the lull from the back-breaking work that called our lives . . . I couldn't help thinking of the squire's daughters, and the Grover girls, sitting about all day with their books and piano lessons, and even Miss Frobisher with her orderly hours in the schoolhouse . . . I thought I could have been clever too, given half a chance. Like Ellen. If you weren't clever you worked with your hands for a living and that seemed to be my path. But I wanted the horses, and if I was clever I would make money that way, which would be better than book-learning. To breed a horse like Marshland Shales, a Sampson, a Driver, a Pretender – that would make my father proud of me! And when I thought of my lovely Rattler, a shiver of delight ran through me. The owl flew away, its white wings beating slowly over the shaved fields, and I went to bed, putting my cold body against Margaret's fever, my thoughts torn in all directions.

* * *

Margaret met Nat again at the village harvest fair. She wore her blue silk dress and put ribbons in her hair and I walked with her along the road. I offered to saddle Tilly for her to ride, but she said she wouldn't be seen dead on that old scarecrow, so although I walked with her I maintained an offended silence. What a rebuff! But Nat came up on Crocus, and then she was lifted on to the front of the saddle and I was left without so much as a good afternoon from her lover. What a pair! I wondered if Father ought to challenge Nat himself in the autumn and put Tilly against Crocus again, or should we wait for Nat to renew his challenge? Give him another two years and we could put Rattler against him! I skipped along at this thought and was soon sitting on the green with Martin, listening to the brass band from town and watching everyone in their finery wandering amongst the pedlar's wares and the sweet stalls and the coconut shies. Father was in the Queen's Head with Jack, and Ellen was bowling for a pig. We had two already and I'm sure I didn't want another to feed, but she wasn't very good, luckily. I could see Crocus grazing at the top of the green, tied to the vicarage railings, and Nat and Margaret sitting on the bank, very close.

'They say Grover's gone down to Leiston to buy a threshing machine,' Martin said. 'That'll cause a rumpus, if he gets one.'

'He was bound to be the first,' I said. 'He's got a sowing drill already.' We had seen the Grovers' drill in action, but it didn't seem very satisfactory, Nat having to do the work himself as they had no one to trust well enough to work it. Judging from their crops, it sometimes sowed very thin and sometimes let out a great dump, perhaps due to how fast the horse was walking, or if he stopped to let out some dung. The workers scorned it, and said machinery would never work on the land, but the threshing machine was rather different. It worked in the yard, powered by a pair of horses, and did the job by itself in a week or two – a job that took many men and women all the winter to get finished, hand threshing with a flail.

'So what happens to all his workers in the winter, when he's got his machine?' Martin said disparagingly. 'He'll lay them off and they'll all starve.'

'The farmers who bought threshing machines up north got them broken up by their workers,' I remembered. 'Perhaps that'll happen here.'

'Yes, and they got transported for their pains. One got hanged.'

You could be transported to Australia for quite small things, stealing and poaching; girls were sent as well. It was a terrible thought. The journey on the ship took three months and it was said to be like a slave ship, all starvation and beatings, and you never saw your family ever again. Just imagine! No wonder few people stepped out of line; hardly anybody was that brave. But it made your blood boil to think of Grover going into machinery. He didn't give a damn for his people.

'You must get Margaret to talk to that Nat of hers. Everyone says he's mad for her. Maybe he'll persuade his father not to.'

'She's not bothered with things like that. She hates the farm,' I said.

'Yeah, she's not much good, your Margaret,' Martin said.

A visitor came up with a horse then and Martin got up to take it to the inn, and so I wandered up the green towards the vicarage to see if Nicholas was coming out. I tried not to see Nat and Margaret but no one could miss the handsome couple holding hands and laughing on the bank. Unfortunately the vicar was at his gate with Nicholas and could see them only too plainly.

Not wanting to make a direct reference to them, he tried obliquely to steer our family into better ways.

'Perhaps after such a good harvest, your father might see his way to coming to praise God for it on Sunday?' he said. 'It will be the Thanksgiving. And you too, Clara – it would give me great pleasure to see you in church.'

I felt myself going red. I only did what Father said, and he said believing in God was a load of rubbish. No one had prayed to God more fervently than our father when our mother was ill; in fact he had been a church-goer all his life, but now he would have none of it. The last time he went to church had been for our mother's funeral. Most people in the village went to church, or to the weird chapel that had opened down the far end by the water mill. That was said to be more fun, with strange firebrand preachers who shouted and thumped, not like poor Reverend Bywater, who was very quiet and dull. The poorer villagers felt more at home there, away from the eye of the squire and his family and his botanic lordship, and the Grovers in all their finery.

'I'll come,' I mumbled, to appease him. I could see him looking at Margaret and Nat and trying hard to stop himself saying something to me about it.

'I would like to speak to your father. Will you tell him? Even if he doesn't come to church. I know the way he is thinking, but he gets no comfort from it, I feel.'

I knew he was doing his job, but Nicholas looked uncomfortable and we were both pleased when a lady we didn't know came up and greeted him, and we were able to peel off down the green.

'Sorry about that,' Nicholas said. 'He doesn't like to see people escaping from his clutches.'

'No. But I can't help it about Father. He won't go, whatever I say.'

'No, don't bother.'

I wondered if Nicholas, likely to meet God pretty soon if there was one, believed in his father's convictions. I remembered my mother's empty eyes and my feeling that she had gone somewhere else. Where? Even when a hen died and I held it and saw the light go out of its eyes, I thought it had a soul that escaped to heaven. But if there was no God there was no heaven and no anything, and I didn't really like to think that. That was why I tried never to think about it. I just thought that nature was very beautiful and gave me my best feelings, and maybe that was God, in

110

a way, the land and my horses. And if it was God who made them, well, I was a believer. But it had nothing to do with all the things that were said in church, about us all being miserable sinners and suchlike. I couldn't bring myself to say it, asking forgiveness for being a miserable sinner when I spent all my life working for the good of others, especially Margaret. And keeping my temper. I thought I was fairly angelic in the scale of things. The biggest miserable sinner in church was Eb Grover, and he was rewarded with riches beyond belief. No wonder my father thought God was not to be trusted.

Nicholas went to church of course.

'Well, I have to, don't I? There's no point upsetting Father. But I can see what your father thinks. Good people suffer and wicked people thrive. I'm good, after all, and look at me. If I thought I was going to heaven soon I wouldn't mind so much, but how can anyone know?'

'I think there's a paradise to go to, for good people,' I said. 'There must be.'

'And good horses too?'

'Yes, of course! Beautiful sunny fields full of rich grass and shady trees and lovely streams and no work and no whips – yes, they must have their reward when they die.'

'And for me there will be big fields with great big hedges to jump and great big ditches and dear Prince who will fly them all,' Nicholas said.

I remembered little Nicholas, as he had been, on his mud-splattered pony, Prince. The gleam of remembrance in his eyes made me feel terrible. I wished we had never started this conversation.

'I'll come to Harvest Thanksgiving to please your father,' I said. 'But I doubt whether I'll get Father to come, nor Jack either. Margaret will come, if she's well.'

As if she'd heard me, Margaret got up from the bank, and Nat and she came together down the green towards us, Nat leading Crocus.

'Nat wants to talk to Father,' Margaret said. 'Is he in the inn?'

'Yes, I think so.'

They neither of them acknowledged Nicholas, beyond a nod.

'Will you fetch him?' Nat said to me.

I was stung. 'No, I will not. I'm talking to Nicholas. Fetch him yourself.'

'Clara!' Margaret shrieked.

Whatever was it about? I wondered. Was he going to ask for Margaret's hand in marriage? Judging from their canoodling, it was high time. But the way he ordered me made my blood boil.

But he smiled then and made it all right by saying, 'Of course. I will go myself. Perhaps you would hold my horse for me?'

Of course, nothing would have pleased me better. I took the reins. And I could not help seeing Nat as Margaret saw him: so masterful and strong, an oak tree in her fragile life, who could supply her with the comfort and fine living she craved. When he smiled he showed perfect white teeth. His sunburned cheeks grew a quick stubble, shaved close beneath the curling black sidepieces, and his eyes were dark as a gypsy's with lashes like a girl's. Yes, he was handsome, as desirable as a man could be.

What a pity he was a Grover.

They strolled off towards the Queen's Head, Margaret hanging on his arm. All eyes turned to watch them.

'That put him in his place,' Nicholas said, smiling. 'Is he going to ask for her hand in marriage?'

'They would never allow it! Not Eb Grover! Nor my father either, I doubt, for his hatred of the Grovers.'

'It would be a way of taking your land, perhaps.'

'What about Jack? He would kill Nat first.' I laughed then and said, 'But it would be good to have this horse in the family. Isn't he a beauty?'

I loosened his girths, which of course Nat had omitted to do, and watched him as he cropped the grass. Yes, what a match he would be, not for old Tilly, but for my Rattler in a couple of years!

'He'd make a rare hunter if he learned to jump,' Nicholas said longingly.

We soon learned what Nat wanted Father for. Jack and Martin came bounding up and said Nat wanted to match Crocus against Tilly again.

'And beat her fairly, he said. He said he wasn't happy about last time, winning through default. He thought now Crocus was stronger he had the beating of her.'

'Oh, does he just! We'll see about that!' I shouted.

'Father said give Tilly a couple of weeks rest from harvest and Nat could name his date.'

'I'll start feeding her up,' I said. 'Poor old Tilly!'

But I was excited at the thought, longing to put Nat in his place. Though when I lay in the grass with Crocus grazing by my head, I could not help but notice the new muscling that had grown on him since last autumn, and the stallion's crest. He was strong! And for the first time I feared for poor old Tilly, the worn-out mare with a heart too big for her own good.

Ellen came up then with Miss Frobisher and we told her the news.

'Poor old Tilly,' said Ellen.

'Is your father here?' enquired Miss Frobisher.

'Yes. He's in the Queen's Head.'

I saw Miss Frobisher gently shake her head, and realized that she, like the vicar, wanted my father redeemed, cleansed of his bad ways. Poor old Father. He had so little joy in life now. And soon it was going to be so much worse.

'He's all right,' I said defensively. 'He's worked so hard.'

Was it my imagination or did Miss Frobisher colour up slightly? But she said, 'Yes, of course. Harvest is a hard time.'

When we were at home later, and Father and Margaret had yet to come in, Ellen said, 'Miss Frobisher says everyone is talking about Margaret and Nat.'

'It's nothing to do with her,' I said angrily.

'But everyone says.'

'Let them say! It's Father's business, our business, not theirs.'

'Mother would—'

'Be quiet! Don't say anything! Don't!'

Margaret deserved some life before she died, but I couldn't say that to Ellen.

10

I went to fetch Tilly in from the field. She was with my dear Rattler, and I must admit my eyes were all for my pride and joy rather than for Tilly, although this was her day of reckoning, her match against Crocus. Father had said to put her out for a couple of days beforehand. It was late October, and warm and sweet, and certainly she could keep gently moving over the wide water meadows, working her ever-stiffening joints. Rattler followed her like a lapdog, but kept well clear of her heels. He had grown and now looked far more mature, deep through the chest and short in the leg, a true Norfolk trotter. His winter coat was coming through, gleaming and dark as polished ebony. His funny bony head was full of character, but could not truly be described as handsome. But the eyes were large and curious, full of intelligence. What more could I ask? He had a generous nature and, I hoped, a brave heart. The looks were no good without the heart, and the heart came wrapped in all conditions. All my dreams lay with Rattler, for there was precious little else to look forward to.

I was not very confident about this match. Tilly seemed to have mellowed, grown softer; I could not quite explain it. And she had worked so hard through the harvest and lost her good summer condition, while Crocus with only light riding work had grown into his full maturity. If he had been impressive a year ago he was even more so now, and I knew that most bets were going his way. I told Father not to rely on Tilly winning, but he looked so dark at me that I said no more.

I think Jack agreed with me.

'Don't press her too hard,' I said. But I knew we needed the money, as usual.

But irrepressible Jack put on his best riding clothes: his red waistcoat and white stock and his old-fashioned cutaway jacket (once Grandfather's) and I brought Tilly out as shining as I could manage, and Hoppy in the side-saddle for Margaret, as she refused to stay at home and hadn't the strength to walk. Father and I had to walk.

It was a soft, perfect day, warm and still. All the girls were still in summer dresses, collecting on the green, and even Nicholas had put aside his woollen scarves and was sitting on the rectory gate in his shirt-sleeves.

'You'll be boiled,' Margaret said to Jack.

'Yes, and your lover boy too. Look at him,' Jack said crossly.

For Nat was dressed for the occasion too and looked magnificent on his powerful little stallion. My heart sank at the sight of them. Worse, as well as my feeling of bitterness I was aware of an uncontrollable pang of excitement as I laid eyes on the fine figure Nat made. Like his horse, he had matured, lost the uncertainty and gangliness of youth. He had a very powerful and authoritative presence and was obviously a magnet for all the silly village girls, which included myself and Margaret. Margaret queened in the delight of her favouritism, before all eyes, as Nat rode to greet her. I, at Tilly's head, scowled angrily and he had the gall to laugh at me and say to Margaret, 'Your little sister looks as if she's swallowed brimstone.'

Margaret said, 'She's a sour one, like Tilly.'

The traitor, after all I did to help her!

Jack said angrily, 'She's worth six of you—'

But I cut him off and said, 'I'll tighten your girths. Move your leg.'

Sim was checking over Crocus, Nat not bothering, used to being waited on.

'Take him steady, Mister Nat. Keep his strength for the last five miles.'

Sim couldn't help himself saying this, but only got a sharp retort for his pains: 'I'll ride how I think fit, thank you.'

Sim shook his head. He loved Crocus. As Nat rode off he said to me, 'A pity he's not in better hands. He deserves it.'

'I think he'll beat Tilly today,' I said.

'If that braggart uses his brain, maybe.' Sim paused and then said, 'That colt you've got – is he going to be as good as Tilly?'

'Yes,' I said firmly. And laughed – how could I tell?

'He's a good'un by the looks of him.'

'What if he can beat Crocus, in a few years' time? My ambition—' As if Sim didn't know.

'Good luck to you, lass. You do a good job with your horses.' He could have added, 'You should have been a boy,' as it was implicit in his voice, but he was too kindly. How often had I heard that? Too many times.

We went to help see a fair start. Tilly was very quiet. I was worried. But she went off in her usual business-like way, not needing Jack's heels for she was watching the starter's handkerchief. She was almost human in her ways, so experienced and cunning. Crocus was all over the place and had to circle for breaking even before he was out of sight. Sim shook his head. The spectators on horseback clattered off in pursuit and the farmers all retired into the Queen's Head. I went to see if Margaret was all right and took Hoppy from her as she wanted to sit and rest. I gave her Tilly's blanket to sit on. She was very weak. She looked up at me and I saw her expression, quite different from the glowing face she had turned to Nat. Desperation, despair.

'I think Nat will win,' I said, to comfort her. Nor did I lie.

'What does it matter?' she whispered.

I could not bear it.

Luckily at that moment Nicholas came up, and Margaret, who never showed her weakness to anyone but me, her night companion – and in the night the terror prevailed – turned her bright face to him and said, 'Who are you gambling on, Nick? Or don't vicars' sons gamble?'

'This one does,' Nick grinned. 'Crocus, I'm afraid. But truly, I'd prefer Tilly to win.'

'Well, that's honest.'

'Yes, well, vicars' sons have to be honest, don't they?'

He sat down beside her and I left them together, torn as always, seeing all the great galumphing village youth in glowing health sauntering past them, some stopping to talk, laughing, carefree. How *unfair* it was! It choked me.

When the two horses came back for the halfway turn, Crocus was well in front. But as he went round the post, Jack said to me, 'She feels good, don't worry. I reckon Crocus will tire before she will.'

He rode so neatly, not like Nat thumping down on the saddle: it was worth a good deal in a long match. (But Crocus was so strong!) Tilly had her mulish look, a good sign, her ears back and her face sour. Her great shoulders worked in easy rhythm, like clockwork; she never broke. Crocus had broken several times, but still he was several hundred yards in front.

After they were out of sight again I was so anxious I could not talk to anybody. I led Hoppy up the green, up and down, and let him graze, but no one came near me. I could see Sim too, standing on his own, sucking a piece of straw like a yokel. The farmers started to come out of the inn and stood around waiting, and some of the horsemen were coming back, having only gone a little way, milling about, shouting. The atmosphere was very tense.

Then a shout went up.

'Crocus!'

And, almost immediately, a great cheer.

'Tilly! Tilly!'

Oh, dear God, so close! Crocus was done in, you could see, lathered and his action gone, but Tilly had her head down and was moving in the same machine-like way some fifty yards behind him. But not gaining. Jack was sitting still, not using his heels because he knew she was giving her all, she knew the job. Nat was using his spurs, bloodying poor Crocus who hadn't the experience to know what was being asked of him. I prayed for him to break, and in his disarray it was very likely. It was the only chance Tilly would have of passing him, if Nat had to circle. But Nat, as well as spurring, was holding Crocus's mouth cruelly to prevent such a disaster. It would not happen.

Sim came down to me, his face dark with anger. 'My poor horse!'

'He's won,' I said dully.

'Your Jack's a grand lad,' Sim said.

I think he guessed that with spurs and a whip Jack might have made it, but Tilly was too good to be treated like that. She passed the post the same fifty yards behind Crocus, and pulled up of her own accord, with no sweat on her save the dampness caused by the warm day; no sign of exhaustion, not even of anger at losing, which was normal on the rare occasions she had met a better. She nearly always bit them when they went past or lashed out at the post, such was her nature. But now she was all disdain, calm, strange.

Jack slid down and I hugged him, trailing Hoppy behind me.

He gave me a rueful smile and said, 'She's had her day, I think. But she went well, I couldn't ask for more.'

Crocus stood head down, covered in white sweat, steaming, bleeding from his sides. Sim was loosening his girths, his lips tight and silent, else he'd lose his job. Nat's admirers crowded round, shouting and cheering. Our father came up, unsmiling, and clapped Tilly on the neck.

'Good girl. Good girl,' he said.

And Tilly lifted her ugly head and gave him a nudge, a sign of affection I had never seen from her before.

Jack grinned at me. 'At least Margaret will be happy.' He wasn't angry at losing because the mare hadn't failed, after all. 'I'll take her home, if you like.'

'Oh no. I will.' I knew he wanted a long glass of ale and talk with the farmers in the Queen's Head. But that was what was so nice about Jack, he wasn't selfish. 'There's Margaret though, and Hoppy. Tell Nat to take her home.'

I put Hoppy's reins in Nat's hand and led Tilly away down the road, just stopping to take her blanket from Margaret and throw it over her back.

'Nat's got Hoppy,' I said.

I didn't wait to see what happened. I knew Nat would want to celebrate his win with his friends in the inn. Margaret was at his mercy. I didn't care now, but set off for home with Tilly. People passed, going

122

home, and gave me the time of day, and one of them was Prosper Mayes on his white mare.

He pulled up from a canter to walk with me, and I felt myself going red and my heart start to thump in a most peculiar way.

'Your brother's got sense,' he said. 'I admire him for not winning.'

Heavens, he was gorgeous! Why ever hadn't I chatted to him earlier when I had the chance? Now you could see he had to restrain his mare who wanted to get home. He had very light horseman's hands, not like Nat's, and held the mare as if on cotton threads with long brown fingers. He was bare headed and his hair was tied roughly back in an unfashionable way with what looked like a piece of string. He sat so easily, as good a rider as I have ever seen, and the eyes he turned so kindly on me were appraising, making me blush ever harder. He was only a boy, fourteen perhaps, like Nicholas, yet he had such authority and elegance he seemed like a man. I found him quite bewitching but couldn't have explained why in a hundred sentences. Well, in my conscribed life, where had I ever seen such grace in a male before, even counting the squire and the gentry from Oakhall? Apart from the string, he was well dressed in shabby but fashionable clothes, his breeches and boots tight and his cravat severe, yet he was in no way pompous or autocratic like Nat.

'She's twenty-seven,' I said. 'Ten years ago, even five, she'd have won.'

'She's a marvel. I love to see her go. I don't come

here to bet, only to see a good match. It was very close. I wish she'd won.'

'I don't think she'll go again. It's not fair to get her beat.'

'No. She doesn't deserve that.'

His mare pranced impatiently and he laughed then and said, 'I'll be getting on. Good day to you!' And all I could see was the snowy swirl of the mare's tail as he released her and cantered on down the dusty road towards the turnpike.

His time of day to me had banished my disappointment in the afternoon's work and I gave a little skip and laughed aloud. Tilly's walking stride was so long that, tired as she was, I had to hurry to keep up with her. As usual I unsaddled her and took her straight down to the river so that she could drink and cool her legs. She always liked that.

She stretched out her neck and lipped at the cool-running stream, and I leaned on her withers, thinking daft thoughts about the lovely Prosper. And as she drank I saw the most amazing thing: a sharp movement in her belly. And then another. I stared. No more.

But it was enough. I knew immediately what it was. Tilly was in foal! Who to? It could only be my colt Rattler! She had been with no other.

I was filled with such joy and excitement I could hardly contain myself. I threw my arms round her neck (filling my boots with water) and hugged her madly. The subtle change I had noticed in her behaviour, her unusual lack of aggression, even the nudge she had given my father, was now explained. She was getting motherly instincts already. Oh, if we had known, would we have matched her? How terrible if the exertion aborted the foal!

But no, Tilly was used to hard work, and was not in the slightest bit exhausted, not like poor Crocus. I stood bursting with excitement, hardly able to believe what I had seen. Or was it my imagination? No, surely, for I hadn't been looking for it. It had been so strong I couldn't have helped but notice. My thoughts soared: a union of Tilly and Rattler! What blood to mix, the best with the best! No breeder could have found better. And Rattler – so young, none of us had even supposed it a possibility. How potent he must be, a fine indication for his future. Father and Jack would be thrilled with the news, a finer reward than winning the match.

I was longing to tell someone, but the house was empty. No one came. I took Tilly back to the yard and rubbed her down and told her how marvellous she was, and gave her a small feed. Then I turned her out into the field. Rattler came trotting over, neck arched, every inch the proud father, and put out his muzzle to her. But Tilly, ever Tilly, turned her back to him, flung up her heels and trotted away down the field. He followed. Two trotters, showing their paces loose, as fine a sight as any proud breeder could wish to see. And that was me, the breeder. I was so proud I thought I would burst.

When I went to bed that night, I dreamed that Prosper Mayes' white mare had a foal and it was the spitting image of Tilly. Prosper Mayes turned up at our farm and was very angry and blamed me. But even in his anger he was gorgeous, and I just looked and looked at him and didn't say anything. It was a lovely dream.

11

Margaret was sobbing. On and on, non-stop.

'Margaret, you'll give yourself a haemorrhage. Stop it!'

We were in our bedroom, the door shut, our terrible secret contained. It was late November and, as if to mock our despair, the sun was shining, the birds singing as if it were May, and the trees in Gridswood a riot of wintering leaves, tawny and gold against a pearly-blue sky, not a cloud to be seen. Jack was mending the cowshed roof, hammering away and singing, Ellen was at school and Father was tending to threshing in the big threshing barn.

Everyone in the village could have told you the reason for Margaret's distress. Nat had gone away on his Grand Tour of Europe, not to return for a couple of years. It was what well-educated young men from rich families were expected to do, save that Nat was not well educated and culture was as foreign to his nature as the countries he was to travel in. Everyone was amazed. The desire to extend his learning was very sudden. Maybe some of them guessed. But only I knew.

Margaret was pregnant.

When she told Nat, he was away to Paris within the week. Whether he put up any argument we did not know, but with parents like his even the strong and arrogant Nat would have had little chance. They no doubt threatened to cut him off without a penny if he married Margaret. Why – *why* – I wondered, couldn't they have done the kind thing and let nature take its course? What would they have lost by it? Their cruelty was incredible. The birth was surely going to kill her, if she didn't go before. They could have waited, seen it out. They could have shown compassion when it would, after all, hardly have inconvenienced them. It was unlikely to be a live birth, even if it went full-term. How the frail seventeen-year-old girl could have conceived in the first place was a mystery, and the news must have staggered them as much as it did me. But they were a tight family. Our family as yet knew nothing about it, only me.

'You've got to tell Father,' I said. 'You can't go on like this.'

Nor could I, the only confidante. It was killing me. Every night she clung to me, great stifled sobs shaking us both.

'I shall tell him if you won't. You need help and nursing. I can't do everything!' I heard my voice rising with anger. 'It's not fair!'

The eternal complaint, not fair. But it wasn't fair that Margaret was how she was, it wasn't fair that the evil Grovers could do this to her. Nothing was fair in this life.

Father had been so happy about Tilly – what a ridiculous thing by comparison! It had put new life into him. I couldn't bear to see this bring him down now, so soon afterwards. I thought it would extinguish him completely. And what if Margaret died and the baby lived? How would we cope then? Would it be my job to look after a baby too? I wanted to scream.

'I'm going to tell him, tonight,' I said.

'He'll go mad,' Margaret said.

'Yes, but you can't put it off for ever. And he will be kind, I know he will. He will look after you and cosset you. You need it, Margaret, you need a doctor, you need help. I can't do it.'

'Tell him then,' sobbed Margaret. 'What difference does it make? He can't change anything.'

Surely Father must have noticed Margaret's decline, I thought, how her brightness was all extinguished, her face drawn, her hair snarled and dirty. She needed kindness and care. I wasn't capable.

I trembled to tell him. I told Jack first. Jack went white.

'A bloody Grover in our family!' was all he could say. All the stuffing seemed to go out of him. If this was Jack, how would Father take it?

'Don't, Jack. Don't be angry with her. It won't survive, how can it?'

'It won't! I'll strangle it first!'

'Jack! It's an innocent thing!'

'That swine, Grover! Lucky for him he's in France. I would kill him, I can tell you. No wonder he legged it when he knew – couldn't get out quick enough, and no thought for Margaret. My God, what a swine!'

I told Mrs Ponder. Jack told Father. Ellen told Miss Frobisher. It was all over the village. Wrath against the Grovers was universal. People asked us if they had given Margaret any money to see her through her confinement, to pay for nursing, but we had to say no, they hadn't. They never got in touch with us at all. People blamed Father for letting her go so free with Nat, but I knew perfectly well why he had allowed her. He had never supposed she had health enough to conceive, even if she had gone that far with her lover, and he wanted her to be happy before she died. If Nat had not gone abroad, either Jack or Father would have killed him, I think. Or even Martin out of loyalty. Hatred for the Grovers was so great that Margaret's promiscuity went relatively uncriticized, although the sin was generally cruelly condemned. Our family was treated with great kindness and concern.

Father's distress was terrible. He stopped going down to the Queen's Head, only going to the village on farm business, and he worked outside from first light until after dark, never halting. Any spare weight he had ever had fell off him and he looked as bad as Margaret, his face drawn and haggard, his eyes lustreless. He hardly spoke a word. People came to visit, his farmer friends who came with excuses, to discuss business that didn't need discussing, to show embarrassed friendship, but in their kind ignorance it was only the embarrassment that showed. Mrs Ponder, a religious woman in our irreligious family, was deeply

130

disapproving, but her loyalty stopped her from defecting, thank goodness. I think it was through her that we received a visit from the Reverend Bywater, Nicholas's father. He came to try and persuade Father that it was God's will and all that, but Father wasn't having any. I heard Father's voice raised – they were talking in the parlour – and Mrs Ponder, standing over the range, shook her head and pursed her lips. Surprisingly the Reverend had brought Nicholas with him in his gig. It was a mild day. He was going to stay outside in the gig, but I went out and tied the horse up and brought him into the kitchen.

'He wants me to talk to Margaret,' he said gloomily.

'Why? Are you practising to be a vicar?'

He laughed. 'Thank God I'll be spared that.'

I saw Mrs Ponder now looking shocked. I really liked Nicholas.

'Margaret's asleep,' I said. 'Talk to me instead.'

'How's Tilly?' he asked at once, and we talked about that for a bit, then Nicholas said his father's sister was coming to live with them. 'Aunt Agnes. She's an ogre. Ogress. I dread it.'

'Why? I thought she lived in London?'

'Yes. Why doesn't she stay there? She says Father needs help in looking after me. She's coming to look after me!'

'You don't need looking after!'

'No. That's what I said. Not anything Jane can't do.' Jane was their maid, a jolly girl who helped their rather ancient housekeeper, Mrs Norton.

'I think she's short of money. *She* needs looking

after. So she's latching on, pretending she's a do-gooder. Father doesn't see this – he doesn't think ill of anyone, part of the job, I suppose. I wouldn't mind if she was decent. But she's horrible. And *living* with us – we get on all right, Father and I. We don't want her.'

It was true that Nicholas and his father were good friends. His father never fussed him, and treated him like an adult. He was a small, round, kindly man, mild by nature, yet he could deliver a powerful sermon. He was said to be a clever scholar and certainly Nicholas could speak French and Latin and write a beautiful letter. But I remembered Aunt Agnes as quite different, formidable and ugly. She had come for holidays sometimes. We had giggled, Jack and I, in church at the sight of her. Those were the days when Mother took us to church, like good children.

Luckily, at this point Mrs Ponder went out to hang out Margaret's washing so we had free rein to discuss Aunt Agnes, and then this led on to how things didn't turn out how one wanted; look at Margaret, for instance, and what if we were landed with a Grover baby? And Nicholas said gloomily, 'You always love them, from what I gather,' and I said firmly, 'I won't, and I won't look after it either,' and Nicholas said, 'Your father, for all his spleen now, will dote on it, I bet.'

'Rather dote on your Aunt Agnes,' I said, and then we got the giggles, and then Mrs Ponder came back so we went outside. Efficient as she was, Mrs Ponder was rather a dour woman, not very loveable. I told Nicholas about Father not wanting someone who had designs on him and Nicholas said, 'He ought to marry again, your father. Then you wouldn't have to do it all.'

Odd, but I had never thought of such a thing. 'Who?' I asked.

And he said, 'Miss Frobisher.'

I nearly fainted. '*Miss Frobisher!*'

'Why not? She's nice, and I'm sure she wants a husband. Maybe my father ought to marry her. I'd like that better than Aunt Agnes.'

We got the giggles again at the thought of the Reverend marrying Miss Frobisher – he did seem awfully old, Nicholas's father – but I must say I was rather taken with the idea of my own father marrying her. I remembered suddenly how she had made him laugh that day. Why had I never thought of it? And Ellen liked her especially.

'I want to marry Miss Charlotte,' Nicholas said. 'I've told her so and she laughed and said all right, but of course she knows it won't come to that. She's really the nicest person I know.'

'After me.'

'All right. Yes. After you.' But he didn't say he wanted to marry me, like he had once.

I didn't know how long Nicholas had got, but I did realize that he was gradually getting weaker, and he now had the bright colour of the consumptive in his drawn cheeks. He wasn't coughing now, but he often did, and I suppose he had the bleeding as well sometimes, like Margaret, because there were times when he had to stay in bed for a few weeks at a time. I knew he was in love with Miss Charlotte, he had told me so. How nice of her to agree to his proposal! Like a proper squire's daughter she did good works amongst the poor in the village and was well liked. She had two older sisters who never did good works but were always off to London and Bath and parties, but apparently Charlotte didn't care for parties and preferred to go hunting. That was where she and Nicholas had got so friendly, crashing over the jumps behind hounds.

Nicholas having put the idea of Miss Frobisher joining our family into my mind, I looked out for her the next time I went down to the village. I wanted to have a particular look at her, consider her in the role of stepmother. Ellen doted on her, so that was something. She could easily invite her home if I suggested it.

Strangely, while I was considering this, she came of her own accord. One afternoon after school she arrived at the door with Ellen and said, 'I thought I would call to see if I can help you in any way. I have heard of your trouble from Ellen.'

I asked her in. Mrs Ponder had gone home early because her husband was ill, but luckily the kitchen was tidy and there were some fresh-baked scones on the hob. Margaret was lying on the couch by the fire where she usually was, making a pretence of sewing a dress for the baby (I usually finished her sewing) and she too, thank goodness, looked better than usual, her hair combed out and a clean blouse on.

I didn't know what to say to make conversation. I told Ellen to go and fetch Father, who was out cutting hay with Jack and Martin quite close at hand, and went and washed myself in the scullery so that I could serve tea. They always said I smelled of horses, but I liked the smell and didn't mind. When I came back, Miss Frobisher and Margaret were talking without any awkwardness, and I could see that Miss Frobisher had a very straightforward way with her. Although not really pretty, she had a fine slim figure and clear pale skin. Her brown eyes were very direct, her teeth even and white, her thick brown hair severely fastened back into a slightly unruly bundle on the back of her head. Down and free, it would be spectacular.

'I didn't know about the baby, not till I was five months gone,' Margaret was saying. 'I never expected it, you see, and I hardly have any bleeding – that sort – at the best of times, so how could I tell?'

'So when will it be? Do you know?'

'Oh, quite the worst time, about February, I think.'

'It happens to many. At least you're not alone in your trouble. Not like many poor girls.'

Her voice then was bitter, and I had a sudden instinct that she spoke from the heart. Had she herself . . . ? I hardly dared wonder at it, yet some inner prompting came quite unbidden. But Margaret droned on, noticing nothing, and I dismissed my shocking imaginings. Margaret, after all, thought of no one's life but her own, nor ever had. It never occurred to her how bitterly we, her family, were facing the imminence of a Grover in our midst. Now that she knew her place was safe within her family, she was living only for the wonder of producing a Nat substitute. At least, thank God, she had something to look forward to. We none of the rest of us thought it would come to term, our only salvation. Nor she survive. Margaret and Tilly too – the most unlikely mothers!

I buttered some scones and Father came in, not willingly I could see, but polite enough. He went to wash in the scullery and came back as I poured the kettle on the tea.

'It's kind of you to call, Miss Frobisher.'

I could see that he was out of habit with women's talk, although he had joined in quite happily with Mother's friends once, laughing and joking – how long ago it seemed! Oh, I did so badly want Father to get on with her! I grabbed Ellen by the arm and whispered, 'Come outside with me!'

They were all served with tea and I slipped out of the door. Ellen followed.

'What is it? What's wrong?'

'Leave them alone, Ellen! Let *Father* talk to her. If we're there he won't say a word.'

'Why? Can't we all talk? I want to be with her.'

'I know. But—' I sighed. This was all Nicholas's fault. What a stupid thing to have to explain.

'Nicholas said—'

'What?'

'What a good thing it would be if Father and Miss

136

Frobisher got – got friendly. You know. He said Father should remarry.'

'OH!' Ellen clapped her hand to her mouth and shrieked. They must have heard her inside. Her eyes glittered. How pretty she was, I noticed suddenly, just like Margaret, so vivacious, with all her spirits shining out of her bright blue eyes.

'How wonderful it would be! What a marvellous idea!'

'Sssh! They'll hear you. I thought it was a good idea too. And then she just turned up, with you, barely after Nicholas had suggested it.'

'Oh, it would be wonderful!'

'Yes, but for heaven's sake, don't let on you're thinking that. That I told you. Father would be too frightened to talk to her at all if he had any idea. You know what he's like.'

'Do you think she likes him? It was her idea to visit. I never said anything.'

'That's a good sign then. She wouldn't come if she didn't like him.'

'Oh, it would be so lovely! Why didn't I think of it? Clever Nicholas! He is clever, isn't he? Everyone says so.'

'Yes, he is. Poor Nicholas.'

'I hate home, without Mother,' Ellen said.

I never gave Ellen a thought: she was always romping about with her friends, away from home. She helped very little on the farm, save at busy times when all the children worked.

'It's so gloomy indoors, with Margaret. And now

Father so awful – I can't bear it. Miss Frobisher asked me why I was always in the village, never at home, and I told her. Do you think that's why she's come? To see for herself?'

'Probably. She cares for you.'

'She's always nice to me, even when my work's bad, that's why I like her so much. I think she's wonderful.'

'Yes, but don't bank on anything. With Father, I mean. He won't think of anything but Margaret until—' My voice trailed off. I couldn't say it.

'Until she's dead?' said Ellen.

'Yes.'

And Ellen said, 'That's why I hate home. With Margaret.'

I could understand that. She was only a child, after all, and Margaret wasn't stoical, accepting, like Nicholas. No. We all suffered. But I couldn't blame her as Ellen did.

'I hate it. I wish it was all over,' she said.

'So do I.'

'But I'd like the baby, even if it's Nat's.'

'You're mad!'

But I laughed. I was beginning to think of the baby more kindly as time went on, although I swore I wouldn't look after it. How did we know? It might look just like Margaret, not Nat, or our mother, or Father. Or me! Poor little thing.

But Ellen stayed outside with me until Miss Frobisher took her leave, and then we saw Father come out with her and heard him thank her for coming, and she said something and he laughed – he *laughed*! – like he had the other time she came, and my heart leaped up like a baby inside me.

When we were all indoors together later, he said, 'She's a kind soul, your Miss Frobisher,' to Ellen.

Ellen glanced at me.

I kept my eyes on my dinner.

12

Miss Frobisher came a few times after that, but not often enough to seem forward. If Father saw her he came in, but usually he didn't see her, and she stayed and talked with Margaret, which was the object of her visit. If Margaret was in bed she went upstairs. What they talked about I have no idea for I could never talk with Margaret for more than five minutes without wanting to do something else, but sometimes Miss Frobisher was up there for an hour.

Nicholas's Aunt Agnes arrived and Nicholas lost his sense of humour.

'Call on us, Clara,' he said, 'and see for yourself.'

I called.

Jane answered the door and I gaped, for she was in a proper maid's uniform which she had never worn before, tight and black and with a white starched apron.

'I have to put the apron on to answer the door,' she said. 'It's clean, to show the visitors. What larks, eh?' She laughed. 'I think I'm in for the sack, because I'm not polite enough. And she says

Mrs Norton's too old and slow.'

I was horrified.

'Nicholas – sorry, Mister Nicholas – is in bed. He won't get up while she's around. You'd better go up.'

I ran up the stairs and knocked at Nicholas's door. 'It's me, Clara.'

He shouted at me to come in, so I slipped inside and closed the door softly. Already I guessed Aunt Agnes would not allow this sort of thing. But Nicholas's room had always been his refuge, for it was a study too and filled with books and his things, his old pony's saddle over a chair, his kite hanging from the ceiling, his cricket bat and suchlike. He had a battered armchair in front of the fireplace, where a fire was burning merrily.

'Did you see her?'

Nicholas was sitting on the side of his bed, still in his nightshirt. He was breathing with difficulty and coughing and I could see blood on the handkerchief that he held to his mouth.

'She's made you worse,' I said. I hadn't met her yet but already I hated her. I fetched Nicholas his dressing gown and helped him put it on. Nicholas managed to laugh and cough at the same time.

'Yes. I am worse. Yesterday she turned Charlotte away, saying I needed to rest, and when I heard that I was so angry I had a haemorrhage. That was all her fault. Father was out or he wouldn't have let it happen.'

'If she tries to turn me away, I will say I'm a skilled

nurse.' This, I realized as I said it, was the truth, for I knew exactly how to help Nicholas in his distress. I had lived with consumptives all my life, first my mother and now Margaret, and there was nothing I didn't know about how it affected the patients.

'Yes, that's a good line. She doesn't know anything. When I started coughing, she shrieked out for Jane to help. She couldn't cope at all, she was frightened.'

'Has she got to stay? Can't your father get rid of her?'

'No. She's got no money. She couldn't pay her rent in London and got turned out.'

'She could sew, couldn't she, or take in washing, like ordinary people do?'

'Oh no, she's much too refined.' Nicholas tried not to laugh, to stop his coughing, but he couldn't help it. I helped him to the armchair and sat him down and went to the bathroom and fetched a bowl of water and some towels and mopped him up. The water swirled with blood.

'Oh Nicholas! You mustn't let her do this to you!'

His coughing fit subsided gradually and I stuffed cushions behind him to sit him forward so that he could breathe. As I leaned over him he said, 'You do smell lovely, Clara.'

'What of?' As if I couldn't guess.

'Horses. Lovely horses. Like my darling Prince.'

Prince had been his pony, the pony who would jump a house, who gave Miss Charlotte a lead over the stiffest country. I came nearer to crying at that moment than I had for a long time. It was so *unfair!* That old word again. Why Nicholas? Why Margaret? Several other people in the village were dying of tuberculosis too, but these were my own people.

I sat in the hearth watching the fire, as you do, not talking. Nicholas's rasping breath was the only sound. The rain rattled the windows; it was bitterly cold and the fire barely warmed the big room. Nicholas would be better downstairs in the little study with his father, but the regime was changed. Aunt Agnes would surely kill him.

'Will you come as often as you can, Clara? If I can't get out – and her fussing – I will go mad.'

'Yes, of course.'

'And would you – could you . . .' He hesitated. 'I don't know if you see her ever, but Charlotte – I want Charlotte to come. She mustn't let that woman turn her away. Can you get that message to her?'

'Yes, I will. I promise.'

I had no idea how, as Miss Charlotte didn't cross my path at all. Would I have to call at Friar's Hall in person? Yes, I thought I would. My heart sank. But for Nicholas I would. I would do anything for Nicholas.

I stayed until I could see that talking was too much for him today, so I made up the fire and left his books by him and slipped out. I was hoping to see Jane and tell her to keep an eye on him, but by bad fortune just as I was coming down the stairs Aunt Agnes came out of the dining room.

'Who are you?' she boomed.

She was a gaunt ugly woman in her sixties, tightly corsetted into a severe and boring dress. She had a thin-lipped, downturned mouth and a large mottled nose. Her cold grey eyes spat disapproval. I think she expected me to curtsey. But, remembering her cruelty in turning Miss Charlotte away, I stood my ground and glared back at her.

'I am Nicholas's friend, Clara Garland.'

'Who let you upstairs?'

'I went myself. He needed me. He's not well today.'

'I shall call the doctor! You've no right to go to his room.'

I stuck my chin out. 'Dr Roberts can't do anything more for him than I can. I know how to nurse him. I'm used to it.'

'You're only a child.'

At that moment I felt about sixty years old. A child! If I was a child I certainly worked like an adult. I hated this woman.

'Nicholas needs his friends. He's dying,' I spat at her. 'His friends are all he's got.'

I turned round and rushed at the door. Luckily I knew its awkward locks and was able to pull it open and fling myself out. I let it slam hard behind me. The horrible woman had got me into a spat in just two minutes. No wonder she had given Nicholas a seizure.

I was so worked up I turned immediately towards the gates of Friar's Hall, set on seeing Miss Charlotte. How dreadful if she never went back, put down by the horrible Aunt Agnes! I would not let it happen. I went through the gates and started up the long drive. It obviously wasn't designed for people on foot, making great loops on its way to the hall in order to show off the lake and the avenues and the pretty little white temple on its knoll. The squire was said to be short of money, his daughters needing to 'come out' and spend their seasons in London and Bath, a very expensive business, and then to find good (rich) husbands. That was why he wanted to sell the water meadows, so the story went. God help us if he did.

By great good fortune, I was saved my long journey to the hall by meeting Charlotte on the way up. She was on her lovely little hunter mare, Fairylight, riding her briskly into the cold wind. When she saw me she turned off the grass and came over.

'Clara!'

I bobbed at her politely and said I had come with a message from Nicholas.

She reined the impatient mare in sharply and said, 'He's all right, I hope? That awful aunt of his turned me away.'

No wonder Nicholas was in love with her, she was so pretty and kind. Her sisters wouldn't have given me the time of day. She was the same age as Margaret, seventeen, but glowing with health and vitality, the colour in her cheeks whipped by the weather, not fever. She was small and slender and needed no tight corsetting under her elegant black habit.

'I came to tell you not to let her turn you away! Nicholas was terribly upset and now he's not at all well. He asked me to tell you – don't stop visiting.'

'She just stood there, in the doorway, and said, "Master Nicholas is busy at his lessons. He's not receiving visitors." I was so surprised I didn't know what to say. Then she shut the door. I thought her very rude.'

'She's horrible. But Nicholas needs you.'

'Yes, now you've told me how it is, I'll make sure I get in next time. I'll have a word with his father. Poor things! The dear old Reverend will have a job to stand up to her if she's so bossy. Poor Nicholas! They didn't need someone to come between them, they get on so well together.'

I was relieved she was so sensible about it, and I admired her mare, and she enquired after Tilly. She knew she was in foal. I told her about Black Rattler and she rode back down the drive beside me while she chatted. She was really nice, not a bit high and mighty.

'Everyone gives you great credit for your horses,' she said. 'They say there's no one in the village as good as you.'

I looked up, surprised, and saw this vision of the lovely girl on the thoroughbred mare and I felt for a moment quite overcome with jealousy. A fierce, biting anger almost stunned me. Miss Charlotte, without raising a finger, could ride her beautiful mare in her leisure time in this glorious park, with a groom to do the chores, whilst I had no riding at all and only the chores, the chores, the eternal chores. If only I could ride my Rattler when the time came, astride in his matches – if only I had Charlotte's freedom! But my horses belonged to a man's world.

'Oh, if only—' But I daren't say anything.

And then Charlotte said, 'I wish I was free like you. To do what I want, do my own horses, work in the stables, talk to whom I please, go about where I like. Instead of this dreadful season thing and being fitted out with dresses and going to boring balls to meet awful boring stupid boys – you can't image how awful it is, what a waste of time. That's why I like going to Nicholas because he understands how I feel. We have wonderful conversations, about how it ought to be, how we could be if it had been different.'

I was so confused at this that it took me all the walk home to work it out. Did anybody in this world have what they wanted? Or, if they did, did they recognize it? And then, thinking about it, I realized I wouldn't truly want to change anything in my life – except Margaret, of course. I loved the farm and my family and the horses and the life. But the work! And if I could ride out astride like a man! A side-saddle would do no good to a trotter's back; I would not take the risk. Short distances perhaps, but not for serious training. Oh, curses, curses ... that Margaret and Nicholas were dying, that my father was so unhappy, that I was a girl instead of a boy ... my head was spinning.

It was hard to take time off but I spoke to my father and told him about Nicholas and he said I should visit him, if he wanted it. So I went down on Hoppy, and Aunt Agnes was overruled, although she was usually there in the hall to make some unpleasant remark. In the end I made a timetable with Miss Charlotte, to go when she didn't, and we got Nicholas through that awful winter, and in the spring he was much better and able to go out again.

Which was more than could be said for Margaret, poor Margaret, who died when her baby was born.

13

Dr Roberts had told Father that Margaret could not possibly survive the labour, as by Christmas she barely had the strength to move. She was nursed devotedly by Mrs Ponder and at night Mrs Ponder's sister came and slept with her. I was turned out and slept with Ellen. I protested as it was the night when Margaret needed me. But then I saw that Margaret was past needing anyone, and Father told me to stay away.

'See to Nicholas. That's enough for a lass like you.' He said I had had no life, what with Mother and Margaret, and he wanted to spare me any more nursing. He had never spoken to me like this before.

'You've seen too much suffering in this house.'

I guessed that Miss Frobisher had told him this. She now came quite often to sit with Margaret. If she had her eye on Father it did not show, for she was very quiet in her ways and never went out of her way to cross his path, attending only to Margaret. But I noticed Father generally came in when she was around, and then sometimes she came down and cooked the tea, or made some scones. We loved having her there, Ellen and I. Ellen had always adored her, and I appreciated the way she referred to me, not as a child, but as someone who was mistress of the house. Nor did she boss Mrs Ponder, but asked her what she should do. She was as different from Aunt Agnes as it was possible to be. Nicholas assured me that sooner or later my father would marry her.

'Her name is Ann,' he told me.

But it was impossible to think of anything beyond Margaret. Miss Frobisher (Ann) was there when Margaret felt her first labour pain. She came down and told Father, and Father told me to get on Hoppy and go and tell Dr Roberts. I did as I was told, shaking with fear.

After that, things got confused. When Dr Roberts came, Miss Frobisher went home and took Ellen with her. Mrs Ponder and her sister stayed, and Father told Jack to take me to the Reverend Bywater's and leave me there, and for himself to go and stay at the Queen's Head. Jack harnessed Hoppy to our old cart, and we trotted away together in the darkness, our light bobbing cheerfully. Not how we felt. When we came to the Grovers' gateway, Jack pulled Hoppy up and said, 'I've half a mind to call. To tell them their grandchild is being born.'

'Jack, don't be so stupid!'

At the top of the long manicured drive we could see the house lights shining. Was Maggie Grover thinking of her grandchild? Or had she – most likely – scrubbed her mind clean of her lovely son's alliance with a farm-girl far beneath him? She had been in the same boat as Margaret once, but Eb Grover had at least married her, ugly and poor as she was. Of all people, she must understand Margaret's plight.

'Oh, how I hate them!' I shouted.

'One day,' Jack said, 'we'll give them their comeuppance, I swear to it, God help me.'

'He'll have to,' I said.

And then we both laughed, because what else could we do?

Hoppy bowled along, rocking us through the muddy ruts (what a good buy he had proved!) and we came to the village and the faint candlelights in the cottage windows and the lantern over the door of the Queen's Head.

'Drop me here. I'll walk up to the vicarage.'

'No. I'll take you up. How do you know Aunt Agnes will have you? She doesn't like visitors.'

'The Rev will have me. And Nicholas.'

Jack drove up the green and came to the door with me. The Reverend himself answered, thank goodness. Jack explained that Father wanted us out of the way.

'Of course, my dears. Come in, come in.'

Jack explained he was for the Queen's Head with his pals, thank you, and I saw Reverend wondering whether to attempt to persuade him out of his bad ways and entice him into the vicarage. Then I saw that he knew it was a forlorn hope.

'Very well, my boy. God be with you.'

'Thank you, sir.'

And then, before he turned to go, Jack clasped me suddenly and we embraced. All our feelings were in that embrace – something we had never done in all our lives before. It was more than an expression of words. We clung to each other, briefly, and then Jack was away, reaching out for Hoppy's reins. That left me crying. The Reverend put his arm round my shoulders and gave me a hug.

'There, it's God's will, my child. We must do our best to understand it.'

If even he found it hard, I found it impossible. I was angry with myself, yet I longed to cry and scream into the night. Nicholas would understand. He appeared at that moment, ambling into the hall to see what was happening, and his face lit up when he saw it was me. He guessed what was happening.

'Well timed! Aunt Agnes is in bed with a chill. Come in by the fire.'

'I'll get Mrs Norton to make up a bed for you, and light a fire in the guest room,' said the Rev.

'Oh no, please, I'm not used to a fire in my room. Don't put her to the bother.'

But he bustled away and I went into the cosy study with Nicholas where I could unload all my fears and make a fool of myself. We were used to this with each other. The awful part of it was that Nicholas was not a disinterested party. Everything I was grieving for – it was for him as well, in the not too distant future, and the irony of it choked my words and made me pull myself together.

Of course when the Reverend came back, we had to kneel down and pray together, and for once I truly did pray, and hung on his every word, and wished with all my heart that I could see that God taking Margaret was a blessing, as he thought. But all I could think of was Margaret's wild happiness with Nat, and her laughter and brightness when she rode in his grand curricle, and how she loved her silks and tatters and pretty jewellery and how her great eyes glowed with pleasure when she had danced at the harvest in years gone by. Margaret was all for living and loving. She wasn't a boring little working girl like me. No one would ever have said of Margaret that she should have been a boy.

Father had told me not to come home until sent for; he would do the horses. But I wasn't sent for for three days. By the time Jack came I knew that it must be all over. He stood at the door in the frosty morning, turning his cap in his hands.

'She's dead,' he said.

'And the baby?'

'Dead too.'

Even when you know something is going to happen . . . when it happens, and the words are spoken, it is a blow like a great oak tree falling. The sky is blotted out, roots torn, the landscape changes.

I just stood, cold, staring at him. He had Hoppy harnessed to the cart at the gateway.

'I think Father wants us now,' he said.

I went and fetched my things and told the Rev and Nicholas that I was going, and they came to the door with me.

'I'll be along presently, to see your father,' said the Rev. 'God bless you all.'

Nicholas just stood silent, his face frozen. I could not speak to him.

We drove off. I was aware of a great relief at hearing that the baby was dead, but also an instinct of regret alongside that I could not understand, a heartfelt grief for something unknown. My mother's grandchild. The child was a part of our family, whether we willed it or not.

My father was in the kitchen, and Mrs Ponder was at the fire, stirring something. She looked very tired, and my father looked terrible, so white and haggard, like an old man. I went and put my arms round him and he stroked my hair and said, 'My poor little girl.'

I knew I had to go and see Margaret, but I didn't want to. I looked in the parlour but she wasn't laid out there, as Mother had been.

'She's upstairs still. I'm having no visitors,' Father said. 'No one's coming to gawp this time.'

But they would all come, and it would be my job to turn them away. Great, I thought.

'Just your friends, in the kitchen,' I said. 'Or I could light a fire in the parlour. But not to see Margaret, no.'

He didn't seem to hear me. I looked at Jack. He shrugged, and we went upstairs to see our sister. This time the holy words made sense, rest in peace, for she did look very peaceful, the shell of her, just as Mother had been. The person wasn't there any more. Mrs Ponder and her sister had done the job well, for she was dressed in her favourite turquoise silk dress and covered in fresh white sheets, her faded gold hair spread out on either side of the pillow. A small vase of snowdrops stood on the table, and a white candle burned. I didn't cry this time, I felt glad. It was awful but I felt as much relieved for Margaret as I did for myself.

And the baby.

It lay in a makeshift cot made out of a drawer, all wrapped in white save for its face looking out. It was the image of Nat. Its features were perfectly formed and fine curly black hair covered its head. It was small, and a very beautiful little baby, like a little wax doll. My heart gave a great lurch as I looked at it, and it seemed to me the worst thing of all, the tiny baby not having any life at all, not even the happy years of childhood which at least Margaret had enjoyed. I wanted to take it out of its drawer and cuddle it, to give it warmth and life. How Margaret must have wanted it too. Did she ever see it?

I asked Mrs Ponder later and she said yes, but it was dead, and Margaret held it in her arms until she died. It was a boy.

'All for the best,' said Mrs Ponder hoarsely. I did not dare to think otherwise. But I grieved for the baby as much as for Margaret, I could not understand it.

But then a terrible thing happened.

Father got out of his chair with a wild look on his face and went upstairs. He came down with the baby in his arms. 'Get me a basket,' he said.

Such was his look I ran to obey him. He thrust the baby into the basket and put his jacket on.

'What are you going to do?' I shouted at him.

'I'm taking this brat to Grover's, where it belongs.'

He stormed out, slamming the door. I opened it again and shouted after him but he was off almost at a run. He did not turn round.

'Oh my God!' moaned Mrs Ponder.

Jack swore, white faced. 'What a terrible thing to do!'

'It's Margaret's baby. She wants it,' I cried.

The three of us all stood staring at each other in horror. I was trying to imagine what the scene would be when he hammered at the Grovers' front door. The maid would surely faint. Would he charge in, shouting?

'We can't let this happen,' I said to Jack.

'Shall I go after him?' Jack said.

'I think you should.'

'The poor man's crazed out of his mind, all we went through here,' Mrs Ponder said. 'Thank God you children were out of it.'

'I'll go,' Jack decided. 'Even if I can't stop him, I'll see to him afterwards.'

He pulled his jacket on and ran out. It was a grey, miserable day with rain on the wind. I wanted to go to the horses but I couldn't do anything till Jack came back, I was so on edge. And Mrs Ponder too. She made tea and we sat together in front of the fire, not talking. I did not want to hear what she might tell me. My mind wandered on to the outcome of all that had happened, and I realized we could have a new start now and maybe things would be a lot better – as long as Father weathered the blow. I hoped Miss Frobisher wouldn't stop coming. I longed for the spring, and for getting on with my Rattler, and seeing Tilly's foal. I was glad it was all over.

Jack came back within the hour, distraught.

'I couldn't stop him. I ran after him but he was coming back when I got to the drive. He said he had delivered the baby to Mrs Grover herself and told her to "see to her own kind" and came away without stopping. He was in a wild state and making for the Queen's Head. I couldn't stop him.'

'Lord save us, he'll get drunk,' said Mrs Ponder.

'Perhaps it's a good thing, like old times,' I said. 'He hasn't been down there for months. Seeing his friends and getting drunk is better than sitting here saying nothing and looking like a madman.'

I spoke boldly, but a cold dread lay behind my words – that Father might return to his heavy drinking habits.

'I don't think he'll be home for a while,' Jack said.

My mind then went to the vision of Mrs Grover receiving a dead baby – what a terrible shock for her! I even pitied her. They must have heard gossip of Margaret's ordeal, but not a word from them. What would they do with the baby? The longer I sat and thought about it the more perturbed I felt. The baby belonged with Margaret, not with them. If they gave it a funeral it would lie alone, a little Grover, instead of by Margaret's side where it belonged. She had died with the baby in her arms. It was hers.

I got up and said, 'Father was out of his mind, taking the baby up there! It should be with Margaret when she's buried.'

'Of course it should,' said Mrs Ponder.

'I'm going to fetch it back!'

Jack looked at me in astonishment. 'You're mad!'

'It's Father who's mad. It belongs here, to Margaret.'

'Indeed it does.' Mrs Ponder agreed with me; not that she was going to do anything about it.

I should have waited for someone to intercede for me; the vicar when he came, or even Miss Frobisher, but in my distress I did not wait. I was off down the drive as fast as Jack earlier, running, spurred on by the strength of my determination. We should have stopped Father. He had acted so fast we had been left gawping like loonies, and now I had to put things right. For Margaret.

I arrived at the Grover door and knocked loudly. A maid came, looking very distressed and I said, 'I've come to take the baby back.'

'Oh lordy!' whispered the maid, and let me in.

It appeared that Mrs Grover had fainted and been carried off to her bedroom, where she was still being revived by her personal maid and the housekeeper. The baby, still in the old basket, was on a table in the hall, surrounded by the younger Grovers, two girls and a boy. They were silent, either entranced, hypnotized or terrified, I could not tell. But certainly fascinated. For a fleeting moment I thought I could just pick it up and go, but as I approached, Eb Grover himself came out of his study door to see who had called.

He must have suffered a shock as great as his wife's, I realized, being presented out of the blue with a child the image of his son, but it did not seem to have changed his charging-bull demeanour. I got my word in first.

'My father did not know what he was doing. He is out of his mind with grief. I've come to take the baby back. It belongs to Margaret.'

Eb came up to the table, looked at the basket and bellowed to his children to make themselves scarce. They fled, leaving me face to face with this dreadful man with the dead baby between us. I put out my hands to grab the basket but he said, 'Not so fast, young lady.'

I stopped in my tracks and glared at him.

'It belongs to us. My father was wrong.' With such a sense of right on my side I found I could be surprisingly bold.

'So, it looks like a Garland, does it? Like its mother? Its harlot of a mother?'

'A harlot?'

'How would you term it? Flaunting my son shamelessly in public, enticing him with her beauty. Yes, beauty she had to offer, I admit. Young men can't resist beauty and that was how she tempted my son.'

'Your son tempted her! He came riding past every day and called out to her. I was there. I saw it. She never *enticed* him.'

'She behaved entirely without decorum and your father did nothing to stop her. You are shameless, the lot of you, and you have reaped what you sowed. You have only yourselves to blame.'

'Nobody's to *blame*,' I said furiously. I didn't want

to discuss all this. I just wanted the baby. 'My father shouldn't have brought the baby here. He was wrong. I just want it back, that's all. It belongs to Margaret.'

'I suppose your father wants us to bury the fruit of this catastrophe with a fine funeral? Is that his reason for bringing the child here, so that he can take pride publicly in his union with our family? Certainly if that is what you want, this child shall have a fine funeral and be buried as a Grover, but not with the harlot his mother lying beside him.'

'My father is disgusted with our union with your family. He hates this child. He is throwing it at you because he wants nothing to do with it. He said he was taking the brat back to where it belongs. But he's wrong. It belongs to Margaret. I've come to take it back for Margaret's sake.'

Oh, what a muddle! Eb Grover was as mad as my father, the tack he was taking. Did he really think we wanted them to bury the baby with full Grover honours? The poor little mite, all alone in the ground without its mother? He stood over it with his hands on the basket like a great blown-up turkey cock, jowls quivering with righteousness, narrow dark eyes squinting at me. Would this poor baby have grown up to look like his grandfather and have his terrible grasping, stupid ways? A good thing it died, in that case.

But he wouldn't let me take it back. I was left to stumble home, weeping. Jack was furious and said he'd go, but Mrs Ponder said it would be useless and we must fetch Reverend Bywater to sort it out.

'Failing that, for he's not a very forceful man, we'll get the squire to put his oar in. Of course the child must be buried beside Margaret.'

The squire! Well, the Grovers would certainly buckle their knees to Sir James. The story was all round the village in no time. The outcome was that yes, the squire did go up, along with the Rev, and they brought the baby back to us in person. The squire himself pulled up in front of the farm in a closed carriage with a pair of beautiful horses and while the coachman and groom waited with the carriage, he got down with the Rev and came in, carrying the baby in its basket himself.

I nearly fainted.

Father, sitting in his silent gloom by the fire, looked up in amazement. He got up quickly, his mouth dropping open.

The Rev said quickly, 'The child belongs here, Garland. I prevailed upon Sir James to accompany me when I called on Mr Grover for, in truth, he is a very frightful man and I needed authority. I am not so brave!'

He smiled, the dear man.

'I acted out of haste,' Father said. 'I regretted it afterwards, especially that Clara was put to the task of calling on him.'

'She is a strong girl, your Clara,' said the squire. 'You are blessed, sir, with your children in spite of your terrible losses. I hope fortune will treat you better in future.'

'I hope so too.'

The Rev took the baby and went upstairs with it to say his prayers, but I made the excuse of staying to invite the squire to a drink, for I could not face praying. It had been such an ungodly argument. I was so relieved the baby was back. I actually felt *happy* at last.

I went to fetch the drink and Father asked the squire to take a seat and they started talking in a quite ordinary way about farming. I don't know why we stand in such awe of the nobility when in fact they seem quite like us, at least on common ground like farming and horses. Not about dining and wining and going to London perhaps, but Father was actually talking about the water meadows and getting assurance that they would not be sold. I could see that the news was a real tonic, for his face lightened and he actually smiled.

'I would be badly pressed without them, sir, for the grazing. I have been very nervous at the thought they would go to the Grovers.'

'Trust me, I would never do anything to accommodate the Grovers – save buy that fine horse off them, if they were to sell.'

'Crocus? Yes, he's a champion. He will rule here now Tilly is past it. But Clara has a youngster we have great hopes of, Black Rattler. We'll be into matches again when he's broken if all goes well. And he's put Tilly in foal, would you believe – after all our attempts with the best stallions!'

I was thrilled to hear Father talk with such

animation – he who had scarcely spoken a word for months save to give orders. The squire's visit was spurring him to life. He had grieved for long enough, God knows, for Margaret had been a long time dying. He was more than ready to start life afresh, as we all were.

The squire's intervention was the talk of the village, and Margaret's funeral, instead of being the quiet and private affair we had envisaged, turned out to be a huge occasion with virtually the whole village attending. It was not what we wanted, but it had the effect of jerking Father out of his grief, finding so many people supporting, applauding him. I had a cynical conviction that it was sparked by the business of the squire interceding for us against the Grovers, everyone revelling in the knowledge that the Grovers had got their comeuppance over the baby, and attending the funeral to celebrate our victory. But perhaps that was an unkind thought, for there were many heartfelt tears, and our mother was remembered too, when Margaret and the baby Nathaniel (for she had called him that before she died) were laid beside her. Of course the Grovers were the only family not represented at the funeral.

Afterwards the vicar very kindly put on a tea for some of the ladies while the men went to the Queen's Head with Father. Miss Frobisher came to the vicarage, with Miss Charlotte and her mother Lady Alderbrook. As I left the churchyard, Martin came up to me before veering off to the inn, and said, 'I'm glad that's all finished, poor Margaret. But now you are clear at last and we can have the summer to get your colt going.'

'He's only two—'

'He can learn to be ridden. Billy weighs no more than a straw. He'll do him no harm, set him up early.'

Yes, I thought, Billy could be a trump card in Rattler's future, such a shrimp and yet so confident and brave. I would have no grown man riding Rattler until he was three but Billy would be fine. My mind too, even with one foot still in the churchyard, was full of the future and our hopes for the horses. We had had so much misery for so long, it was surely time now for things to go right? I looked at Martin and saw again the cheerful face I had almost forgotten amongst all the grief, Jack's right hand and friend of our childhood ever since I could remember. Brother, as good as. I felt a surge of affection for him, excitement for the future, a sudden leap of such optimism and joy after all the sorrow that I just stood there and laughed. It was very unseemly, with people still around all in black mourning, but it burst out of me and I could not help it.

'Oh Martin, yes!'

I wanted to hug him, but I didn't. He stood, laughing too, and looked at me with his old funny expression which sometimes frightened me, there was so much in it that I wasn't ready for. Or maybe I was but wouldn't admit it. I had Margaret's example before me, God knows, all too clearly. I turned away and said, 'I've got to go and have tea with Aunt Agnes. Think of me!'

'Poor you.' Then a pause, and then, 'I love you, Clara.'

And I laughed again and so he laughed too, and I went in to have tea and he went down the green, whistling.

14

I think it was the support shown to our family over Margaret's death that helped Father out of his misery. And also the quiet friendship of Miss Frobisher, who still came to call once a week, to bring little presents: sweets or newly-baked pastries or a cotton scarf. Was she courting Father? I don't know, but he responded, nearly always coming in when he saw her.

He had gone back to work with a will, and did not drink too much, which is what I had feared. Since the war ended, farming was not in a good way, not even for the Grovers, the price for corn having halved and the demand for food and goods dried up since the army was disbanded. When Father had first married, it had been at the peak of prosperous farming and I remember that Mother had always had nice things and we had had a smart gig (now in the shed badly needing repair) and the house had been shining and welcoming and full of polished brass and pretty ornaments and bright curtains and cushions. When I looked at it now, I was ashamed. I realized that Margaret's long journey to death had sapped all our ambition, along with the depression in farming.

'Times are hard,' our father said. 'But at least I have the squire's word that he's not selling the water meadows.'

I think that had a huge part in cheering him up, the fear having lain over him for so long.

'He might sell them to us, if we make enough money,' I said.

'You're thinking of your young colt? I can't see as how we're going to make that much money out of farming.'

'Tilly made you plenty of money. He's going to be as good, I know he is. Better than Tilly!'

Jack was as keen. 'It can happen. What about Phenomena? She won two thousand pounds for a match!'

'Yes, for nineteen and a half miles in an hour!' said Father. 'You'll never see that again in a lifetime! She was truly named Phenomena.'

'And we can make stallion fees if he's good. Five guineas a mare,' I said.

Father laughed. 'He's got to be good for that! And proved. More like two guineas round here.'

'And Tilly's foal – that'll be worth a bit,' put in Jack.

'We'll not be selling that,' Father said.

'No fear!' I shouted. And then, ever-hopeful, 'He might get her in foal again.'

We were full of optimism, even Father. I could not believe how wonderful life seemed at last. I had always dreaded that Father would go back to his drinking ways after Margaret's death, and now that this fear was lifted I was so relieved I felt I was back to being a twelve-year-old again, instead of feeling fifty.

And the farm – and my chores – got a lift one day when I was coming back from the village and came across Soldier Bob. I would have passed him by, unseeing, but a soft moan from the roadside bank made me stop.

'Please.'

A broken voice, a last appeal. The man was at death's door, a tramp I supposed, but sick and unable to go any farther. There were plenty of tramps about but they were usually strong enough, living on people's charity, and we gave them a meal when they came to the door, or a penny to go on their way. But this one wasn't going any farther. He wasn't local, I didn't know him. But it didn't take much intelligence to see that he wasn't going to go anywhere any more without help.

'Hey, what's up with you?'

He was about fifty, I thought, with a sabre scar across his face, but there was nothing fierce about him. I was on Hoppy, so slipped off and went to him.

'I'll take you home if you can get up on my horse.'

I didn't know what Father would say, but no one could pass by a man in this state (save perhaps Eb Grover). The offer galvanized his last reserves of strength, and by standing Hoppy in the ditch I was able to help the man off the bank and on to the saddle. He couldn't have walked. As it was he swayed alarmingly as I walked on home, but determination prevailed and we made our back door where he fell off in a heap on the step.

The outcome of this was that we took the man in and nursed him until he recovered. He had a high fever and would no doubt have died of pneumonia if he had stayed where he was. He was one of Wellington's soldiers. He had been all down to Spain and back with the Duke and had fought at Waterloo. The army had been his whole life since he was a lad, but he had been thrown out without a penny, like thousands of others. He had lived by begging and the odd job that had turned up until the day I found him so ill. But he was an intelligent man and we all got to like him, and when he was better he came to be very useful, so Father offered him a place on the farm. We made up a room for him in the outhouse behind the scullery which had once housed a few geese at night. I cleaned it out thoroughly, Jack whitewashed the walls and knocked up a wooden bed, and I made it nice with a pretty old quilt over the covers and a picture of the Prince Regent, before he got fat, on the wall. Bob thought it was a palace.

'I've landed lucky and no mistake!'

I would have liked Billy to work for us, as although he was only seven, he was forced to earn his pittance. But he was a Ramsey, closely related (either illegitimately or incestuously, I'm not sure which) to Martin's family. And Martin's awful father Mr Ramsey, the ganger for Grovers', insisted that he worked there with his mother. The more people Ramsey got working for Grovers' the bigger his cut, so Billy never had a chance. He never went to school. He came to us after work or on the odd days off, when he was so tired he could hardly move, and sometimes fell asleep in the straw. When he had sat on Rattler's back for a few circles of the yard and helped me with a bit of grooming or feeding, which he loved, I would take him home riding Hoppy. He would sit up in front with me holding the reins, but sometimes, often in fact, he fell asleep on the horse, and I would ride along with him cuddled in my arms. He was such a funny, innocent, sweet little boy, in spite of his terrible upbringing, that I was only too happy to feel motherly towards him. As Martin was always saying, he could be a little goldmine to us if Rattler turned out good enough to do a fifty- or hundred-mile stint for a wager. Horses at three could do this with a very light weight, although I would never risk a horse of mine if it lacked the strength.

I was riding back from the village one evening after taking Billy home, slack-reined on Hoppy and dreaming of what the future might bring, when Hoppy's ears pricked up and I saw a horse coming towards me. The evenings were drawing out now and the hedgerows full of new growth; there were plenty of people on the road going back from the fields, but few riders. This horse was Crocus. I recognized him at once and expected to pass time of day with a Grover groom, but to my amazement I saw that the rider was Nat.

The Grand Tour was supposed to last two years, one year at the very most. But now, with news of Margaret's death, he was back. I was so angry, so choked, I had no idea of what I could possibly say to him. But he reined in as he came alongside and bid me good day.

And out of the blue he said, 'I am so sorry, Clara. Tell your father. I did love her.'

I was struck dumb. I could not believe I had heard these words from a Grover. I gaped like a loony.

Whether through foreign travel or heart's turmoil, Nat had changed since I last saw him. He was sparer, quieter in his bearing, his face more fine-drawn. He was even more handsome in his maturity, very brown, his hair longer, his eyes bluer and less haughty. I had a sudden vision of the two of them together, Nat and Margaret as they had been last summer, her golden radiance against his dark happiness, and the shattering of it came freshly, as if I hadn't known. I had never given a thought to Nat's suffering, never supposing he had cared so deeply, but now I saw differently. There was no doubting his sincerity.

After I got my wits back, I just nodded. I put my heels to Hoppy's sides and we rode on our ways. But my head was reeling. From being my most hated person in the world, Nat had taken on suddenly a new persona which disturbed me deeply. He had revealed a part of himself I hadn't known existed.

When I told Jack, he said angrily, 'If he loved her, then he should have had the guts to stand up to his father.'

Recalling my clash with Ebenezer I knew it was a hard man who could stand up to him. It was Ebenezer who had decided that Margaret died in misery. With Nat by her side she would have died happy. I hated Eb! But now I did not feel quite the same about Nat.

Of course the great excitement was Tilly's coming to

term and the birth of her foal. She did not foal until June. We had no idea what to expect. She was too old and the sire too young, and it was her first foal. We tried to keep an eye on her but she was a wily beast and foaled one dawn morning out in the field after I had despaired of keeping her in, waiting day after day. She had seemed imminent for a week, running with milk, but like so many mares she only foaled when we took our eyes off her. Fortunately the foal had a safe arrival. I went out to fetch the farm horses in and there was this wispy tottering thing by Tilly's side, coal-black and as ugly as sin.

I ran to fetch Father, and Jack and Ellen came out too and we all stood round looking. I can hardly say admiring. Father was deeply disappointed.

'What a runt! What sort of a foal d'you call that?'

But Tilly was proud. Her ears pricked up when she saw Father, and we had to laugh at her proprietorial air. She nudged and licked the little thing without stopping.

'She likes it anyway,' I said. But I was not impressed by Rattler's produce. He would have to get better than this if I was to sell his wares for good money.

'Well, Tilly's no looker and she's good enough. You don't know how it'll turn out,' Jack said sensibly.

'Aye, it must improve,' Father decided philo-sophically.

We had to choose a name for it. Father said, 'Garland's Disappointment,' but he laughed, all the same. (Yes, he was beginning to laugh again.) So I said, 'How about Garland's Better Times?' And Father gave me a quizzical look and smiled and said, 'Why not?'

So Garland's Better Times became Timmy and whatever he lacked in looks he made up for in character, for he was as self-opinionated as his dam and frightened of nothing. Father took to him after his first shock and used to stop and play with him on his way back and forwards past the field, and Tilly looked on approvingly.

I used to go up to spend time with Nicholas two afternoons a week, the days Miss Charlotte didn't. Even when we were very busy, Father encouraged me to go up to the vicarage for he thought the refined life up there might rub off on me. He was afraid I was getting too manurey – that's what Jack and Martin called it.

'She needs to know how the gentry live,' Father said. 'She'll never learn here.'

When I told Nicholas, he said, 'Your father should come and court Aunt Agnes. Take her home and she'll teach you to be gentry. She's always teaching me.'

Poor Nicholas! Having Aunt Agnes in the house was a dreadful pain.

Then he said, 'I told you – he ought to marry Miss Frobisher. She's nice.'

'Do you think *she* would?'

Nicholas considered, and then said, 'Yes, I think so, unless there's things we don't know about. She might be married already. She's very secretive about her past. She never speaks of what she did before she came here, not even where she comes from. And never of any family.'

No, when I came to think about it, that was true. Nobody knew anything about Miss Frobisher, which was strange, given that she was now so much a part of our village. But Father was no womanizer. He never sought women out and all his friends were men. I did not think it very likely that he would think about remarriage.

When Nicholas and I drove out I usually took farm tracks and sometimes went over the river and round the back of the water meadows. One day we were jerking over a bad patch in the woods when a wheel nearly came off and the cart had to be abandoned. Jack and Martin would have to come out and mend it before we could get it home. I stripped off Hoppy's tack, save the bridle, and Nicholas got on. I was going to walk, but Nicholas hardly weighed anything so I got up as well.

'Oh God, how lovely it feels to be on a horse again!' Nicholas shouted, and he immediately put Hoppy into a canter. We were bareback of course, and heading for home and Hoppy put in a buck of excitement and took off like a racehorse. I nearly came off but of course Nicholas sat like a rock – he was always a superb rider – and we galloped flat out along the track through the woods, ducking branches and splashing through drains. It was wonderful, and funny, but at the end when we pulled up, poor Nicholas started to cough, and then he had to get down and lean against Hoppy's shoulder, holding on, whilst he coughed and wheezed helplessly. Thank God no blood came up but it sobered us up, and when he felt better I got him back on and we walked home quietly.

'Don't tell them,' Nicholas whispered.

'No fear.'

But we decided to go to my house first to give him a chance to recover. Jack and Martin were in; it was a hot day and they had come for a beer. Mrs Ponder had gone home luckily. Jack got Nicholas a beer too and we told them about the abandoned cart. It was nice all being together without any old people. Afterwards we rode back to the vicarage on Hoppy, at a walk this time. I sat in front and Nicholas had his arms round me.

He said, 'You're a really good egg, Clara. If I wasn't going to marry Miss Charlotte, I wouldn't mind marrying you.'

'Aunt Agnes would prefer Miss Charlotte,' I said. 'She's gentry. She smells better.'

'Yes, since she found out that Charlotte is the squire's daughter she falls over herself to be nice to her. She's really gruesome when she's being nice. Charlotte gives me an imitation, we have a good laugh.'

She certainly didn't fall over herself to be nice to me. She was waiting with a face like thunder. We had missed tea of course – as if it mattered. When she started her diatribe, Nicholas just grasped the stair rail and started up the stairs, which I could see was a great effort for him. He did not make any attempt to reply to her. She shouted after him for his breach of manners but he gained the top landing, gasping for breath, went into his room and slammed the door. I longed to follow him but thought it might make it worse for him. I explained about the accident.

'It's very unseemly that you two should gallivant about the countryside together,' she said. 'I shall speak to my brother about it.'

'He's always allowed it!'

'You're not children any more,' she snapped.

I couldn't think of a reply to this. What difference did it make? I was twelve and hardly a siren.

I turned to take my leave, and as I opened the door I found Miss Frobisher standing on the doorstep.

'Hullo, Clara. I've brought some books for Nicholas. Have you been visiting?'

After what Nicholas had said earlier, I found I was flushing up with embarrassment at our presumption. The idea of her being my stepmother was so enticing. Was it possible? Her eyes were kind and friendly as she smiled at me.

'We've been out together. He's just gone up to his room. He'll be very pleased to see you.' I said this last defiantly, seeing Aunt Agnes about to come into the attack.

'He's exhausted!' she snapped. 'Clara does him no good at all, roving round the countryside with him. I shall complain to her father about it.'

Miss Frobisher said sweetly, 'It's very good for Nicholas to get out. He enjoys Clara's company and she's a splendid influence, I can vouch for it.'

I said, 'I've known him all my life. He's my friend.'

Agnes gave a sort of snort and said, 'You've too much to say for yourself, young woman. Manners wouldn't come amiss.'

176

'There, she's a country girl, Miss Bywater. You must excuse her. She's only telling the truth, after all.' And with a winning smile and bob to the horrid old woman, Miss Frobisher swept up the stairs to Nicholas's room without waiting for another snub.

I left immediately, thrilled by Miss Frobisher's triumph. I daydreamed then about her becoming our stepmother. I told Jack to give Father a nudge about it. I felt that Miss Frobisher was willing, else why should she call as she did, when she had work enough to do at home? The drawback, I realized, was Father's great love for our mother, and his probably thinking she was irreplaceable. But she had died five years ago, a fair length of time. Before then, Father had been a funny, outgoing man, making light of any trouble, generally whistling about his work. Even the advent of the Grovers when they bought their place did not worry him greatly. When they were new he had called to be friendly and come away with a flea in his ear. He had not even been asked in, presumably because he was on foot, in his working clothes. Mrs Grover made it plain that one called only when invited, after leaving a card beforehand on a salver in the hall. This behaviour in a farmer was new in our experience and we had a good laugh about it. Even the squire and his funny old lordship at Oakhall would come to the door, but not Eb Grover and his scrawny wife. Father thought them ignorant more than rude, but later when he saw how they treated their workers his amusement turned to a deep-seated dislike which strengthened steadily over the years. Eb Grover had bought, along with the farm, a row of broken-down cottages on the edge of the village, and if any of his tenants couldn't pay their rent he evicted them. Nobody had ever done this before in our neighbourhood and when he turned out a widow with two children, the ill-feeling in the village was such that a few bricks sailed through the Grover windows one night. The vicar took in the evicted family and found them a new place but after that everyone heartily disliked the Grovers. And since our mother's death, Father had let the threat of the Grovers get him down.

A new partner, especially one as strong as Miss Frobisher, would surely give him a fresh outlook on life. Every day he was more like his old self. I tried to see him as Miss Frobisher might see him, and the picture was quite encouraging. He was a good bit older than she was, of course, but fit enough apart from the rheumatics and not at all lined and grey, considering what had happened to him. Without a mother and without any grandparents I always thought we were somewhat lacking as a family. Compared with Martin, who had about twenty aunts and uncles and thirty cousins and two full sets of grandparents, we were very quiet. All our grandparents had died young; we had scarcely known any of them, save I had a memory of Father's father who left us the farm. He died fairly young in a carting accident, and Father had had no siblings. Mother apparently had two sisters in Scotland but we never heard from them. Perhaps they were dead, for her family had all been consumptive. Fortunately, Father, Jack, Ellen and I were immune to the infection, or too tough and hardy to catch it. At least Miss Frobisher was healthy, with her strong walk and good eating habits.

It was Ellen, not Jack, who made the breakthrough. I suppose Jack and I had more memories of our mother than Ellen did, which inhibited us. Ellen scarcely remembered her at all.

Ellen was getting into trouble from our father for staying out too late in the village, and he made the mistake of saying, 'Your trouble is you miss a mother's upbringing. There's no one to put you right and I'm sure it's not my job. Clara doesn't give me these worries.'

'Get me a mother then!' Ellen shouted, very put out. 'I *need* a mother, and it's all your fault I haven't got one.'

'It's not my fault your mother died!'

'It's your fault you haven't got me another.'

'Another!' Father blazed up at this and I thought for a moment he was going to hit Ellen. 'You don't know what you're talking about, girl. Keep a civil tongue in your head or I'll give you a thrashing.'

We all sat tight and looked at each other. The anger drained out of Father as quickly as it had come.

'You don't know what you're talking about,' he repeated.

And Jack boldly said, 'But she's right, Father. We would all like another mother.'

'Really? And who do you suggest? Miss Charlotte? Mrs Ponder's sister? Peggy Masters?' Mrs Ponder's sister was seventy and had a crooked back and Peggy

Masters was gone in the brain and dribbled.

'Miss Frobisher!'

I think we all said it in chorus. He had asked, after all. He looked dumbfounded. It was obvious that it had never entered his head.

'She's a lady,' he mumbled.

'A school teacher,' corrected Jack. 'She's not gentry. She's got no family, she's lonely, you can tell.'

'I bet she'd love to marry you!' Ellen shouted.

'Yes, she would,' I said.

'You're all out of your minds!'

But at least the idea was in his head.

He was a slow worker. By the time he married Ann Frobisher after the harvest the following summer I was fourteen. Rattler was full-grown and ready for his first trial.

15

The wedding was meant to be a quiet affair, but it turned out just like a second horkey, the whole village dressing up and between them all providing food and drink on the green. I think it was because Miss – Ann – Frobisher was so well liked, and because Father had suffered such dreadful tragedies, everybody wanted to show their support and affection. It was quite wonderful, the happiness that flowed from that day.

The squire gave Ann away. Nicholas had asked Charlotte to see if he would, and of course he agreed. Ann made no mention of family. Maybe she had told Father her circumstances, I don't know. But certainly nobody else knew. She was a mystery. She said she belonged in the village now, it was her home. Of course, marrying meant she had to stop teaching, which was a certain grief, but the children's loss was Small Gains' gain. Ellen and I were bridesmaids, and Jack was best man.

The wedding day was in October, and it turned out to be one of those perfect, sunny, very still, slightly sharp days with the gold just starting in the trees and the sky almost colourless. The green had been mowed and the church filled with flowers by the school-children. We went down from the farm, all of us, in the cart pulled by Tilly, with the colt coming on behind. Father insisted on Tilly although I said the foal would make us look a bit silly, but he just laughed. Tilly was looking good, having been given an easy time as a nursing mother, and we all looked amazing in our wedding clothes. Ann had made the dresses for Ellen and me. They had the fashionable high waists and straight-down skirts and I must say I thought Ellen looked lovely, the cream, flower-sprigged material setting off her slender child's figure and loose brown curls. But I felt stupid and would have preferred my ordinary clothes and comfortable boots. Ann said I looked lovely too when we tried the dresses on, but I think she was just being encouraging. If any of us gave Margaret a thought we kept quiet, but when we walked through the churchyard past her fresh-looking grave and the stone over our mother, we all hesitated. Father turned towards the graves and said something in a low voice, but I didn't catch his words. I saw Jack give his arm a squeeze.

He said to him, 'Mother would be happy for you today.'

Sometimes Jack was very adult in the middle of being a daft boy. These words seemed to reassure Father, for he smiled then and walked on. Ellen and I went back to wait by the gate where Martin was un-harnessing Tilly to let her graze until she was needed again. Everyone was already in church or else – the ungodly – milling around the green. The squire's open carriage was standing outside the cottage where Ann lodged, with the liveried grooms in attendance. It was hardly necessary for the distance to the church but the squire had insisted. How splendid for her! I was sure he wouldn't have done it for everyone, nor would Nicholas have asked if she wasn't someone special. I still couldn't believe how our luck had changed with Ann agreeing to become our step-mother. The burden lifted from me was incredible. Now I only had the horses, my work, to think about. I would be as carefree as Rattler in his field, my lost childhood returned. No more nursing, no more cook-ing, no more worrying over clean clothes for Ellen. I felt like bursting into song, jigging about with im-patience by the church gate, waiting for the carriage.

How lovely it looked, the beautiful grey pair stepping in unison, the squire smiling and Ann Frobisher veiled and mysterious – my mother! Ellen was dancing up and down, squeaking with admiration.

'Hush,' I said. 'We've got to be serious.'

We hadn't much idea of what we had to do, save walk behind. There was no train or trailing veil to bother with, thank goodness. The groom opened the carriage door and let down the steps, and the squire helped Ann down and we glimpsed a smile for us through the veil. The squire held out his arm for Ann and they set off through the churchyard with Ellen and me following.

The church was packed to the doors, and Edmund from Oakhall, no less, was playing the organ. This was very special for he rarely played at home, only in Cambridge where he worked. The kindness shown was moving and made me feel weepy as we shuffled up the aisle. I felt conspicuous and stupid but the events overcame my own misgivings and I forgot myself in seeing my father being made so happy. At last.

The only people missing were the Grovers.

Or so I thought until, when the service was over and we were progressing back down the aisle in a blaze of triumphant music from dear Edmund, I saw a figure slip out of the door before us and make away. It was Nat Grover, who had obviously slipped in at the back at the last minute. It made me think suddenly that he had a little boy of his own lying by Margaret outside, and that this man being married today was in a sense his father-in-law. Nat had links with our family which he was privately respecting. I think I was the only person who saw him, and I never mentioned it. I didn't see him again that day.

Nat got on Crocus, keeping his head down as he made his way through the crowd that was thronging round the churchyard to see the bride and groom come out. A few people called derisively after him and he could feel the hostility that followed him as he rode away from the festivities. He left the village and made for the woods beyond Oakhall, slowing to a walk as the trees closed round him. He felt very disturbed and wanted to be on his own.

The woods were silent save for the distant burring of a woodpecker, and his horse's hooves made no sound on the deep pad of fallen leaves. He followed the paths the charcoal burners had made into the heart of the forest, and pulled up in a glade. Crocus, out of habit, pulled the reins through his fingers and started to graze, and as he did so Nat felt the tears rise hot in his eyes. His blurred vision saw only Margaret lying on the grass, laughing at him, the lovely flower that had filled him with such happiness that he could scarcely believe such emotions existed. He had seen very little love in his life after all. His love for Margaret and hers for him had seemed like a miracle. It was hard to believe that it was finished. Following the ways they had ridden together, he always believed she would be there again, laughing and teasing him. But seeing her fresh grave again crucified him. He could not picture her in the cold ground with the baby beside her. Extinguished, bloodless, still, after the love she had given him. She had given him her life.

Grovers were powerful and showed no weakness. Nat had had this beaten into him since he was a child, but now he got off Crocus and cried like a lily-livered idiot because the vision hurt so much. He was stupid to have come back to this place, the place where their child had been conceived. And yet he stayed, feeling that he needed it, a silent space to grieve in. The tears healed. He could never have had her, after all. It was doomed to be fleeting, and all the more painful for it. Even their love would one day have grown cold, he guessed, or – worse – ground down by the all-powerful Ebenezer. Margaret would not have thrived in his parents' company. She had no steel, sweet Margaret.

But Clara, the little one, she had steel.

Nat, his outburst of grief subsiding, found his thoughts wandering as he rode home. He rode out behind the squire's park, a long way round over rough common ground, thinking about the Garland family to which he was inevitably linked, whether it was acknowledged or not. Seeing Clara today in her bridesmaid's dress, her hair let loose from the unforgiving braids, was a revelation. She was small, but straight and strong like a good sapling, with a challenge in her eyes that had fazed him in the past. They all said she should have been a boy, the way she handled her horses, but no one saw a boy in the graceful child who had followed Ann Frobisher into church. Nat had seen something that intrigued him, and the thought consoled his grief. There was the future to look to, as his parents were always telling him.

So after the eating and drinking on the green and the speeches and celebrations, we all drove home in our cart with Tilly pulling, and our family was complete again. Ann, with her veil thrown back and her hair starting to come loose, her colour bright and eyes wide with excitement, was laughing on the front seat with Father and we were all larking about in the back, Martin as well, and singing stupid songs. When we got home, we found Mrs Ponder had made a homely meal in the kitchen to welcome us, with special delicacies from her own oven, and jugs of her good home-made ale. A vase of late roses stood on the table, and the kitchen was sparkling clean, as good as when Mother was alive. For all her grumps, Mrs Ponder had been a stalwart friend during our bad times and Father did not want to sack her. He said Ann should talk it over with her, for perhaps she would be happy to go; if not, she could help out, for there was no shortage of work.

I never forgot the happiness of that day. It was the start of a brief period in our lives when everything was right, not a single thing to worry about. When I watched Tilly's colt growing, throwing off his initial ugliness – although he was never going to be handsome – I thought that his name had been made in good faith, Better Times (and after a while he came to be called Betty, not Timmy, because Timmy was too like Tilly). But later I came to think he should have been called Worse Times, for although we had lovely Ann, we still had the Grovers across the way.

16

When Ebenezer Grover ordered a threshing machine from the makers at Leiston, he was told that demand was so heavy they would be unable to deliver until the following winter. And late at that, possibly into the new year.

'They can't make the damned things fast enough. Maybe that's the business to be in, Nat, developing machinery. Shame you're not clever enough to go for that sort of money.'

'You didn't want to waste money educating me, remember?' Nat said sharply.

'Aye – I educated Philip and where did that get me?'

'They taught him enough sense to leave home,' Nat muttered, but not loud enough for his father to hear. His elder brother Philip had gone to Eton and hated every minute of it. Shortly before Nat was due to go, Philip had been expelled and sent home, where he was beaten by his father nearly to unconsciousness.

'I got beaten at school, but never like that. Goodbye,' said Philip to Nat, and that was the last any of them had seen of him. Nat had been crushed and terrified by the whole business: the wailing of his mother, his sisters' screaming, his father's fury, the sight of Philip's tight-lipped anguish. He had hero-worshipped Philip, a tall slender youth, as blond as Nat was dark, with a sweet temperament that he must have inherited by chance from a distant ancestor, certainly not from his mother or father. Nat was only too aware that he was a 'chip off the old block' as his father loved to hear people say. But not Philip. Philip had been fiendishly clever and top of every class at Eton. His expulsion was for deflowering his house-master's daughter, quite something to be proud of in Nat's eyes. But that was several years ago and Philip would be in his mid-twenties now. If he were to come home and make peace, he, as the eldest son, would inherit everything his father had built up, a possibility that lay heavily on Nat's ambitions. Eb never spoke of him, but his mother was always to be seen red-eyed on his birthday.

Nat fetched the port decanter and two glasses and put them beside his father's chair. They were waiting for supper to be served and the port was a ritual, reviving his father after a hard day outside. Eb was showing signs of his age, the red veins threading his cheeks, the nose purpling. Nat wondered if he would look like that one day. What a thought! He was proud of his looks and doubted if his father had ever been as hand-some as he was. He poured the port.

'The machine will be too late for this year's thresh-ing then,' he remarked.

'Yes, dammit. I was looking forward to getting rid

of those cackling women. Threshing out there all through the winter and me paying for their hours of gossip. The sooner it's all machines, the better.'

'You'll have to watch your back. They've been rioting up Wymonden way and breaking up machines. There's people in this village would do the same to you, if they get half a chance. Putting all those people out of work in the winter, just when they need the money.'

'They'll swing for it if they come here.'

'That Firmin fellow was in the Queen's Head last night, talking to Jack Garland. He's said to be a trouble-maker, was caught firing a rick at Diss. But he got acquitted by some miracle – they said his mother had been the judge's lover a few years back and he let him off for old times' sake.'

'Young Jack would row up with a firebrand like that. He's raring for trouble, that lad. I'd see him hang if he brought a tinderbox into my yard.'

'It won't come to that.'

Nat spoke against his intuition. He did not like being so unpopular in the village, unable to take a drink at the inn without the conversation stopping, aware of men spitting close to his feet, women turning away when he was ready to bid them good day. He liked to think it was due to his father, rather than himself. He had few friends. He sometimes felt he didn't belong anywhere. When he had had those few months off in Paris and Rome he had felt a total fish out of water, thrown in with some acquaintances of his father's who were far better educated and higher up the social scale than himself. Nothing he had seen of their way of life attracted him. Yet it was supposed to have been a great opportunity, as well as sundering his affair with Margaret. Maybe Philip had had the best idea after all.

'You keep an eye on that Garland,' his father said.

'Jack's all right,' he said.

'Jack is after getting even with us because of that damned sister of his, you mark my words. At least you can trounce that horse of theirs with Crocus the next time you meet, put them in their place. The old bastard needs taking down a peg or two, marrying above himself, an educated woman. She needs her brain examining, going to live in that pigsty.'

Grover heaved himself out of his chair as his wife announced dinner. Nat was used to listening to him spitting venom and scarcely listened any more. Only as they went into the dining room the next salvo brought him up short.

'And tomorrow you can call on the Harrises and say unless I get their rent arrears paid up in full by Christmas, they're out.'

'Father, he's had pneumonia! And he's gone eighty. How on earth can he earn anything until the spring?'

'That's not my business. My cottages need to pay their way. I'm not a philanthropist.'

No indeed!

'Can't you go? You're the landlord.'

'Have you ever heard the saying, "Why keep a dog and bark yourself"? You're the dog, Nat. I keep you and you do what I say.'

Stifling his fury, Nat followed his father into the dining room. He noticed the poor little sluts from the village hired as maids fidgeting with fear as the master took his seat. They came and went like flocks of sparrows, generally reduced to tears within hours. His mother had no idea about handling staff, never having lived in a well-run household, and her life seemed to be given over to interviewing and hiring new sluts as the frightened ones departed. His mother was more or less a failure at everything, although she was said to have been a good dairymaid once. After Nat's birth she had lost three babies before managing to raise the two girls, Elizabeth and Henrietta, who were now thirteen and twelve, a secretive, whispering pair. Then the ultimate son George, now aged ten. George was his father's pride and joy and was disgustingly spoilt by both parents. He was as fair as Philip had been, but by no means as sweet. Nat loathed George. Of the three sons only he was the dark one, the used one, the put-upon one, never praised or appreciated. Philip, until his expulsion, had been as doted upon as George was now. But Nat had always been the second best. He felt it. He supposed Philip's departure had scarred his father bitterly, but he still felt it was no excuse for the way his father used him.

So with this latest chore to look forward to in the morning, he sat down at the table with a heavy heart. He had learned from his father to be impervious to the suffering he saw amongst the poor in the village, but evicting a couple in their eighties was surely going to be unpleasant. He knew, since Margaret, since growing up a bit, that his feelings were susceptible. He wasn't the braggart boy of a few years back. But while his spirit struggled to free itself, he feared that he was bound to become more like his father every day. He had no choice. As they all said in the village, he was a chip off the old block.

It was all as dreadful as he had feared. He rode down to the village on Crocus and pulled up outside the Harrises cottage. He felt the village breathing down his neck, women coming to their doors to shake mats or scrub steps, on cue for his appearance. Two old girls stopped in the street right outside the Harris door to have a chat just as he knocked for admittance. It was like being on a stage.

Mrs Harris came to the door. When she saw who it was, she seemed to crumple before his eyes.

'Oh Mr Nat, sir . . .' She shrugged, unable to finish her sentence, holding out her arms as if in surrender.

'My father says—' He found it as difficult to speak as she did. He cleared his throat. 'My father says unless you pay your rent arrears, you must leave by the last day of February.'

'Leave!'

The whole street heard this cry of dismay. It was like a howl of a whipped dog.

'Where can we go? Our children are all dead – we've nowhere! For God's sake, let us die here! It won't be long!'

She started to cry. She was a round, tough old soul, who probably had another good ten years yet. Nat found himself thinking like his father – another ten years with no rent. Yet he remembered this same woman picking him blackberries out of the hedge when he was little, the biggest and juiciest which he could not reach.

He could not look her in the eye. 'My father told me to deliver this message. It's not to do with me.'

'Oh come, Nat! You're a Grover. Of course it's to do with you!'

The voice was sharp and familiar. He swung round to see Charlotte, the squire's daughter, sitting there on her lovely horse Fairylight – not a trotter but a thoroughbred as elegant as herself. She had cantered down the green and pulled up sharply, knowing without being told what Nat's visit was about.

'Mr Harris has had pneumonia. Surely you know that? You can't expect him to work again until the spring at his age? Go home and tell your father he'll get the money in the summer. He's not so hard up that he can't wait that long, surely?'

Her scathing tones scorched Nat. Instead of telling her to mind her own business, he felt himself colouring up.

'I have to do my father's business, whether I agree with it or not. Go and speak to my father, not me.'

'No thank you! But believe me, if he turns these people out, there will be trouble in this village.'

She spoke bravely but Nat knew the law was on his father's side. It did not make him feel any better about it. Charlotte looked so fine, sitting there with her eyes blazing, her cheeks whipped pink with indignation, that he longed to act on his mother's prompting to court the squire's daughter. There would be no impediment to a marriage in that department!

'I can't help it, Miss Charlotte. Don't tar me with my father's brush. Maybe your father should speak to mine.'

This ploy was the right one. His honesty obviously appealed to Charlotte for she now looked at him more kindly.

'I must say, I wouldn't want your job, working for your father.'

'If you're riding towards the turnpike, may I accompany you?'

'I'm going that way, yes.'

'You can call in at home, if you like, and put your views.' But he smiled as he spoke and she smiled back. He vaulted back on Crocus, excited by her compliance. This was worth the unpleasantness with Mrs Harris. He bid Mrs Harris good day, and was aware of the neighbours closing in behind him on Mrs Harris's doorstep as he rode away. The tongues had plenty to wag about now.

'Your father should watch his back,' Charlotte said. 'They say he's ordered a threshing machine. That will be as popular in the village as evicting the Harrises.'

'Yes, I'm aware of that. Can't we talk about something else?'

She turned and smiled at him. 'All right. When are you challenging the Garlands for a match against their new horse? Everyone's agog to see the two of them against each other in the spring. He's so fine, that

Rattler, they have such hopes of him. Clara is a marvel with her horses. You must fix it, make a date.'

'There's plenty of time.'

'Yes, but make a date. People like to have something to look forward to in this dreary village. And then you have a goal too, to get your training in.'

'Give everyone something to look forward to – yes – the Grovers getting beat. How the village will cheer if Rattler beats Crocus!'

'Oh come, everyone loves Crocus. They will cheer for Crocus!'

'But not for his rider!'

'You've just got to be nicer, Nat. Kindness gets more out of a worker than cruelty, surely you can see that?'

'Go and tell it to my father, not me.'

'You've got to stand up to him.'

'Oh Charlotte!' It was impossible to describe the power his father had over him. He was nineteen, but his father still hit him. He no longer beat him, but his huge fist would land a cruel blow when he was angry. He hit all of them, save George. Once when he had hit his mother Nat had stood up to his father, but received a blow in return that all but knocked him out. His father was not yet fifty and strong as a lion. No one ever stood in his way. Charlotte had no idea of the brutality that ruled behind the closed doors of the Grover farmhouse. Her own father was as gentle as a dove.

'You don't know how it is,' he said roughly. He could do without Charlotte in her missionary mood.

Charlotte then remembered how her father had

had to broach the evil farmer during the bizarre affair of the dead baby and what he had said about him afterwards. Her father had said he had never met a more brutal man. He had come home quite shaken, and the dear vicar who, although timid by nature, sailed through great difficulties in the sure knowledge that he was no more than God's servant, had had to restore him with a large draught of brandy.

'Well, no, I don't,' she said more sympathetically. She, after all, had to do her father's bidding, without being physically coerced. 'All the same, you could still challenge for a match.'

'Clara won't allow it until he's fully mature. You know how she is. But I still reckon I'll have the beating of her. That horse of hers is powerful but he hasn't got the class of mine.'

'Well, class tells,' Charlotte said.

When she had parted from Nat, Charlotte wondered if he had taken the remark personally. It made her laugh. She found Nat incredibly attractive but her strong common-sense held her back from succumbing to his charms. His was not a family one would wish to be associated with.

17

'Now sit tight, Billy. I'm going to make them stretch.'

Billy's eyes fairly glittered. 'Faster! Faster!'

He gave Rattler what he thought was a vigorous spurring, drumming his little heels against the dark flanks. Rattler hardly felt it, but as Tilly started to pull out beside him he lengthened too. Billy laughed with delight.

'Faster!'

'Remember, if he breaks trot—'

'I pull him up.'

I was riding Tilly, with Rattler on the lead rein. I did not trust him yet not to take off with little Billy, who was like a sparrow on his back. Only hammered-in obedience on Rattler's part would make the pairing viable, for Billy could do nothing by the commands of his body. He was only ears and a big smile, after all.

We did these training sessions as often as we could find the time. The objective was to run Rattler over a timed course in the summer and see if he could do two miles in five minutes (very optimistic!) and later to try him farther. He had only turned three in the spring, and I was determined to be careful and only run him on suitable ground. But there was no immaturity in his looks. All his yearling gangliness had furnished out into a splendid symmetry and his action was faultless. Having been seen out on the road a fair deal, he was already well known amongst the local sporting farmers, and his name had been mentioned farther afield too, for he had the advantage of Tilly's reputation to follow.

Without Billy, I would not have started so soon. Billy was our secret weapon.

We did most of our training out in the water meadows beyond the woods where no one would see us. I could ride astride and handle Rattler more easily. We needed the space to get up into a full fast stride and there was room out there, although the going left something to be desired. I preferred the road, but didn't want to be seen. We used the road in the evenings when it was nearly dark and there were few people about. I didn't want Nat to see what a good horse we had.

Billy loved these sessions. Where he got his strength from I shall never know. Father had offered him a job on our farm but his mother insisted on being with him and Father said he wasn't having that harpy on his land. And it meant crossing Martin's father Ramsey, which wasn't wise. So poor Billy was a Grover child, and driven by Nat in their bleak fields, hoeing and weeding and carting in the rain and the wind, not even having the shelter of a barn when they ate their bait, whatever the weather. Two of the girls died that winter. They were only eight and ten.

Billy said Eb Grover had gone to Leiston to see about buying a threshing machine. The village was full of this rumour, for it would mean half of them being put out of work if the machine came in. Threshing corn to get it ready for the miller to grind was the longest, steadiest winter job, done indoors too, and no one could credit what life would be like without this work.

Eb had also sent Nat to evict the Harrises from their cottage. This had caused such disturbance that the vicar had had to intervene, and with the squire's backing had got Ebenezer to postpone the eviction. People said Miss Charlotte had engineered it, having seen Nat on the doorstep delivering the dread news. What with that and the news of the threshing machine, the Grovers' reputation had sunk to an all-time low.

'If Grover brings one in here there'll be trouble,' Jack said.

I had a feeling Jack and Martin would be leading it.

'It's not worth being hanged for,' I said. Or transported, which was almost worse, being sent in a ship to the other side of the world, never to see your folks again.

'You can't stand by and see the labourers starve,' Jack said.

But Father said he wouldn't half like a threshing machine himself, and where would that put him? They could argue about such things for hours. Ann was a pillar of calm, saying nothing. I suppose after a classroom full of children our boisterous family was nothing much, and she knew better than to take sides between Father and Jack. Jack, nearly eighteen now, was throwing his weight about. Father couldn't beat him any more.

But Billy, reporting the news, was untroubled: the only thing he thought about was riding Rattler. Having Tilly to train him with was a fine advantage, for I would never have dared send the little boy out alone, not until the horse was older and sensible. But this way Rattler learned sense very quickly and he had to really use himself to keep up with Tilly. It seemed in no time we had him educated, and I let him off the leading rein and gradually drew away from him so that he trotted alone. And he never tried to get Billy off, caring for him out of affection.

I rode him too, of course, the light of my life, generally at dusk when my work was done and there was just light enough to see. Then I took him on the road and asked him to go, using his great shoulders and powerful quarters. How strong he was! The hedgerows flashed past and the blackbirds panicked across in front of us as his big round hooves threw up the gravel; then, as he worked himself in, he seemed to flatten and find an even longer stride. I knew I had a champion. As good as Crocus. In the summer evenings, I felt my own sap of excitement rising as I sniffed in the dewy night and saw the first stars appearing: I had a future now, with my lovely horse and all the horrors of Margaret's dying fading into the past. I would walk home, cooling down, mulling over my luck. I rode astride, not thinking to meet anyone who mattered, but occasionally I saw Nat on Crocus, no doubt on the same task as I was, getting the training in. I think he would have spoken but I would not linger, passing him with a nod. Meeting him disturbed me deeply, I cannot say why. I didn't feel just pure hate, as I had once, but I remembered seeing him in the church, and I remembered him say that he was sorry, he had loved Margaret. I didn't dare speak to him.

But it was lovely going home after these rides, not having to hurry in the stables, doing my round to see all was well and not being bothered about the others waiting on my cooking. Ann cooked, and very well too, and it was like old times to all sit round the table together to eat, with everything set nice, and freshly baked bread in the basket and home-brewed ale to drink, just as when Mother was in charge. And Father all smiles, looking ten years younger. The polished candlesticks were back, with bright candles throwing a shine on picture glass and ornament. It was a real home again.

So why, then, were Jack and Martin getting worked up about what did not concern us, talking of rioting and rick-burning? They said they would join in if it happened near us.

'Because they are hot young men, bored with their work,' Father said. 'Why did all the young men flock to go to war twenty years ago, to fight an enemy who was miles away in another land? They wanted a bit of excitement.'

Jack disagreed. 'They went because there was no living for them here. They were out of work and starving. And that's what will happen here when the Grovers and their like all have their threshing machines and their drills, and need employ scarcely any labour.'

Father took a different view. 'The poor devils that work for Grover will be well off if it finishes, the way he treats them. Find some other work.'

'Like what?' Jack shouted. 'What work is there round here, tell me?'

'Learn a trade, lad. Learn to be a carpenter, a thatcher, learn to shoe horses – there's always work for a good tradesman.'

'And how do the poor devils go about that, when they're so ignorant?' Jack said angrily.

Jack was so impatient these days, and angry about things that didn't concern him. He seemed to fill the room with his presence, always on the move. He was strong and hard working, yet all the work he did had no effect on his immense energy. The farm work was arduous and boring, the hours long, and his active brain, not much extended, seemed always to be looking for something more to apply itself to.

Ann said it was his age, the age when young lads went wild, and later on he would settle down. Sometimes I wondered whether keeping house for us lot was frustrating for her, hardly extending her skills. But love came into the equation and it was clear that she was happy. She looked after old Soldier Bob too, and most nights he came in for his supper.

'But for the likes of you, where might we all be now under old Boney?' she would say. She surprised Bob with her knowledge of soldiering. Where did it come from? I wondered, but I did not ask.

But that summer, when Rattler was three, Jack's restlessness fixed itself on my horse and he told me Rattler was ready to compete.

'Come on, Clara, let's make some money out of him. Let's get him going.'

'You're not competing him yet! Not till he's got his full strength.'

'Well, get Billy going then. Everyone's talking about him round about. I can't wait to take Crocus on again.'

'Next year at the soonest! But perhaps we can do a time trial with Billy now.'

'That won't harm him, that little shrimp on board. I'll borrow a stopwatch off Tucker.'

'It will only be a trial for ourselves,' I insisted, but when the time came on a Sunday morning after church, there was a whole group of interested farmers waiting in the Queen's Head. Our measured two-mile track was made from outside the inn and round the squire's park, finishing back at the Queen's Head. This, with the permission of the squire, was the standard two-mile in our parts and had always been used for tests. The Squire's Two-Mile, as it was known, was very fair, the turn back towards home very wide and gradual.

We rode down on Rattler, Billy and I, but I slipped off before we got to the green, not to be seen astride. Billy rode proudly and Rattler stepped out calmly. If he was surprised at his reception he showed no temperament. I saw the informed eyes squinting over his fine body critically, the heads nodding. I knew they could find no fault, and he looked his best, my stringy arms having raised a fine shine on his silky coat. His intelligent eyes took everything in. The betting was in full swing, mostly as to whether he could get the distance in under six minutes. But there were variations, some of the richer farmers betting on a specific time. Betting was a big entertainment – if such it could be called – for the farmers' lives, after all, offered little excitement. This betting on horses was one of the ways to get the blood running faster.

It was certainly making my blood run faster, for I had no idea whether Rattler was kind enough to look after young Billy once the wide acres of the squire's park opened up in front of him.

'If he bolts with you, Billy, just sit there and let him run himself out, then bring him back and we'll start him again. Don't try to stop him.' For I knew his efforts would be in vain.

So none of us knew what to expect, least of all myself. Jack and Martin came to the start, Jack holding the stopwatch. One of the farmers took it off him, to see fair play and there was a bit of an argument. I told Jack to say we wanted a flying start, for that might well count, Rattler not being experienced like Tilly in getting into his stride immediately. So they cleared the road and Billy rode into the backyard of the Queen's Head in order to get a straight run up the green. I held Rattler's bridle, turned him round and held him, for he was now on his toes and beginning to sweat up with excitement.

'Take it easy, Billy, we don't want him to break if we can help it. The time doesn't really matter. You're teaching him, remember, for the future.'

But Billy's blood was up too and he shouted at me, 'Let go!'

I let go.

Rattler leaped forward at Billy's shout and did a great plunge out of the yard. The spectators scattered, but Billy sat tight and by his determination got Rattler's stride contained by the time they had crossed the road and passed the post. The farmer with the stopwatch set it with Jack hanging over his shoulder, and everyone started chasing up the green. Rattler was at the top before I had crossed back on to the green, and Jack said to me, beaming, 'Perfection! What a start! Let's just hope Billy can hold him when the grass is under his feet.'

But we had practised, the three of us, night after night in the long dusk, and I knew now it was paying off. With a rider so powerless, obedience was everything, and that had not come about by chance. Rattler had learned to listen to voice commands and I could almost hear Billy's little squeaking: 'Steady, steady, you big oaf!' Rhythm was everything, to get the long stride going like clockwork.

I couldn't see what was going on for the crowd round the squire's gates, but I heard no shouts of dismay so assumed all was going well.

'You're a marvel, Clara! If he does it I stand to

win a packet. And Father too.' Jack was at my side.

'You're crazy,' I said.

'I can't wait to ride him!'

And when he said that, a great pang of jealous rage shook me – that I couldn't ride my own horse after all the hours I had put in! Yes, I certainly should have been a boy, just like they all said. I had never felt it over Tilly because Tilly was Father's, but Rattler was mine. *Mine*. But I was in a man's world here and powerless.

'We'll take on Crocus in the spring, eh? That'll be a day to look forward to!'

'Let's see him come home first, before you start saying those things,' I hissed at him furiously. But he put a great arm round me and gave me a hug.

'You're a great girl, Clara. I'll do it for you, all for you.'

I had to laugh. 'What about Billy? You'll not get him to give up in a hurry!'

'What he weighs, we could both be up.'

My heart was beginning to pound now with nervousness. Four minutes had gone. The farmer with the stopwatch was down at the post calling out the time, and the men at the top of the green were shouting at the little boys running about, calling them to order. Billy must be rounding the course safely. I was jumping from foot to foot, straining to see the squire's gates.

'Five minutes, thirty seconds!' shouted the farmer.

And as the words left his lips, Rattler came flying through the gates and down the green. My heart nearly burst with pride to see him, the way he moved with his head down and his great shoulders swinging, his tail high and the action in his back legs propelling him with a force that made the old farmers cheer. Everyone scattered. Billy's face was white and he was hauling on the reins, but I could see that Rattler wasn't going to stop.

'Turn him, Billy! Turn him!' I screamed.

The farmer at the post shouted, 'Five minutes, fifty-five seconds!' and leaped backwards, almost turning a somersault. Billy, hauling with all his strength on his left rein, turned Rattler on to the road. Rattler skidded round, the dust flying. It was a wonder he didn't fall and for a few desperate seconds Billy was half out of the saddle. But at least he was on the road and heading for home, not crashing into the backyard of the inn, where innocent passers-by were gathered wondering what on earth was going on. They would have known well enough if Billy hadn't steered so well.

Headed for home I knew he would take some stopping, but Martin on a borrowed horse went galloping after him and caught him up, Billy's shouts of 'Whoa! Whoa!' having taken effect.

I stood waiting in the middle of the hooley which was taking place outside the inn. The time keeper insisted the time was under six minutes, but the farmers who had laid money against were objecting, some of them having timed the course themselves and added a bit on at the end. Jack shouted that the official time stood: five minutes, fifty-five seconds. The few people who had betted for under six minutes were to get their money. Cheers and boos and a fair bit of brawling: it was always the same. At least in a five-minute trial they hadn't had time to drink too much, so the fracas soon died down, and Rattler arrived back at Martin's side to take his plaudits. And Little Billy too. I pulled him down and gave him a great hug.

'You're a marvel, Billy? Did he break at all?'

'No, not once!' Billy was shaking with excitement and nerves, his face white, all eyes. I wished he was mine, to look after like Rattler, to feed up and cherish. His awful mother was beside him, giving him a shake.

'What do you say to Miss Clara now? What did I tell you?'

'I won't,' said Billy.

His mother gave him a clout round the head. 'You say as you're told now!'

'No, I won't.'

I knew all about Billy's stubbornness. I pushed forward, feeling very angry.

'What has he got to say? You can say it if he won't.'

'You owe him, Miss Clara, for all the work he done for you. And for winning. You owe him summat.'

Perhaps the woman had a point, but I hated her so much I couldn't find an answer. Luckily, Jack pitched in and pushed me out of the way.

'See to the horse. Leave her to me.' And I did, gladly, taking Billy with me.

Rattler had a crowd round him, mostly farmers, some of them from quite far, come to see a possible star. Well, I reckoned they had seen one.

'His first outing is it, miss?' one of them asked.

I nodded and he said, 'You take care of him. He's got a future, that one.'

My father was holding him, Martin alongside, and taking all the congratulations, but when I came up he said loudly, 'This is Clara's horse. She's done all the work, the credit is hers.'

I was pushed and patted and showered with compliments, and Billy was boosted back on to Rattler's back and given sweets and apples, and I felt so proud, so shaky with spent nervousness that I just stood smiling like an idiot, clutching on to Rattler's mane in case I fell over. It was an amazing success, I knew that – under six minutes in his very first outing! He was valuable already, after this, his first showing. But he was sweating up at all the excitement and getting uneasy, and I took his reins and said, 'I must take him home.'

We went, Billy and I, and left all the argument to make our way home down the quiet road. I walked, half-listening to Billy's prattle, feeling Rattler's soft muzzle by my shoulder, tasting my pride and ambition like nectar on my tongue. Maybe it was too good to be true, our first outing, but savour it as it came. I knew it wasn't coincidence: we had put the work in. Yes, we had worked! Anything could go wrong – with horses it nearly always did – but now everything was sweet and perfect.

And to add to it, amongst the people passing down the road on the way home, I heard the sound of hooves close behind me and, glancing up, found myself face to face with Prosper Mayes on his mare. He was coming the same way, and reined in from a trot to stay with me.

'That was a great performance. You must be very pleased.'

He sat so easily, so gracefully, again he reminded me of Nicholas, how Nicholas would be if fate had not decreed otherwise. He had the same unselfconsciousness, not trying to impress, or being shy. Most boys were such clods, but not this one. And so attractive, looking down at me with his lively, long-lashed green eyes. I tried not to look too bowled over but could feel my jangling blood reddening my face. He had caught me out in my horse gear, careless of everything but my triumph. I should have been side-saddle in a skirt, looking across at him, calmly beautiful like Charlotte. But I just laughed – what was the point of bothering?

'He's so promising, I can't believe it. This was his first showing. I never dreamed he'd get it in the time.'

'You must have done some work on him for the little chap to handle him so well.'

'Billy's great, aren't you, Billy? Yes, we've worked.'

'We're not into trotters, more's the shame. It's hunting for my father. I reckon a good trotter is a good hunter too, as often as not. This mare of mine, you think she's too pretty to do anything, but she can hunt all day and not stop at anything. She goes for ever.'

I laughed. Prosper spoke as if he had known me all my life.

'Where's your farm?' I asked.

'Oh, not far. Twenty miles. I take Gibbet Lane, before the turnpike, and it goes all the way.'

I had never been farther than the turnpike in that direction, although as far as Norwich the other way.

'Will you be travelling him as a stallion? If you do, call on us. Great Meadows. My father would be interested,' he said.

'Yes, yes, I will.'

He doffed his hat to me like a real gentleman and rode on at an easy canter. I watched him go. He had been so civil, so friendly, not a bit superior like Nat – although he was younger, of course. No more than sixteen, I thought. How lovely that he had been so friendly! My day was made.

The afternoon was still, fading, the autumn chill coming out of the ground as the sun went down. Sunday, the day of rest . . . I could hear the bell tolling for evensong, but I had to get all the big horses in from the field; it was their day of rest too. Billy helped me, bringing two at a time. When I opened the gate, they came into the yard, like the cows, without being led save for the two young ones, Boney and Blücher, who liked their freedom too well. We rounded them up, Billy laughing and capering after them, and brought them in. I stood and watched them, the double row in their stalls, noses deep in the mangers which Soldier Bob had filled. It always brought me a deep feeling of satisfaction, taking in the rounded, shining backsides, the air of calm and contentment. Yes, I was good at my job. My stable, if not quite so perfect, was in every way as good as the Grovers as far as the horses were concerned. We had no rough words, no punishments, and no reason for them either.

I gave Billy a hug and he set off for home, making a beeline across the fields. And I went indoors dreaming of Prosper, and my wonderful horse.

18

Aunt Agnes herself answered the door. Presumably Jane had left, as she had threatened to do many times. I gave her my polite bob and scurried inside before she could say her piece. It was all about the young 'gel' being alone in Nicholas's room without a chaperone. The vicar, shocked, could not believe we needed one – poor dear trusting man. He was beginning to take a stand against Aunt Agnes now that he saw that she was making Nicholas ill. When Nicholas got angry against her strictures, which was often, it usually resulted in his taking to his bed, feverish and coughing.

I ran up the stairs and knocked on the door. 'It's me, Clara!'

'Oh, good.' He was sitting in his armchair, grinning. I remarked on Aunt Agnes lowering herself to answer the door.

'Yes, we are maidless. Jane has spread the word and no one wants the job, only the desperate. And Aunt Agnes, of course, wants a woman with "class", as she puts it.'

'She hasn't got class,' I said.

'No. She thinks she has. Dear old Papa is starting to stand up to her. At last he is seeing the light.'

'But will he get rid of her?'

'That's the rub. He's too kind to put her in the workhouse, and where else can she go? She could easily get a job as a housekeeper in a farm or some-where, but she's such a snob it would be beneath her.'

'I hate her!'

'Don't we all? Never mind, let's not talk about her. No doubt someone without a brain will apply for the job eventually. How's Rattler?'

I loved going to see Nicholas because, in spite of his weakness, he was always interested in what was going on, funny and informed. He kept mostly to his room these days, where Aunt Agnes was not allowed, and Jane had kept him in supplies, keeping his fire in, and bringing him titbits between meals. He would miss her terribly. But if he did not want to talk about it, neither did I. I had great news for him.

'Wonderful! This is what I want to tell you: Nat came looking for Jack in the Queen's Head last night, and said he wanted a match with Rattler in the spring. Crocus and Rattler, twenty miles. That would be with Jack riding, of course, not Billy. Rattler will be four in the spring and really strong and so we agreed. They even agreed a date, weather permitting, at the beginning of March.'

'Wonderful! You've just *got* to win!'

'I know. I am going to train him all the winter. He'll be working on the farm as well – Pa's got him going in harness, so that will build him up, and then near

215

the day we'll rest him and feed him – oh, I can't wait!'

'Poor Billy's losing his ride?'

'No. I promised him another trial against the clock whenever the weather suits. A long one this time. Jack says fifty miles, but I'm not sure. Billy is dying for it, of course.'

'It would be a great advertisement for Rattler, if he did well. You can travel him as a stallion then, in the spring.'

'And do a hundred, Jack says. A hundred miles in twelve hours and we'd get all the mares in East Anglia.'

'With Billy?'

'Yes, it would have to be a lightweight. Whether Billy could do it is another matter.'

'You could do it, you're not heavy.'

'I'm a girl!'

'Oh, yes, a stupid girl. I'd forgotten.'

We laughed. I put some more coal on the fire and saw that the scuttle was empty. Nicholas was always cold when he hadn't a fever – just like poor Margaret – and sat in his sagging armchair with his old horse blanket round his shoulders. The name 'Prince' was sewn across one corner. He always had books near him, supplied by his father and Charlotte and Edmund from Oakhall. Everyone loved Nicholas, and grieved that such an intelligent, bright character could not be delivered from his fate. He was plainly growing worse, but never spoke about his health, at least not to me.

I went downstairs and filled the coal scuttle. Aunt Agnes came out to see what I was doing but said nothing. Would she have filled it, I wondered, or left Nicholas cold? Perhaps Cook would have done it. She did not allow anyone in her kitchen, even the Rev, so she wasn't bothered with Aunt Agnes.

'You'll have to have another maid. You need someone. Does your father fill your coal bucket?' I asked Nicholas.

'Yes, he does when he's here. He'll be back shortly. He's only gone down to see the old Harrises. Grover has served that eviction order on them again. He says he can't wait any longer, but they still can't pay their rent. And now of course they can't bear to go to the workhouse and be separated. You know how devoted they are.'

'I can never understand why husbands and wives can't live together in the workhouse.'

'It's to make it beastlier, so no one wants to go. Cheaper if no one goes.'

'Surely the Harrises won't go? They're so old – it would finish them off.'

'Grover can't wait. You know how he is.'

'There'll be trouble if he evicts them, surely?'

'Lots, I should imagine. But no one wants to lose their Grover jobs, do they? So it won't be enough to bother him. Listen, guess what Charlotte told me – would you believe? Nat Grover is making overtures.'

'Overtures?'

'Advances, you know. Asking her to go for a ride, saying how pretty she is.'

I didn't know what to say. On reflection, it was not surprising: Charlotte would be the obvious choice, and not only because she was lovely. Old Eb would love such a connection. The squire wouldn't, though. Poor Charlotte, if she fell for Nat!

'Did Charlotte accept his advances?'

'No. She's being true to me.'

Half the time I didn't know whether Nicholas was joking or not. He sat there looking smug, laughing.

When I got home I told Ann that Nat was trying to court Charlotte.

'Poor Charlotte!'

'Maybe his father put him up to it.'

'He wouldn't need much telling. Charlotte is a lovely girl. But the squire won't stand for it.'

'Suppose she fell in love with him?' I was thinking of Margaret.

'That would be very hard. It would have been hard for Margaret, had she lived, for your father would never have allowed her to marry a Grover.'

What would Margaret have done, I wondered, if she hadn't been so ill? She had been wilful all her life.

As if Ann knew what I was thinking, she said, 'Nat would never have married Margaret. She wasn't a big enough fish, his father wouldn't have allowed it. Eb would have cut him out of the money and the farm, and Nat couldn't have taken that. He would have stayed away on his Grand Tour and come back engaged, or even married, to someone his father thought suitable. That's the way of it, Clara.'

Ann was sitting at the kitchen table preparing vegetables for supper as she spoke, and I had sat down opposite and by force of habit had taken a knife to help her. We were alone in the kitchen. Some mutton bones simmered on the range making a familiar homely smell; the men were not in yet, although it was getting dark. Ellen was out milking the two cows, her job in the evening.

Ann said now, quietly, 'When you marry, Clara, don't throw yourself away. Use your ambition.'

I was startled by this remark. I had always assumed I would probably marry Martin; it was so obvious. He was already part of the family, and always making passes at me when we were alone. I fought him off, although I knew all about kissing and fondling. Who didn't, after all? Our country life did not give us drawing-room manners.

'You are too clever to link yourself to someone who will be doing the same thing when he is eighty as he is at eighteen.'

That sounded like Martin, of the hopeless Ramsey tribe. He had got nowhere so far with trying to be a coachman. He was impetuous by nature, like Jack, and perhaps not suited to the long, cold, responsible hours of the stagecoach driver. I knew he was fairly empty-headed, but he was nice with it.

'Don't be in a hurry, Clara. Look around you first. To marry for convenience is all very well, but to marry for love, to know passion, is what makes life worth living, for all its dangers.'

I was so surprised I kept my eyes down on my onions, my knife slipping dangerously. Ann was such a quiet person. I still felt I did not know her well, save as a sort of homely wall, now shoring up our heretofore hopeless domestic life. That she was happy with Father was obvious. But I had not noticed that their love was this she spoke of: passionate and dangerous.

'How do you know?' I asked. I looked up, suddenly bold, reddening as I spoke.

'I have married three times. Once for convenience, once for passionate love, and now for love and security. I speak with great authority.'

I nearly fell out of my chair. Three times! Our quiet village schoolmistress!

'Your father knows this, don't worry,' she said. 'And I am only telling you because your time is coming soon, that you will marry, and I want you to know that you have choices in this life, Clara. I don't want you to make the mistake I did, to marry for dreary convenience when you are very young.'

'Why did you?'

'My father was a vicar. My mother died when I was young and I had no siblings – rather like our Nicholas. My father had a curate, John, a nice young man, and he wanted me to marry John, to see me settled, before he died. Because my father was old, you see, he was fifty when I was born. And when he was approaching seventy, he worried about my future. He had no money to leave me, and John would get the living, and my life would be secure. So I married John. I didn't love him. It was the marriage of convenience.'

I was waiting eagerly for the marriage of passion. 'Then what happened?'

'Very soon after I was married, a company of soldiers was billeted in our village, waiting for a ship for Spain to join the fighting there. It was only for a short time and we all had to take them in. We took four, and one of them – one of them – oh, Clara! I can hardly describe it to you. We just looked at each other – it was the same for him as it was for me, like being bewitched. He was an officer in the Dragoons, an Irishman. His name was Fergal. He lived with us for three weeks, and then went out to join Wellington just in time for the battle of Salamanca. He fought all through Spain right up to the end, and came home when Boney capitulated and was taken to Elba. I went to him then.'

'But what about your husband?'

'I had told him. I didn't deceive him. And he died before Fergal came home, which left me free to marry again. But don't think, Clara' – and she lifted her head and looked at me fiercely – 'that I didn't suffer through guilt and compassion, for John never did me harm and died loving me. He died of pneumonia, quite suddenly. I nursed him and when he died I had the freedom I so wanted, to go to Fergal. But it was a terrible way to find happiness. John's last words to me were, "You will be so happy now." Not bitterly, but kindly spoken. And he was right, but the cost was heavy and the guilt never left me. When Fergal was recalled and killed at Waterloo I felt that the scales had been balanced, that I now suffered as John had suffered. Oh, how I suffered! I loved him so! God forbid that you should ever have that pain, Clara.'

She held her head low now and I could see that her eyes were full of tears. She wiped the back of her hand over her face, and got up suddenly, gathering the cut vegetables and taking them over to the range.

I sat, mesmerized by her story. Nothing like this had ever come my way. Certainly some of the women in the village had lost husbands and sons in the war but I hardly remembered that. The war had only affected us by the prices we got for our produce; it might never have happened apart from that. But to have been married to a man going out to fight that last great battle, to wait for news, to know nothing but silence, a great void ... even I could picture the agony of it. News came so slowly, if at all, and if one was lucky, eventually, by a government letter from the mail coach. If you loved someone like that ... I did not know about that kind of love, the love that Margaret died for. Not yet.

Ann said, 'Your father loved your mother as I loved Fergal. He understands. We are lucky to have found each other to heal up the wounds. I am a very lucky woman.'

And she turned back from the range, smiling now, and gave me a soft caress.

'Don't look so stricken, Clara. It's all over now. We live on. I just wanted you to know how it can be. You ought to know. There's glory to be found out there, if you're lucky.'

I thought it was chance, after pondering about it in bed that night. If Fergal hadn't been billeted on the vicar, it would never have happened. Would Ann have fallen in love with somebody else later on, bored as she was with the curate? But who knows whether another attractive man would have come along?

But the next time Martin called – only the next day, of course – I studied him with more attention than before. He and Jack were full of the latest news: the Grover threshing machine was on its way, due to arrive that afternoon. Everyone was planning to turn out to see it. Martin and Jack were full of excitement. I would have joined in, but kept thinking of Fergal on his charger, scything down the French. Now that was excitement surely, compared to a mere threshing machine? Martin could well have been on his way to spear a Frenchman, the way his blue eyes blazed. If I hadn't known him all his life and he just appeared at the door one day, like Fergal, would I fall passionately in love with him? It was hard to say. He was handsome enough, well built, active and agile, strong, laughing – all the right attributes. But it was true that his mind was fairly simple. There were no complications with Martin, no hidden depths. Probably that was why I liked him so much. It was confusing, Ann's argument, that one looked for something better. Like who? Nat Grover? If the love she spoke of was the sort that stirred the loins, Nat Grover was the candidate. I hated him, yet something in me was very susceptible to Nat Grover. To a cruel man, a bully, a man who didn't treat his wonderful horse properly . . . how did this make sense? There was no sense in love, I concluded. The man who answered all my criteria was dear Nicholas, and there was no sense in that either.

We all turned out to see the threshing machine arrive. It was a huge beast, drawn on a low cart by four heavy horses. There was no sign of any Grovers to meet it. They were lying low, no doubt not wanting to meet the crowd in the lane. Someone managed to throw paint on the body of the machine, but had no chance to write a slogan, and a lot of stones were thrown which chipped the bright surface. But when one of the horses got hit, the stoning stopped. The enormous ugly machine turned into the Grover's drive and no one could follow it any more, so the crowd dispersed, gossiping angrily. It was the biggest excitement since news of Waterloo.

Father stirred up the boys by saying he would like one too, but he was laughing. Later he said, 'No good will come of this in the village. I can see trouble ahead.'

How right he was.

It was coming spring and most of the threshing had been done, but Grover had held some corn back in order to try out the new machine. Gossip, easily had, confirmed that it was difficult to work, having teething troubles. It was powered by three horses going round in a circle pulling a beam that moved the machines, but it seemed that it was very hard on the horses and the horses were replaced so often that the rest of the farm had to do without. The horsemen resented their horses being taken up by the threshing machine, for they then had no job. The threshing machine only required a couple of men to feed the sheaves of corn into the revolving drum: the machine did the rest. Several of the women who usually did the threshing were sacked; also a couple of the horsemen who complained to Nat.

The village, never having much to talk about, was agog with the goings-on, and reports came in daily from Jack and Martin. Eb Grover, being the man he was, did not sack his workers with any kindly handout, and the ones who lived in his tied cottages mostly had to leave, having no money to pay the rent. They were evicted and left the village on the carrier's cart, their few possessions roped in place, children and dogs running excitedly behind. Some had relations to go to, others found a cottage by the river, ruined by flooding; two old men went to the workhouse.

Father could not afford to take on any more labour, much as he would have liked to. One small family lived in our barn for a week before moving on, fed by Ann, and a boy moved in with Soldier Bob for a few days before going to find his fortune in Norwich.

But the eviction that caused the most outrage was that of the Harris couple, both in their eighties, the eviction Nicholas had mentioned to me.

When I visited Nicholas I told him all about the unrest in the village and about the Harrises. Of course his father knew all about it too, but I suspect he did not tell Nicholas everything. Nicholas was not to get upset, it made him ill.

'We've got our own drama going on here,' Nicholas said. 'You will like this story.'

He started coughing and could not go on for a bit. I fetched him the foul brew Dr Roberts had mixed up for him, more than familiar to me, and gave him a dose, and presently he continued.

'Father couldn't help but notice that I was getting

worse, not having Jane to pander to me, carrying the coal, bringing me those potions she liked to cook up and all that. And no one else will take the job because of Aunt Doom.' (That was now Nicholas's name for Aunt Agnes.) 'We were at supper the other night and old Doom said my visitors excited me and were bad for my health – this was after Charlotte had called, and I think Charlotte snubbed the old girl. She's a great snob, Aunt Doom, and lickspittles to Charlotte in a gruesome way, which makes Charlotte snub her, you see. It's natural. So spiteful old Doom suggested Charlotte should stay away, and I lost my rag and then that gave me a great fit of coughing and blood and everything, and to my amazement Father jumped up and shouted at Doom to fetch a basin and cloths and things – you know how good Jane was at all this and now there was nobody to help. And he *shouted* at her, Clara – have you ever heard him shout in all your life? Because I hadn't. And then, in the middle of it all, he shouted that he was taking in the Harrises when they were evicted and maybe the old folk would look after me, and old Doom could move out of the best guest room because that was where the Harrises were going—'

Nicholas had to stop for breath and another coughing fit at this stage, but I was sitting there agog, picturing the wonderful scene . . . the old Rev *shouting*, come to the end of his tether at last. How wonderful!

'She said how could he think of having dirty old peasants in his house, sleeping in the best guest room, and he said Mr and Mrs Harris were the salt of the earth and worth ten of her, and the obvious solution was for him to take over the Harrises cottage and pay the rent for her to live in it. You should have seen her face, Clara! But the great thing is, he is sticking by it. That is what he is going to do. She's leaving, Clara, she's leaving!'

I could hardly believe it, that dreadful snob Aunt Agnes going to live in a pauper's cottage in the village! Surely she would fight against the decision with all her spiteful, selfish might?

She did, but the dear old Rev, seeing at last how Nicholas was declining, held by his decision. He did not wait for eviction day, but brought the Harrises into the vicarage, had the cottage quickly renovated, painted up and nicely furnished, and when it was ready, the squire's house-carriage called with two grooms to transport Aunt Agnes and her luggage. The village was tactful enough not to turn out in their hundreds to gawp, but faces were at every window and all doors were opened a crack, with amused eyes glittering. Everyone knew the story, of course.

When the carriage had departed the Rev went down in person and stayed some time, probably trying to placate the old girl now he had got his way. But how wonderful that he had stuck to his guns! Jane went back, of course, and the old vicarage looked smarter and the atmosphere there noticeably lightened. The old Harrises, grateful beyond belief, quickly regained health and strength and in a very short time the old vicarage looked cleaner then ever I could remember it. The old man tackled the overgrown garden, and mended the rotting window-sills, and Mrs Harris got the brass gleaming, the dusty curtains washed and the old dark furniture gleaming with polish.

Nicholas was waited on hand and foot. But for all the care, I could see his time was nearly up. I knew the signs only too well. His demise was something I could not bear to think about and my visits now made my spirits so low when I came away that Ann remarked on it.

'You don't have to hurt yourself so much,' she said.

'You mean stay away? How could I?'

'You are still a child, Clara. It's three times now that you have suffered this – it just seems to me too much. I think you could spare yourself.'

'I can't.'

My spirits weren't much compared to life itself. I knew that I loved Nicholas more than anyone I knew. But everyone called me Martin's sweetheart, so who was I to disillusion them?

19

It was then, in the middle of March, that the black clouds came rolling over. It is hard to imagine how quickly one's life can change. We thought our future was bright now and our hearts were set on Rattler's coming match with Crocus. It was a busy time on the farm with the sowing starting and the growth coming, the sheep lambing and the year's pattern starting into flower. But that was the routine we all took in our stride. The great excitement was the coming match. That was, until a greater excitement came to override everything.

Billy was clamouring to do the timed ride over fifty miles. Whether his strength was up to it I did not know, but his feckless family was full of support and I had never seen Billy show frailty, even though he looked as if a puff of wind would blow him away. Certainly he could fall asleep suddenly at the end of a long day when there was nothing else to do, but that hardly showed weakness. I promised him that he could do the timed ride after the match with Crocus, when obviously Jack would ride. Of course Billy wanted this ride too, but it was out of the question. The weights carried had to be fairly even.

Meanwhile, of course, he was working all day long at Grover's. Eb Grover was boasting that the threshing machine could be worked by a child. This child was Billy. He stood on a box and fed the sheaves of corn into the revolving drum. It was only poor corn that Eb had set on one side to try the machine. Most of his threshing had been done the old way by hand, before the machine came. Such was the demand for the machines that the manufacturers could not turn them out fast enough and the delivery to Eb Grover had been too late to catch the harvest.

'It's all very well you joining the protests,' Father said to Jack and Martin, 'but you might as well stand on the beach and tell the tide to go back.'

'And let the workers starve!'

'The workers can get jobs in the factory making threshing machines,' Father said.

But I think Jack and Martin were looking for trouble. They liked a bit of rioting if their cause was just. As Ann said, it was their age. There was no doubt that feeling against the Grovers was running high and we, as a family, had more reason to hate them than most.

It was late afternoon, just going dusk, and I was in the stable waiting for Billy to come and ride. It was a chore for me, as Rattler was already well exercised, but if Billy wanted to do the fifty miles he had to get his riding practice in, to be fit enough. I usually went with him on Tilly but he was perfectly able to go on his own, such was his confidence now. We rode out on the road, four or five miles out and the same back, and in the dim light no one saw a girl riding astride. Billy loved it. He had such appetite for a little shrimp, he never ceased to amaze me with the fire in his parched body.

The workhorses were in – they came in early in the afternoon at this time of year – and were quietly munching their hay. I always loved the stables at this time, the warmth coming from the big creatures, the soft sound of their eating and the chink of the brass tethering buckle against the mangers: an atmosphere of contentment, so familiar, the great part of my life which I would not want to change. No, I would not change it for anyone. I was thinking this, reaching up to the rack for Rattler's saddle, when I heard a distant noise, a screaming which made me stop in my tracks.

It was far away but so piercing and agonized that I ran out to see what was going on. Ann was just taking some washing in from the orchard, and dropped the basket in alarm.

'God in heaven! Whatever's that?'

'It's from Grover's,' I said.

We ran out past the house and looked down the driveway, but of course could not see far enough, but the screaming was still continuing and we could make out shouting and signs of dashing about.

'Heavens, what can have happened?'

I am only human. I hurried down the drive to poke my nose in. At the same time I saw Nat coming along the road on Crocus, home from his exercising (Crocus

too was being worked hard to get fit for the match).
Hearing the noise, he put spur to Crocus and trotted
full pelt into his home drive. One of the grooms was
coming down on a hack and I heard Nat shout,
'What's going on?' The man shouted something in
passing and came cantering down towards me.

'What's happening?' I shouted.

'An accident. I'm going for Doctor Roberts.'

Oh well, accidents happened all the time. But the
screaming was awful, hysterical. And there was a
familiarity about the shouting that went with it. I
stopped and listened and, with a dreadful feeling like
a physical blow, I recognized the coarse, shrill voice as
that of Billy's mother.

Billy!

'Oh my God!' I breathed. 'Not Billy!'

I started to run.

As I went up the drive, I saw the workers of Ramsey's
gang trailing out for home, coming towards me. They
were all chattering excitedly and some of the women
were crying.

'What's happened?' I shouted. 'What is it?'

One of Martin's sisters came up to me, tears streaming down her face. 'It's little Billy. He caught his arm
in the machine and it's all wrenched off and his
mother is going berserk, and Billy is crying, "Clara!
Clara!" Go to him, Clara. Eb Grover won't have him in
the house, for all the blood—'

I nearly died on the spot. The horror overcame me.
All the world turned round on me and I staggered. A
man came up and held me in his arms. It was Sim.

232

'Steady on, lass, steady on, my dear.' Like to a horse, his soft words calmed me. 'He'll live, the little devil, if the doctor comes fast.'

I thought, if Dr Roberts is away on a visit, Soldier Bob knows all about shattered limbs and blown-off legs and how to deal with them: it was one of the yarns the boys loved to listen to.

And then Nat reappeared coming towards us on Crocus, and in his arms in front of the saddle he had Billy wrapped in a blanket. I couldn't see Billy's face, but he was quiet, the bundle of him shuddering in Nat's arms.

Nat pulled up and said shortly, 'Get up behind, Clara. He wants to be with you. I'm taking him to your house.' It was a command.

Sim bunked me up. So there I was, astride the gorgeous Crocus, pressed against Nat's expensive black jacket, the smell of the man's sweat in my nostrils, my head reeling with shock, taking the strangest ride of my life up my own driveway. I reached my arms around Nat to find Billy, to clutch the shivering blanket, to find a cold hand to hold. But now there was only one hand and I couldn't find it, and my own hand came away warm with blood. I wept.

And Nat turned his head and said to me, 'We'll do our best by him, Clara, I'll see to that. Don't be afraid.'

But Eb wouldn't take him in, so as not to mess up his house. I would never forget that.

Ann came running, white as a sheet.

'It's Billy,' I said slipping down. 'His arm is torn off in the machine. Is Father in?'

'Yes.'

'Billy wants Clara,' Nat said. 'And he's best here with you, if you'll take him.'

'Of course, of course!'

Father came out and heard the story and took Billy from Nat's arms. Nat handed him down tenderly, as gentle as Sim. What a puzzle of man, I thought. I couldn't help it, and looked up into his stern face as he straightened up. And he smiled at me, just a quick passing of a smile, and said softly, 'You're the good 'un, Clara.' How strange!

'I'll go and hurry old Roberts,' he said, and rode swiftly away.

So we were left with this bloody little wreck of our dear Billy, the three of us, cradling him into the house. We were all shocked stupid. Father lay the bundle on the table and we tucked him round with what cushions we had, and under his head. Ann went to open the blanket, and said to me, 'Go out and find Soldier Bob, Clara. Bring him here.'

She didn't want me to see, nor did I want to see. I went out into the yard, blind with shock. All Billy's plans . . . how could he be a horseman with one arm? The shock might take his frail life, dear Billy. And so much for the wicked machine, gobbling lives as well as livelihoods! I found Bob and told him what had happened and he said, 'We put stumps in hot tar, to bind them over, but that would probably kill the little chap. But I know a trick or two.'

He went in.

To my relief, Dr Roberts came shortly after, belting

his poor old cob with his whip as the gig rattled down the drive. I ran to take the reins and busy myself with the cob, afraid to go in. But then the worst job came to me, fending off Billy's mother as eventually she came stumbling down the drive supported by a posse of the awful Ramseys. She was in high drama, not unnaturally, and in dire need of Dr Roberts herself, but I managed to waylay her for a little while, telling her what good hands her son was in. She quietened down gradually and I told her relatives to go away, and when I could keep her away no longer I took her into the house.

Billy lay in his rags on the table, unconscious. I saw his stump of an arm, cut off just above the elbow, but sewn now like a piece of meat on the butcher's counter. Dr Roberts was cleaning up, with Bob as his assistant, and Ann was gathering all the mass of bloody linen that covered the table. Billy's mother, at the sight of him, fainted, but I just managed to ease her from hitting the floor too hard, and Father laid her out straight and put a cushion under her head.

'That woman is not staying here, Billy or no Billy,' he said firmly. 'You can see to her, Doctor, and take her home. We'll keep Billy.'

'That would be best. He'll soon get infected in that filthy house she keeps.'

The drama was over now that Billy's blood was staunched in its flow and the stump heavily bandaged, and after the clearing up, Father fetched the doctor a drink of ale, and something stronger in a small glass.

The doctor was getting old now for such excitement, but the village depended on him utterly. He saw everyone into their graves as kindly as he could, and saved many a poor person without any payment. He was a grumpy man, but sometimes acted kindly, another puzzle in life. Certainly there was no money to pay for this latest drama, as he well knew while he worked.

The ghastly mother recovered consciousness and started weeping again, saying, 'They wouldn't take him in! They turned him away from the door and the blood running everywhere and that Grover woman afraid for her carpets—' And streams of terrible language followed which Father put an abrupt stop to by pulling her to her feet and giving her a good shake.

'Now pull yourself together! Billy is saved and we will nurse him here until he's ready to come back to you. You can see he can't be moved now. Calm yourself, woman.'

'And Billy'll be no good to me no more! How can he earn money without an arm?'

Dr Roberts shut her up by giving her a stiff draught of something unpleasant out of his bag, and she went groggy after that and sat down muttering to herself. Father meanwhile carried Billy gently upstairs and he was put in my bed with a hot bottle at his feet. I would lie with him that night, because he asked for me. He wanted me.

But life changed after that. Billy's arm was the spark that set light to the tinder.

20

We knew Jack and Martin were up to something. And not alone, for we saw them with strangers, mostly young men of a rabble-rousing nature. Father lectured Jack sternly about not getting mixed up in trouble, but Jack set his jaw and did not reply, did not even argue. He had grown so big of late, into a man, and Father looked almost the weaker of the two, lecturing him.

'He'll not listen to me,' I heard him say to Ann, and she shook her head and said, 'You can't change nature.'

All I thought about was the coming match between Rattler and Crocus. Jack was all set for it, and rode out Rattler of an evening to get himself into the way of it, and to learn to control his stride. He was used to Tilly, but Rattler was new to him. Tilly used to do all the thinking for herself but Rattler did not know how, and Jack saw that he was going to have to work harder on Rattler than he used to on Tilly.

'Nat's been out on Crocus every night. He's dead keen,' he said. 'We'll have a job to beat him.'

'We will if your heart is in it. I can't get him any fitter than he is. He's out of his skin as it is.'

But Jack's heart was elsewhere, it was only too obvious.

'What are you up to, Jack? Don't bring any more trouble on Father. He's had enough.'

'We can't let these swine off scot-free, Clara. Grover's made no reparation to Billy, not even a visit to his mother.'

Well, I knew that. Grover didn't want blood on his carpets, wasn't that enough?

'It's not just me. It's a whole crowd of them from as far as Wymonden and Diss, they've been treated the same. A man called Firmin . . . he's very brave, he calls the tune. He wants me in. Grover's in the running for trouble, not just from me. He's a marked man.'

'You'll get the blame, if anything happens!'

'I'm not stupid, Clara. I look after myself.'

But he was stupid when it came to a bit of excitement, I knew it. And Martin was worse. What if they were hanged or transported like the others? What would it do to Father? Father was so transparently happy these days, a new man. He wasn't laughing and jokey as he had been with Mother, but an older, wiser, quietly contented man, working hard and full of optimism. He came in at meal times to a warm, shining house with good food prepared – how different from the days when I was in charge! And the love and affinity between him and Ann was plain for all to see.

'Don't spoil anything, Jack,' I pleaded. 'You don't have to get involved.'

'I do, Clara,' he said stubbornly. Then he laughed and ruffled my hair in his old stupid way and said, 'It's only a lark, Clara. Don't fret.'

But I knew it wasn't.

So I laughed too and said, 'Well, keep out of prison until after Rattler's match.'

And he said, 'Firmin calls the tune and he don't care about horse matches.'

My heart sank into my boots. I felt this was a warning. After all my work! And half the county now had its eyes on our date and were going to descend on the village en masse come the day.

But it was out of my hands.

I had enough to do keeping Rattler in full fettle and looking after Billy, who stayed with us and followed me about like my shadow once he was back on his feet. So tough was he that he recovered very quickly from the accident and the wound healed cleanly without infection, thank God. He cried with frustration at all the things he couldn't do but I knew his quick little brain would conquer the disability quite soon. But he couldn't ride Rattler with only one arm. Rattler was far too strong.

'We'll buy you a pony, Billy, for your own. How would you like that? A kind pony who will do what you want.'

'Oh yes!' His face lit up. 'For my own?'

'Yes. You can keep it here and ride out with me.'

His mother had claimed him back, but now he could no longer work at Grover's he came to us every day and helped in the stables as best he could. Father paid him the sixpence a week he used to get from Grover and agreed about the pony.

'Old and cheap,' he advised.

Poor Billy! After Rattler an old dodderer would come hard. But I thought – and told him – he might ride Better Times in another year, for, though the son of indomitable Tilly and high-mettled Rattler, Betty was as amiable and lazy a yearling as they come. He might as well have had a donkey for a mother. I could have been bitterly disappointed by this offspring of my great Rattler, but there was something so endearing about funny, kind Betty that one could not regret anything. Like Tilly he was a roan, a dreadful colour, at present a dark browny-grey with spots of paler grey sprinkled at random round his rear and shoulders. His black mane stood up on end and his tail was as poor and ratty as his dam's. He would hardly fetch a bid at market. But his eyes were bright and kind and his nature the same. He was very affectionate, quite unlike his parents. Rattler, so keyed up now like a Newmarket racehorse ready for the Derby, was anything but affectionate, but he was being prepared for a job and needed the aggression to be a winner. I understood him and he understood me.

So Billy lived on the promise of a pony – which I would look for when the match was over – and took to Betty as his own property for the time being. He was able to halter the dozy animal with one hand and lead him in from the field to be groomed and fussed over. Billy was happy, truly happy at last, even without his arm. How strange the consequences of disaster!

* * *

But Billy losing his arm, along with the Harrises
eviction, brought to a head the feeling against Grover,
and when the faction at the Queen's Head decided to
act, there was nothing we could do to dissuade Jack
and Martin. Jack didn't come home that night, not for
supper, nor later. We none of us said anything.

'Drinking,' Father said, and shrugged.

Ann looked at him, but said nothing.

I did my usual round of the stables before I went to
bed, carrying my lantern. It was a cold night and
foggy, with a light breeze. I thought I could smell
spring in the moisture-laden air and my usual little
bug of optimism sprang happily in my breast. I sur-
veyed my lovely horses eating or dozing in their stalls.
If there was anything wrong, this was usually the time
to see it first, a restlessness or unaccustomed lethargy.
Rattler, as usual, turned to me, still munching his hay,
and I gave him a caress, feeling the hard muscle of his
strong, crested neck under my palm. The match was
less than a week away, and I didn't think Crocus stood
a chance against him. Rattler had grown into an
altogether larger stronger animal than Crocus. Yet
Crocus had a quality that made me love and admire
him, a distinction, a sort of classic self-possession, as if
he knew himself a cut above. Hard to describe.

There was nothing untoward in the stable and I
came away, shutting the door behind me.

There was nothing to suggest there was anything
wrong, but my content unaccountably turned to
anxiety. There was a feeling in the air – was it my

imagination? A dog barked in the distance; a faint
lantern bobbed on the road away across the fields
where some late-night traveller made for home.
Otherwise silence. Where was Jack? All good people
were in bed by now. When I went in there was a candle
left for me on the table, the room empty. The fire was
in embers, the glowing ash fading. I sat there a
moment, warming my hands, then I climbed upstairs
and got into bed beside Ellen.

I slept.

'It's the dogs as'll bark,' said Martin. 'If anything
catches us out, it'll be the dogs.'

'Once we've got it going, they can bark their heads
off. We approach from the fields behind, and the dogs
won't sniff us. The wind's blowing the other way.'

'We've waited long enough for the right wind, that's
for sure.'

'That was Firmin's orders. He's a right professional.
Done three of these in Norfolk.'

'No wonder he gave us the job this time! If he's
caught—'

'He's for the long drop.'

Jack and Martin were keyed up, wanting to babble,
as they crept along the hedgerow skirting the Grover
stackyard. They had never done anything as exciting
as this in their lives before, with the strong element of
danger unfamiliar. They only knew of danger from
Soldier Bob's stories of waiting to fire till the last
minute as the French army approached in a great wall.
Firmin had given them the flint and tinderbox and a

bag of powder which he said was nearer to gunpowder than made no difference. 'Make sure you run for it when you throw that.' No wonder their pulses were racing.

The object was to set fire to the threshing barn and destroy the machine inside it. The barn was huge, a fourteenth-century granary built of wood and mud and thatch. Once it caught, no man would stop a fire there. But it was part of the stackyard and nearest to the house where the dogs roamed, and the idea was to set fire to the nearby hayricks and hope the wind would carry the fire to the barn. A nice dry rick, as Grover's were, would be hard to stop too, once taken.

They knew they mustn't be seen. Grover might guess who the culprits were but without proof he couldn't prosecute. The family would swear they were in bed. But the hedge was high and thick and took them along to the gate into the rick-yard. They lay there a while, making sure no dog was sniffing about, no tramp keeping warm between ricks. No lights shone anywhere. A rat ran across under the gate, the only sign of life in the world.

'It's clear,' Jack whispered.

He was shivering, whether from fear or cold he had no idea. They had to climb the gate, which creaked softly to their weight. The nearest rick was twenty yards away, half cut with loose hay beside it and a pile of thatching pegs. But the damp hung heavily.

'We'll have a job to get it started.'

Exposed, they were both frightened now, the bold talk in ashes. Nothing in their lives had prepared them to find cold courage. Jack's fingers trembled as he pulled the fire-making equipment from the sack he carried.

'Got the powder?'

'Yeah, here.'

'Get those thatching pegs, they'll burn. We'll make a hole in the stack, get to the dry inside and stack the pegs up.'

Making fire was a commonplace, with a flint and tinderbox, but it took time. There was plenty of dry tinder in the sack which Martin pulled out and arranged under a wigwam of thatching pegs in a cave pulled out of the stack. The hay was good and sweet-smelling and both of them were aware of the terrible thing they were doing. They had a deep revulsion towards their own action, yet a firmer conviction of the need for justice.

'Bloody murderer, it's what he deserves.'

'What did Firmin say we did with this powder?'

'Stand back, he said. Sprinkle it above the fire.'

The tinder had taken hold now and was flaring up, engulfing the thatching pegs. Some of the hay caught, flared, and died.

'Go on. Use it.'

The damp was in everything. Jack's voice was urgent, wanting the job done. He groped in his pocket for a rag, his eyes running from the smoke, and heard something drop. He groped around, just as Martin threw the first handful of powder. There was a roar as good as an explosion and the flame shot up in front of their faces with a fierce scorching crackle. The hay above broke into happy flames. The two boys staggered back, feeling their hair scorch, eyebrows shrivel, hearts leap with exultation. Martin threw the rest with a cheer and the conflagration sent them running. What magic! They could not help resting by the gate to admire their handiwork, feeling the heat from twenty yards back.

'Whew! What was it? Gunpowder?'

'Nearly blew us up!'

'God, the dogs!'

A racket of barking broke out from the granary and from the stables a horse whinnied, no doubt smelling smoke.

'Get down! We must leave!'

The two boys leaped over the gate and ran down the hedgerow the way they had come. But coming towards them was a horse trotting fast, with a rider in dark clothes outlined against the glowing sky. They had no time to do anything but fling themselves face down in the ditch under the hedge. It was full of nettles with the drainwater running hard in the bottom, but there was no time to choose anything better, only dive and keep face down, still as a corpse. The hooves reverberated in the ground above them, throwing clods, then hesitated. Jack felt his throat tighten with fear. He dared not look up, but was aware of the horse prancing close by his head, not going on. He heard the whip come down and a curse.

'Get on, you fool! Smoke won't hurt you!'

It was Nat, as he had surmised. Crocus let out a snort, but shied away, not towards the ditch, thank

God. What a predicament if he shied again and Nat landed in the ditch beside them! Jack had never known fear as he knew it now, yet it was a pounding, exulting emotion, half triumph, half terror – perhaps how Soldier Bob had felt facing the French. Jack felt his dull life was exploding, bursting into flame like the hayrick. But Nat's whip cracked down again and Crocus went on, passing so close that Jack got an eyeful of mud.

The two of them struggled on to their knees. The first rick was really roaring now, in a manner that confirmed no pathetic chain of buckets could possibly confine it. Not that any villagers would come forward to help. To watch, certainly, to pass comment, and smirk. But no one would lift a finger to put it out.

'We'd best get clear,' Jack said. 'We don't want nobody to see us around.'

The dark night was no longer so concealing, the great glow from the fire lighting up the landscape. They got their heads down and ran on down the hedge, keeping in shadow all the way. They crossed the road into a field of their own beet, at last finding darkness again. But the inferno they left behind danced on the horizon and kept on growing.

'We done a good job,' Martin said as they stood admiring it. The candle in the Garland cottage glowed close at hand.

A good job, safely completed.

'Old Firmin'll be proud of us,' Jack said.

They both laughed.

* * *

246

It was still dark when I woke, yet I knew it was nowhere near morning. There was a smell in the room which had woken me, a smell of burning. I sat up in alarm, thinking it was the house, but the house was dark and silent and the ashes downstairs dead. The smell was from across the fields. I lay there, too frightened to look farther. This is what they did, those people from Wymonden and Diss, the man called Firmin: they set light to ricks and barns and the army was called in to hunt them down. And they were nearly always caught, and hanged or transported.

I got up and went to look in the tiny room under the eaves where Jack slept. His bed was empty. His window looked on to the road and as I stood there I could see the light of fire between the trees, coming from Grover's stackyard. Even as I watched it was growing brighter.

I quickly threw on my clothes and ran downstairs and went out. The smell of burning thickly overlaid the foggy night, and out in the orchard I could hear the roaring of the fire. Once hay and straw caught and the fire held, how they burned! I knew only too well, for we had all seen rick fires caused by bad making. I could hear shouting, men's voices, the frightened whinny of a horse. There were voices on the road too, coming from the village. But no one from the village would be anything but glad at what they were witnessing. They certainly weren't coming to help, as they would if it had been any other farm.

Jack, oh Jack! I would have been glad to see this terrible act of the workers' revenge if only Jack wasn't involved. But I knew he was a prime mover, a natural leader, the man who knew the landscape, who knew how Grover's was guarded. He was the local knowledge that the hard men like Firmin used in their business. Where was he now?

In answer to my questions, there was suddenly a commotion, a sound of boots, running, and a laugh, and Jack and Martin came haring out of the darkness, nearly knocking me over.

'Clara! You should be in bed!'

Jack got hold of me and swung me off my feet. He was deliriously happy, no doubt at the success of the night's work. The great idiot! The oaf!

'Have you no sense?' I shrieked as my skirts flew.

'Sense enough to do for him, my darling, make him dance with rage. What a lovely fire we made! What a pity we couldn't stay and enjoy it, eh Martin?'

'Aye, it went well,' said the idiot.

'Just the smell of you – all your clothes – for God's sake, what are you thinking of? They'll come looking, for sure—'

'And you'll say we were sound in bed. No one saw us, we were so careful!'

'You both stink of fire. Get washed, for heaven's sake, and give me those clothes—'

I was so angry. Of course Father and Ann woke too, and poor Jack's joy was quenched by Father's rage, just like water over flames. Not that there was any saving of Grover's, for a chain of buckets formed by the servants was of little use against such a force of fire. Thank God the stables were not close to the ricks, but the great threshing barn had been fired, and whether Grover was able to save his machine we none of us knew.

'He'll call the army in, that's for sure, and all the special constables he can lay hands on,' Father swore. 'How are you both so sure no one saw you?'

'We crept in like little mice,' crowed Jack. Father's rage could not cow him for long. His pleasure kept breaking out. 'Oh, it was so lovely!'

'Yeah, lovely,' Martin agreed.

Then, even Father could not help but enjoy the night in spite of his forebodings, for we could hear the commotion on the road, the whole village having arrived to take stock. We heard afterwards that no one offered to help, save old Ramsey and a few of the most grovelling of his workers, no doubt hoping for a reward. The rest just stood there grinning, as if it were a Guy Fawkes night, and it was said they could hear Ebenezer's swearing from a hundred yards away. The fire roared steadily through all the ricks that remained after the winter – not many, in truth, but enough to make everyone happy – while Nat and his father tried to drag the threshing machine to safety. Unsuccessfully, apparently, for the roof of the threshing barn caught fire from the ricks. We saw the tall building start to burn from our driveway and we all let out a cheer. For indeed, the spirit of the night had got into all of us. Remembering Billy, and the Harrises, who could help but cheer when the comeuppance came? We heard the cheering from the road too.

No one was going back to bed. We went into the kitchen and Father drew up the fire. We made Jack and Martin wash and change clothes to get the smell of fire out of them, and I hung their jackets and trousers out of sight in the feed shed, to ingest the smell of hay and corn instead of fire. We sat round discussing what they should do.

'If we scarper away, it'll make us look guilty,' Jack said. 'I swear no one saw us, so why don't we just go to work as usual?'

'The blame will fall on you and your crowd, but they'll have to find evidence.' Father was doubtful.

Ann said, 'Knowing Grover, he'll have the authorities out in force.'

'He's got to raise them. Special constables don't come that easy, unless he puts out big rewards. He's got enough clout though, to get the Metropolitan police up here.'

'None of us are planning any more – it was only Grover. They won't use the army just for the one burning,' Martin said.

'That's true.'

We all sat round surmising the state of shock in the Grover kitchen as dawn broke. I can't say we showed any kindness or sympathy. The tea we drank seemed sweeter than usual and the potato hash Ann decided to cook was definitely a form of celebration. All seemed quiet up on the road. The flames had died but a great stench lay over the fields. Smoke hung in the damp air, sour and clogging, veiling the sun as it rose into a clear sky. I had fed the horses and the men were in, grooming and harnessing up. Father had to go out and give orders. But just as he rose from the table, there came a knock at the door.

So unusual was this, and so uncommon the circumstances, that Jack and Martin went out the back way into the dairy, suddenly frightened. Father opened the door.

It was Sim.

'I come down to tell you summat, sir. You should know.'

'Come in. What is it?'

Sim entered, looking round shyly. He looked tired and agitated, as well he might if he had had to deal with the frightened horses all night.

'It's to tell you as Mister Nat picked up a clasp knife of Mister Jack's this morning. His name is writ on it. It was lying in the rick-yard. It shone, like, amongst the ashes.'

Father groaned. We all knew Jack's clasp knife, his trophy from a fair long ago on which he had scratched his name. It was always in his pocket.

'He's going to come down, I reckon, quite soon, I thought as you should know.'

'Yes, well done, Sim. You've done us a good turn.'

'I must get back. I'll get the sack if he sees me.'

'Go back behind the hedge, through the beet field. You won't meet him that way. We'll get the boys away at once. You're a good man, Sim.'

Sim left and a fair pandemonium broke out then in our kitchen. Our triumph turned to horror as we realized the implication of what Sim had told us. Jack and Martin came out and heard the news, and all the stuffing went out of them. They looked like what they

251

were: two frightened boys who had been up all night playing with fire. The party was over.

'We've got to get out,' Martin said. 'But where to go?'

It never occurred to him that he wasn't directly implicated, so close was he to Jack. He could have gone home and kept his head down. But it wasn't in his nature.

'Out the back way into the woods, for now,' Father decided. 'We can work something out later. If Nat's on his way, the sooner the better.'

Ellen went to keep watch on the drive and we loaded the boys with bread and cheese and a can of tea and hustled them out of the house. They ran off towards the river. There was an old charcoal burner's hut deep in the trees that few people knew about, a makeshift shelter for the time being. But what of the future?

'If Nat's coming, we must go about our work as if we don't know anything. We can talk about it later.'

'But what to say if he asks where Jack is?' Ann asked. 'We must have a common story.'

'I'll say he's working in the Road Eight Acres, and if Nat goes there and finds he isn't, I'll say that he's supposed to be and, if he isn't there, how the hell do I know where he is? That'll have to do for now. And you can all say he was here last night until we were awoken by the fire and he went up the drive to see what was going on. That would be natural. And if we're lying, it's for Jack's life, as well you all know. How his knife came to be in the stackyard – well, we have no idea. Maybe he lent it to one of the arsonists.'

We were now all in deep confusion and fear, and trying to go about our everyday jobs was terrible. We all wanted to stay and face Nat but that was Ann's job alone, and Ellen's if she was in the dairy. I was out in the stable, grooming Rattler and Tilly, trying not to tremble. I could only think of seeing Jack and Martin being hunted like criminals by the special police who were bound to arrive in a short time, beating through the fields with their sticks and dogs. And, as I worked on Rattler's already gleaming coat, I felt sick at the thought of the impending match and how the bottom was dropping out of our world. Would Nat call it off, or would I, now I had no rider?

Father was in the barn seeing to the loading of seed when Ellen came running for him to go back to the house.

'He's here. He wants to talk to you,' she cried.

Father went back to the house. Spying, I saw Nat shortly emerge, mount Crocus and ride up the track to the Road Eight Acres. He was soon back, as it was only too obvious the field was empty. By then Father was back working in the barn, pretending he wasn't worried about anything.

I heard him say roughly, 'I'm not his keeper. He's supposed to be seeding that field today, and if he's not there I don't know where he is.'

'I think he's on the run,' Nat said.

'And why should that be?'

'You know perfectly well why that should be, Mr Garland.'

Nat was in rough clothes, unshaven, red-eyed and

dirty, no doubt exhausted from his night's labours, but his voice was cool and sounded infinitely menacing. I thought of the power of that evil family, no doubt at this very moment talking with magistrates and rounding up (and paying) special constables and perhaps, through influence, a contingent of soldiers. I was peeping out of the stable door, and when Nat turned away from Father I shot back in to groom Rattler. But as Father drove away with his cart of seed, my doorway darkened and I turned to see Nat standing there. He came down the stalls and stood looking at Rattler.

'A pity about the match, if you have no rider,' he said.

'I'll have a rider,' I said.

I could feel myself trembling and tightened my lips fiercely, not to give way.

'My father will see Jack hanged if he puts in an appearance. You know that, don't you?'

I was too frightened to reply. I turned my head to Rattler's dear hide and tried to keep the tears from rising. Oh Jack! The stupid, *stupid* dearest brother in the world! To go under to the evil Grovers – it was more than I could bear to think about. I put my head against Rattler's sweet-smelling coat, and felt a determination like an iron rod steal into my panic. Never! Never! And the answer was under my hand even as I stood there. It came to me like a flash of summer lightning out of a clear sky. I nearly laughed then. Nat had given me the answer.

'My horse looks well, don't you think?'

I turned and saw Nat's surprise at my sudden riposte. Then he laughed.

'Yes, a rare horse, I'll give you that. I'd trade Jack's life for your horse, Clara.'

'Never!' The word sprang from me without my thinking. As soon as I had cried out, I realized what I had said and clapped my hand to my mouth.

Nat then said, 'But my father wouldn't.'

'Get out! Get out!' I screamed. His words shook me to the core. 'We all hate you! Why are you so cruel? Why do you treat people so badly? Why—'

But Nat came up to me then and took my wrists in his hands and held me like Jack used to hold me in teasing play, laughing.

'What a pity,' he said, 'you're not as pretty as your sister.'

His grip was like iron. I couldn't move. I looked into his jeering blue eyes and shouted out, 'You bastard! You bastard!'

'That I'm not,' he said. Then, 'You Garland girls have such spirit. I love it. I could love you, Clara, ugly as you are.'

At that I went berserk. I spat in his face and kicked wildly at his shins and did my utmost to get my knee up into his crotch. But he held me away, laughing. I screamed.

And Nat suddenly let me go with a shout. Billy stood behind him with a pitchfork which, with his one arm, he had stuck into Nat's buttocks. There was no force in it, but enough to have the desired effect, for Nat sprang away. He made a swipe at Billy but Billy dropped the pitchfork and ran. I leaped forward and picked up the fork.

'Get out!' I screamed. 'Get out!'

Nat retreated. But he was laughing again.

'I'll see you at the match. Billy can ride!'

He was lucky I didn't stick his guts there and then and lose his entrails on my stable floor. I was trembling so hard with rage I hardly knew what I was doing. But Nat saw the danger and slipped out of the door, and was on Crocus and away before I got myself in hand. Billy came running back and I gathered him in my arms and wept.

'You're a real little trooper! You saved me, Billy.'

'If I had two hands I'd have killed him!'

'I bet you would.'

'I hate him!'

'Yes, we all do.'

'But they burned down his farm last night! Did you see? It was wonderful.'

I calmed myself in his excitement, hearing his story from the village point of view. I sat in the straw, hiccuping, my brain in turmoil, as Billy prattled on. I must see Father ... the wonderful idea that had bowled me over was to take Rattler out to the woods and see Jack speed away to safety. No one would ever catch him, not on Rattler, not with dogs nor all the army in England.

I ran out and spilled out my tale to Father, who was lurking behind the barns waiting for Nat to ride clear.

'The boys must go! They can go on Rattler and Tilly.'

Father saw the sense of it. 'But where to?'

'To Harwich and take a ship to somewhere, and then no one will ever find them. And when it's all died down, they can come back. They can leave the horses in a livery yard and when they're safe away, I will go up and fetch them back.'

Father stood considering my plan. It was a good one, I knew it. There was no safety in staying in the wood.

'They can take them to the inn in Manningtree,' he said. 'That's just a stone's throw from where the ships dock. Even if they just take a hay barge to London they'll be safe, I reckon.'

He stood there rubbing his chin, looking old and weary again, like before he married Ann.

'Oh, the stupid boys! When will they be free to come back? Never, if I know Ebenezer Grover. What shall we do without Jack?'

He sounded broken. I could not bear it. I went up and put my arms round him and said, 'He will be safe, at least. They can't be after him for ever.'

'Only if we pay reparation. And how shall we ever do that? And even then, Ebenezer is an evil man. He would see a man hang and laugh.'

'Father, he's not caught yet. Let's see him safe first. It might turn out all right.'

I couldn't see how, as we all knew Jack was guilty and the evidence was there. Maybe if they caught the Firmin man they would forget about Jack. I wouldn't tell Father of Nat's offer: Rattler for Jack's life. Was it made in all seriousness? And my own shout of 'Never!'

I did not want to think about it, and thrust the memory away. Best to think of his jibe: my ugliness. That filled me with the necessary gall to spur me to action.

'If I take Rattler and Tilly out to them, they can be away within the hour.'

'All right. Go and saddle them. I'll go and tell Ann.'

It would take Eb a while to round up his constables and soldiers. The magistrates would have to be called on first. No doubt Nat was now away on Crocus to town. We could already see the Grover workers set to scour the hedgerows and common, but they were unlikely to report anything even if they found any clues, and the ones that approached our boundaries got short shrift from our men. The morning was grey and dull with rain in the air, yet the smoke still curled sullenly from the night's work and the ash from the ricks came like moths from the sky.

I decided if Billy rode out with me on Tilly we would look as if we were doing our normal exercising, keeping Rattler fit for the match. We often rode through the woods so why would anyone who saw us suspect we were doing anything different? So we mounted, the two of us, and Ann came out of the house with a bundle of food. Father gave me a packet of sovereigns in a leather bag. Ann was crying and Father not far off tears himself.

'Tell him to keep in touch, that we might get him back when it's safe. Not to go without a word. Tell him that.'

'Yes, I will.'

'Tell him—' But his words were lost in his choking voice.

I rode away and Billy followed. I was blind with tears. It was all so sudden, this misfortune, when everything had been so shining in our lives at last. All I had had in my head for weeks was the excitement of the match. It was only three days away, and now I had no rider and very likely no horse. My world was shattered as completely as Jack's. But nothing was of any importance save the boys' lives.

We crossed the river and took the muddy track into the woods and came to the charcoal burners' hut. Jack and Martin were lying low but when they saw who it was they burst out, grinning like schoolboys.

'Here you are. You can get clear away in a day to where no one's looking.' I slipped down and handed over the money and the food.

I explained about leaving the horses in Manningtree where they were close to the shipping quays.

'You can get a ship there, to London or the north. Or the west. Wherever.'

To two boys who had scarcely been farther then thirty miles from home all their lives, and that perhaps once a year, it sounded like going to the far side of the world. They stood staring, jaws hanging.

'We thought Norwich,' Jack said.

'Ebenezer's got family in Norwich, you know he has! You'll need to go farther than that. It's a hanging matter, Jack, don't you realize?'

I don't think he did, the idiot.

'You've got to get away where they can't find you.

Just up the road's no good. If you're in Manningtree tonight you'll be well away from any searchers.'

'How far is it?'

'Sixty miles about. If not Manningtree, you can go on to Harwich where you'll have all the ships in the North Sea to choose from, and then they'll never find you.'

Martin looked more excited about the adventure than Jack. He would be glad to leave his horrible home, I knew, whereas Jack had a good time of it working for Father and cosseted by Ann.

'We could go to America, Jack. They say there's all the riches in the world to be found there.'

'Don't be daft. I don't want to go to America.'

'I wouldn't mind.'

'You can go. I'll be home as soon as I can.'

'Be careful, Jack. Ebenezer will have you, you know what he's like. And the evidence to hand. Nat – Nat's not so bad—'

I couldn't bear to repeat the sarcastic offer Nat had made and my wild answer. It shamed me.

'And what about your match, Clara?' Jack asked sadly. 'I didn't mean to do this to you, I didn't think. We'll go safe, and you'll have no horse for the match and no rider either.'

'It's not important,' I lied. 'I'll fetch the horses home when the coast is clear. Don't worry. You go now, before the searchers arrive.'

So Martin got on Tilly, and Jack vaulted up on Rattler and took the parcel of food. Martin reined Tilly round and said to me, 'Don't go off with any other fellow till I come back, Clara. Promise?'

I shook my head. He could take it for a yes or a no as he pleased. I was beyond thinking so far ahead, just bereft now at seeing them go, the awful tears streaming again. There were tears in Jack's eyes as well.

'I'm sorry, Clara. Tell Father I'm sorry.'

So they rode away. Billy and I walked back. It was still early and I felt bereft, my horses gone, my mind in turmoil.

I told Billy he must tell no one of what we had done, on pain of banishment from our yard for ever.

'It's Jack's life, you understand?'

Billy swore he understood.

'No pony, if you breathe a word. Say we exercised the two horses as usual. Round behind the woods and through the water meadows. That's all. Just the same as always.'

But there was nothing the same as always about the house and yard. Father could not work and stayed in the house, Ann was crying, Ellen gone to the village to see what everyone was saying. I was so restless I could not settle to anything and went back to the stables. There were only Hoppy and Better Times in their stalls, Hoppy not working. He had been very useful all the winter and was fit and strong now. He would be used, no doubt, to go to Manningtree and fetch Rattler and Tilly back, so it was just as well he was fit. Father would not want to stretch the journey to more than two days.

And as I stood there, thinking how well he looked, I suddenly thought that I could go to Manningtree to fetch the horses back. I knew if I asked my father he wouldn't let me. He would say it was too dangerous for a girl to travel alone so far. But I had no fear and, the idea once seeded, grew and filled my whole brainbox. I had some money of my own, enough to stay a night at an inn, and it would stop me mewling about the place pining for Rattler. I could not bear to think of him being in the charge of strangers. I would not tell Father and Ann, for I knew I would be forbidden.

I told Billy. He could tell them later, when I was well away. I fetched my money, saddled Hoppy and rode away. It was quite simple.

The consequences were so unexpected, so completely opposite from anything I could have imagined, that I still find it hard to believe what happened. But it happened, for I have the proof of it inside me.

21

I will not dwell on that terrible ride. My great idea was stupid, for I did not know the way. The names of towns had no meaning for me, save Harwich. I knew it was south, that's all. If I kept the sun, such as it was, in my eyes, I was heading south. Did Martin and Jack know any better? I doubted it. Fast as their horses were, it would probably take them days wandering round the countryside, and they would be wary of asking the way. I could ask but I had taken the cross-saddle and men looked at me askance, a female riding astride in breeches. I was very careful who I spoke to. Tramps were best, or old road-workers. Women didn't seem to know; they just gaped. I knew I needed Bury and then Sudbury, or Ipswich, one or the other. Opinions varied. A roadman drew a map in the dust with a stick.

'Manningtree, that's the river crossing. Harwich is at the mouth of the river, twelve miles farther on.'

Going through villages I sat sideways and drew my leather rain apron over my breeches so that I looked less conspicuous, and few people then threw me a glance. After a while, through asking, I got my route into my head and was able to follow signposts and read the milestones: forty, thirty, twenty . . . But all the time I was wondering how Jack and Martin had got on. My lovely Rattler was a conspicuous horse, and a lot of people knew Tilly through her fame. Keeping low, not knowing the way, would have been well-nigh impossible. How many people already knew about the passage of the two idiots and where they were heading? The farther I rode, the more stupid my wonderful plan seemed. Or had I got it all wrong and was Jack far more prepared and intelligent than I gave him credit for? I had no idea. Suppose I never found Rattler and Tilly again? The panic rose in my throat and I had to force myself to keep steady. I was too far away to turn round and go back and with every mile I cursed myself for my stupidity.

Having been up all night, riding sixty odd miles came hard. Ordinarily it would not have worried me, but with the excitement and my anxieties I found myself getting very tired. Hoppy seemed tireless – I knew he was very fit, for like all our horses he worked hard and was well fed, but by the time it grew dark he was getting hungry, like me. By this time I had found my road. Hadleigh was well behind me, the lights of Manningtree ahead. I could smell the unfamiliar mud and ooze of the tidal river. They called it the Stour. I had come by it a few times on my way and pretty it was, but now in the growing dark it opened out into a vast expanse of hostile water. I had never seen the sea in all my life, and this estuary seemed to me a terrible place. I smelled the salt air and heard the gulls crying like the bereft souls of all the exiles who had taken ship away from England. I cried as I rode, shaking with hunger and despair.

But when things are that bad, they can only get better. Fortune favoured me at last and I came upon the livery yard on the edge of town that Father had told Jack to find – a jobbing sort of inn not unlike our Queen's Head at home, that let out post horses and hacks.

I slid off and led Hoppy into the yard at the back. My heart now began to thump with anticipation: were Rattler and Tilly here? The cobbles were untidy, straw-strewn, and several carts and gigs filled most of the space. But lanterns shone in the stables and I led Hoppy eagerly to the door. I stood there, blinking, looking in.

It looked full, a long row of stalls all showing hind-quarters. Hoppy nudged me, smelling food, and suddenly let out a shrill whinny. Instantly came an answer, and then another. I recognized the two voices immediately, coming from down the row. Rattler and Tilly!

All my weariness and misery was banished in a flash. My journey was not in vain, and Jack and Martin had made it to sanctuary. No one was going to catch them now, and the dear horses were safe. I flung my arms round Hoppy's neck, laughing.

A dour old groom came up behind me and said, 'We're full up. You'll have to move on.'

'Oh no! Two of my horses are here already – I've come to fetch them. Surely you can find room for this one till we're rested and fed and ready to go again?'

'Which two is those then? The ones the lads came on?'

'Yes.'

Shoving Hoppy's rein into his hand, I walked down the stable to Rattler and Tilly. Rattler gave me an effusive welcome, slobbering chewed oats all down my front, and even Tilly pricked up her old ears for a moment and her nostrils quivered acknowledgement. The stalls were wide enough.

'He can stand in with the mare here. She hardly ever lies down and they're good friends.'

'On your head be it,' said the old man.

He led Hoppy down to Tilly and clapped the old girl on the hindquarters to make her move over for Hoppy. Hoppy barged in and stuck his nose into her feed and she bit him.

'Hey up!' said the old man.

I laughed. 'I'll see to him, if you just fetch him a feed.'

I stripped his tack off and brushed him down with some brushes the old man gave me, and made him comfortable, an old blanket over his back, and when he was happily feeding I went to talk to darling Rattler, almost crying again with relief at having found him. My fears at the end of that ride, of never finding him and Tilly again, had been terrible. I was pleased to see that after his long journey he looked as if he had been resting lazily in the stable all day, not a sign of weariness.

I was just as hungry as Hoppy and needed a good

supper. I could stay at the inn and get away early in the morning: that was my plan. I was looked at askance, naturally, a girl alone, dressed like a man – the landlord called me 'Sonny'. I didn't expect to be in any danger from my feminine allure, and, having secured a room in the attics with a cleanish bed, came down and took my place in the dining room. I sat in a dark corner away from the men drinking round the fire and the few travellers, and the landlady brought me a wonderful plateful of beef stew and dumplings and a hunk of bread, with ale to drink it down with. I felt just like Hoppy, plunging his nose into Tilly's feed: I was so hungry. All my strength and spirits came back as I ate, and the warmth mellowed my cold bones. Nothing seemed quite so terrible as it had in the morning, even the boys going. They would surely come back before too long: Ebenezer couldn't hunt them for all their lives, surely? But then a shiver ran through me, because I thought: Yes, he could. Of all people, Ebenezer was the most evil man in Christendom. I sat hidden in my dark corner, tired now, but enjoying the warmth and comfort after the long ride. I had done well, I knew it, and if Father was tearing his hair over me now, he would be really happy when I got home and told him Jack and Martin were safely away. Oh, I had done well! The knowledge kept me steady, for all the calamity that had fallen on us. And I had, for no reason, a sudden vision of poor Nicholas, dying, with all that fire and intelligence soon to be quenched, and I thought of Margaret, and I felt sad and confused, that life should be like it was. So *unfair*. I did not believe in God.

Maybe that was a mistake, for just as I was sitting there puzzling over these conflicting emotions, the door opened and Martin walked in, sent by God, I realized. He went to the bar and ordered himself an ale without seeing me.

'Martin!' I called. I could not help myself. He turned round and I saw his astonishment, then the excitement of seeing me.

He came over. I stood up and we hugged each other rapturously. I told him how I had left home to follow them without anyone knowing, and asked after Jack.

'Where is he? Is he here?'

'No. He's on board a ship here in Manningtree. We've been really lucky – secured berths – but we don't sail until the tide turns at three in the morning. We've got to work our passage. God in heaven, Clara, we didn't tell 'em we haven't even seen the sea before, let alone been on it. Jack sent me back – he thought I should give that ostler a good tip, tell him we'll be back in a couple of days. I think he got the impression we were clearing off, the way we were talking, and Jack got worried just now and told me to come back and sweeten him up. But now you're here, that's taken care of.'

'Where's your ship going?'

'Plymouth.'

'Where's that?'

'I don't know, but it's a long way and it's still in England, so it suits us well.'

'Oh, Martin!'

I was half-laughing, half-crying. The boys were safe

but to be so far away ... Ann would know where Plymouth was.

'You must always let us know where you are. Don't ever lose touch. It would break Father's heart to lose Jack.'

'And yours to lose me, Clara?'

'Yes, it's breaking now!'

I laughed. It was so wonderful to see Martin again and hear the good news. From being so downcast an hour ago, I was now up in the clouds, my body tingling with excitement.

'Have you got a room here, Clara?' Martin asked.

I nodded.

'Let me kiss you up there, before I go. It's the last time, Clara, for ages – please. To say goodbye. I love you so much. I don't want to leave you.'

Only an Ebenezer Grover could have said no to such a plea, and we slipped out and up the dark stairs. The landlady had left me a candle in the bedroom, a tiny slip of a place with straw falling down out of the thatch and the rustle of mice above. But the brickwork of the big chimney from below formed the inner wall and the room was cosy and dry. Martin latched the door shut and turned to me. I went and put my arms round him and buried my face in his sweaty shirt. My head only came up to his collarbone. For all my strength I was still a little thing.

'I do love you, Clara. You are so beautiful.'

'Not me, Martin. I'm not beautiful.'

'Oh yes, you are. Not like Margaret. But brown and strong and clever and lovely. I think you are beautiful.

I don't know anyone else like you. You know I love you, more than anyone in the world.'

He was so sweet and the fact that he was now going to leave me, perhaps for ever, made my feelings for him swell up inside me, so that when he kissed me I responded in a way I had never allowed myself before. What did it matter any longer, to keep him at bay? I was fifteen now and all the girls in the village of my age had been with boys by now, I knew it, for I wasn't so wrapped up in my work that I didn't go down to the green in the summer and gossip with the rest of them. And what else did they talk about, save which boy was the best lover?

And I was so happy now, having been so afraid and miserable all day, that to lie on the bed in Martin's arms seemed like the most wonderful thing in the world. And so precious, for it would not happen again, perhaps not ever.

So, in that little room, I learned the great secret, to turn me into a woman. Ah well, it seemed very quick, and I didn't quite see how marvellous it was, but it seemed to round off my amazing day in a fitting way.

The pain and the weariness was now deep in my being, and even Martin's endearments could not keep me awake any longer. I told him he must go, but fell asleep still with his arms around me. To catch that tide was his business. I could do no more for the boys. And I awoke later in the night, and he was gone, and I was alone and cold in the bed. The mist and rain seemed to have cleared, for a full moon shone in the little gable end window. I got up and opened it to look out, for I sensed that it was high tide and the ship for Plymouth would be moving now on the ebb, taking Jack and Martin. The smell of the estuary came strongly, of salt and mud and seawrack, and I prayed – in spite of not believing – for their safe passage. At least it wasn't a transportation ship, bound for Australia. The cruelty of that punishment kept many a brave family man from taking revenge on the injustice of life. Thank God, I thought, that it wasn't myself being wrenched from everything that was my life.

It was quite silent in the night; nothing stirred, but that huge expanse of mud was now a sheet of silver water with the far side only to be seen faintly in the moonlight. Sails moved like ghosts over the shimmering surface, barely filled. The air whispered spring – that special intangible scent that comes in March or even in February sometimes, just a moment's whiff, enough to touch the heart. It makes you wonder: where are we in the scheme of things, so infinitesimal our little lives that seem to us so earth-shaking? Spring always comes, whatever calamities we suffer. But I was still too tired to philosophize and I went back to bed and lay for a moment or two, thinking of Martin, and then I slept.

22

I woke late. There was the sound of horses departing below from the yard, and by the light I knew it was well into the day. I lay wondering for a moment where on earth I was, then all the events of yesterday came crowding in.

I groaned, laughed, then jumped out of bed and hurriedly dressed. I could not wait now to get home and tell Father all was well. Disaster and deliverance, it was all the same to me now. The journey ahead would be a triumph. I had to overlook the fact that another sixty miles did not exactly speak delight to my poor body, but I would make the best of it.

I noticed there was blood on the scruffy sheet we had lain on, but I pulled the blanket over, and wondered on my initiation into adult life as I went down the stairs. It had not been the great delight that Margaret seemed to have discovered, nor – I gathered – that many of the village girls enjoyed, but maybe one needed practice. And I had to admit that my love for Martin was more sisterly than loverly, which might make a difference. I was glad it had happened, for it made me feel good about myself, that somebody desired me, at least. But, in a way, it was a great disappointment.

I went out to see that the horses were all right and found them fed and comfortable. I told the young boy mucking out to saddle them up ready to go in half an hour, and went in for my breakfast. In broad daylight now I had to endure more stares, but I made my face vacant and let my jaw drop so that I looked like an imbecile, and no one made advances, only let drop a few remarks that I tried not to hear. So Martin thought I was beautiful – dear deluded Martin! I ate my bread and cheese and thought of them fumbling with the ropes on board their ship, now well on its way south, for the tide had run right out and was on the flood again since they had departed. I heard some sailors talk, so knew this. This so-called sea was once again a huge expanse of mud, not water. This sailing business was very strange. Jack and Martin must be fast learning all about it, poor lads, but it was no longer any concern of mine.

The day was clear and warm, quite different from before, and I knew my way now and rode cheerfully. I rode Rattler and had Tilly on a lead on one side and Hoppy on the other and my only problem was to keep Rattler back to a pace that Hoppy could keep up with. If I had just had the two trotters I could have been home in half the time. But in the warm air I decided to enjoy my ride and not hurry overly. Rattler found this very puzzling, not often asked to go slowly, and he started to pull so hard that my good intentions were rather scattered. We trotted on and poor old Hoppy had to canter to keep up.

But I was tired too and eventually I pulled Rattler up to a walk and held him in hard to have a rest. The sun was shining and the hedges all breaking into leaf, full of birdsong, and great white clouds sailed overhead making ever-changing patterns of light and dark across the fields. I held my face up to the sun and felt again the pleasure of succeeding so well in my task.

So content, I didn't hear the approach of another horse from behind until it was nearly upon us, and Rattler tried to wrench himself free from my hand to start up again. I turned hastily, pulling Rattler in, and as I took in our pursuer I nearly fell from the saddle in horror, for it was none other than Crocus, with Nat astride.

My instinct to kick on was quashed – how could I beat him now, with such a handful of horses? I pulled up instead, and waited, for there was no way I could avoid his company. My mind was reeling, horribly curious to know what he had seen of my doings over the last few hours. I feared the worst.

He pulled up beside me and raised his hat like the gentleman he was – or at least had been brought up to be. Far from the dirty, fire-blackened Nat I had last seen, he was now smart and freshly shaved and looked as if he had just left home. He looked pleased with himself, just as I had been a minute before.

'What brings you out here?' I asked grimly.

'I could ask the same of you, dear Clara, save I know the answer already. Let me give you a hand and take one of your horses, as no doubt we are riding to the same place.'

I hadn't much choice but to let him take Hoppy's rein, which at least left me more free to constrain Rattler. Crocus walked kindly with his long swinging stride – what a gentleman *he* was – there was no doubt there. Rattler, seeing he was not to be overtaken, settled kindly at last.

'I suppose you've been spying on me,' I said bitterly.

'Of course. When I saw you set off on your bay horse here, I guessed there was something in the wind. I wasn't sure what, but I found out all I wanted to know after you retired into that inn. I saw Martin come back and waited – rather a long time, Clara, which surprised me, but we won't dwell on that . . . I followed him back to his ship and found out where its next port of call was. Plymouth. Well, it will be simple to put mail on the coach to the magistrates in Plymouth to apprehend the two of them when the ship arrives. There will be plenty of time.'

I found all this hard to take in.

'You followed me? But I never saw you, or heard you—'

'I don't think you turned round once. I was well out of earshot and most of the time out of sight. After you turned from the London road, I was pretty sure where you were going. One only has to put oneself into the minds of the people one is pursuing. It isn't difficult.'

'And you followed Martin on Crocus?'

'No. I followed Martin on foot. I really enjoyed myself. There was a lot at stake, after all. He went straight to the ship. I found out its name and destination, came back for Crocus, then went into town and stayed at the best inn there, not the fleapit you chose, Clara, and came away this morning to follow you at my leisure.'

I was so choked with anger that I could not reply. All our endeavour in vain, for the ship to be met in Plymouth by the constables! Jack and Martin to be so cruelly disappointed and now, after all, in danger of being hanged.

'You can't!' I cried out. 'You can't have them hanged! After all the brutality your father gets away with! How can you be so cruel?'

'It's for my father to say. For myself, I'd let them go. As long as they stay away, who cares?'

'It's nothing to you – not Margaret, nor Billy, how you've harmed them, and you take no blame.'

'Don't speak of Margaret,' he said angrily.

'Yes, Margaret. And now Jack. If your father played fair, Jack would never have harmed him. Evicting those old people, not caring for Billy, those little girls dying – the whole village hates you, can't you see? Jack's only done what they all want and aren't brave enough to do themselves. Nobody came to help you, did they? They just stood there loving it.'

Nat coloured up at my words and did not reply. He looked like his father in his anger, with flushed cheeks and quivering nostrils but no turkey-cock jowls – in fact, with jutting chin and tight lips he looked incredibly handsome. I noticed this even in my distress. I saw what Margaret had seen, and hated myself for it.

'We all loathe you!' I screamed furiously. 'You want *everything*! And now Jack's life – his *life*—'

I choked myself on my rage. I tried to pull myself together but I was shaking and felt as if I would pass out and fall in the mud. Rattler, scared, pulled hard against my hands and I let him trot on fast, forcing myself to recover. But Crocus was beside me. I wept. I loved Jack so – and Martin – I could not bear to think of them hanging.

But I think Nat was disturbed by my outburst for he did not come back at me, although his face remained very proud and angry. We rode for a long time in silence, the horses' trot matching, poor old Hoppy rolling along in our wake, jerked crossly from time to time by Nat's hard hand. I just wanted the miles to be over, to lie in Ann's arms and sob out my tale of woe. It should have been glorious!

But the morning was so lovely, the air alive with larks, the sun bursting free of the huge white clouds, that after some miles I found my senses again and began to think of ways to cajole Nat into keeping our secret. I remembered only too well his suggestion: Rattler in return for Jack's life. And during the long ride I came to acknowledge that this could be the way out. I cannot say this conclusion brought me any joy, only the deepest grief, but it was a spark of hope for Jack. If I struck a bargain with Nat, it would have to be before we arrived home, for I'm sure once Ebenezer knew the story Jack would stand no chance at all. Eb would not bargain. So when in the early afternoon we came to a big coaching inn, Nat's suggestion that we stopped for something to eat was a welcome one. I was hungry again and beginning to feel very tired.

We rode into the yard and the ostlers took the horses. Nat led me into the dining room. It was the sort of place I wouldn't usually have ventured into myself, where the landlady would ignore people like me but bow and scrape to one of Nat's appearance. So it was pleasant to be bowed and scraped to in my turn, in spite of my rare outfit, and seated at one of the best tables. Nat took this sort of treatment as his right, of course.

I was too frightened to instigate the conversation that was in my head, and thought a good meal first would strengthen me. Nat poured me wine which of course I wasn't used to, but I took a few sips thinking it might loosen my tongue. We had very good beef and mounds of potatoes, and Nat said no more than I did, eating hungrily. But when we were finished he made no move to go. He sat watching me in rather a strange way. I tried to broach my bargain, but my voice would not work.

He then said, 'You're a rare girl, Clara.'

There was no answer to that.

'It's a pity about the match on Saturday, that you have no rider. It will be a walk-over if you don't find someone.'

I had for the moment forgotten all about the match.

'I'll find someone,' I muttered. Maybe Father, I thought. He was out of practice, but knew more of the game than anyone I knew.

'I can't think about it,' I said. 'It isn't a big thing, compared with Jack's life.'

'I made you a good offer earlier.'

'Do you still stand by it?'

He did not answer. He poured himself some more wine. As I had drunk very little, he had had most of the bottle.

'I'm not sure. It's hard on you. I might make a better bargain.'

'What would that be?'

'You yourself, Clara. In return for Jack's life.'

'Whatever do you mean?'

'Oh come, Clara, you're not so innocent. Didn't you lie with Martin last night?'

I could not believe what he was saying. I just stared.

'I would like to lie with you,' he said.

It must have been the wine, I could think of no other explanation.

'I am ugly,' I retorted. 'You said so.'

He laughed. 'And when you get angry, you aren't ugly any more, but beautiful like a little wild pony, all eyes and spirit. I love your spirit, Clara. I don't know of any woman, let alone girl, who would have done what you've just done, for Jack.'

He was certainly intoxicated. When I thought about it, his life was very boring, just overseeing the workers on the farm. And maybe this expedition, chasing us to Harwich, spying in the darkness, had livened him up a little. But I thought he was talking out of his head. I didn't answer, not sure if he meant it. Was that my choice, to go to bed with him in exchange for his saying nothing of Jack's whereabouts to his father? It seemed (after my experience with Martin) a much easier deal than losing Rattler.

But I found I was trembling. There was far more to it than that.

'Would you not tell your father then, that you found where Jack was going?'

'If you are kind to me, yes.'

'I don't believe you.'

'How can I convince you?' He leaned across the table then and took my hands, which were toying with my wineglass, in his. My hands were not like Margaret's. They were hard and calloused, the nails short and none too clean. But he held them in a way that made me feel as if I were some sort of princess. He stroked them as if they were white like Margaret's and precious and soft as silk. I was going to snatch them away, but couldn't. I looked up.

'Wild little pony,' he said.

I was going to jeer at him, but couldn't.

This was nothing like Martin.

'Think about it, Clara – what a simple way to save Jack! I promise to you I will tell my father I lost him on the road, that I never saw you. And I will make you happy too, that's another promise.'

I could well believe this already, the way my senses were leaving me. His face was close to mine across the table and his dark eyes were regarding me with a light that seemed to spark into my own.

'It's not true that you're ugly. I only say it to see you

angry. I think you're lovely, Clara, so brave and strong. I wish we could be friends.'

'We can't be friends,' I said. My voice sounded very strange.

'Let me love you, Clara. Be kind.'

I tried to say what did he know about kindness, but the words did not come. He got up and pulled me after him. I followed him across the room. He said something to the landlady and she nodded towards the stairs with a shrug. She seemed to know him. Then he took my hand and led me up to a bedroom.

I cannot explain now what happened, for it is beyond my comprehension. I hated Nat, yet he made me love him. Yes, I loved him, in the four-poster bed inside the embroidered hangings, I loved him as if he were a long-awaited husband, a lover such as Ann had, returned from the war. I loved him as Margaret had loved him, all my being awakening into this amazing realm, like paradise, so long discussed and now, at last, experienced. Nat, the vile tyrant, so beguiling, led me gently, gently along the way, and the low spring sun slanted in under the eaves and made a halo round his dark head. I could not see his eyes or his expression, but I could feel his hard hand gentle on my body and smell the sweat of his hard ride and the scent he used to cover it. I heard his heartbeat over my breast. I hated him and loved him and let him love me, in exchange for Jack's life. It was a good bargain but it left my mind in turmoil.

He fell asleep, and I still had my arms round him

and his head lay on my shoulder. It seemed to me impossible, what had happened, yet I lay there and felt his breath on my cheek and the tickling of his curly black hair making me want to sneeze, and he was as real in my arms as any man would ever be. Who could I tell what had happened? There was no one. I would not even dare tell Ann. Nicholas, perhaps Nicholas, but he would not respect me any more. But for Jack's life? If I were ever to tell Jack, he would kill Nat, I know that. And be hanged for my saving his life!

It was impossible to give it any clear consideration, so I decided to enjoy it instead. My life was not very full of enjoyment. No wonder the village girls all longed for this marvellous thing. How many found it? Very few is my guess, in their hurried couplings under the hedgerows with the ignorant village boys. But my brain had swung so dizzily with fear, disappointment, triumph and disaster in the last twenty-four hours that I, like Nat, fell asleep almost immediately. When I awoke it was late afternoon, the sky already darkening and a thin rain creeping down the windows.

Nat was standing in front of the window, smiling. He had wound and tied his cravat and was shrugging into his black riding coat. I found myself staring at him like a mesmerized rabbit, with my mass of tangled hair (which he had lovingly unbraided) in an unfamiliar blanket over my shoulders.

'Much as I want to stay with you, it's too dangerous here for us to be seen together. The London coach is due and I want to be away before that. We must go our separate ways now. I shall tell my father Jack caught a ship for the north, to honour our bargain. I promise I shan't breathe a word of this to anyone, if you will promise me the same. We never met, nor saw each other. My father will kill me if he finds out the truth.'

'I won't say either. Not to anybody.'

If I were to tell my father, I know he would approve my action, for Jack, but I would be besmirched in his eyes. It would make him deeply, hopelessly angry, and he did not deserve that grief.

'I will ride on fast, and you can come on at your leisure. I shall pay the bills here, and they will treat you like a lady.' He laughed at his dig.

'Thank you,' I said, trying not to be sarcastic.

I could not bear to look at him now, trying to be glad that he was going, trying to suppress the wild instinct that longed for him to stay. With dark coming on, the candles lit, the flames reflected in his black eyes . . . my mind was wandering like a lunatic's, trying not to recall the feel of his body against mine. Oh Margaret, I thought, if only I had known! Poor Margaret, a moth to a flame, she had been quite helpless. But at least he had loved her. I was just a game.

He went.

Shortly I heard the clatter of Crocus's hooves on the cobbles outside, and the departing trot, fast fading. I lay back, feeling quite exhausted. But I believed what he had said, that Jack was safe, and after a while my senses calmed and my satisfaction returned. Jack and Martin were free. That was all that mattered. Of my adventures I would say nothing, not a word to anyone.

23

I went to see Nicholas.

I needed desperately to get out of the house, away, alone. I longed to take Hoppy or Tilly in the old cart and ride through the woods with Nicholas as I used to, talking, talking, but Nicholas was now too ill to leave his room. But at least, with him, I felt free of the terrible guilt that was bearing me down. Why guilt, when I had saved Jack's life? I suppose because I enjoyed what I did with Nat so much, and could not stop thinking about it. I felt cursed.

I was going to tell him, but in the end I didn't. I didn't tell anybody. I think Ann sensed there was something going on that I wasn't revealing, for she gave me a strange look when I was on my way wearily to bed, and said, 'Is there anything else? You seem—' She shrugged, did not finish her sentence, but came up to me and put a hand on my forehead, gently pushing back my untidy hair. Then she kissed me.

'God bless you, Clara. You take too much on your shoulders.'

My father had shed tears of joy when he heard of

the boys' successful escape. That was what mattered, none of the other things. Not to them.

I dashed up to Nicholas's room, as if for sanctuary. He was sitting in his old armchair, blue-lipped, his breathing painfully shallow. He surely had only a very short time left, and I could not bear for him to go. To lose Nicholas was even worse than Margaret, whom I had never loved, after all.

I kissed him and hugged him and told him that Jack and Martin were safe. I told him the story.

He said, 'They say Nat went down to Harwich looking for them. Lucky you didn't meet!'

I turned away, feeling my face reddening.

'My father went to see Ebenezer. He tried to tell him he had brought it all on himself. But you can imagine the answer he got.'

'He's brave, your father!'

'Yes, well, he's got God on his side, hasn't he? It makes a difference. You do it for God. You speak by proxy.'

Darling Rev, I thought. How dreadful for him when Nicholas died. They were so close.

'He told me – you wouldn't believe – that it would be a blessing if Eb were struck by a bolt of lightning. My father to say that! He thinks Nat is not nearly so bad as Eb and if he were in charge things would be a sight better.'

'Yes, I think so too.'

How could I disagree?

'Another thing that's happened since I saw you. Jane told me. Can you believe, Aunt Doom is getting friendly with Mrs Grover, that old cow of a dairymaid. Mrs Grover invited her to tea. Aunt Doom has made out how badly she's been treated, and how she's a cut above the rest of the cottage people, and Mrs Grover believed her and now they're friends.'

'They make a good couple! Ugh!'

'I suppose they neither of them have any other friends. We should be sorry for them really. Father prays for them, of course. Not very hard, not like he prayed for Jack and Martin. And you.'

Saying all that tired Nicholas out, and he lay back in his chair and shut his eyes. I looked at him and a great hard lump came into my throat. He was as close a friend as anyone could have, my only true friend apart from Martin out of my family, and what was I going to do without him? He had, as always, the old pony blanket wrapped round him with the faded name, Prince, embroidered in the corner. He swore Prince was now in paradise. Soon he would join him. Would they gallop together through the Elysian fields in eternal sunshine as once they had galloped after hounds through the depths of earthly winter? How I would love to believe it! My memory of him, glowing with spirits and health on the mud-spattered little pony, was still fresh even when his gangly, emaciated body was at my side. He was just sixteen, a year older than me. And God is love, said the Rev!

I sat beside him for a long time. I took his hand and held it and kissed it and he opened his eyes and smiled.

'And what about the match on Saturday, now you've no rider? Everyone wants to know.'

Two days away. I had not given it serious thought, so much on my mind. It was too late to cancel it, unless Father had already done so, or perhaps another contender was in line to challenge Crocus . . . I must wake up and find out.

'I need a rider—'

'Why don't you ride him? There's no rules against it.' The old spark came for a moment into Nicholas's eyes. 'Women hunt, after all. What's the difference?'

It was true that this possibility had crossed my own mind. I had just ridden a hundred and twenty miles without even thinking about it: I was certainly not incapable. And, above all, I knew Rattler and his ways. He knew me as a rider better than anyone else. But would Father let me? It might be considered shocking in such a man's world, and Father was not a radical man. He liked the proprieties.

'I'll have to ask Father. It's the best idea. There's no one else I would trust.'

There were certainly men who would jump at the chance if I asked them, but Rattler was young and green, not an old pro like Tilly. Tilly only needed a rider to make it legal, for she did it all on her own, knowing when to take a breather, when to fight, how to put the other horse in its place. Rattler was far from battle-hardened like the old mare. He was still learning and I didn't want him to win at cost to his future. A professional man might whip him into winning and put him off the game for life.

It depended on Father, for if he forbad me I would not argue. If he forbad me, he would have to take the ride himself.

'Yes,' I said, the excitement rising suddenly. 'It's a great idea.'

'Oh Clara, do! *Do it!* Beat Nat yourself—' He started to cough, laughing. Coughing.

'Oh Nick, you idiot! Why do you have to die!' It just burst out of me, from my heart which – if hearts do break – was breaking then. I helped him, supporting him forward, reaching for the towel and all the while he was coughing he was laughing at me. His eyes were bright with fever.

'If you do it,' he whispered, 'beat Nat – I can die – happy.'

'You will die happy,' I promised.

When the spasm had passed he lay back, eyes closed, barely conscious, and I slipped out. Jane saw me and came to the foot of the stairs.

'I will watch him,' she said.

She was so loyal and loving, he was in good hands. Thank God the Rev had had the courage to throw out Aunt Doom and get Jane back. I told her what he had said.

'If I tell my father, it's for Nicholas to die happy, he'll have to allow it!'

'Oh why not, Clara? There'll be a huge turnout if it gets around that you're riding. Everyone will come to gawp. And if you beat Nat – everyone will *love* it, that he gets beaten by a girl. Imagine Ebenezer! Oh what bliss! Your father *must* allow it!'

288

I was very doubtful myself, but it was a good argument to persuade him, making Nicholas happy. I told Ann first, so that she would support me. I could see from her eyes that she was excited at the thought.

'Your father said he'd pull out, but I don't think he's spoken to Nat yet. I told him half the county is coming and he'd be very unpopular to cancel it – they all love a day out so – and he said he'd try Arthur Simmonds. Whether he has or not, I don't know.'

Arthur Simmonds was a farmer in the next village, an accomplished horseman. If Arthur said yes, I wouldn't stand a chance.

But Arthur – oh heavenly bliss! – had to go to his sister's wedding in Norwich. Ann and I put our idea to Father, and I told him Nicholas's words.

'He's dying, Father, it would be so wonderful for him. And me to do it. If I was a boy, you wouldn't hesitate, and everyone says I'm as good as a boy. Better than a boy! You let me do a man's job, after all. Nobody will be a bit surprised if I ride.'

I knew this was true. It was a long argument, Father so recalcitrant, and when he eventually gave in we had an even longer argument about riding cross-saddle, which I wanted so badly.

'You know perfectly well if I ride side-saddle, it will be a huge disadvantage. He's not used to it and it will be much harder to balance him properly.'

Ann took my side, but so tactfully that Father did not notice. He agreed in the end but with much misgiving. I hugged him with joy and he kissed me and said, 'It's not that I doubt you. In fact I know you ride better than Jack. It's just not a lady's job, that's all.'

'I'm not a lady!'

He laughed. 'No. That's the trouble.'

So the word went round that I was going to ride Rattler, and the betting started in earnest. I had to forget all my late adventures, my secrets, and concentrate on the job in hand. Rattler – my dear Rattler – was going to make good, he *had* to, even if it was his first match. I knew he was fit enough. But to beat the admirable Crocus was asking a lot, and anything could happen with a youngster. The crowd and the atmosphere might get to him, he might be frightened by spectators alongside or even – how did I know? – might not have the bottle to dig deep when it mattered, when he was tired and it was beginning to hurt. He might not be a true champion after all.

But when I went into the stable and saw him, dozing in the evening dusk with his lower lip hanging down and his bony old nose drooping over the empty manger, I was suddenly filled with a great thrill that this was my horse – he was a champion, there could be no doubt. His silk coat bulged with hard muscle; there wasn't an ounce of flab on him. He was like a Newmarket horse, primed for the Derby.

But Crocus was too, I reminded myself. Perhaps the match was between the two riders, the cruel and strong Nat Grover, and the weakling girl. I thought all the bets would be on Nat. But I would show him . . . how it mattered now, after all there was between us, that I should come out on top! (But I could not stop myself thinking about that afternoon at the inn. All the time it kept coming back to me, not with the disgust it should have raised, but with a secret joy that I could not keep from welling up.)

I did not see Nat before the match. I heard a lot of gossip, about Jack and Martin getting away and Nat chasing them, but nothing about myself. I was known to have gone to fetch the horses back, no more than that. Everyone was thrilled that Jack and Martin had escaped, after the special constables were out combing the countryside and the military up from Colchester. The general feeling was of great joy that Grover's had been torched, the threshing machine badly damaged, and the boys away scot-free.

So when the Saturday dawned there was already a festive atmosphere in the village, everyone awaiting the appearance of Nat, the villain, and me, the heroine. It was not how I would have wished it. The weather was perfect, calm and sunny, with the ground soft but not muddy. Father had given the men a day off and they turned the old horses out for an extra rest and no one would allow me to work, only on Rattler. He was already as shining as a really fit horse should be, although he still had his winter coat. Ann and Father himself had gone over his saddle and bridle and Ann had found me a black riding jacket with skirts that would hide most of my unladylike breeches, and a pair of black boots that had been Jack's several years back now stood all buffed up waiting to receive my delicate feet. Father tied me a hunting stock like Miss Charlotte's and pinned it with a gold pin, and Ann braided my hair tightly and pinned it up and topped me off with an amazing riding hat (borrowed I'm sure from Charlotte), black and jaunty with a little feather at the side and a veil. I refused the veil, wanting to see where I was going after all, and Ann stitched it up out of the way. I must say I looked terribly smart, and my blood warmed at the thought of the impression I might make on Nat (if he recognized me at all).

We all rode out together, me and Rattler, Father on Tilly, and Ann and Ellen on Hoppy. Billy came running up the drive and I scooped him up so that he rode in front of me, all the way down to the village.

When I saw the huge crowd that had gathered there I must say a great scare came over me and my heart plummeted. After all this, to lose out to the Grovers! It would be a desperate defeat. And I could not be unaware of the fact, from all the shouting going on, that Nat and Crocus were clear favourites. The fact that Rattler's rider was a girl was not popular, except with the village people who knew me and the circumstances. The old horse-masters and breeding farmers were shaking their heads, no doubt thinking their sport degraded. I saw their eyes light up with appreciation when Nat and Crocus arrived, and could not help but blink myself at the splendid sight they made, both so handsome and confident. Nat rode up to me and his eyes raked me up and down, insolent and – I think – angry. He did not want to be pitted against a girl. It made his position slightly derisory, I could see.

But I greeted him politely. Billy slipped down and

went to Rattler's head, my staunch groom. The stewards started clearing the road, and Father came beside me on Tilly and said, 'There's always another day, remember. The horse is more important than the race. Be sensible, Clara.'

Tilly was getting excited, no doubt thinking that she was about to race, and Father had to ride her out of the way then, but his words sobered me. It wasn't about Nat and me, it was the horses. It wasn't about Jack, and Billy's arm, and Margaret's death: it was between two good horses. The thought settled me.

'Are you ready?'

The timekeeper came over to us and we followed him to the post outside the inn. The green was filled with people right up to the squire's gates, but when the timekeeper shouted at them, a hush fell. Nat rounded up beside me on Crocus. I could feel Rattler trembling, and myself too, seeing Nat so strong and arrogant and remembering – God help me – his body on mine.

'Steady . . . go!'

My heels came down sharply, my hands gave, and Rattler went off with a leap to a great roar from the crowd. We had practised starting, not to break, and he was foot perfect, straight into his long trot, tossing his mane up, twitching his rabbity ears to the noise behind him. I heard my name shouted on all sides as we went down the street between the cottages, but not one cry for Grover. Outside the Grover farm gate, old Ebenezer stood watching, leaning on his stick, scowling as ever. This was not sport to him, but an opportunity for revenge. I went close, hoping to throw mud in his eye. He took a step back and I laughed. I couldn't help it: Rattler felt so marvellous, so strong, and with the action I was now all happy and optimistic. Wasn't this what I had always wanted – to ride my own horse in a match? It may have come about through the most terrible misfortune, but now I was doing what I had always wanted. So I laughed, and Nat beside me gave me a strange look and said, 'I hope you'll be laughing at the end.'

I could tell now that he hated me, for putting him in this position, riding against a girl, and I think he knew that – even if I was a girl – it would be no walk-over. I knew he respected my horse and my riding. But now, in public, he was all sneers and hate. It helped me, so that I could hate too and forget my terrible instincts. I put all that out of my mind and concentrated on working up a good strong rhythm to make it easier for Rattler, to get him swinging, eating up the ground. I think he had a longer stride than Crocus if I could coax him to find it. Crocus went ahead, very fast, while I was trying to find the right cruising stride, settling Rattler, getting him to concentrate. He was still all ears and eyes around him, not attending to the job in hand. The big crowd and the jostle of people behind us and the cheers of spectators as we passed was all new to him and distracting. I spoke to him, steady, steady, my words mostly rubbish but my voice encouraging, sing song, to the beat I wanted. Once he settled, I thought he would go for ever. Our training had not been in vain.

Having ridden a hundred and twenty miles in the last few days, a mere twenty, even at racing speed, did not deter me. Rattler was a very comfortable horse, like all good trotters, and when I got him going I was able to enjoy myself. Crocus was ahead of me but I did not bother about that. Nat was not a judicious rider and lacked experience. I had been brought up to it by my father, a great practitioner in the art, and it stood me in good stead. He had always brought Tilly on at the end, conserving her strength in the early stages so that she was able to trounce the other tired horse near the finish. Rattler had the turn of foot to do the same. That was the plan. But whether it would work or not remained to be seen.

We passed Rattler's birthplace. His old dam was staked out on the common, but she did not know him, scarcely lifting her head as we passed. But the old farmer and his wife stood at the gate shouting like mad people and waving a Union Jack, along with all their neighbours. It was fun riding to the cheers of the populace. I think more people had turned out than usual because it was a girl riding, and astride too. For all the cheers were for me. I think Nat was really hating it. I could see his straight back and Crocus's red tail swirling, not close enough to get spattered by the stones and mud of his passing, but nicely out of reach. Close enough.

When he went round the five-mile post and came back past me, then I saw his determination. He did not smile, nor even look at me, watching for stones ahead on the road. He had Crocus fairly bowling along, but I could see as usual that the little horse was being slightly overpressed. Too soon. It raised my hopes considerably. Rattler was steady as a rock now, and the rowdy spectators we met on the way back did not faze him. His big hooves were going *bang bang bang* in perfect rhythm and he had his head down in his characteristic fashion. I was still talking to him and my heart was swinging in time to his going. He needed Tilly's killer instinct to beat the other horse at the end, but it was too soon yet and perhaps he didn't know about killer instinct. But I think he did. I would see.

As we approached the village again, word had gone ahead from the riders as to who would be the first to appear. Crocus got a rousing cheer but not nearly so big a cheer as Rattler got. Rattler of course thought it was the end of his effort and started to pull up as he approached the Queen's Head. He was most surprised at my lusty chiding and skidded round the post, nearly losing his feet. At this point Crocus was about fifty yards in front of me. Father rode alongside on Tilly and said, 'How does he feel? He looks good.'

'Yes, he feels great.'

'Don't lose any more ground, but you needn't come up to him until round the last post. Then work at it. But if he's spent, Clara, don't force him. He's only a baby.'

'We must beat him, Father.'

And Father grinned, pulling Tilly away. My blood was up now, every stride inching a fraction nearer to the flying hooves ahead. Now the road was straight and clear ahead, I could feel Rattler going in that long, low, raking way that I loved, game for ever. Twenty miles was nothing, after all. Rattler was a good horse – I knew it! All my hopes were going to be vindicated. Jack avenged. For Nicholas! Oh Nicholas, how I wish you could see me now! How I wish you were beside me on that pony Prince! Dear Nicholas was going to die happy, the least I could do for him.

When we went round the post out in the country after the completion of fifteen miles, I was considerably closer to Crocus. Nat noticed with a deep scowl and I saw his spurs scrape into the sweating flanks as he came past. Rattler made to turn and join him and I had to check him sharply, but then the post was there and he stumbled round it, not very elegantly but at least without breaking step. I gathered him sternly and got him balanced again and set him off. This was serious now, the time when steadily, steadily, he must gain on his rival. The home run. I must not leave it too late; he needed every chance.

There was no sweat on his coat at all, only flecks of foam specking my black coat from his soft mouth. But Crocus was sweating up quite badly, more I think from the feel of Nat's tension than from lack of condition. He had not yet broken into a canter but I felt sure that if Nat went on niggling at him, as I could see quite clearly he was doing, he was very likely to do so. That would make my task easier but I could not depend on it happening.

'Come on, Rattler, lengthen, lengthen!' He had to understand, like Tilly, that the horse in front was to be overtaken, the whole point of the game. If not now, very soon.

We began to get gravel thrown up from Crocus's hooves flicking at us and I edged Rattler to one side a little to prevent it. Nat glanced round. He must have had a good and frightening view of us, hardly two lengths away. Still Rattler showed no sign of fatigue, but I was getting drips of Crocus's sweat on my jacket. I saw Nat's spurs dig again, and saw the drops of blood drawn. I wore no spurs at all, nor ever had, and I felt for dear Crocus, but my own blood was up now and no compassion was going to stand in my way: we *had* to beat Nat Grover. Not just for Nicholas any more, but for Margaret, Jack, Billy and everyone the Grovers had harmed, and for me too, to expunge the guilt I felt at submitting to Nat. I had my eyes on his elegantly suited back and saw the black hair hanging sweatily over the edge of his cravat: Nat was rattled, I could tell. What a splendid word – rattled! I could see it by the way his head kept slightly turning to see my approach, by the high colour in his face and the clenching of his lips. To be beaten by a girl . . . it would be the final humiliation, in the view of half the county!

The spectators were coming at us from the green now, with ridden stewards flanking the way, and I felt Rattler's attention erring. Crocus shied suddenly, at a stupid boy on a grey cob coming too close, and broke stride. Nat yelled out and yanked Crocus cruelly into his circle and – just as my heart swung in celebration – Rattler decided to put in a couple of canter strides as well, and a buck for good measure.

'Rattler!' My scolding voice surprised him, for he made his circle obediently. I had so rarely had to practise this manoeuvre that I was frightened it would utterly confuse him. Crocus, yanked round on his skittering hindquarters, was quickly back into his trot, but my circle lost me a couple of lengths. And Rattler was now unbalanced, inattentive, attracted by the shouting spectators. Had we thrown it away? My heart was in my mouth, seeing Nat's grin as he glanced behind.

But I could see that Crocus, unlike Rattler, was now very tired. He was highly strung and Nat had never had a calming influence on any animal. Crocus had fretted his strength away. Rattler, by contrast, showed no sign of fatigue at all. So I dug in my heels and spoke to him sternly to attend to the matter in hand, and I got him going and balanced again and pressed my knees hard into his sides to make his great shoulders power to their utmost. And he obeyed me, perhaps recognizing my scolding for his canter strides, and his head went down and he fairly flew after Crocus. Maybe now he knew what was wanted, that the horse in front was to be trounced, for his whole action suddenly seemed intent on just that. His ears were pricked up, flicking back momentarily to hear my encouragement.

After nearly twenty miles flat out I realized that I was beginning to tire, but my competitive spirit was galvanizing me to ride as well as I knew how. I could see that Crocus was falling apart but Nat's strength was compelling him to make the post now only just round the next bend.

'Come on, Rattler!'

I could hear the cry, and the words from my own lips, and Rattler came up to Crocus's flank. My knee was within inches of Nat's. He glanced round, his face contorted with anger, but my eyes were on the road ahead and the first glimpse of the swinging inn sign. Our presence by his side seemed to dash Crocus for, whatever his effort, his stride shortened and he stumbled. Nat wrenched him cruelly together. Rattler sailed on, head up now to hear the wild cheering from the green, and we passed clear by Crocus and left him with a thick black tail whirling in his face.

We came powering down to the post alone, and it took me to the far side of the green to pull up, so eager was Rattler's going. There was shouting all over the green and a great crowd came to engulf us as Rattler at last slowed to a walk. He put his head down and shook his mane and gave some great snorts and stopped to scratch his nose on his foreleg, as if the whole match was just in the ordinary day's work. He wasn't even blowing, nor sweating at all. A lot of farmers I didn't know came up to pass remarks and enthuse over my horse, and Billy came pushing through the crowd to take my rein, so proud, I could see, that he was almost swelled up with it. I slipped off to loosen the girths and let Billy keep the honour of leading him back. It was so little compared with what he would never do. I did not want to come face to face with Nat, for I was sorry for him, stupidly, now the deed was done.

Father and Ann came through the throng, their

faces wreathed in smiles. I felt very conspicuous now I was off the horse and wished I were back in my skirts, but Father didn't seem to care any more. He was ecstatic at our performance.

'No one could have ridden him better. Your timing was lovely – why, I don't think Jack could have done more, lost his head more likely when he broke stride! You're a wonder, Clara, and the horse could be one of the greats, who knows? His first match, and to beat that Grover horse, that's a real feather in his cap. First time off, eh?'

I had never seen Father so happy, in spite of all that had happened. But maybe he was thinking, if Jack had been here to ride, it might have turned out differently. Jack was into a new life now. I suddenly thought that there was no grief after all in what had happened, for Jack had been bored with life and now he was starting a new one. Who knows what would happen to him next? He had his way to make, but was free of persecution, at least. I had Nat to thank for that. But Nat was the last person I wanted to see.

'I must go and tell Nicholas,' I told my parents. 'Billy will see to Rattler.'

'We'll follow along then. And see you at home.'

'Tell Billy not to let him drink too much straight away . . .' But Billy was well trained, I needn't have worried.

I guessed Ann would go home and Father would go to the inn. He wouldn't want to miss the celebrations, and take the opportunity of advertising Rattler as a stallion.

So I pushed my way back through the crowds and made up the green to the vicarage. I felt very conspicuous in my clothes, no longer being on a horse, but Nicholas was bowled over by my outfit.

'I know you've won – I could hear the shouting! Oh, you're a marvel, Clara! I knew you'd do it.'

'I didn't, not till right the end. Oh, *he's* the marvel, Nicholas! He's wonderful!'

I realized I was very tired suddenly. My legs felt all wobbly, and the dear Rev said, 'My dear, come and sit down and have some tea. You must be exhausted. It is so kind of you to call, when everyone is shouting for you.'

I had found Nicholas in the front garden, watching all the shenanigans. His face was bright with fever and his eyes seemed to glitter. Perhaps it was the excitement but I didn't think so. I took his arm and we went in together. Jane had set a lovely tea in the study, in front of the fire. We all sat down. It was such a sudden contrast, the eternal quiet of this familiar room and the respectability of the tea set, the white lace cloth, the lovely old china, the Rev's old-fashioned manners, that I felt I was suddenly in another world. A very comforting world, far from the ardours of my own. It reminded me of what Ann had said about bettering myself. Fresh from the extremes of the rough masculine world I was familiar with, I felt the contrast sharply, almost with a pang. For what might be? Did I want, like Jack, something more from my life than Small Gains offered? But I had no education, only my animal skills. The thoughts whirled through my head as I took my place at the table.

'You're mother,' Nicholas said, nodding to the teapot.

'I'm a bit smelly,' I said, realizing that my hands were hot and sweaty, my face covered in dirt. 'I ought to wash.'

But, having sat down, I didn't think I could get up again in a hurry.

The vicar laughed, reading my thoughts, and said, 'It's all right. Aunt Agnes is with us no longer. A nice cup of tea is what you want.'

How right he was.

'It seems God saw fit to punish the Grovers for their behaviour in a very satisfactory way. Although I doubt that they will change their ways. Nicholas insisted on coming down to watch.'

'I sat up on the squire's gates and had a very good view. You were splendid, Clara. I knew you'd win though, all along.'

'That's more than I did then. But the way Nat rides – he frightens Crocus, instead of giving him confidence.'

'That's his way, bullying,' Nick said. 'But you're a cajoler. Isn't she, Father?'

'I don't think there's any such word as cajoler. But if there is, yes, she's a cajoler.'

'She cajoles me,' said Nicholas.

The Reverend looked slightly worried at this and Nicholas added, 'To keep well. She's very good for me.'

'Yes, I know that. You are fortunate in your friends, if not in much else.'

'True,' said Nicholas loftily.

I laughed. 'I think Ann borrowed my hat from Miss Charlotte. Do you recognize it?'

'It's her style. She has a great array of hats, mostly cast off by her sisters. She's not much into clothes, like you, Clara.'

'No, and nor are you, wrapped in Prince's old blanket every day.'

'We have a mind above such things,' Nicholas said.

It was so strange, coming into this teatime banter after the rigours I had just experienced, that I felt as if I had changed into somebody else. I felt just at home here, yet it was a world away from my own. It was so beguiling, this taste of civilized living unwed to farming, independent of weather and seasons and animals' needs, where one could talk of hats and suchlike rubbish, and eat little cakes with icing on instead of the great slabs of fruitcake that graced our table at home. My head spun with the doubts and longings it set up in me, the contrast so sweet just at this minute, when I was fresh from rigours I sought in my own life. I didn't have to pursue the path I had chosen, after all. I could always make a change, like Jack, even though his was forced on him. I wasn't sure how, but Ann had half encouraged me with her talk of bettering myself. Marriage was usually the key to change, like the dairymaid Maggie to the powerful Ebenezer, but I saw no such partner anywhere on my horizons.

My weary brain flitted over these unfamiliar

hallucinations – as surely they were – and left me feeling disturbed and almost faint.

'I must go back,' I said. 'They will be expecting me.'

'You look tired,' old Bywater said. 'I wish I had a horse to drive you. It was kind of you to call in when I'm sure your family wants to celebrate with you.'

I remembered my vow, to win so that Nicholas could die happy. Well, it was done and the dying seemed fairly imminent, Nicholas so obviously feverish, hectic colour over his prominent cheekbones.

I shed some tears as I left the house, loving Nicholas so much, but then as I came to the road the fresh hoofmarks so deeply indented reminded me of my amazing victory. My exhaustion dropped away to be replaced by a strong, crazy exhilaration and a wild surge of love for life, my life, which then I would not have changed for all the richest opportunities in the land. I capered down the road in my daft clothes, and all thoughts of little iced cakes dissolved in the cold spring breeze.

A week after the match, news came that Eb had sacked Sim. He said he was too old.

Father said the time was ripe for Rattler to go travelling as a stallion and Sim would be just the man to travel him, experienced and trustworthy. We had had quite a few enquiries about Rattler's services after the match, and knew that a tour of the locality offering the stallion's services would make us quite a lot of money.

'Sim would be grateful for the job,' Ann said. 'He'll die if he has to go in the workhouse.'

'Can I go with him? Rattler needs me around, you know he does.'

'It's not a job for a girl.'

'Nor was riding him in the match! Nor going to Harwich after Jack! Father, you know I'm not a lady – you said it yourself. I am Rattler's handler – it *is* my job!'

I could see perfectly well why I couldn't travel Rattler myself, staying in strange places every night, unattended. But with Sim it would be perfectly acceptable. Or so I thought.

'I must admit, your name's got around as a strange one, after the match. No one would be surprised at your travelling with the stallion with Sim, I daresay.'

Ann laughed. 'It would be a nice break for her, like a holiday. Seeing new places, meeting new people. If she goes to farms where we're known, no harm will come of it, I'm sure. It will be good for her.'

All I could think of was visiting Great Meadows and seeing Prosper again in his own home. He had, after all, more or less invited me. I told Father the Mayes wanted Rattler to visit. I told him Prosper had mentioned it after one of the matches. This seemed to help persuade him that the idea was a good one and he started to make out a list of likely farms, putting them in order so that we made an itinerary, going on from one farm to the next. I noticed Great Meadows was last, on the way home. The stallion stayed at each farm for a few days and farmers brought their mares in to him, and the stallion minder – or minders in our case – stayed at the farm and handled the matings.

Father sent out advertisements to the papers and posters which an errand boy took out and pasted up in the relevant places, and I got ready for my royal progress. I wasn't going to wear breeches! A travelling stallion was not ridden, but led in side-reins, all spruced up to be admired by everyone he passed. I only hoped no one knew about scraggy old Betty, his first and only produce, little Billy's darling. Now Betty was a two-year-old and could be broken to ride, Billy was not bothered with a pony. He said he would prefer to have Betty for his own. I promised him he could have him. He needed a better name, Billy decided, and I agreed. 'You think of one. Just don't link it with Rattler, that's all.' The quieter we kept about Betty the better. I convinced myself Betty was a freak, and such a produce would not happen again. Of course, Rattler was totally untried. He hadn't got Tilly in foal again. But people liked a new stallion. If it proved good, they could boast to have had the seeing eye. We had reckoned we would have plenty of takers when we took to the road. I just prayed that Rattler wouldn't let us down.

Father was missing Jack and Martin on the farm and I was slightly worried about him when I left. We hadn't heard anything from them in spite of their promises, but it was early days. They might not write if they had no good news to give, but we all worried about what they were up to. Nat had obviously kept his promise about not telling his father where they had gone to, for Ebenezer was still complaining bitterly about the damage done, and no culprits caught. The man Firmin had torched a machine in Norfolk since and had been apprehended this time, and this seemed to have calmed Eb down a bit. His threshing machine had been sent back to the makers for repairs. If Firmin hanged, we predicted that there would be no more attacks in our district.

But Sim and I put all this grief behind us when we set out with Rattler on a beautiful morning at the end of April. Since our match, my slight fame, or notoriety, as a female rider had spread around and everyone recognized us even when we were quite far from home. Travelling along the road we made quite a triumphal progress. Our first port of call was fifteen miles away, all along the main road to the east, to a farm that had promised to make us welcome. Rattler was puzzled by having to walk, unridden, but after several bucks on the end of his gleaming brass chain he settled down and jig-jogged along beside us. Sim carried a pack with our belongings, and some food and drink, and I had a bag of sovereigns strapped round my waist. I had dressed carefully, smartly for me, in a new dark skirt and fine boots, not the cloddy ones I wore round the stable. I wore a good black jacket and a navy-blue spotted hunting stock over my blouse, and my hair was pinned up, Ann having decided I needed to look as old as possible.

'Responsible,' she said, and laughed.

I felt responsible. To be in charge of Rattler, high-mettled with the spring air heating his young blood, was no mean duty. But dear Sim, calm and silent, plodding beside me, could be relied on if the horse became troublesome, for he was an expert horseman. I couldn't have asked for better.

People turned out to chat to us as we passed and most farmers seemed to know who we were. There was a gratifying response to Father's advertisements, for at our first stay we received five mares for Rattler to cover. We were made welcome in the farm and I was given a room to myself, very small, but clean and comfortable. We ate with the men. It was a big, hard-working farm, not given to airs and graces, but it had an air of prosperity, different from our own farm which I thought always gave the impression of struggling. Perhaps not so much lately now that Father was a much happier man, but there never seemed to be enough money for a new waggon or a whole set of harness, only enough for patches and mending. This farm had lovely freshly painted waggons and the farmer had a drilling machine and was interested in buying a threshing machine. He knew all about Eb Grover and he knew that Jack was my brother, on the run.

'He was wrong, your Jack,' he said. 'You can't stop progress. Go along with it and make it work for you.'

'It was Mr Grover, more than just the threshing machine. He treats people so cruelly. If he had been a kind man, he wouldn't have been attacked.'

'Aye, I know his reputation. I don't have dealings with him, he takes advantage. No one shed tears for him when his ricks were burned, that's a fact.'

Having scarcely left the village all my life, I found my stays on different farms eye-opening. I suppose we mostly lodged in the bigger, more prosperous farms which had spare stables and barns for the business of mating mares to a stallion and could put up with the bother, but they made our Small Gains look very small beer by comparison. The houses were much bigger and the living easier with servants in the house; the children were educated by governesses and there were hunters in the stable as well as workhorses. We were treated kindly, and Rattler was much admired. Word went ahead quickly and he was well patronized. Word had also got round about our match with Crocus, and the fact that I had been the rider made me something of a freak show. I was glad Ann had togged me out to look like a female in spite of the job I was doing. I found I was quickly able to disillusion the men who came preparing to treat me like one of the boys. In fact I learned a great deal about how to handle myself during the tour, meeting so many different people.

One morning when we were due to move on and I had been sleeping in a smart bedroom, I was unaccountably sick as soon as I climbed out of bed. I was never sick, and was so surprised I nearly didn't grab the chamber pot in time. Horrified that I had so nearly spewed all over a very fine carpet, I was then embarrassed as to what to do with the contents of the chamberpot. I didn't dare put it in the slop bucket, smelly as it was. I looked out of the window and luckily there was a rose bed below so I tipped it into that and hoped the lady of the house wouldn't be inspecting her buds that morning. I supposed it was something I had eaten, although I couldn't think what. I felt slightly dizzy and ill, but nothing that the fresh air wouldn't cure. We were due to walk on another twenty miles that morning.

I washed and dressed and went out to Rattler. Sim had already fed him and he scarcely needed grooming, so shiny was his coat. His pleasurable job was obviously suiting him for he was full of spirits. When we brought him out, ready to leave, he was prancing about like a foal. He had served four mares at that farm, and the sovereign bag round my waist was getting quite heavy. I would have to unload some of the money on to Sim at the rate we were going on. Sim was a great man for knowing how to get from farm to farm. Without him I would have got lost many a time, but he knew all the roads and mostly knew the farms we were visiting. Unlike many countrymen, he had worked as a horseman all over the neighbourhood. He said he got bored if he didn't move on, although it did not pay him in advancement. There were many good places he could have stayed put in, and been looked after in his old age.

'I'm paying for it now,' he said. 'With no security. When you're gone seventy, not many farms will take you on when they don't know you. That's why I had to take the job Grover offered.'

And, travelling myself for the first time in my life, I understood how curiosity might get the better of you, to move on. The job itself was much the same on every farm, and could get boring after a few years. To meet new people would always be a lure.

'I tried my hand at Newmarket as well. I worked in racing and saw the first Derby run at Epsom in seventeen eighty. Won by Diomed it was, but no one knew then what a big race it would become. I've worked as an ostler in coaching inns, I've been guard on a coach, I've been stud-groom for a duke, farrier for a while . . . groom to a vicar. I haven't been bored.'

'Do you know the next farm, the one we're going to tonight?'

'Great Meadows? I know of it. Old man with seven sons. All hard workers but how can one farm support

312

seven families? I don't think any of 'em want to leave home.'

'No daughters?'

'Not one.'

I had cherished the prospect of visiting Great Meadows ever since setting out, the thought of it making my blood run faster every time I pictured the lovely Prosper. I felt sure that I was bound to be disappointed, for my romantic imaginings were running away with me. But what else did I have to think about, stepping out the miles on the soft spring mornings with Rattler on the quest for sex? The sap was rising and mine was too. Being away from home was a great release for my spirit. I had never stayed away before, apart from the three days before Margaret's death. That now seemed an age away, with all that had happened since. But coming to Great Meadows I felt an excitement out of all proportion. From two or three sightings and a shred of conversation I had fallen in love with Prosper.

When we approached, late in the afternoon, I could see that having seven sons at work paid off, for the farm was as well groomed as Rattler himself, its hedges expertly laid, its orchard flowering in exact rows, its potholes filled, its ditches scoured. Everything spoke of high standards, and wealth. The farm itself lay in a bowl of late afternoon sun surrounded by softly rolling, wooded hills. As we came over the last brow on the long road, dusty and tired, Rattler gave a bound beside me, and snorted at the smell of mares and food and all the comforts of life he now took for granted, and old Sim laughed and said, 'You've both got spirit after a long day, I'll say that for you.' I think at his age, the journeying was beginning to tell on him.

We walked down the long driveway to the house. There was a beautiful garden at the side and trim barns and cowsheds set in two big yards opposite. A man came out to greet us, followed by what I presumed was most of the family, several well-built young men, and the old man, the father, John Mayes. I stood Rattler out for them all to admire, and he arched his neck and chewed on his bit in splendid style. He had learned to show off, big-headed that he was, and loved the attention. His big lively eyes took them all in as they appraised him, his ears pricked to their voices. It seemed they had three mares of their own which they bred from, and several of their produce had been successful in matches. They were very knowledgeable, and knew all about my riding against Nat.

'Trounced up young man – we were all glad he were beat,' said Mr Mayes. 'Not that we don't rate that horse of his, mind you. That's a nice little beast. But he hasn't the presence of this one. Take him in the stables now. There's a place ready for him.'

The stables were wide and airy, all the workhorses back for the evening, groomed and fed. We put Rattler away in a separate stallion box, Sim brushed him down and fed him and then we were invited into the house for supper. I was shown a bedroom, very fine, with a lovely view over the fields. Mrs Mayes was a large, spare woman with a lined face and black hair taken severely back. She was kind, and seemed tired, but had the say in the house, giving orders to her husband as well as the sons. Mr Mayes was on the fat side, but strong, like the Suffolk Punch horses in his stable, and very affable. I got the impression he left most of the work now to the boys, but supervised, and I wasn't surprised they none of them wanted to leave home when the atmosphere was so pleasant. It was quite the nicest place we had been invited into. They were all very kind to me, the boys eyeing me as if I were a new horse, so that I felt I should trot out for them. There were six of them round the table, the eldest looking to be in his late twenties, the youngest about eighteen.

'This is all of us, save Prosper, our youngest,' Mrs Mayes said to me. 'He's not very good at timekeeping, I'm afraid.'

'He's ridden out on that mare of his,' one said.

'He knew we were having guests. It's rude of him to be late.'

It was very smart to be considered guests, I thought, me and old Sim. Did Prosper know that I was travelling Rattler myself? He would have been waiting, I had hoped. Idiot girl!

'He didn't know what time we were coming,' I excused him. 'We might have been much later.'

'He pleases himself, I'm afraid, whatever time he's told,' his mother said.

'He was keen enough to see this Rattler. He wants to put his own mare to him.'

'I thought he wanted a thoroughbred for her?'

'He changes his mind as often as the moon rises,'

said the old man. 'It'll be something else tomorrow.'

'Not when he sees Rattler, I think.'

'No.'

I was grateful that this highly intelligent family all seemed to agree on Rattler's superiority. In spite of not seeing Prosper I was content after the good meal and the long day's walk, and afterwards I helped Mrs Mayes clear away and wash the dishes in the scullery, although she told me to go and rest. I felt tired but still stirred up in this strange way and I went out to talk to Rattler as I often did in the evening. It was going dusk, but there was a new moon rising over the wooded horizon and the wonderful smell of dew-drenched soil from the ploughed and newly sown fields. Mr Mayes had a drill from the look of the young corn in soldierly lines, no doubt a threshing machine too. I thought of my own poor Small Gains by comparison and ached for my hard-working father who had had so much to bear in his life. I did not feel envy, more just longing for something out of reach, whatever it was I could not tell.

And while I was mooning in the stable with these stupid thoughts, I heard a rattle of hooves on the cobbles outside. I went to the door and saw Prosper slipping down from his white horse. Again I was struck with the thought that he was like Nicholas, if Nicholas had still possessed the strength and animal energy emanating from Prosper. And when he spoke, even his voice was like Nicholas's, soft and humorous, inquisitive, friendly.

'The stallion girl, vanquisher of Nat Grover. How nice that you're here.'

Close up, even in the dusk, I could see that he was as lovely as I remembered – the large greeny-grey eyes, the straight, aristocratic nose and fine brown skin, not a spot nor blemish. And such self-possession, a manner so easy and elegant, as unlike my rough brother Jack and lover Martin as it was possible to have. I stared at him, in a daze. I had never experienced such delight as at that moment.

'Your horse is lovely,' I murmured.

'Yes, she is. She goes back to the Alcock Arabian. I got her from Mr Dobito, you know, who breeds a few.'

I didn't know, but I didn't say so.

'How is your horse bred?'

The worst question he could have asked. 'Nobody knows, not even the breeder. She was tethered out, and he never knew she was in foal, till she dropped it.'

He laughed. 'He has a great reputation all the same. We've heard all about your match with Crocus. I wish I'd seen that! I wasn't able to come that day, more's the pity. Father is very pleased you've brought him here.'

He led his mare in and unsaddled her and tied her up, then came over to the stallion box carrying a lantern. Rattler came swinging to the door, nosy as always and I haltered him and made him stand out. How lovely he looked with the lanternlight playing over his gleaming coat, showing himself in his cocky way! He had learned all the tricks, and with the way he looked at us and pricked his ears to our conversation I felt he was in agreement with everything we said.

'Yes, my word, he's fine.' Prosper spoke with enthusiasm.

'Would you use him on your mare?'

'I don't want her in foal. But who knows, I might change my mind. He would give more substance, and she would give quality.'

'It would be a prince!'

'Or a princess.'

We both laughed. My heart was hammering with excitement at this mundane exchange. I felt I had gone mad, but I was transfixed by Prosper. I suppose it was what is called love at first sight, something I had always deemed unimaginable. Or was I overtired after my long walk and being sick earlier? A sickness of the heart, I could not explain it.

We went in together and Prosper got into trouble from his mother and was given a cold plate of the mutton roast we had enjoyed, to eat in the kitchen. Mrs Mayes gave me a branch of candles to take to my room, but Prosper said, 'Oh, stay here a bit and talk to me.'

'The girl is tired, let her be,' Mrs Mayes said.

The she looked at me, and smiled suddenly. What showed in my face? I wondered. She put the candles down on the table and went out, closing the door gently.

So we talked. The candles played on Prosper's face and showed flame in his eyes, gilded his cheeks, and I could not take my gaze off him. He told me he was the youngest and there was nothing for him at Great Meadows and his parents wanted him to go to university because he was clever but he refused to go. He didn't know what he wanted. He thought maybe he would go to Europe now the war was over. He would have joined the army, but now there was no war that would be dull. His brothers all thought he was mad, as they never wanted to go anywhere. But he rode miles away on his mare, all the way to the sea, and he visited the house where Nelson was born and wondered if he should be a sea captain. You could go to the Indies and be a pirate and make a fortune by lifting treasure from vanquished ships.

'Or get run through, or thrown in prison,' I said. But it sounded wonderful all the same. I hadn't ever wanted to do these things, but I often wanted what I couldn't have in the same dreamlike way, fantasizing as to my future.

Prosper laughed. 'I daresay hunting is the most excitement I shall ever get out of my life.' He shrugged. 'My parents are too good. Why should I run away or displease them? They give me everything. Even if I decide to go to India, they would pay for me. I asked and they agreed. That would be a great adventure, I think.'

'Oh no!' I don't think I said it out loud but all my being cried out for him not to go to India. I was going mad.

'So tell me about your place and your Rattler, and that good mare Tilly of your father's.'

It was my turn to tell the story of my life. So little! He knew all about the Grovers and sympathized that they were our near neighbours. How near, did he but know it – I could not bear to talk of Nat. He knew Jack and Martin had flown, he thought to Newcastle, so I was wise enough not to correct him. How news sped around on the grapevine! It was astonishing, even if not always true. I told him about Margaret and even Nicholas, my dearest friend. That sobered him, to think how easily he might be in the same situation.

'We had two sisters, who both died of it, the wasting disease. They were six and eight. It was terrible for our parents, our mother especially, to lose her little girls.'

The sad talk turned back to horses, and Tilly's exploits. She was famous everywhere I had travelled and her renown was a good way in for Rattler, her replacement. I didn't tell Prosper about Betty. We talked until one of the brothers came in to make up the kitchen range for the night. He laughed when he came upon us and said to me, 'You be careful of young Casanova here. He's the black sheep of the family, I'm warning you.'

I didn't quite know how to take this, but it was a signal for me to take my leave. I picked up the candles but Prosper took them off me and said, 'I'll show you the way.'

The house was huge and rambling, all up twelve stairs and down two, with huge beams to duck under in the long corridors, but I was lit safely to my room and Prosper stood the candles on the dressing table.

'There. Sleep well.' And he departed.

There was a mirror behind the candles and I stood there looking in it, to see what Prosper might see in me. I suddenly longed to be as beautiful as Margaret, although I never bothered before, but I could see quite clearly that my longing in that direction would never be satisfied. She had always worn her hair loose, such a nuisance I had always thought, impossible when there were horses to groom and all that dust flying about. Mine was always firmly braided, worn in a thick long plait down my back. So I undid it now and brushed it out so that it stood out round my face. (Nat had done this when he made love to me.) It was very thick and shining, as good as Rattler's mane, and it curled too, like Margaret's, but had never been given the chance to show itself. It certainly made me look quite different. My eyes were brown but not dark. They could, if you were feeling romantic and stretching a point, be described as golden. This thought made me laugh – the presumption! Light brown, boring, not large and glowing, but more shrewd and observant. I frowned quite a lot and my brows were low, not exquisitely arched like Miss Charlotte's. (Did she pluck them? Probably.) But my skin was clear and healthy, not pink and white like Margaret's but more pink and brown. Pink and gold? That sounded delicious, but I wasn't delicious, just healthy and ordinary but maybe not as plain as I was, now that my hair was loose and I was in love.

Yes, I thought I was in love. I had never felt like this before. I got into bed and lay thinking about Prosper until I fell asleep.

25

In the morning I was sick again. I was mortified, as a
servant girl caught me in the act, vomiting into the
chamber pot when she came in with a jug of hot water.

'Oh my lordy, are you ill?'

She brought me a wet flannel to wipe my face, and
a glass of water from the washstand.

'Shall I tell the missus? She's got cures for everything.' Then she laughed and added, 'Not for what
you might have though.'

'What do you mean?'

'Not if you're expecting, I mean. That's usually what
it means, if you're sick in the morning.'

I stared at her in horror. 'I can't be!'

'Well, you should know. Just lie still for a bit. It
usually settles. I'll bring you something up if you like,
some dry toast or summat. Would you like that? The
missus won't mind.'

'No. No, I'll be all right.'

I felt faint now, as well as sick, at what the girl had
said. It wasn't as if I didn't know this fact of life. I had
seen it with Margaret. But it hadn't occurred to me

322

that it might be the reason for my own sickness. I felt so ill now at the contemplation of what might be in store for me that I fell back on the pillows and lay like someone bludgeoned. That's what I felt like, bludgeoned.

The girl departed, humming a happy tune. I lay looking at the window where the sun shone in and the first house martins were already flitting up and down looking for the best nesting place. The sky was blue and clear, the world in perfect mood. I remembered Prosper. I wept. It was impossible! I was fifteen, my life hardly started, pregnant at my age! And by whom, Martin or Nat? The horror that it might be Nat's baby left me feeling weak with disgust. Surely God could not have willed such a wicked trick on me? No wonder I had given up love for God long ago, in league with both Nicholas and my father. I howled, burying my face in the pillow so that no one would hear. The house creaked about me with the rising of all its inhabitants, but I could not move, destroyed by the maid's cheerful diagnosis.

After a while I began to think of Prosper again, and how bewitched I had been the night before in that spring dusk, and in the candlelit kitchen. How would Prosper stand up in the cold light of day? I wondered. And what good would it do me if he was still as beguiling, when I had this dreadful future already mapped out. I didn't even like babies. I hated babies. There were ways of getting rid of them, I knew. I would find these out as soon as possible. Maybe Ann would help me, as I knew she was a woman of the world, and I was only just into pregnancy, scarcely a month in. I had missed my bleeding but I had put that down to the rigours of so much riding and not given it much thought. I was never regular anyway.

Possibly it wasn't true, the maid's scaremongering. I might have some malaise, or an upset stomach. But all my instincts told me that the maid had got it right. I was pregnant.

Eventually I got up and washed and dressed. I did feel ill now but more with what I knew than what I had. I went into the kitchen where a few of the brothers were still sitting round the table with Sim, but Prosper wasn't there. They moved up for me and started talking about the timetable for Rattler. They had three of their own mares wanting his services and some more were being walked in during the week we were to stay. With all this help and interest I saw that I wouldn't have much to do myself. This did not please me for I did not want time to think, although perhaps I would have time to spend with Prosper if he wanted it. My heart still fluttered at the thought of Prosper.

When I met him again, I knew that nothing had changed. My condition didn't preclude falling in love with Prosper. In broad daylight he was even more beautiful than in the dusk, to my eyes at least. All the brothers were attractive, but Prosper had some sort of magnetism, for me at least. And, from various remarks I heard during the week, not for me alone, for there were joking illusions to the broken hearts around the neighbourhood and cruder remarks from the brothers that I sometimes overheard which I will not repeat. Yet Prosper made no undue advances to me but treated me during the week in a friendly, respectful way, quite often seeking my company to ride out, or go fishing, or to deliver goods in the farm wagonette. I spent quite a lot of the time helping Mrs Mayes in the kitchen, and Prosper would seek me out. While I was beating up mix for the large fruitcakes that were turned out daily, he would sit picking out raisins and licking the forks when I laid them down.

'I think you should offer her a job, Mother, she's very useful around the kitchen.' He smiled mischievously. 'Good in the stable too.'

'God forbid the girl should want to spend her time feeding eight greedy men, you stupid boy. If she's any sense she'll keep away from housekeeping for a living, at least till she's had some fun first. My mistake was to marry at sixteen and have Jake so soon after.'

Her words struck despair into me, even as I desired her lovely Prosper, whose green eyes laughed at me across the table.

'Come on,' he said. 'Let's go for a ride. You can ride your own horse and show me how he trots out. He's got no work to do until Mr Miller brings his mare this afternoon.'

'I haven't got a saddle with me, or my clothes.'

'You can borrow Ma's clothes, and we've got saddles.'

'A side-saddle?'

'Yes, of course.'

I wasn't going to show my masculine style of riding to Prosper. A lady, even a fat ugly one, looked elegant side-saddle, and I wanted to look my best. So we rode out, me on Rattler and Prosper on his Arab mare, Cobweb, and Prosper led us through several fields until we came to a fine long track going up over a hill, at least two miles to the horizon.

'Go now, and I'll keep up with you.'

'You won't!' I shouted, and I sat down into Rattler and gave him the office and he immediately strode forth into his long-striding trot, racing style. I saw Prosper riding beside me, cantering, so easy and graceful in the saddle, the wind blowing in his hair, his face alight with pure pleasure, and a great pang went through me as I recognized Nicholas again in his bright boyhood on the brave Prince. He had looked just the same, so easy and fearless and happy, and I felt that in some way Prosper was his reincarnation. Prosper would thrive and Nicholas would die. As I loved Nicholas, so I now loved Prosper, although I scarcely knew him. I was thrilled to find this sub-stitution, as it seemed, for my dearest friend, but thought my mind was cracking to be coming up with such a strange analogy. The shocks of the morning had unhinged me. I felt unreal, on another planet, yet the powerful horse beneath me was my own familiar Rattler, my life, and his great stride my pride and joy. I was laughing with pure pleasure as he pulled away from Prosper's mare, the hill steepening but my fit horse finding no bar to his flying progress.

Afterwards I thought I should have been more

prudent and let Prosper win, to make him happy, but Prosper did not let me down by complaining. He was astonished by Rattler's prowess and full of praise, not angry as Nat would have been, nor sulky like most boys at being proved wrong.

'If he passes on his style he'll be the most sought-after stallion in the county!'

We pulled up on top of the hill and stood breath-less, laughing. White clouds bowled across the sky, casting capricious shadows along the valley below us, but the sun shone on our faces with the warmth of summer coming. I could not but feel happy, in spite of everything, as we turned back for home down the hill. We followed a path beside a clear-flowing stream, rimmed with masses of marsh marigolds in full flower. Prosper stopped by a little bay under the willow trees and told me to watch for trout. Thin lines of weed streamed in the current and the first dragonflies darted across the water, blue sparks in the sunshine. All life was brimming in the spring, and me too, I was part of nature's irrepressible reproduction process, dragged willy-nilly by biology into the teeming scheme of growth and progress. Life must carry on, nature was so cruel! To fertilize a seed so wantonly sown . . . I sat there on Rattler looking for trout, and my eyes filled with tears at the disaster that had overtaken me. I was so happy, with Rattler and Prosper in the soft spring morning, and so devastated by my secret knowledge. I could say nothing to Prosper, but pretend a sneeze and wipe my eyes.

'There, do you see? A beauty!'

He pointed and I pretended to see through the mist of my misery.

'I come here fishing, it's my favourite place. My brothers don't care about it, but they like eating the trout I catch.'

He was so full of enjoyment, taking life's pleasures with both hands, that I was enamoured of him still more. His presence was all warmth and exhilaration – I was falling deeper and deeper into love by the minute and the deeper I was in love, the more dreadful seemed my predicament. I told myself it made no difference, I would be away within the week and Prosper was unlikely to pursue me. I told myself I would very likely miscarry. I told myself I could hide away and farm the baby out. Or, if I had it, what difference would it make? *But whose was it?*

'You're very quiet,' Prosper said as we rode on.

'I think I'm pregnant,' I said.

I was mad to tell him, but my brain was so full of it I could not help myself.

'Oh, bad luck,' he said, not looking at all surprised. (Had any girls said it to him? I wondered with a pang.) 'I bet you don't want it.'

'No, I don't.'

'It's rotten for girls,' he said.

Was that sympathy or complacency? Of course it was rotten for girls, while nobody ever blamed the men. Servant girls were forever being dismissed after getting made pregnant by the son of the house, but everyone said they were only getting what they deserved.

He told me all the ways he knew of getting rid of them (however did he know?) and said he knew of a draught for mares that got covered by a roving gypsy colt when out at grass, and it would probably do the job for a girl.

At this I couldn't help laughing. 'Get me some!' I said.

He said, 'They all like the baby when it comes, however hard they've tried to get rid of it. Well, nearly all. A servant girl we had here in my grandparents' day drowned her baby in this stream. I think the father was the butler. We had butlers in those days, not like now.'

'How dreadful! That's wicked.'

'She had no family, I suppose. What could she do? She got her job back afterwards but the butler married someone else. Your family will look after you, surely? Unless you marry?'

'Yes, they will. I'm not marrying though. He's gone away. I won't see him again.'

If it was Martin, I added to myself.

To Prosper I said, 'I shouldn't have told you. Don't tell anyone, will you? Not your mother. And maybe it's not true. I might be all right.'

'Do some more trotting! Another match. I'd love to have seen that Nat Grover's face when you beat him!'

So our conversation rambled on, and during the week I found I could talk about anything to Prosper, always receiving attention, and in return hearing about his hopes and fantasies, his ideas, his past history, his relations with his brothers, his education, everything. I found that he was as honest and sympathetic as his looks were so heavenly, and my love at first sight consolidated into love pure and simple. I loved everything about him.

A week seems a very short time to have this happen, but I know I am not alone in finding out this magic. Ann told me how it had happened to her, and she was far more intelligent and steady than I am. We were very young and I suppose silly, but by the end of the week I could see that Prosper was as keen to be with me as I with him, and the brothers took to making sly remarks and the mother looked worried.

On my last day, when we were due to set off in the morning for home, Prosper asked me to walk out down by the river after supper. It was a calm, warm evening with the sun still casting long golden shadows across the grass.

'Don't be long,' Mrs Mayes said somewhat sharply. 'The lass has a long journey tomorrow.'

'Trot all the way, that might do it,' Prosper whispered. He took my hand and we went out across the orchard. This was the first time he had touched me, or made any advance. I was brimming with love for him; it must have showed, for his mother watched us go, her lips tight. Perhaps the servant girl had told her of my sickness, perhaps she was remembering her own early fall from grace and advice to me. If I ignored it, she had done her best. The evening was full of the smells that dewfall brings out of the ground, sweet familiar smells of cut grass and apple blossom petals and the musky passing of a fox. The sun still touched the far slopes and our shadows were miles long as we ran together down to the little bay under the willows, Prosper's favourite place. Had he brought many girls here?

'I love you, Clara,' he said and put his arms round me and kissed me gently on the mouth. Gently, and then more ardently.

'I want to see you as you are,' he said. 'I want to kiss your hair and your breasts.'

He unplaited my hair and shook it out loose all round my upper body, and took off my jacket and my blouse and my bodice. I was all bare above and the cool air made me shiver. But I was shivering more with joy than with cold. He ran his hands all over me and I nearly died for love of him, pressing myself close and murmuring his name.

And then I thought of Martin and Nat, and my condition, and the look on his mother's face, and I thought I was a slut and a sick girl and I couldn't do this thing again, even though this time it was motivated by love, pure and simple.

'Don't do it. I can't.'

'Sit down,' he said. He took off his jacket and spread it for me to sit on.

'I'm cold!'

'You can have my shirt.'

I took it off him, undoing all the buttons, and slipping out his arms. He put it round me and now he was bare above. His body was white and so slender, yet hard and strong, and his hair, untied, hung in curls on to his shoulders. He stroked my hair and kissed my ear and my neck and I turned to kiss his lips.

'I do love you so.'

'Yes, and me you.'

And then we laughed, because it was so lovely, and we lay down and kissed and explored each other, but he didn't make me do what I didn't want, he was so kind. Then it got cold and we started to get goose-pimply, so we sat up and got dressed again, and he braided up my hair back to how it was before. Not as tight as I did it.

'I love your hair, Clara. I love your face. You are lovely all over.'

'Yes, and you too. I love you. I don't want to go home.'

But there was no way to avoid it. Our time was up. Prosper said he would ride over to see me, but I didn't think he would. We lived nearly twenty miles away and he was too young to be a suitor. I didn't doubt that he loved me now, but I thought his love would quickly fade, whereas I knew mine would last for ever.

When we set out in the morning, Sim and Rattler and me, the whole family turned out to see us off. Rattler looked magnificent in his side-reins and show-off bridle and curvetted at my side, making stallion snorts. I had to let the lead rein loose so that he could prance without treading all over me and was so much taken up with his behaviour that I hardly had a chance to say goodbye to Prosper. Perhaps it was just as well, in front of the whole family, who stood there laughing, admiring. We had said goodbye lying in the grass under the willows, and perhaps that was how it should be, given the predicament that lay before me.

26

Sim had been a good companion on our travels. I had
talked to him about my hopes and fears as he had told
me a lot of his life story, but I didn't tell him on the
way home that I was in love with Prosper or that I was
pregnant. He might have guessed the first but I hoped
he didn't know the other, unless the servant girl had
gossiped. I knew Prosper would not betray me. Sim
told me of his regard for the Mayes family – 'Good
old-fashioned people, not your trumped-up money-
grubbers like Grover.' But I didn't need to be told.
Great Meadows had been a glimpse of paradise in
farming terms: solvent, thriving, well stocked, beautiful. Could we ever make Small Gains like Great
Meadows? But with Jack and Martin gone, it seemed
unlikely.

I realized how Father was missing Jack when I got
home. He looked tired and dispirited again. Jack had
taken more and more of the work off him, and now
the load had descended again just at the time of year
when so much needed to be done. But his face lit
up when we arrived and there was a great celebration

of Rattler's success. Ann got out the best ale and Sim and Soldier Bob came in and Ellen was hugging and kissing me.

'We heard news he was getting plenty of mares. I heard he was well liked – word came back to us,' Father said.

I pulled out the leather bag from my waist belt and tipped a stream of sovereigns on the table.

'There, that's how popular he was.'

Ellen's eyes shone. Father pushed her a sovereign and said, 'Go and buy yourself something pretty.' He laughed, cheered by the prospect of making money so easily. Then he pushed the clinking heap across the table to me.

'It's yours, my little horse-master. Your horse, your success.'

'I don't want it! It's for the farm.'

'Towards a threshing machine?' Father laughed.

We all drank and Ann made a meal and we had a jolly evening, but all the time the knowledge that I had to tell my parents my awful news kept me subdued. I should have to tell them of Nat's involvement as well as Martin's and I thought this would almost kill my father. But my cause was just, how could he blame me? I had saved Jack's life by my submission to Nat. Ann thought I was tired and chivvied me to bed, but the next morning when I woke up I was sick again. Ellen, my well-educated sister, sat up in bed and said, 'Hey, Clara, what's wrong with you? Are you expecting?'

'No!' I shrieked. 'Mind your own business!'

'It will be, if you are,' she said.

I knew I could not put off telling Ann. Father went out to work and Ellen to school (she was ready to leave but had been kept on by the new teacher to help with the young ones). I had done my outside work and let Rattler out into the field to give him a well-earned day off. It was another beautiful spring day and I thought of Prosper and our evening by the stream – oh, if the baby were Prosper's, how happy I would be! The thought of what I had forgone wrenched me. Without Martin, without Nat, my first experience of love would have been magical. I dragged my feet up to the house and went into the kitchen. Ann was chopping up vegetables for soup.

'I have something terrible to tell you.'

'I thought you had something on your mind. What is it?'

'I'm expecting a child.'

'Oh, my dear.' She laid down her knife and gave me a searching look. Perhaps my dread showed for she then said, gently, 'That's not so terrible.'

'It is, when you hear the whole story.'

I told her, and then she agreed that it was about as terrible as it could be. 'Not to know whose – that is the worst. If it is Martin's – why, that would be simple. But if it's Nat's—'

'It's bound to show when it's born, whose it is. Margaret's baby was the image of Nat. It will kill Father.'

'Not when he knows how it came about. And that you offered Rattler – that was the noblest sacrifice!'

'I wish he'd taken it.'

'Now you might, but not later, Clara. These things that seem so terrible at the time generally work out all right. Time softens cruelties. A child is a child, whoever sired it, and why do you not suppose it might be the image of you! Another Clara – that would be a bonus indeed.'

And she put her arms round me and hugged me as if I were her own.

'Think, if you hadn't given in to him, Jack would be in prison now, waiting to be hanged.'

'How do we know he kept his word?' I wailed. 'We haven't heard from them, that they're safe. Jack promised to write.'

'I think we'd have heard, if they'd been taken.'

But very shortly, in fact the same day, we found out what had happened to them. Ann made me feel a good deal better about my situation, and said she would tell Father.

'Why don't you forget all about it and go and see Nicholas? He must have missed you this last month.'

So I went down to the village and called at the rectory. The Rev was there and when he had welcomed me he said he had a letter for me. The envelope had been addressed to him but inside was another letter addressed in Jack's terrible scrawl to 'the family Garland'. The Rev hadn't opened this envelope.

'I was going to bring it down this afternoon. It only came on the coach this morning.'

'Oh, I must open it! It will say what's happened – we're all dying to know what's become of them both.'

I opened the letter and read:

'Dear all, I am sending this vi the revrend in case it falls into rong hands. Martin and me are working in a tin mine. Its dam hard I can tell you but we got good mony and good hom. Will rite again son. Your loving Jack.'

'Oh, what good news! Look.' I gave the Reverend the letter. 'They are safe, that's the main thing.'

It made my trouble the more worthwhile, as it showed Nat hadn't gone back on his word to me. My sacrifice had not been in vain. Sacrifice? As I remembered my feelings during the night in question I felt the colour rising in my cheeks in shame.

'I'll go and tell Nicholas.'

'You'll see a change in him, my child – just to warn you. He's sinking fast.'

The Rev's words put all other thoughts out of my head. My troubles were nothing compared to what was happening in this household. I ran upstairs and knocked at Nicholas's door.

'It's me, Clara! Are you decent?'

'Yes! Come in!'

I had opened the door a crack else I wouldn't have heard his voice, it was so weak. He was lying in bed, propped on pillows. He was now a shadow of his old self, thin and fragile. His face was bathed in sweat, his hair damp and clinging to his skull. Fever burned on his cheekbones and glittered in his eyes, but he scarcely had the strength to lift his hand to mine.

'Oh, Nicholas!' I cried out, trying to hide my

distress as I embraced him. 'I did miss you while I was away. It seems ages since I saw you.'

'It is ages, the way my time is going.'

'Don't say that! I will come every day now I'm back.'

'Tell me' – he was so breathless he could scarcely speak – 'everything. All the gossip.'

So I sat on the bed close to him and told him everything. About our journey with Rattler, about Martin, about Nat, about Prosper, and about being pregnant. Everything I didn't tell him before.

'I know you won't tell anyone about this last thing. You can tell your father, but not Jane nor Miss Charlotte. Promise.'

'I promise.'

I knew I could trust him utterly.

'Jesus, Clara, you're in deep water.' He reached his hand out to mine. 'I wish – oh, I wish – I could—' His sentence ended in an incomprehensible wheeze. He fought for breath.

'I wish—'

It was impossible. Tears of frustration filled his eyes.

'Clara!' he whispered.

Now I could see, for the first time, how frightened he was. All the gloss he had always put on dying, the joking bravado – he was beyond that now. He was at the end, and knew it.

I just held him in my arms. I didn't know what else to do. He was like just bones, hot as fire. And as I lay there with him, Jane came in and said, 'Doctor Roberts is here.'

I got up slowly. Jane looked at me, stark. 'He's come to bleed him.'

I felt angry at these doctor's tricks, the way they spun it out. Jane shook her head too, but there was nothing we could do to help.

'I'll come tomorrow,' I said to Nicholas.

Sometimes bleeding made them better for a few days, although I always thought the poor skeletal sick needed every drop of blood they possessed. To take it away seemed weird, a whole big jugful at a time. Jane had to stay to help, so I went back to the Rev and collected the letter from Jack.

I went home with it and was cheered by being the bearer of good news. But when the first euphoria was over, I told Ann about Nicholas.

'He's nearly gone. I can't bear it, to see how awful it is for him.'

'No, poor lad. The world needs people like Nicholas.'

'I wish my baby was his!'

'Yes, he would have been a fine match for you, Clara. His brains and yours together. You would have made a fine couple.'

'Have you told Father?'

'Yes.'

'What did he say?'

'Oh Clara. I'm afraid he wept, in case it's Nat's. What you did for Jack – he has nothing but admiration for you.'

At this I felt my terrible shame again, remembering the pleasure of it. This was one secret I would never admit to anybody. Even to myself it was hard. I had had enough of horrors.

'Is Billy here?' He would cheer me up.

'Oh yes. He's been here every day handling Betty – or whatever it is we have to call him now. His name's been changed again. I can't remember what. Your father calls him Billy's Bad Luck. But Billy dotes on him. It's astonishing what he can do one-handed now. Sim says he's worth a full hired man.'

'Don't tell his mother!'

'Heavens no!'

I went out to the stables and found Billy bridling his colt. He said it was called Good Fortune.

'Whose?' I said, laughing.

'Mine.'

He did up the buckles with one hand and his teeth. The colt kindly put his head down so that Billy could reach. Billy didn't bother with a saddle but slid on to the horse's back from the edge of the water trough.

'Look, I'll show you.'

This was the tonic I needed, to see Billy riding our funny colt round the field. He sat so easily and with his one hand he neck-reined, occasionally using his stumpy arm to shorten up, hooking up the loop in the reins. But with his body and legs, perfectly balanced, he had the colt circling at trot and canter like a lady's hack, beautifully bent to the bit, kind and willing. Good Fortune indeed! What a treasure our runt had turned out to be! I could see that it was Billy's skill getting the results, but the animal was so kind and willing to please. That was his temperament, nothing to do with Billy. And strange, with his two strong-willed, big-headed parents. Good Fortune was a most unexpected produce, proving what a toss-up breeding was. As in horses, so in humans. (Who knew what I was going to produce?) I was agog to see the results of Rattler's work from our recent foray round the countryside, but that would be a long wait. If the foals were really good, there would be a big demand for him next year. But if they were like Good Fortune, there would be no demand for him again.

I had to admit that as a two-year-old, Good Fortune wasn't quite so ugly. His roan coat was mostly steel-grey but brownish over the quarters, flecked with paler spots (very strange! Where did they come from: a circus?) and his mane and tail were black. He had white socks but no white on his head. There was an outside chance that he might grow into a decent horse, but he would always be a dreadful colour.

'You're a marvel, Billy,' I said when he came back to the gate. 'I would never have believed you could get him going so well.'

Billy beamed. He still only came up to my waist, and I'm not tall.

'Can I try him?' I asked, thinking he would be honoured by my request.

He looked doubtful and said nothing but I got on all the same. I turned the colt away and sent him up the field at a long trot, but the next I knew I was flying through the air. The bucks were so unexpected I hit the ground before I had time to do anything about it. Billy put his hand to his mouth and gave a piercing whistle and the colt came cantering back and stood like a lamb at his side. I staggered to my feet and stood uncertainly. The thought flashed through my head that perhaps that evil seed inside me had been dislodged. Good Fortune indeed! But should I be so lucky? It was doubtful. I staggered back to Billy.

'I'm sorry,' he said.

I laughed then, for Billy looked so comic, saying the right thing but obviously quite pleased that the colt had bucked me off. The colt was *his* and that was how he wanted it.

'He's a one-man horse, Billy, is that it? I won't want another ride, don't worry.'

And the beam came back. Billy and I understood each other.

Nicholas slowly came back from the brink of death, stayed for the present, but was irrevocably nearer. He got back into his armchair, but his frivolity had faded, and our conversations now were difficult, about serious things. One of the serious things was my future. This was something I was not keen to discuss, preferring to live for the present, ignoring the now inevitable swelling of my waistline. The little beast was healthy in there, not to be budged by a little violence. Now Martin had gone, I did not really miss him, and certainly did not want him for a husband should he return, having tasted the ecstasy of true love. I thought of Prosper all the time, but talked of those thoughts to no one, not even Nicholas.

We talked of the baby at home and it was obviously

going to be welcomed, even if it was Nat's. Not perhaps by my father, but both Ann and Ellen were full of excitement about having a baby in the house. I had thought once that Ann might have a baby herself, but she did not get pregnant and did not talk of it to me, so perhaps there was a reason why she could not have one. I don't think my father would have minded having more family.

Ann said to me, sternly, 'Even if it's Nat's, the child itself is what we make it, and completely innocent of the hate the Grover family arouses. The child is innocent, remember that. And it will be well loved here.'

It was almost a lecture to me, for she knew I harboured great resentment at my situation. I didn't want the child, and never experienced any of the maternal desires and delights I saw in other expecting girls. That sort of glow – it wasn't in my nature. I was prepared to endure it, and hopefully hand it over to Ann afterwards while I got on with my real interest, the horses. Over the coming months I was busy with taking Rattler out to local mares. My condition was known, even if it didn't show much, and everyone assumed the father was Martin. This was all right by me, but I did hear of it being referred to at times as 'poor little bastard' which caused me pain. For it was true, a bastard had a hard life and was not respected in society. A bastard was always an outcast unless it moved away from its home and started a new life somewhere, and even then if it wanted to marry and had to state who its father was, the secret would be revealed. Suppose it was a girl, with all that scorn and taunting to endure in the village and at school? A boy could fight for his respect but a girl could be branded for life.

Ann had obviously been thinking along the same lines, for one evening she said to me, 'I was talking to the Reverend Bywater this morning. He suggested something that gave me a great shock, and I expect it will shock you too. The idea, apparently, is Nicholas's.'

'What is it?'

'That you and Nicholas should marry.'

To say this idea was a shock is an understatement. I could feel my mouth hanging open, speech petrified on my tongue. *Nicholas!* My dearest, dearest Nicholas, whom I would love to marry with all my heart, suggesting such a brilliant way to give my poor baby a name! . . . It was a possibility that had never crossed my mind. And if it had, I would never have had the temerity to suggest it.

Ann smiled. 'When you think of it, it's a brilliant solution.'

The brilliance, of course, lay in the fact that I would only be a wife-in-name for a matter of months, if that, and then be quite free to get on with my life. Nicholas of course knew that perfectly well. But my little brat would get a name, and a splendid name at that, child of Nicholas Bywater. The village could think what it liked as to who the father was, but we would have our baby's name written in the church records, which no one could dispute. In short, no one would be able to call it a bastard. There were few children in the village who could boast better anyway, most having been conceived out of wedlock and born as premature babies. Nearly all babies born in our village were 'premature', some by as much as six months.

I went to see Nicholas and accept his proposal. It made him laugh again and we were quite stupid with making frivolous suggestions for our married life until the jokes started him coughing as usual. The Rev came up and we made a date, only seven days hence.

'In the church,' Nicholas said.

'Oh my dear, will you get there?' asked his father. 'We could easily have a little ceremony here in the bedroom. We can make an altar on your desk.'

'No, I want it done properly. I want Clara to walk down the aisle, and Edmund to play the organ.'

Jane said starkly it would kill him off. 'But as long as you get the wedding in first, I suppose it will be a good way for him to go.'

I was shocked. 'Do you mean that?'

'I think it will kill him, yes, the way he is. Maybe that is one of the reasons he wants to do it. As well as doing you a favour at the same time.'

It sounded dreadful the way she put it and sobered me utterly. Afterwards, it struck me that perhaps she was in love with Nicholas herself, and this wedding, farce that it was, was a blow to her. But consumptives were notorious for the ups and downs in their illness and I thought she was speaking out of turn.

I gave Nicholas the opportunity to cry off, but he was adamant he wanted to marry me.

'What about Miss Charlotte?' I asked. 'I thought she was the one you wanted to marry?'

'Yes, but she's too old for me. And I like doing you a good turn, Clara. You need having a good turn done to you, you must admit.'

'Yes, I do.'

'My life is so boring now. It will make a nice break.' He was taunting me. 'A nice wedding, and then—' He shrugged. I nearly finished for him, 'a nice funeral' but bit the words back. He knew. He laughed. He was back to being my old Nicholas.

'I want you looking pretty. Not just in from the stable.'

'Yes, truly. I will be a credit to you.' Ann had her old wedding dress somewhere, I was thinking. I was sure she could cobble it about to fit me.

'Ellen can be a bridesmaid, and Edmund will be best man, between playing the organ.'

'No guests,' I stipulated. 'Only ourselves.'

'Yes, only ourselves.'

Not surprisingly, I felt very excited and nervous. At home, Ann and Ellen and I went through our finery and spent hours pinning and tucking and all those things Ann knew about. I could sew after a fashion, but not beautifully like Ann. We didn't have a closed carriage and I refused to go through the village to my wedding all on show, so it was arranged we should dress in the vicarage.

'But not to let Nicholas see you,' Ellen said severely. 'Not till you get to the altar. It's bad luck.'

'Yes, well, the vicarage is big enough for us to be well separated.'

Then we only had to slip through the garden to the gate into the churchyard and no one need see us. It was not put about that we were to be married, as we didn't want the whole village to turn out for it as they surely would, agawp at the scandal. Clara Garland's bastard getting a name! I could just hear the tongues wagging. The Rev got a special dispensation to forgo the banns. We just prayed that Nicholas would be strong enough to see it through.

So on the appointed morning, Father drove us all to the vicarage with Tilly pulling the cart and all our smart clothes in a trunk at our feet. Jane let us in and showed us into the front parlour where she said we would be private and unseen.

'I have to help Nicholas,' she said.

The Rev came to greet us and my father changed quickly into his one good suit and went back with the Rev into the study. I heard the chink of glasses as the door shut behind them. Ann set about getting me into my finery. I was hooked tightly into her dress and my hair was brushed out in a heavy cloud down my back. Ellen fussed around with the veil and orange blossom wreath thing which kept it in place. I felt idiotic and wondered why ever Nicholas hadn't opted for a quick kneel in front of a makeshift altar in his bedroom. Whatever had got into him to want all this fuss? When I caught sight of myself in the sideboard mirror I found it hard to realize it was me, so unearthly did I look, so far from the stable, so utterly unlike the usual Clara Garland. Nicholas would wonder who he was getting. However I had to admit that I paused longer than necessary and my thoughts went to Prosper. If he were to see me now would he be impressed? I wasn't as ugly as I thought I was.

But Prosper was now a dream and Nicholas was truly the person I wanted to marry above all others, so when I walked down the aisle on my father's arm, I felt calm and almost singing with happiness. How strange that I was able to shut out completely the future and the heartbreak ahead. But it was the moment that mattered. I saw that the church was not entirely empty, for Miss Charlotte and the squire himself sat in a pew with Jane, and funny old Lord Fairhall was blowing his nose on the far side, while his son Edmund played the organ as Nicholas had requested.

And Nicholas was standing at the altar, alone. If I feared he would not recognize me, I in turn would scarcely have known it was my dear Nicholas, dressed no longer in a horse blanket but in white breeches and a beautiful dark high-collared cutaway jacket with a snowy cravat fashionably voluminous, above which his high colour glowed, whether with love or disease it was hard to tell. What it must have cost him to get himself up like this I cannot tell, but it was what he wanted: his last joke is rather how I thought of it. And when I came up to him I turned to him and laughed, and I could see that he wasn't at all serious and was grinning too, in spite of his desperate breathing.

Edmund stopped playing the organ and scurried down the aisle to turn into the best man, and the Rev got up and commenced the marriage service. I think he shortened it for it seemed to go over my head in no time at all. We knelt at the altar rail and stayed kneeling for Nicholas's sake, while he put the ring on my finger and we exchanged our vows. 'Until death us do part' seemed to ring out cruelly in the almost empty church, and I think everyone was in tears except us two. Ellen lifted my veil up over my head and we kissed and Nicholas whispered, 'Good idea of mine, eh?'

Yes, it was.

How Nicholas got through it, nobody could understand. We walked down the aisle arm in arm, and Father supported him on the other side. Charlotte kissed us both and Jane kissed Nicholas but not me. She looked terrible, I thought with a pang, blotchy with crying. When we got into the house Nicholas was put into an armchair in the dining room at the head of the table. A lovely spread of cold meats and jars of chutney and home-made bread had been laid out by the cook, and a great array of cakes and bottles of wine. We Garlands ate hungrily and when the toasts were made, the Rev made one to 'distant friends, Jack and Martin'.

'Jack would have enjoyed this,' Father said.

Nicholas ate nothing but had a few sips of red wine. It was such a strange wedding that nobody knew exactly how to behave. The squire and his lordship talked hunting and my father held an uneasy conversation with the Rev about the rights of the villagers to common land. Edmund talked to Ann and I sat with Nicholas, wishing he was back in his bed before he keeled over. I caught Jane's eye and she jerked her head upwards, suggesting the same thing, so we left the company and staggered upstairs with him. We took off his jacket and cravat and propped him up on his pile of pillows. Jane was more practised than I and I felt myself resenting her. I had never felt this before.

'There,' she said to him rather severely. 'You've done for yourself.'

'Getting married, you mean?' he said.

'Going to church and all. You could have done it here.'

'I wanted it proper,' he said.

'You'll pay for it.'

She left us and Nicholas said, 'What's got into her?'

'She wanted to marry you herself.'

'Really?' He was surprised. 'You're the lucky one then. Poor Jane.'

Then the strain of it all overtook him and words died on his lips. He was deathly pale and had obviously carried through the whole charade by pure guts. His eyes were now closed and he was struggling to breathe. Yes, he was paying for it. Jane was right. I went downstairs and called her.

'He needs you.' I said. 'I don't know what to do for him.'

Margaret had never fought as Nicholas had. Even at her worst she had never tried to be anything but an invalid, but Nicholas had fought all the way. Right to the end. I suspected that Jane's words were true, that by doing me a good turn he had decided to use it for his own ends. If so, it went according to plan, for when I called in the morning he was dead. Jane said he had

351

a huge haemorrhage in the night and died before Doctor Roberts arrived.

'He died in my arms,' Jane said.

And I saw the glitter of triumph in her eyes. I respected her for it and kissed her.

'You have been so good to him.'

And we went upstairs together.

27

Marrying Nicholas for the sake of my child might have been a good move on the face of it, but emotionally it made his death much worse. Expected as it was, even prayed for at times when he suffered so, when it came it brought me more sorrow than I could ever have imagined. Sometimes I wondered whether without the marriage I would have accepted it more easily. But the marriage, sham as it was, seemed to have bound me to him truly as a partner, beyond mere friendship. At least that is how I perceived it, but I was partly out of my mind afterwards. Ann took to dosing me with laudanum at nights. Father said it had been a crazy idea. Whose was it? It was Nicholas's, perhaps his last joke.

I went to the funeral and afterwards I was ill for several weeks. The funeral was as beautiful as Nicholas would have wished it, nothing spared: the squire's horses, Miss Charlotte red-eyed with weeping, Edmund's organ softly playing in a church decorated by the village women with wild flowers and leaves and grasses. The bishop came, because the poor Rev was too overcome to take the service. He had aged overnight and was scarcely coherent. I sat with him, holding his hand, and Jane sat next to me, in the front pew. Then when it was finished and Nicholas was buried under a pile of white lilies by the gate into the vicarage garden, I went home and went to bed with a raging fever. I did not get up again for what seemed half the summer.

During this time Father took Sim on to take my place, and with him and Soldier Bob and Billy no one missed me in the stables. No one missed me at all. Who would? I wished my beastly child to die but it thrived and kicked inside me. The movement reminded me of seeing Tilly's flanks move the evening I had taken her down to drink in the river, and that made me laugh. We were all such a helpless part of nature, living, conceiving, dying in such a tangled and disorderly way, we humans no better than our animals, that I gave up trying to work it out. Prosper was now an impossible dream and best forgotten. I seemed to have no future at all save for reluctantly giving birth.

Ann said, 'I think you're getting better.'

'I'm not really ill. Just a lead-swinger.'

'Come and sit in the orchard. I've never seen you so pale. You need the fresh air.'

Gradually Ann encouraged me back to health. I felt so tired, but sitting in the orchard in the July sunshine improved me. The first hay was being cut and my horses were at work in the hay waggons. Sim and Billy were out in the fields with them, carting. The very old and the very young between them were trying valiantly to make up for the lack of Jack and Martin, but it was a hard act to follow. Ann and I cored strawberries for jam-making, sitting together under the apple tree where once Margaret had wasted her life away. It seemed a century ago.

I could not help asking, 'Have you seen anything of Nat lately?'

'I see him in passing. He doesn't acknowledge me. I see that old aunt of Nicholas's waddling up to the farm with her daily parcel of gossip. I suppose she's your auntie too now, by marriage – think of that!'

'No, I won't think of it! Do you want me to have a relapse? Does Nat know about the baby? He must do, as all the village knows. He must know it might be his.'

'The whole village thinks it's Martin's, so he can't have opened his mouth. He's not such a braggart as I always thought. Some good qualities tucked away perhaps. If he wasn't so much under his father's influence he might be quite a reasonable young man.'

I did not answer.

'But God help whoever he marries, having such in-laws!'

Nat might have said I was beautiful that night but he didn't come looking for me down the trackway as once he had sought out Margaret. I was just fair game for that strange evening.

But someone was coming down the trackway now, a young man on a white horse.

'A stranger,' Ann said, getting up. 'Whoever can it be?'

I nearly fainted clear away, as even from the distance

I recognized Prosper. I felt the colour flooding my face, my whole body trembling. I started up, spilling my strawberries violently into the grass.

'It's Prosper Mayes!'

Ann gave me a strange look and said, 'What frightens you so?'

I just moaned, like a lunatic, and then Ann saw the light and laughed.

'I do believe—!'

And Prosper rode straight into the orchard through the open gate, seeing me trembling there, and slipped off the mare. He gave Ann a polite little bow and introduced himself in his lovely mannerly way.

'I'm Prosper Mayes, ma'am. I've come to see Clara and ask a favour of her. I hope my calling isn't inconvenient?'

'Not at all,' said Ann. 'I'm only too pleased to meet you. I'm her stepmother, Ann Garland.'

They shook hands. I could see Ann taking him in, charmed, amused. He turned to me then, and a look of alarm came over his face.

'You look ill! Are you all right? What's happened?'

'She did too much,' Ann said firmly. 'She has been ill, but she's better now. Sit here. I'll put your horse away and bring you a glass of ale.'

Prosper did not argue, looking at me in no doubt the same way as I was looking at him, red and tongue-tied.

'Are you – have you—?'

'Truly, I'm better now. I'm all right. I – I've missed you—'

356

'And me you. Oh Clara—'

We were both incoherent, unable tō make a sensible conversation. He sat down in Ann's chair and stared at me.

'You're so pale and thin!'

He by contrast was weatherbeaten and strong, taller and more beautiful than I ever remembered him. I was completely besotted all over again. Perhaps he would not love me pale and thin!

'I'm getting better fast! I've been in bed. I'll soon be back to my old self.'

'I do hope so! I don't like to think of you wilting, Clara. It's not the baby, is it?'

'Oh no, the beastly baby's still there! If only—'

'No, don't say it. You mustn't wish things like that. My mother jumped off a haystack to get rid of her last one and it was born dead and was so pretty, a little girl. She cried and cried for weeks.'

I had heard many of these sobering stories and did not want to hear another.

I said, 'I am glad to see you again. I've been so miserable.'

'If I'd known you were ill I would have ridden over. I've thought and thought about you.'

'Why have you come now? What is it, this favour you want?'

'I'm going to India. I want you to take my mare while I'm away.'

'To India!'

As far as I knew India was halfway round the world. People went to India and died. People scarcely ever came back from India. *India!*

'Oh Prosper, why? Why must you go away?'

He looked quite surprised and said, 'Only for three or four years. It's a great opportunity for me. A great-uncle has offered me work on his tea plantation, to take it over if I'm any good. I've no prospects here, after all, being the youngest of seven. Only go into the church! You wouldn't wish that on me.'

'No, but India! Oh Prosper, for so long! So far away!'

'Yes, but I'll come back. It's not so dreadful.'

I pulled myself together with a great effort, for I had no claim on him. Why ever shouldn't he go to India if he wanted? Hundreds of young men did, all the time. Better than to Australia on a convict ship.

'Perhaps you'll make a fortune! I'm very happy for you, if this chance is what you want.'

'I have no job at all at the moment and no chance of anything here. I'm not clever enough to go to university even if I wanted to, which I don't. I could go to sea, or join the army, or go stockbroking in London – I've thought of everything and this appeals to me most. And my parents give it their blessing. He's a nice old codger, this great-uncle, so they say, and there's lots of riding. He's got a fine stable, and you can play polo and hunt big game – not bad, Clara, when you think of it.'

Oh yes, I thought, all those hearsay things our family knew nothing about, for the rich and ambitious! If I loved Prosper, I was loving out of my league. I thought he was a country boy but a few years of playing polo in India and earning lots of money would bring him back in the squire class. He would buy a place and keep good horses to hunt and go shooting, and marry the likes of Miss Charlotte. And forget me, surely.

'It's great for you, Prosper, yes. I can see you wouldn't want to turn a chance like that down. And if you want a home for your mare while you're away, of course I will look after her for you.'

At least when he came back he would have to call and collect her. I would see him again.

'Good, I hoped you would. No one at home cares about riding horses, only breeding them, and I don't want her turned away for that long time. I thought you might use her to breed something useful, or ride yourself. She goes in harness too. How's Rattler?'

'He's working out in the hayfields just now. He's fine.'

I got myself back on an even keel gradually. It was so wonderful to have him by my side again, but the thought of India was terrible. I was torn, racked with love and despair. I felt so weak, drained.

Ann came back with the ale and some bread and cheese for him and we sat talking, the three of us, under the tree. It was civilized, entertaining a neighbour, chatting as if we had no cares in the world. Maybe the other two hadn't. But I had.

Prosper said it would be as well to leave the mare now, if it wasn't a nuisance: I could turn her out and he would walk home. I said that would be fine. Ann said why didn't I take him back part of the way driving

Hoppy to the trap. I think she saw how the land lay and wanted to make me happy, so pale and wan had I become. She said she would harness up Hoppy for us, but in the end we all went out to the stables and Prosper helped her, and I turned Cobweb out into the field. She was a lovely mare and ordinarily I would have been thrilled to have had the loan of her, but my mind was so full of her owner that I hardly saw her. Prosper kissed her goodbye. I could see that he loved her, and I was honoured to be trusted with her. We got in the trap together.

'Not all the way, Clara,' Ann said. 'That would be too much for you. I shall expect you back by four at least.'

'Yes, I promise.'

So we set off. I felt it was the last journey, something like the last supper, a journey into a future that wasn't going to happen. It was a perfect summer afternoon, the road in perfect condition, not too dusty, and dear old Hoppy trotted along without my having to guide him, only to turn him off the main road into the lane that led, eventually, to Great Meadows. Ancient elms arched over to make a tunnel of shade. Grass grew in the ruts and buttercups and Queen Anne's lace in a white froth on either bank.

'It won't be like this in India,' I said darkly.

'No. It will be hot and dusty and while I'm sweating on an elephant under the sun I shall remember this perfect afternoon with you, Clara.'

'Will you?'

'I will.'

I didn't even know what an elephant looked like, save it was very large.

When we got to a little crossroad six or seven miles away he told me to pull up and he would get down and walk. The moment I had dreaded.

'I can see you look tired. You should be back at home, resting. I don't want to get into trouble from your stepmother.'

'I don't care!'

And he smiled, and kissed me, very gently, and got down. He walked away and I just sat there watching him go while Hoppy grazed on the vergeside. I watched till he disappeared out of sight round a bend in the lane. He turned just before the bend and waved, his hand held high, and I waved back. And that was it. Hoppy went on grazing and I just sat there in the heavy shade, my head in my hands. Waiting, I thought. For four years. Waiting.

Hoppy realized that he could do what he pleased, so shortly turned round and headed off back the way he had come without my touching the reins. I sat there watching the rise and fall of his homely back and the set of his hopeful ears, and thinking we had come a long way since I had bought him in that snowy market. Things had been pretty black for him that day, but life had turned out to his advantage. Perhaps the same would happen for me.

The elms petered out and the shade gave way to a deep swathe of afternoon sunshine as if taking up the same theme, warming my bleak thoughts. With every step my spirits lifted, realizing that I had Prosper bound by keeping his horse. He would have to come back, with a bride or an elephant in tow I knew not, to claim the white mare. And at that thought, I smiled and my feeling of illbeing seemed to dissolve. My illness was the result of my widowhood and I was glad I had grieved properly for the person I had loved so dearly. But now that time was over. I was on my way home and I thought, at last, I was strong enough to resolve the problems that lay ahead. How I knew not, but my strength was back, and my optimism rising.

Perhaps Hoppy caught my mood, for he broke into a canter, heading for Small Gains.

ABOUT THE AUTHOR

Kathleen Peyton is a highly acclaimed author of
more than fifty novels, her most successful
being *Flambards* and its sequels which won the
Carnegie Medal and the Guardian Award. She
lives by the sea in Essex with her husband.

C⊕RBENIC

CATHERINE FISHER

Cal has struggled to cope with his mother's drinking and psychotic episodes since he was six; so when he finally leaves home to live with his uncle he is ruthless about breaking with the past, despite his mother's despair. But getting off the train at the wrong station, Cal finds himself at the mysterious castle of the Fisher King; and the night he spends there plunges him into a wasteland of desolation and adventure as he begins his predetermined quest back to all he has betrayed.

In this intriguing reworking of the Grail Legend, the award-winning author Catherine Fisher has created a gripping novel that moves between myth and a contemporary journey of self-knowledge until one becomes indistinguishable from the other.

'An elaborate and intricate reworking of the Grail Legend...an absorbing story' *BOOKSELLER*

Shortlisted for the Tir Na nOg Prize

DEFINITIONS
Price £4.99
0 09 943848 8

I CAPTURE
THE CASTLE
DODIE SMITH

*This wonderful novel tells the story of seventeen-year-old
Cassandra and her extraordinary family, who live in
not-so-genteel poverty in a ramshackle old English castle.*

Cassandra's eccentric father is a writer whose first book
took the literary world by storm but he has since failed to
write a single word and now spends most of his time
reading detective novels from the village library. Cassandra's
elder sister, Rose - exquisitely beautiful, vain and bored -
despairs of her family's circumstances and determines to
marry their affluent American landlord, Simon, despite the
fact she does not love him. She is in turns helped and
hindered in this by their bohemian step-mother Topaz, an
artist's model and nudist who likes to commune with
nature. Finally there is Stephen, dazzlingly handsome and
hopelessly in love with Cassandra.

Amidst the maelstrom Cassandra strives to hone her writing
skills. She fills three notebooks with sharply funny yet
poignant entries, which candidly chronicle the great
changes that take place within the castle's walls, and her
own first descent into love. By the time she pens her final
entry, she has captured the heart of the reader in one of
literature's most enchanting entertainments.

DEFINITIONS
0 09 984500 8

Remembrance

THERESA BRESLIN

Summer 1915, and the sound of the guns at the Western Front can be heard across the Channel in England. Throughout Britain, local regiments are recruiting for Kitchener's Army. And in the village of Stratharden, the Great War has already begun to irrevocably alter the course of five young lives...

'It's up to us now. I can't wait to get to the Front and be with my friends. I hope it's not all over before I get there.'
JOHN MALCOLM

'I'm not trying to look respectable, I'm trying to be useful. I intend to volunteer for nursing in France.'
CHARLOTTE

'I am strangely unafraid of death . . . what frightens me more is the death of spirit, that I have so quickly become accustomed to the sights and sounds of war . . .'
FRANCIS

'There are opportunities for women now, and I mean to take them. I am set to determine my own course in life.'
MAGGIE

'I may be too young, but I am going to enlist.
And I will get away with it.'
ALEX

An epic novel from the award-winning author Theresa Breslin.

Read it - and remember...

CORGI BOOKS
0 552 54738 7

jan mark
Something
in the Air

Ever since a visit to the dentist, Peggy has been hearing the oddest noises reverberating in her head. It's not clanging water pipes, or creaking floorboards from outside, or music, or humming in her own mind. In fact what it really sounds like is Morse code – a rapid staccato of dots and dashes of the sort used by radio operators in the Great War just a few years before. But why would anyone be transmitting Morse code that fast – through Peggy's head?

Who can Peggy confide in? The only possibility is her young aunt, Stella – a true friend and trusted confidante. But instead of the reassuring response Peggy expects from her aunt, Stella has an uncharacteristically disturbing explanation for the strange sounds.

Could the noise in Peggy's head really be a message from the past, from a world beyond the grave?

A finely wrought picture of a girl's life in 1920's England from Jan Mark, twice winner of the Carnegie Medal.

DEFINITIONS
0-099-43234-X
Price £4.99

LINDA NEWBERY

THE
SHELL
HOUSE

When Greg stumbles across the beautiful ruins of Graveney Hall, he becomes intrigued by the story behind its destruction. He and his friend Faith are drawn into a quest to discover the fate of Graveney's last heir, Edmund, a young soldier who disappeared in mysterious circumstances during the First World War.

But Greg's investigations force him to question his own views on love and faith, and reveal more about himself than he would ever have imagined.

A beautiful portrayal of love, sexuality and spirituality over two generations.

'Intelligent and perceptive'
GUARDIAN
'Newbery writes wonderfully'
FINANCIAL TIMES
'This is a novel to read, think about, and then read again'
INDEPENDENT

SHORTLISTED FOR THE GUARDIAN CHILDREN'S FICTION PRIZE
SHORTLISTED FOR THE CARNEGIE MEDAL

DEFINITIONS
0 099 45593 5